Bats Out of Hell

Barry Hannah

BATS
OUT OF
HELL

Grove Press
New York

The following stories were previously published elsewhere: "That Was Close, Ma,"
"Herman Is in Another State," *Esquire*; "This Happy Breed," "Dear Awful Diary,"
"A Christmas Thought," *Chicago Review*; "Upstairs, Mona Bayed for Dong,"
Southern Review; "Nicodemus Bluff," *Carolina Quarterly*; "Evening of the Yarp:
A Report by Roonswent Dover," *The Quarterly*; "Hey, Have You Got a Cig,
the Time, the News, My Face?" *Santa Monica Review*; "The Spy of Loog Root,"
"The Vision of Esther by Clem," *Oxford American*.

First published in the United States of America in 1993 by Houghton Mifflin Company
Grove Press paperback edition published in April 1994

Published simultaneously in Canada
Printed in the United States of America

FIRST EDITION

Library of Congress Cataloging-in-Publication Data
Hannah, Barry.
Bats out of hell/Barry Hannah.
ISBN 0-8021-3386-X
I. Title.
[PS3558.A476B37   1994]   813'.54—dc20   93-43692

Grove Press
841 Broadway
New York, NY 10003

2 4 6 8 10 9 7 5 3 1

For Larry Debord
under the knife and back fresh from Hell

and for my White children,
Shannon and David

CONTENTS

High-Water Railers

THE PIER shook under his feet, wrapped in socks and sandals. He wore huge gabardine shorts and was blue-white in the legs. Yeah, our time's about over, and I was counting the things I hadn't done last night, things I regretted, sins of omission; omitted to *sin*, I mean, ha! He was going on. Lewis, ninety-one, had watched some four-foot square of water for three years. He was still intrigued by what the lake gave up. Storms had been rough through the late winter and spring. This was an oxbow lake. The flooding from the great continental river washed splendid oddities into the channel, some of them carnivorous, some of them simply bottom-suckers of astounding girth, armored with scales of copper. Lewis shook with both palsy and wonder when fish this rare were dragged up or just spotted rolling.

His fine sea-size rig was cast out with a six-inch red and white bobber; two fathoms under was a hooked shrimp from a frozen bag he'd brought down. Lewis had a theory that with hurricanes — they'd had two just lately a hundred fifty miles south — sea life pushed up into the high reaches of the river, then flooded even into this lake and Farte Cove. He considered himself an ichthyologist of minor parts and kept a notebook with responses to fish life in it. There were no entries or dates when he did not catch or witness interesting water life. Like a great many days in a man's life, those days he'd just as soon did not occur at all. He wanted a lot of the exotic and a minimum of the ordinary.

Lewis turned and was deeply unimpressed by old Ulrich staggering onto the pier. This man featured himself a scientist or at least an aerocrat, though Lewis thought him a fraud afloat on a sea of wide misunderstanding. Ulrich was in the process of "studying" blue herons, loons and accipiters in flight and for some nagging reason was interested in the precise *weight* of everybody he met. He thought it happily significant that the old had lighter, hollower, more aerodynamic bones, such as birds had. Having been witness to the first German jet aircraft in the war, a specter he had never recovered from, he "drew on" this reflection time and again, apropos of almost zero, thought Lewis. Unfortunately, he had also been blown a goodly distance by Hurricane Camille in 1969. Ulrich was old *then*, but claimed also to be wiser in special "hurricane minutes" and inflicted this credential here and there, at any time, during his seminar at the end of the pier. There was no gainsaying the man with his "brief flight" and "hurricane minutes." The body was preparing the elderly for the "flight of the soul," said Ulrich. Why, he expected to weigh about thirty-five pounds when he died, just a bit of mortal coil dragged away protesting like a hare under an eagle.

Another annoyance to Lewis — who actually loved Ulrich; almost all the old loved each other at the end of the pier — was that Ulrich, eighty-nine, showed no signs of bad health even though he lit up one Kent after another. This Ulrich attributed — wouldn't it be — to a "scientific diet" such as that literally eaten by birds. The diet of birds was indicated come the senior years. A final annoyance was that Ulrich cherished the word *acquit*, as in "let me acquit myself" or "he acquitted himself well." Though Lewis ignored this as often as possible, he wondered why Ulrich should think a person was perpetually on trial when he opened his mouth, especially given the blather that flew out Ulrich's own. Ulrich, too, was interested in piscatorial life, though fish were "base and heavy," mere "forage in the pastures of the deep." Ignore, look away, pleaded Lewis to himself.

Many eutrophic lakes, their food chains unbalanced by man or nature, simply died. But this old oxbow had come back in the nineties. Bass, sunfish, perch, bluegill, gar, buffalo, carp, and now small alligators popped the surface. Big shad fled and recovered in shoals. Rare wading birds attended the shores and shallows. Hunted duck and geese veterans rested and paddled with only the great moccasins and turtles to fear. The water was a late-spring black, with sloughs going to tannin. Three unrecovered human bodies were somewhere out there, victims of March lightning. In a bad storm, the huge lake could imitate an inland sea, all three-foot whitecaps and evil sail-wrappers. It would also flood quickly and drive mink and nutria to the back roads, where one could make ladies' coats from the roadkills.

Next Sidney Farte, of the old cove family who owned the boat and bait house, came out, barely, humbled by shingles and roaring ulcers, giving a sniff of propriety to the pier, which he did not own but had watched for fifty-seven years through the replacement and repiling in the seventies. The man who'd had the benches and the rail fixed for the elderly was a kind man—Wooten—now dead and discussed only by that one inexorable trait of his, his kindness in little things and big. Nobody knew what experience had produced this saint, and his perfection attracted none of them, so terrible would be the strain, especially considering the fact that Wooten had not been stupid, not at all. Some said that he had been president of a small Baptist college, but for some reason nobody had ever directly put the question to him. There was a holy air about the man, no denying, that brooked none of your ordinary street questioning. Wooten never quoted anybody or any source. He spoke only for himself, and not very often. Such a man—well, even if something enormous and ugly had happened in his past, it would seem rude to know it. Wooten was a tiny man, maybe five-four, with snow-white hair that turned boyishly fore and aft in the wind. He stepped very softly. Next you knew, he was beside you, looking at what you were looking at in respectful quiet.

Ulrich had said that the lake was now Wooten's college, but Wooten himself would never have expressed anything as pompous as that.

"The water looks so fresh and deep this morning!" Wooten would say, a curious sweet medicinal smell reaching you on his breath.

Sidney Farte did not care for his virtue, was made sullen by it, but did not dare attack "Cardinal Wooten" (as he called him under his breath) around the others. He was glad when the fellow passed on. Now Sidney could get back to the regular profanity of his observations. Sidney was having a bad time in his old age, but he rather adored his bad time. Also afflicted with serious deafness, he did not enjoy the reprieve from noise as other old people did, but hurled this way and that, certain that whispered conspiracies and revenges were afoot. The soreness in his chest predicted the weather, which Sidney inevitably pronounced rotten: tornadoes, more flooding and thunder, every kind of spiteful weather. A sunny day filled him with mild horror and suspicion. Sidney had endured lately a sorry, sorry thing, and all of them knew it. A male grandchild of his had won a scholarship to a mighty eastern university, Yale, and was the object of a four-year gloat by Sidney, who had no college. The young man upon graduation had come over to visit his grandfather for a week, at the end of which he pronounced Sidney "a poisonous, evil old man who ought to be ashamed of yourself." This statement simply whacked Sidney flat to the ground. He was still trying to recover and was much more silent than in previous springs. Ulrich and Lewis both worried about him, used to his profanity as a sort of walking milieu against which they fished and breathed.

The other oldster of the core on the rail was late. This was Peter Wren, brother of the colonel who made Wake Island gallant against the Japanese and a chronic prevaricator whose lies were so gaudy and wrapped around they might have been a medieval tapestry of what almost or never happened. He had of course suborned the history of his brother and his constant perjuries held a real fear of the truth, lest the whole tissue of lies crumble when it came forward. It was getting where it seemed dangerous to risk even a simple declarative sentence about the weather or time of day, and Pete Wren was likely to misstate even that. "It's really wanting to rain, you know. Must be near noon" — when the sky was full blue and the time was about ten, latest. People took him to be majorly misinformed, but it was not that: he lived in fear of rupture from the tangled web. So finally he came out with his expensive ultralight rig and crickets. Wren was a partisan of the bluegill, for which — it was heard — he held the state record, but he'd casually eaten the fish without registering it. He was breeding a special kind of mutant cricket in his wire keep that would take the record fish again. There were enormous bluegills in the lake, in fact, and even a liar could catch them. Wren had taken home a pound-and-a-quarter one late one evening, but he claimed it had interbred with a German trout and had disqualified itself.

"Morning, gents," said Wren to the three at the rail. They waited for his maiden lie of the day. Something impossible about his sleep, perhaps.

"A car hit him and that queer just flew away," he said.

"Say it again?" asked Lewis.

"Oh, I rented a video of *Last Exit to Brooklyn* last night. A queer ran out in the road, a car hit him, and that queer just flew straight up in the air away."

"Could I see that?" asked Ulrich, intensely concerned with the flight of human beings.

"I might have lost the tape."

"Already lost it, Wren?"

"It could be in there among my volumes of Shakespeare. I've got all ninety-five of his stories and plays. Given to me by my grandson, who just adores me."

Though he meant nothing by it, Sidney Farte was insulted, recalling the anathema of his own grandson last spring. This began his day vilely, even lower.

"You diarrhea-mouth cocksucker," he said.

"Here now, so early," objected Lewis. A ninety-one-year-old man didn't want to hear such filth announcing the day. That was the sort of thing they did in that vicious far-north horror, New York City. The saintly Wooten had established a certain spirit on the pier that was not recanted at his death. Sidney heard nothing beyond a direct blast in the ear, which Wren was determined to give him. He actually began feeling better now, recovering his purchase on the island of unconscious profanity that was his.

"Puts me in mind of Icarus," said Ulrich.

"Like everything," said Sidney. "Shit, I knew a rat once could fly. Throw that sumbitch cheese in the air. Shit in the air too."

"You look thin today, Sidney. What's your weight?" asked Ulrich, lighting another Kent.

He jumped into something running parallel in his brain: "Thing to do is wait out the pain. Most times it'll pass of itself. Modern man has not let the body heal itself. The downfall was aspirin."

"What in hell are you talking about?"

"Rock and roll kills a lot of men early. We know for a fact that the presence of rock and roll electrons in the air causes plane crashes. Some of that hip-hop stuff will take the wing right off your jumbo jet. Even makes cancer, too. They're looking into it."

"These people you say 'looking into' shit. Count 'em, it just about leaves only us on the pier that ain't doing a survey."

"It's the age of high-priced nosiness all right," said Lewis, whose bobber was going under as if a sucking thing were on. He let out an audible breath in sympathy. "Something's on my shrimp, gentlemen."

"I want to see this sea creature," said Peter Wren, throat red with prevarication.

The huge bobber submerged and disappeared in the blackish green, down to legend they hoped, and the men hovered together into one set of eyes three hundred and twenty-three years old. The bobber came back up again, but Lewis raised the line and the shrimp was gone. Wren began rigging for bluegill, excited.

"A turtle or a gator'd bite shrimp," said Sidney.

"I suspect sturgeon," said Lewis. "They can breathe both salt and fresh. And they migrate long distances."

"Your human being is made like the shark. If he quits moving and doing, he perishes," said Ulrich.

"Now *shark*. I'll eat any shark you catch raw," said Wren. Though a liar, Wren was a man of some sartorial taste. He suddenly observed Ulrich, with a jump. Ulrich wore a brown Eisenhower jacket over blue-striped polyester bell bottom pants — something truly ghastly from the seventies, such as on a boulevarding pimp. Through a flashback of several connected untruths, Wren was visited by a haze of nausea, for everything wicked had happened to him in the seventies. He had lost his wife, his business; thieves had stolen his collection of guns. Music was provided by those skinny, filthy Lazaruses, the Rolling Stones. Carter had given away everything to the blacks and hippies; brought blue jeans to the White House. Every adult became a laughingstock and fool. Old Ulrich here was dressing right into the part. How Wren despised him now for his encyclopedic near-information. The world was in such a sorry state, it made a man lie sometimes to be sane. He tossed his line out grimly. Ulrich had ruined the fishing.

The lake, just alive, now seemed bright warm and dead, just a stretch of empty liquid at midmorning. A bad quality of light had suddenly come over. All of them felt it, like that mean gloom one feels after a pointless argument with one's wife. Nobody spoke for thirty minutes, hearing the call of an unnamed flat accidie.

At last Lewis, back to his daybreaking thought about what he regretted having never done, his sin of omission, spoke. He asked the others what bothered them in this area. Lunchtime loomed — pleasant ritual of the hungry sun. More and more they talked about food, except for Sidney Farte, often too sick to eat.

"I guess what I missed most was having a significant pet," said Lewis. "I was always talked out of them. Would be nice to have an old dog hearkening toward the end with me."

"I guess I missed the Big Money," said Ulrich. "That could have been sweet. Imagine the studies one could pursue. Perfecting one-man propulsion. I could have been the Howard Hughes of individual flight."

"I wished I'd had a heart," blurted Sidney Farte. "I didn't even cry at my wife's funeral. Knew I should, but I just couldn't. My children looked long and expectant at me. Hell, I was like that as a little boy. Look on the worst things without a blink, eyes so dry they hurt. Something left out of me at birth. Begun lying 'cause there wasn't nothing in true life that moved me."

The confession was so astounding to the rest, who had known Farte for a decade and a half, that reply was occluded. His health must be sincerely bad. They all felt a surrender. Now noon, it became darkly clouded; something dangerous and honest seemed to be in the air. Peter Wren had a fish on, but was just ignoring it, reckoning on Sidney Farte. But it was Wren's turn.

"That I could have sex with a child," he said.

"My ugly God," said Lewis.

"I mean a youngish girl, say fourteen. That she would adore me. I would be everything to her."

Was he now adjusting himself to a public? they wondered. Or was he inwardly a vile old criminal, collecting photographs and near to wearing a garter belt? Fourteen was suddenly too legitimate, hardly a story at all. In their youth, fourteen was open season. There were many mothers at age fifteen, already going to fat. Four memories raked through the deep ashes of their desire.

"Shit, I *had* that," said Sidney.

"Was she tight? Did she cavort for you?" asked Wren.

"Yes and yes. Couldn't get enough. I tell you —"

"Shhh!" said Lewis.

Behind them, someone had lightly shaken the pier. In her tennis shoes, she had crept up unheard. The small vibration of the boards was all the warning Lewis had of her. She was right behind Sidney, attentive. It was Melanie, Wooten's widow, the only woman ever to insist on coming among the men at the end of the pier. Farte despised having her near. The others could not quite decide. Something was always suspended when she came around. A sort of startled gentility set in, unbearable to Farte, like sudden envelopment by a church.

"We were talking horses, Mrs. Wooten," said Lewis.

She'd brought them a snack of homemade sugar cookies. You could smell vanilla on her. She was an industrious person who had begun blowing glass animals after the death of her husband. That she came out there was somewhat aggressive, they felt, and she had begun talking a lot more since Wooten passed, finding a hobby and her tongue at about the same time.

"No, you weren't talking horses. Don't mind me, don't you dare. I like man-talk."

"Cloudy noon," Ulrich offered.

"Aren't you going to pull your fish in?" the old lady asked Wren.

When he got the fish reeled in, they saw it was a gaspergou, a frog-eyed crossbreed of bass and bream nobody had seen in ages. Every-body but the sulking Farte was fascinated.

"That's your unlikely combination, a mutant, absolutely," said Ulrich, "the predator and the predatee, crossbred. The eater and the eaten." As Wren unhooked it and laid it out on the planks, Ulrich continued, in an access of philosophy: "An anomaly of the food chain, hardly ever witnessed. We've got the aquatic equivalent of a fox and a chicken here, on your food chain. Reminds you of man himself. All our funereal devices are a denial of the food chain — our coffins, our pyres, our mausoleums, our pyramids. Pitifully declaring ourselves exempt from the food chain. Our arrogance. But we aren't, we're right in it. Nits, mites and worms will have us. Never you doubt it."

They munched the sugar cookies and Ulrich was confident he had produced a deep silence with his gravity.

"I'm not that innocent, lads," said Melanie Wooten. "*I've* cavorted. I was a looker, my skin they said seemed not to have any pores at all. Wootie was lucky. The man stayed grateful, all his life."

"Is that what made him so kind?" asked Lewis.

He acknowledged, looking at her firmly for the first time, that she was no liar. Her skin was still fine for a woman in her seventies. There was a blond glow to her. Her lips were full and bowed — quite beautiful, like a lady in films. The way she broke into life here toward the end he found admirable too. Many women of his generation remained huddled mice. You could not even imagine them straight in their coffins.

"I hope so," said Melanie. "His gratitude. Without, I hope, sounding proud."

"Not at all," said Lewis. "Gratitude is what marks the higher being, doesn't it?"

"But the thing came over him toward the end, which I've never much discussed. It came on just like diabetes. My love had nothing to do with it. In his seventies he turned gay. Isn't that something? All those male students — he had a different infatuation every week. Poor Wootie. They fired him from the college. He couldn't control himself."

"*What?*" asked Sidney Farte, rather meanly. She knew the problem.

"He turned homosexual. *Homosexual,*" she emphasized, as if in a lecture to a pupil.

"Is it true?" asked Lewis.

They were not looking anywhere in particular, the others, when they noticed Lewis was weeping. He shook a little, and his long white face was drawn up in hurt.

"What is it?" Ulrich and Wren begged. "What's wrong?"

"I want a *dog*. I want a *dog*. I get so lonely, nothing anybody can do about it," Lewis cried out like a child.

"Well now, a dog can be *had*. Let's be about getting you a dog," said Ulrich.

"Certainly," Melanie said, taking Lewis's hand. "Did I upset you?"

"Just a dog," Lewis sniffled.

"By all that pukes, get the man a dog," said Sidney.

"That's a dream you hardly have to defer," said Wren. "*That* can be most painlessly had."

They went back up the pier together, Melanie indicating the way to her station wagon. All in, they set out over to Vicksburg to find Lewis a dog.

Two Things, Dimly,
Were Going At Each Other

THE OLD MAN off forty years of morphine was fascinated by guns. He was also a foe of dogs everywhere. They were too servile, too slavering, too helplessly pack-bent, when not treacherous. The cat was the thing. Coots cut at the evening with his cane and wanted to "see a death" in the big city. He had been crazy for death these many years, writing about it and studying it in thick manuscripts. Many, hordes, died in his fictions. He dressed in a suit, often a three-piece, and looked to be a serious banker, with a Windsor knot in his tie. The scratch of the lower Midwest was in his voice. He was looking for a billiards parlor in Manhattan. In these blocks he had heard one rumored.

He knew of an afflicted man playing billiards — Latouche, ninety, a barely retired surgeon. The grofft was getting him. It was a rare Central American disease, making one hunt like a dog, bark and whine, the face becoming wolfish. The old man, Coots, despised the even older Latouche. There was just something, something — what? — about the man, perhaps his comfort, an obtuseness. And, sealing it, he owned a proud Hungarian sheepdog. The thing had gruesomely licked Coots at an underground firing range where he and Latouche shot their exotic weapons. It was their only similarity, this love of handguns. The old men would ardently blast away for hours, exchanging Italian, German, South African and Chinese pieces, barrels all heated up so that they would have made a pop of steam if tossed in water. Hunting and ordering correct calibers was a main part of their lives. Latouche was more the weapons technician, while Coots revered the history of each piece, or even more precisely, what kind of hole in what men in what time, entrance and exit; what probable suffering.

In Mexico once when he was young, Coots had shot his wife "inadvertently when the black thing was on me" as they were sporting around with the idea of William Tell, a glass on her head. Coots was drunk, but he insisted on "the black thing." He believed in spells and even more in guns as he got old. He believed he could think spells on enemies and bring hideous luck to them, or so he wrote in his chilly fictions, where homicide and orgasm were inevitably concurrent and hundreds died in rages of lust and murder; a holocaust of young men perishing was always at least in the background, like wallpaper in a shrine. It was an ancient and beloved tyranny of the cosmos in which desirable bodies were given up religiously.

Coots, queer not gay, was an old-timer who hated "fairies" almost as much as women, or so he wrote. "Queens" were anathema, down there with the dreaded "cunts." His manly midwestern prose would scratch out at them. Physically he was a coward, and as he aged in the big city, his paranoia had a field day and became quite adorable to Coots cultists, who were always at him for interviews. His prose was no hoax. He wrote beautifully, especially when he was telling a straight clean story — something "linear." But too much of this thirties stuff annoyed him and he was apt to launch off into his "genius" — spiteful incoherence, cut-up blather, free-floating time pirates corn-holing each other, etc. He was, though, dead accurate about the century often in this "shotgunning" — it seemed to thousands anyway — as only, perhaps, an old shy queer full of hate can be.

Coots had murdered nobody else (his wife's accident had cost him a few days in a Mexican jail), but he was proud of the three dogs he had shot in a great city park one twilight, two German shepherds and a Rottweiler, just last year. Their hides were on the wall of the composing room in his "bunker," a windowless warehouse apartment tremendously padlocked in a cheap nasty section of town. Coots had claimed an attack, and the young amanuensis with him (they were not lovers) did not deny it. There had been high adventure in secreting the gun, getting the animals back to the apartment in three separate taxis, and arranging for their skinning with a jubilant cultist now ten years on Methedrine. The legend got out to everybody with whom the cultist had a beer, hundreds. Alcoholism was necessary to balance his speed habit, but nothing balanced his tongue. The story had all three animals, escaped from a wealthy high-altitude widow hag on Riverside Drive, tearing unprovoked at Coots' legs, with the amanuensis sprawled in terror, and Coots fast-drawing a .44 from his Abercrombie and Fitch raincoat. Coots, swarmed by his interviewers and even by *Time,* demurred, but there were the three hides on the wall, head shots, no hole in the pelt. Of peculiar literary satisfaction was the fact that the Methedrined skinner died a week later, as if taken off by a curse from the shy hermitic Coots.

Coots was now thinking he had successfully hexed Latouche, a man who at eighty-nine had never had a day of bad health, and now the grofft on him, horrible and unlucky. Latouche was of an almost alarming breed. He seemed never to have made a mistake. Neither with his surgery (famous), his wives (he had outlived two fine women devotedly in love with him), his clothes, his money, his charities (quiet and enormous), or his prosperous handsome doctor sons. At billiards he was a wizard and put away other wizards one fourth his age, some of them precocious millionaires of his pattern. The great violent, greedy and rude city had not put one line of worry on his face. He had been a gallant chief of surgery in World War II, at forty-one, with Patton's racing Third Army, but could have been queer Hitler's Aryan model. Even in his forties he seemed to be the one for whom Grable showed her amazing legs; he could have been her kiddish admirer and our hope for Over There, Lucky Strike thrust into sidelips with the dash of veteranship forced on him. Latouche could have ridden on sheer image, but insisted instead on Johns Hopkins, Harvard, and the Sorbonne, to emerge a surgeon, powerful before age thirty: athlete (impossible endurance, perfect fingers), intellectual (four ontological approaches named for him), and doting lover, amazingly of his beautiful wives alone. Also he had written about guns, and could outshoot Coots, who was almost twenty years younger.

After retirement, Latouche became a student of man, fresh as a ten-year-old. It was the one thing he'd neglected, mankind. He was making fast time, of course, as usual. His Hungarian sheepdog, his curly pal, was allowed everywhere, even restaurants. Latouche was that kind of darling. Folks loved to have him around and hear his voice, kind and modest, and he could have lived free on what people bought for and gave him. He lived in an apartment on Wall Street very near the waterfront, where men loaded and unloaded international goods. Because he was such a distinguished widower, emblem of a nobler time, the owners of the building allowed him to stay on the top floor in a building where everything else was business. With more dedication than others with telescopes, he began watching the men on the docks, studying the poor, the bitter, the disheveled, the union apes, some with bursting muscles, some gone all punk and crooked with labor. He might have seen Coots down there, with his young amanuensis dickering for morphine, heroin, hashish, opium, or just espresso, Player's cigarettes, and Stolichnaya, with a man of trade. Dr. Latouche knew nothing much of drugs. He had never done much biochemistry. Fifty years ago he had quit cigarettes. His three cold martinis every evening, no matter where he was, were the only rise he required. He had been close to being an addict of surgery but why not? He did not like drugs, even when he prescribed them in small amounts. Dr. Latouche had never even had a real headache. In his medicine cabinet were Epsom salts, Pepto-Bismol, iodine, and, for visitors, aspirin.

Coots might have looked back up at Latouche's apartment window, maybe swallowing a Bucet with a fresh cup of espresso if nothing better was to be had. He, just lately, knew where Latouche lived. He was very much on his case, narrowing. Latouche might have mistaken the gaunt, tall Coots in his suit for an owner, a big legitimate importer. Outside his addiction, morphine now beaten, Coots insisted on having his things in order. The shooting of his wife had finally convinced him deeply against sloppiness. The worst of it was the mess. He led a tidy, controlled life. He despised what controlled him. His books railed against control, didn't they, despite the obliquity? Conspiracies of control were the target for his massed attacks, using stacked cords of bodies out front, behind, flanking. Up at seven for his stomach exercises; fruit, espresso, and pumpernickel toast; cold shower, then hot briefly, beating last night's cigarette residue from his lungs like Tarzan with a habit; speed-reading the London and New York *Times*es, especially for dire foreign and space alien occurrences, then more deliciously the personals; next perhaps a novel urged on him by some hopeful who'd pierced through his secretary, a matter of fifteen minutes (Coots had speed-read by sixth grade in St. Louis without realizing it was unnatural). His mind brilliantly plundered the book, storing entire sentences, shucking the rest like a piece of green corn, only a few nuggets in there. Coots cared very little for creative writing other than his own, and was blithely unconscious of any real American literary scene — a part of his charm to his adorers. He would write very slowly and often beautifully, clearheaded, trusting only hashish or a minor barbiturate, with his mild Benson and Hedges cigarettes. At times he would quit one or the other to exercise his control. Coots had lost a rough twenty years stoned, in Tangiers, New Orleans, New York and Mexico, filthy on a mattress, and he wanted to make them count.

Some had called him a genius since the fifties. Now he was a man of adequate means and invited everywhere for very little reason except the sight of him, alive and gray and imperturbable, a miracle of crotchety survival, beyond space and time. By late afternoon, through with his "studies" — diseases, drugs, hieroglyphics (he had no facility with languages and was deaf to music) — he'd be tired, and walk off the funk in the company of his secretary on interesting streets, wanting to "see a death" near him. His cane, really a sheath for a long stiletto, tapped along merrily. New York was getting too expensive, but he had always loved the hate and Byzantine corruption not only as metaphor but directly inhaling them so as to store them as power. He had been among natives and occult literatures and believed in magic as flatly as in chemistry. He had experienced rare days when he could do no wrong. He would sail an envelope, eyes blind, and it would smack right into the wastebasket. He would drop his razor and the thing would tumble perfectly to his toe, clipping a nail that needed it. On his tape recorder certain meaningful phrases would rise in volume for no technical reason, and they would be important to his life and work. He could fast for a week and be stronger. On the streets he was almost sure that if the enemy were persuasive enough, he could cause "a death" and pass by as an innocent bystander. The evidence of this had come clear years ago when an absurdly rude landlady had looked at him and fallen dead right on the stair landing outside his door, the hexed "gash." At night, eating with friends and admirers, some of them world-famous actors and musicians, he was polite and attentive. He would not lie, and he refused to be cajoled into being "strange" by some fresh fool who had misunderstood him entirely. Most of the world was perfectly obvious to him. He would not romanticize the "alien." In his own case, he'd never romanticized being a junkie. Contemporaries in drug and drink had dropped around him like flies — into morgue or loony bin — but a certain dim ingeniousness and regularity had dragged him through, so that his gray eminence punched out like a face on Mount Rushmore. For several thousands worldwide, Coots was one of the true fathers of the century. And greatly tested by calamity. His wife, then their son shooting up like Pop (amphetamines), but lasting only till thirty, liver all gone. Coots was not stone. He fell in love with forlorn helplessness, even now, and would cry like a woman when penetrated by some dreams. Dr. Latouche was in his dreams — not love, not envy, but what? Coots was driven, as not in decades.

When he found the billiards club, an establishment for the Arrived, he snorted. The Britishness. These atavistic beasts he'd had
fun with in his violent satires, but even those books were old. He
reckoned he looked M.P. enough to get in and was very pleased
when the deskman, young, collegiate, recognized him and waved to
the back rooms where all the fun was, offering him the place. It was
dark green and woody, pungent with hearthsmoke, with jolly music
from somewhere like England happening. Low voices drifted from
separate parlors. Coots had no opinion of billiards at all, but the
place made him a little homesick for St. Louis in the thirties: innocent American pool tables, the first taste of tobacco, the swoon. He
was a boy then, just graduated from the neighborhood pond, with
sun-browned cheeks, a string of bullheads, and a cane pole with
black cotton line. Learning to be idle and mock, forever. The heft of
the cue stick always made it seem like a good thing to knock with.
Even Harvard never dragged that feeling from him. The pool hall
had a real wood fire you could spit in and watch.

The first players to his right were neither one Latouche. Coots
could tell by their faces that they were dumbed by privilege and
bucks, and he hissed straight at them, feeling the hidden stiletto in
his cane. How a sweep of it across the throat would tumble them,
gasping Why? Why? Queer angels would then move down on them
with a coup de grace of quick sodomy. Coots' grandfather was a rich
inventor and Coots had never been without a constant monthly sum,
but the frigid regard of certain wealthy raised a fire from balls to
crown in him. And where was Latouche? In another parlor, vainly
ignoring active grofft by placing himself in public at billiards. Coots
had only, with delight, *heard* of grofft in his Central American travels, where he'd made himself fit enough to penetrate the wilds in
search of a storied hallucinogen. The drug was a retching bust, but
the grofft tales were very interesting. Latouche must have *been* there
to contract grofft. Coots had never heard of a white man with it.

A man near ninety could not have pushed into the deeps down
there. Coots remembered the horrible misunderstandings with natives,
the dangerous approach through a white-water creek, the malarial
bottoms, where mosquitoes *were* the air. He had written solemnly
about his explorations, but in the back of his mind he'd since wondered if he was thoroughly had by the tribesmen. Some foliage had
moved, a barking human face emerged briefly, and the thing had run
off lowly like a pointer, having smelled or seen that Coots was not the
right thing. *Grofft!* shouted the natives, terrified. He didn't understand

what was going on, but he was alarmed too, near killed by a fer-de-lance before he snapped out of it. In the University of Mexico medical library he had looked up the pathology. But the entry on grofft read as if it didn't belong, as if it had been written in dread by a haunted mystic of the seventeenth century. The cause: probably the bite of a grofftite — the breath or saliva. Etiology? Symptoms: lupine facial features and doglike barking and whining; quadriped posture; hebephrenia; extremely nervous devotion to a search, general agitation, constant disappointment; lethargy, then renewal. Treatment: Nobody of any medical skill had ever run down a grofftite. History: The skeletons of grofftites had been seen (and avoided) in places near and far from settlements; no uniformity in demise except bones of the fingers, forehead, and sometimes neck were often (twelve cases reported) fractured, the teeth broken; head in three cases planted to jaw depth in dirt, as if thrown violently from a high elevation. And *this*: Grofftites have lived up to fifty years after being stricken. It was claimed infants were taken off by grofftites but these might be mere Indian tales or manipulative responses to the urban interlocutors. *N.B.*: Indians have demanded money to imitate a grofftite.

Coots, peering hard at old Latouche in the last parlor now, suspected it might be a powerful drug that induced grofftism. He was in the country of powerful brews, and he could not shake the idea that it was a vaguely religious, maybe even saintly condition, drunk deliberately down by the devout, enough *d*'s to go direct to disease, the divine. The sight of noble old Latouche, cueing the ball and doing something smooth with it, was making Coots silly.

Thinking back through the years, he had known very, very few people of pure virtue, if that were Latouche's case. In his suit Coots felt rude and small. Latouche — another endearing trait — wore wonderful clothes, but he was a bit sloppy and misfit in them. They loved his rumpled way, his scuffed shoes, the speck of sauce on his tie. What an agreeable granddad of a guy.

The doctor was playing a young man with a built-up physique. The young man wore a blazer. Ribbed socks — Coots noticed — with spangling black loafers. He acted familiar with old Latouche. Coots wondered if Latouche was the ward of this muscular stooge.

"Good evening, our genius," said Latouche, surprised. "You're a billiards man too?"

"Hardly. Just a watcher. Lifelong."

"Order you a drink?"

"Too early. Perhaps a tonic with lime."

"We're just talking about the rumors that God is a woman. What do the literary people say about that?"

"When wasn't it? It's a neurotic hag demanding worship while it lays a pox down. An obtuse monster, a self-worshiping fiend. I know gods, Doctor."

"Should have guessed you'd have an opinion. This is Riley Barnes, Coots. Barnes, the author. Barnes knows your work. I've been reading you. Some difficulty, I confess, for an old sawbones. I liked the surgeon using the plumber's friend in a heart operation. I'd suppose you've known some awfully bad doctors. So have I, but —"

"You have literary interest?" Coots asked Barnes. "I've seen you before, haven't I?"

"Yes sir," said Barnes, knowing Coots too. "I'm a stevedore. The docks."

"You know, I'd spotted Riley. Somehow I thought I must meet him. So I did. Very fortuitous circumstance. I watched him through a telescope. How could I have guessed he was a literary man and wild for billiards? The city always surprises you," explained Latouche.

Coots had written about men like Barnes, one of his physical type of boy. He had them falling through space, ejecting incandescent sperm while being hanged by the neck...Old duffer consuls would gobble it up. Sacrifice of the young to evil, entrenched needs. The way the world worked.

"You and your friend bought...commodities down there. I was in different clothes," said Barnes. "Don't think you'd recognize me, sir. Anyway, it's an honor. I know people who'd pay to be here."

"Go on with your game, please," said Coots to the young man. Was he in his late twenties? Coots wondered. Straight. Off a mural of American Labor in an old union hall, dusty hoarse Commies around being ass-fucked by shark-skinned fat union bosses with stogies. Brando, *On the Waterfront*. What we pansies would have given to jump *his* bones. Stop. Latouche is the mission. The doctor did seem a little depressed, anxious, behind the jolly front. In the old days I'd have shucked him for drugs. Exactly the kind of croaker we'd set up till thoroughly burned down. Some of them were so stupidly moral they believed they were helping my endless kidney stones. Could be literary because I was so good at those riffs. Multiple personalities I developed. Then no personality at all when sick — protoplasm, whimpering, completely dishonored. Working the subways for drunks, at my best. New York, New York! Never again, knock on wood. Paper cup of coffee dissolving at the edge with spit.

Ketchup on crackers, free at the Automat, for weeks. Harvard education. Unfit to attack Hitler or Tojo, thank God.

"How's your dog, Doctor? It isn't here?"

"No." Latouche looked guilty, furtive. "Had to bury her. She got something, poor girl. They didn't know what."

Coots came alive, took a seat in a padded drugstore chair copied from the thirties.

"Was a Hungarian breed, something, wasn't it?"

"I wouldn't talk about the dog, Mr. Coots," interjected Barnes. Latouche *was* his charge, then.

"It's fine, Riley. Really." Latouche grasped the billiard table, his fingers going white over the felt edge.

"I'm a cat man, myself," said Coots. Could he now detect Latouche trembling, his eyes rolling back into his head? Delicious, better than his first horror movies with Lon and Bela in St. Louis.

"Can't stand them!" yelled Latouche. He shot back — reloaded, rather, thought Coots. "Sneaky, conniving!...the *odor* of cat piss! Doesn't that tell you something?" Agitated, pushing the insane, this beat the medical libraries cold. ("A death"?) But I don't have the full persuasion for a spell, really, Coots decided. What do I hate about the man? My own grandfather? Grand patricide? Biting the hand that.

"I'll have to ask you, Mr. Coots." Barnes again. My word, so rapidly the nurse, all the jargon.

"No. I want this resolved and confessed!" shouted Latouche. "Secrets are killing me!"

The cue stick, released, fell over, *plump,* on the rug. Both his hands were on the table now.

"I buried Nana, I had Nana buried with my wives, between them, in Forest Hills cemetery! Riley did it for me!"

"That isn't so bad, Latouche. Isn't there a law, though? The Indians, you know...the Egyptians..."

"We didn't ask. I did it at night," said Riley Barnes.

"He's got grofft, doesn't he?"

"How'd you know?" Barnes bolstered Latouche. "Oh yes. Your travels. Would you know how it's treated? Dr. Latouche, bless him, believes he can just ignore it away."

Latouche was slavering and attempting to drop to the floor, while Barnes was resisting, gently, though all his big muscles were needed. The doctor certainly had his right man. Barnes seemed to care deeply for him. Coots smiled less than he wanted to, hands crossed on his stiletto cane in front, the boulevardier.

"I don't think this is a mind-over-matter case, Barnes" — Latouche actually whimpered like a dog now — "though by what I've observed, the doctor has *civilized* the disease. Perhaps strength of character. Or just being un-Indian, highly Western. I recall the smallpox didn't kill that many of us, but wiped out whole tribes of the Sioux. We've antibodies, but — "

Barnes sadly let the doctor go and raced to the door, pulling it to and locking. The doctor went around the table on all fours, sniffing and pointing, heedless of them. Why was this, Coots asked himself, so charming to him?

Why did Latouche pique such high disgust? Was he an old lifetime closet fairy and Coots knew it? Many great professionals were, no great mystery. Then was it the hypocrisy Coots loathed? The laurels and friendships gained by an, at least, eighty-year false front? But he did not really think Latouche was gay. Some deeply sick, hidden gays were fascinated by weapons, especially on the right wing, the loud NRA and all that, but not Latouche, who loved the technology more than the blast. Latouche acquainted himself with past heroes in dangerous times, as did Coots, who owned in his locker one of Billy the Kid's purported old irons. But Latouche liked to balance the loads, better.

Latouche was all around the room now, scraping at the door and whimpering urgently. Something was out there he had to hunt. Coots thought of a feverish liver-spotted thing whirling in its cage, wanting the quail fields. He had witnessed that once in Texas when he was a failed marijuana farmer. The face of the doctor was working classically, too. His cheeks closed forward, lupine, more than could be done by a well man. Then came the barks and worried low growls, the mutter of need, almost ecstatic.

"How did he get into the Honduran wilds?" asked Coots.

"He didn't. I went for him. The Indians were known for prodigious strength. Please don't let on, Mr. Coots. You're a man of the world, the cosmos. It shouldn't shock you. I'd found a healthy young Indian, I thought. He'd had a fatal accident. I took his blood and brought it back chilled. We transfused Dr. Latouche."

"Extraordinary. Why?"

"It had worked for one of his old colleagues. The man's ninety-five now, in glowing health. Down there, the laws...deep back in there, there *are* no laws. You can *buy* somebody. Never mind, I had the boat connections and the way, so I did it for him. There aren't many Latouches in the world. Like there aren't many of you. He'd been low, depressed, feeble, didn't believe in drugs. This is corny, but he's the grandfather I never had, and the father who left me. I didn't want to lose him right after I'd found him."

"Commendable. So this is the 'secret'?"

"Yes."

"But, my God, boy, he's a horror. How can you have him out here in public playing at billiards?"

"He goes a long time without spells. He's set off by mental... imagery, I think. Especially dogs. Or their enemies. Cats, awful. And sometimes blacks, unfortunately, although Dr. Latouche doesn't have a racist bone in his body."

"He's going to quit this after a while, then?"

"If things go right. But the spells are getting longer. We've got to keep him locked in here. I'm sorry."

"Not at all. I've no other business. So he gave you money, he paid you..."

"Mr. Coots, you'd imagine, but Dr. Latouche doesn't even have that much money. He's given it all away. He should have a better apartment, servants, but he's got none of it. Thousands are *alive* because of Dr. Latouche."

"And he looks a young seventy."

"Doesn't he? I think it's all love and happy work, Mr. Coots."

"*William.* You think so? And nobody knows any more than I do about the disease?"

"Looked everywhere. Only one doc in New York had ever *heard* of it. It's never been treated in South America. We can only be grateful his is milder, so far. If you believe this, Dr. Latouche wants to begin a fund to go in and cure those few pitiful Indians. Not for himself, not in his lifetime."

"Yet an Indian... died. For him."

"That's the worst way to put it. And it was my choice."

Coots lit a Player's. He needed a strong hit. Fifty years of cigarettes now, with no drastic trouble. He was enjoying the smoke no less than the first good inhale in St. Louis. In that pool hall, he remembered now, a strange old man from nowhere had put his hand on his shoulder and said to him, "My lad, you will write masterpieces." One of those magic episodes that had punctuated his life. Now Latouche was grievously scuttling and digging at the floor with his long elegant surgeon's fingers.

"I don't know why you're here, sir. But you are the thing, I hope. Obviously you know medicine and magic. I've read all your books. What can we do?"

"The Indians did nothing. I believe they revered and, I know, feared the grofftites."

"Your guess would be better than any doctor's, I'd bet."

"I could try something." Coots was into the grim clinical zone he often elected for himself. It was obvious he could have been a fine M.D., given any ambition to heal. The other, too. He grabbed at the pertinent file in his head. The delight of the fit was wearing out. He had lost his spite somewhere.

"You might try slapping him a hard one. Be a bigger dog. Canines respond to bald aggression. They're pack animals."

"I doubt I could —"

"Do it. Don't hold back. Otherwise, you could drench yourself with bitch urine. But he might just hump you and bite your back."

Barnes did reach down, turning the doctor's cheeks up, and slap him powerfully, then shut his eyes in pity.

It worked.

Soon enough, Latouche was biped, straightening his tweedy suit back to its original loose rumple, pulling down his vest and replacing his watch chain across the front in the old style. His medical fraternity pin hung there, a small vanity. He was national president in the fifties, the decade of Coots' first grand fame and obscenity trial. The French, who like their authors sick, fell on his book in droves. Coots stayed shyly and happily away, grogged in morpheus. It had taken him years and the help of friends, but the thing was out and he was going to make some money. Manslaughterer, junkie, thief, queer, layabout — the outer and under had won through. He was regent guru of the beatniks, like it or not.

"Little phase there. I seem to have left you. My cheek smarts. Did I fall?" Latouche wanted to know.

"A little," said Riley Barnes quickly.

"Old men get tired. Don't they, Coots? Are you sometimes just *tired?*"

"Yes indeed."

"I think it's martini time. Can almost taste it already, terribly cold, with big white onions. Would you, Riley? What's your pleasure, Coots?"

"The same. Sounds perfect."

"All right, then. Don't want to try the stick?"

"No. Let's sit in the booth and talk, guns maybe. Hard decisions about the forty-four / forty-five."

Coots noticed Latouche did not have that detestable turkeyness under the throat that the old often do. Even in his thinness Coots had one gaining on him. A thing that the aging imp Capote attempted to cure by fellatio, he'd heard. They sat.

"Good. I have one. An eighteenth-century heavy handgun. Short piece, cap and ball, of course. Never shot."

"Bring it on down to the range next Tuesday. We'll rig it."

The martinis came, with Barnes, who had a light beer, imported. A health man. How long was his dick? The drinks were sublime, just the ticket. Coots opened up even more. He was narrowing on the question of his own spite.

"I have the Billy the Kid gun," he said.

"You don't. There is no Billy the Kid gun."

"But there is. I'll show it to you. You must come down to my fort. Say Tuesday instead of the range."

Barnes spoke up, delighted. "He's known for not inviting many, Dr. Latouche. You should feel honored. This could be a legendary evening for us."

Coots looked at the boy, who had become too chummy.

"How about just an old-timers' chat, the two of us?" said Coots. "This is no rebuke, Barnes."

"Sorry. Not at all. I go to the gym, anyway, when he goes shooting. I could be nearby, however."

"Then it's fixed. I'm feeling better all the time," said Latouche. "Let me ask you something. Why did Billy the Kid kill so many?"

"*¿Quien es?*" chuckled Coots. These were the Kid's last words before being gunned down by Pat Garrett. "I'm not sure. It was a sort of war, the Lincoln County thing. It wasn't twenty-one, not nearly that. But I'd imagine it got in his blood, very early, when he was attacked by a bully with a knife. Rather like a drug addiction. I've studied killers. Now let me ask you: When you shoot, who are you shooting, mentally? What kind of enemies does a man like you have?"

The old doctor was surprised. "Well...quite zero. It's *all* mental, a sport."

"Come now. You're too good at it. Some emotion belongs, surely."

"I've no enemies I know of."

"Life has treated you nicely. No malpractice suit, say, totally unjust. The lawyers. You've known *women*. Some yapping gash that bilked you. Tell me too, that somewhere in the world of money there wasn't...And you were in the war, no?"

Coots hardly ever beseeched this much. Even when directly interviewed, for money, he'd not shown this zeal.

"Downrange there you must see some Nazi, some Commie, hippie, queer, black mugger, proponent of socialized medicine, or, really, man a—" Coots almost said *cat,* as a joke. He looked at Riley Barnes, intense and worshipful, vastly enjoying, and lucky. "Mengele, a Stalin, a Klansman."

"Not at all. I'm afraid you're making me sound like a man of no passion. What do *you* shoot, Coots?"

"Everything. Old age."

This created high giggles in the other two. Poor men, was he that interesting to them? A scholar, a dreamer, and rather a drudge is what Coots thought he was. He yearned for the character of William Bonney.

"I suppose people who don't hate don't write," said the doctor. "With surgery, I was rarely conscious of a person. Another thing entirely. Never have I felt the necessity, either, to interpret the universe. It was mainly just one piece of work, then another."

"Then who would you rather have been, Latouche? Please think."

"Umm. Well, actually...Methuselah. I'm not ready to go. I've known hardly a day I've not truly enjoyed. Even the war, I was always up bright and early. Even, do not mistake me, the morning of my wives' funerals. You've made me honest. Is that your function?"

"But, my man, you have..." Coots reflected and checked on Riley Barnes, who was writing something down on a billfold tablet. "You have *grofft.* The only man in North America."

Barnes flashed up, eyes sorrowful. He might want to strike Coots. When he masturbated, looking in the mirror, did he insert his finger in his anus to intensify it? Could he entice women into rim jobs? Many muscle men—*vide* your obsessive weightlifters in the big house—were "anally retentive," thanks, Sigmund. And sex was a way of keeping, owning lovers, having them to play with in the bank vault later. As opposed to the looser lostness of the mere pussy, which invited death and servility. Barnes' big stevedore's hand was on Latouche's wrist.

"Yes, I have it. But luckily, it seems, just a mild touch. I've not been on all fours yet. No barking. Riley watches me honestly."

As with a thirty-year quart-a-day man he'd once met at the Maple Leaf bar in New Orleans: "I have no drinking problem, Coots." Skin flaking off from the burst veiny patches of his face, yellow as a crayon, and his tongue black.

"Then Tuesday night at seven, Latouche."

"Delighted. I'll have Riley bring me around in my vintage Hudson. Now there's an item you might like. Spotless. Forest green. Purrs like a" — Barnes harder on his wrist— "sewing machine."

"The Hudson and Billy the Kid's gun," said Barnes in wonder. "A great American evening."

A couple days later Coots flew to Kansas with his amanuensis, Horton. They planned to live there soon, and had already bought a small clapboard house with a picket fence and a porch in the university town. Coots hoped he might teach a class there, though there was some lack of enthusiasm from the older faculty, to whom he was a profane dope fiend and pederast who wrote gibberish. His secretary friend was attempting to broker him into a place. Coots could use the money. It was a sorry scandal that they would exclude him. In several apparent ways he was a conservative. He loved the plains of the Midwest and was fascinated by the Old West and its worthy guns. He knew Native American culture (Custer's stuffed horse, Comanche, was in the university museum); had the notes for two large books wherein he would explore the West in space-time narratives and by way of his "cut-up" method — not montage, he insisted, but more: common threads of magic in random clippings from various sources, sometimes announced into his tape recorder and retranscribed. He'd not yet got all from cannabis that he intended, either. Coots was a hard worker, putting to shame the energies of the senior faculty, with their emeritus rosebeds and sailing vacations.

It was hard for Horton not to get angry about the matter, though Coots accepted the landscape and l'état gladly as they were away from wearying, impolite and expensive New York. The main point was he was old, damn it, and had been everywhere. He'd never had a thing against roots and a calm place, there was no crime in that. And there would be wide and free places to shoot. He could have a cat or two, his favorite creatures. He was so much like them it was nearly like having children. "The furred serpent," Egyptians called them.

He did not tell Horton about Latouche.

Lawrence, Kansas, occupied them. Coots breathed in his "square" neighborhood: perfect, superb. The air might give him a few more years, a few more books. The scratchy, potent West. The "Johnsons" — trustworthy, minding their own business, nonjudgmental, quick to ally with a fellow in trouble, salt of the earth, loving of land, their house was yours, etc. — Coots had the forgotten shock of being waved at by citizens who didn't know him from Adam. Howdy. Partners in the given day. Suitably, it came a "gusher" while they were there. The rain smelled sweet, rich. Thinking of the golden wheat lapping it up, breadbasket of the world, amber fields of, sunbrowned boy with a string of bullheads, home-dried cut canepole with black cotton line, drilled piece of corncob for a bobber, Prince Albert tin with nightcrawlers in wet leaves for bait.

Horton liked seeing the old fellow this happy.

They were out in Latouche-land too. Latouche was originally from Ellsworth.

It was the land of generals — Eisenhower, Bradley. And Frank James rode through Lawrence itself with the guerrilla slaughterers and Quantrill. Then Coots and T. S. Eliot over in St. Louis, not far from Twain. Ah, dreamed Coots on his porch, his thin hair blowing, to have fucked Huck when the country was young, about to strangle itself in the Big One, sun-swollen teenage corpses in the cornfield. Sherman sodomizes the South. John Brown began here first, Kansas, bloody Kansas, my Kansas. What did Latouche think of it? Had Latouche ever thought much at all?

The doctor was at his door and they walked out to see the Hudson purring at the curb. Barnes, in gym suit, was at the wheel saluting him. The Hudson was a gem all right. A space fiction of 1950, drop-shaped, chubby, svelte too. Barnes yelled something about being careful, he'd see Latouche at midnight. Coots noticed his massive legs. That boy could really hurt you if he wanted. Without him, the car gone, Latouche seemed smaller, with snowier hair, cautious and unbalanced. Coots helped him down the stairs to "the bunker," leaning on the sharp door — like a vault door. Coots gasped, weak himself. Safe inside, Latouche took the sofa and looked about, out of his overcoat. They were alone. Horten was away for the night.

"I've brought this mini–tape recorder, if you don't mind. It's for Riley's sake," said Latouche.

Coots minded. His words were worth a great deal lately. The BBC thing, and NPR. He was to play a junkie priest in a movie soon too. Might as well ham it up toward the end.

Something had clicked one strange tired morning a month ago — he'd been very, very tired, from no direct cause. Coots was going to die soon, the fatigue told him quietly. Some ancient soft voice like that of the unknown man in the pool hall, but this was not an "episode."

This was the dead and dry tone of the inevitable. He didn't know when he'd die, but something announced the beginning of the last lap. The public flies were on him, even worse.

"I thought you'd bring your forty-four / forty-five," he said coolly. Coots could wither, with his scratchy voice and small eyes.

"But I did, in the other pocket." Latouche drew the handsome brute out, size of a good man's organ, laying it on the coffee table next to the minirecorder, a Toshiba. He punched it on. Coots' anger left when he spied the weapon. Lovely little highwayman's surprise, lovely.

"I've loaded the thing. Can't quite figure why," said Latouche.

"The mean streets. It's a bad area."

"No." Latouche stared at Coots as if lost. He seemed really to have no idea why the thing was loaded. Septagonal barrel?

"Barnes knows you have a loaded gun?"

"No. He's a deep pacifist, for gun control. New York law, of course."

"I think he killed an Indian for you." Coots smiled at the little reels turning inside the machine.

"He told you?"

"I gather things. Pretty nasty, and unethical, medically speaking, you know."

"Oh, I do. It's all a bad mysterious thing. And my fault. I found out that Riley has a dangerous loyalty to me. Almost an innocence. If only I could take it back. I'm very shallow with people, I'm afraid."

"But I suppose you've been paid back. The blood of a very wrong Indian. Hmm?"

"Yes. And that wasn't my first transfusion. I've had two others — one for each of my marriages — each done legally. Good Swiss blood, very."

"What do you mean, *for?*"

"For Maggie and Verna both. I was slowing down and I did it for us. To keep up, to prance, to dance. They were both a good deal younger and I couldn't give them an old coot dead on his lounge chair at the end of the day."

"And they worked?"

"My word, yes! You couldn't keep me down. It was amazing, scary, truly. I romanced them, read in erotic books" (Latouche blushed), "rowed down the river with them in the bow. I pleased them constantly, not just with flowers and gifts. In fact —"

"Just a second. I'll have the martinis out. Save this."

Coots prepared the martinis with more care than usual, dropping in Latouche's big white onions, specially bought that afternoon. He waited longer, too, to diffuse the agitation the nonagenarian had got himself into. Coots — Saul on the road to Tarsus — suddenly had an overwhelming light on him; nothing like this had happened to him before. He *liked* Latouche, thoroughly. True friendship was attacking him. He was very afraid the fellow would get too wound up and stumble into the names, the "imagery," and say *cat* or *dog — wolf? snake? Negro? quail?* He was close to saying everything, and in danger. He waited almost impolitely long. When he went out with the tray he stared at the gun. Let's get that thing away, Coots decided. Which is what he did, turning it in his other hand admiringly, his martini hand freezing.

"Fine heft. A real buried treasure. The recoil must be a consideration. Jim 'Awkins and Long John Silver, eh?"

"What?"

"*Treasure Island.* Stevenson. What did you *do* as a boy in Kansas?"

"Oh, sure now. Even I read that one once, I think."

"I dreamed of almost nothing but pirates, myself."

"I dreamed of, can you believe it, Kansas itself. Simply repictured what was around me. The wheatfields, the blizzards, the combines, the awful summer sun. For dreams in my sleep, I never had any. I never dream."

"You've got to be kidding. A man would die, flat out."

"But it's true. Freud would've had no use for me."

"Well, surgery did. But what a fact."

"The transfusions, though —" began Latouche.

"My friend, this is startling too. Yours worked. Mine didn't. I tried to kick morphine with one. No go."

Latouche couldn't know that he had Coots entirely. Coots had a young healthy crush on him, wanting nothing.

"I'm very sorry." Latouche drank deep. Coots was saddened by the unusual sloppiness, gin down the doctor's chin, untended. "But my transfusions, let me tell you, I think, I know — poor Maggie, poor Verna — I was *too* much. How they loved me! What a heavenly benefit, their love. I could not leave them alone, Coots. Finally, I — now I say, the bed, the bed, the bed, the bed. The dances, the bicycling, the jogging, the too-long mountain hikes in rain — they loved it for *me*. Then always the bed, the couch, the shower, even the garage, every which way, all hours! Then I'd be up with their breakfast, waking them. I'd have written up an oncological technique while they slept! Too much, too much! They died."

"What?"

Latouche's pathetic unlined face was sopped with gin, dropping down like a beard of tears and slobber.

Coots dragged his handkerchief out and kneeled to attend Latouche, dabbing away, kinder than a nurse.

"My friend, my friend," he sympathized in his great scratch, softened.

"It's true. I killed them. They were just worn out, is all. Still lovely, both, still should have been in the fine bloom of a woman's middle age, that arousing..."

"But one would suppose that one often destroys the loved one. *I* have destroyed. Have been destroyed," Coots said, trying to aid.

"I don't mean your... fictions, your creative writing! I mean *destroyed!*"

"Yes, but guilt, must..."

"I don't know what brought me to shout it out. I don't know why that pistol is loaded. Something made... *You*. It's you, Coots. You demand terrible buried things, somehow. Calamities. Isn't that it?"

"That's not a condition of our friendship."

Latouche calmed down and smiled. "We *are* friends, aren't we? All our strangenesses and our differences. We are, yes?"

"Doubtless, friends. And for that I'll get a fresh one for you. Take it easy. All is locked, here in the bunker."

Latouche saw the big secured door and nodded, instantly more solid himself.

This drink Coots did thoroughly, a spring in his step, close again to that sunbrowned boy with his string of bullheads, his Prince Albert tin filled with nightcrawlers.

When he came out, Latouche was gone and the door was thrown open. There had been a noise in his writing room, and now only Latouche's things were left, his tape recorder, gun, and overcoat across the arm of the sofa. The front door was unlocked; it must have been thrown open very rapidly, speed quieting the noise.

Coots shut his eyes and knew. He'd forgotten, forgotten, forgotten, entirely the dog hides on the wall of his writing room: the Rottweiler's black one, and the German shepherds' speckled gray. Latouche must have stepped inside, looked, then fled, feeling hunted himself. On the spoor.

Horton's Honda Express, the little city motorbike, was next to the front entranceway, helmet on the seat. Coots knew he should take this. He'd handled it perfectly many times. It would be required, he was positive.

He labored with the big two-by-twelve board on the stairs that served Horten as a ramp. His own long smart overcoat on, helmeted — Horten's humor insisted on a dove aviary painted all over the helmet — and buckled in, he cranked the scooter and rushed precariously upward through exhaust clouds to the sidewalk, then out bumping off the curb, an old man from hell. Wouldn't you know, his pesty neighbor, the junkie dentist Newcomb, antithesis of Latouche, hooked possibly on everything and ever determined to visit, was right in his way, and was knocked down by Coots and the whirling machine. Coots cursed with his last cigarette breath, despising this low absurdity. He thought he saw Latouche three blocks up as the street was otherwise empty. Something was scrambling ahead on all fours, head down, trailed by its suspenders, white shirttails out.

It was Latouche. Coots ran over his jacket in the street. Then there was a boot, an old Wellington boot, straight up, abandoned. Poor man! Coots could hardly breathe — the pity, the terror, the love, and the effort with that board. His adrenaline, if it was there, was wondering where to go. He could hardly get air down. Latouche was faster, or through asthmatic illusion Coots thought he was, and he turned back the accelerator all the way. The doctor was running up into the middle of the city. Soon he'd be lost in neon and street strollers, sloths, pimps, bus-stop criminals, sluts. Coots could see citizens spotting the sidewalks increasingly a quarter mile up.

At last his respiration and vision were easier. How fast could a dog run? He looked at the speedometer: thirty mph, and he still wasn't gaining on him. What kind of dog was Latouche? Something Central American and predacious. Please not a greyhound, pushing forty! The motorbike could hit that speed too, but barely. How, then, could he catch Latouche?

He didn't know it but he passed Riley Barnes, early out of the gym, coming toward him in the Hudson. Barnes flinched and soon U-turned. Coots' frail head in the bird helmet was unmistakable. By the time he came even, Coots was narrowing his eyes, an elderly cavalry scout in spectacles. Latouche had run into the crowd. He was gone. There was only reckoning with his speed now and trying to stay up even. If Latouche took a turn, it was hopeless. The motorbike wobbled into higher speed, but the traffic would have him soon.

Coots felt pure hate for humankind, especially New Yorkers, too cowardly to stay in their rooms; they must be out with their autos, part of the clot, rubbernecking at each other—like dogs. Dogs! Packs of them sniffing, licking balls, consorting in dumb zeal, not a clue, not an inward reflection. The mayor and the police should be shot, for not shooting them. And then this streetlight. He was in a paroxysm of fury.

"Where in the hell are you going, Mr. Coots?" Riley Barnes was next to him at the junction, yelling to him from the high car. "Stop, please."

Coots did.

"He went into the grofft. I swear, Barnes, a horrible inadvertency at my place. He saw some 'imagery' on my wall in another room. He's up there, blocks, incredibly fast."

"Get in the car, quick. He can't be out here!" Barnes was in tears already.

"The car's no good. If he turns, you've no chance. This Honda's the thing. Let me go."

"I'm going too. He's mine."

"Fool. Then get on the back if you can."

"You can handle this?" Great poundage in the rear with Barnes. They sank down.

"I can handle it. Shut up and look."

They were off, riding as if on a wire, given Barnes' body. Every yard was risky and grim. The motorbike wanted to waddle off into the gutter or straight out into the oncoming lanes. Coots' arms were noodles from the effort.

"Don't move! Just look, damn you!" His voice whipped back around the helmeted cheeks.

He looked too, tried to. Hunter of the hunter, pointer of the pointer. It had been ages since he'd labored physically at anything, but Nature had not slighted him in adrenaline. He was handling the cargo nicely after another half mile. But Nature—in Latouche's case, God?—had not slighted the doctor either. Age ninety, ninety! His fitness was uncanny. Coots thought he saw a clot of citizens part, shouting, at something on the ground another three blocks up. Maybe they were gaining a little. Latouche could not be given much more by his heart and lungs. His bootless feet must be awful by now. If only some decent man would just stop him. But where was a decent citizen of New York to be found? It would take a tourist, some Johnson from Kansas.

"Help! Help him!" shouted Barnes, sensing the same.

All Latouche did was gather disgusted glares from both sidewalks.

The thing they feared worst occurred. Plainly, just two blocks up now, a corner crowd parted, faces snapped down, then to the left, some of them pointing down a side street. Latouche had turned. If he began weaving the streets, he was doomed unless he fainted. Coots' grand new friend would be snatched from him by the most horrible chance and he would be forever had by another "black thing" as vile as his wife's death. This plague of one, this Kansan prince of North America, was nearing his end and Coots did not even feel potent enough to be his nurse.

Latouche may have been the only man of pure virtue Coots had ever known. You could not really fornicate somebody to death. That was all just Latouche's elevated code, wasn't it? An anachronism. Guilty for his own vigor, guilty for his own superb gifts. Could be slight atherosclerosis closing on the old gent, who'd buried awesomely too many contemporaries. Left lonely in his luck.

He must have turned yet again. These streets were near-empty, and they saw nothing. It would be merely a matter, Coots feared, of patrolling for his corpse, if they were even that fortunate. They'd have to go to the police and do the official. In the precincts they might know Latouche and get on it with more effort.

The motorbike putted — bleakly — as Coots halted it. The weight of Barnes, at rest, nearly threw them over into the road. But he stood them up with his mighty legs spread. He had not expected to stop.

"Go on! Go on!" cried Barnes in a futile voice as Coots removed the helmet. His hair stood out in wisps. The city had never seemed so unnecessary and odious to him. You could forget there was an old-time Greenwich Village, once worth inhabiting, breathing. And a zoo, the museums, Columbia, the fruitful subway where he'd rolled drunks for dope money. You could "raincoat" a stiff, tying the thing over his head with the sleeves, and have the money without violence; it was quite safe, even for the skinny Coots.

He must meditate the point here, a new one. Where did grofftites want to go? Where would they rest? Where *was* the quarry? There had to be something, he figured. While Barnes was calling the police, Coots tried to voodoo it out, but there was no file in his head about this he could turn to. Bad luck. "Spot of bother" — a refrain of the nasty British colonial — rang silly back and forth in his mind. He had no further sources. Barnes was probably worthless, in his grandsonly adoration. Knock down the maze, what could be the rat's desire? Somebody should have injected rats with grofft gland, offered a number of rat gratifications at the end.

The two of them, Coots and the almost whimpering Barnes — as if taking on symptoms in sympathy — stood foolishly beside the Honda peeping around, statues of the bereaved. Coots had had it with impotence, too old and losing too much by it in the past.

"He was talking about his wives, how he'd murdered them, worn them out with love. He sounded hyper, self-flagellating, caused by a quick suck of gin, maybe."

Barnes stood taller and clamped on Coots' wrist, too hard. You fucking monster. Then Barnes kneeled in street clothes with white bucks on his feet, drew a pen from his coat, and began drawing some route on his right shoe.

"What are you doing?"

"He's talked about his wives before. He could barely stand going to the cemetery with flowers for them. And their birthdays ruined him for days. He was chin-up, but I could tell."

"What cemetery?"

"Forest Hills, and the dog is there too. I know how to get in at night."

"That's ages from here. He couldn't make it."

"He could try. It's all we have. I've got a crow's flight route here on my shoe. We've got to go. Look along the way for him."

Damn the horror between here and there, thought Coots. It's the only mission.

The men wobbled along for a while seeing nothing, then hit an expressway where motorbikes were disallowed and Coots put the engine up red-line, clawing for near forty-five, deathly slow against the eighteen-wheelers. They looked along the highway for the doctor's flattened corpse. He could bake flat like a dog before New York got irritated by the smell. Thank the stars, they were soon off it, buffeted by winds of every rolling thing back there.

The landscape became tree-lined, with residential hedges on both sides where dogs could conceivably sleep in the street for a while, as in Kansas. Coots thought of every possible hazard to Latouche on a run even near here. They were too monstrous to confront. He aimed the scooter numbly, dread age tuckering him again in this long helpless mourning. He wondered if Barnes could feel the cap and ball .44-.45 in his overcoat pocket. He'd forgotten it himself and could not recall why he'd pocketed it. Then it came to him — it was exactly the caliber he'd used to nail the dogs, the favored size of the Old

West and until lately the modern army. So what? Except that plugging the dogs was the last large physical thing he had done.

There was a narrow screened gate in a northern wall before a gravel path. Barnes simply destroyed the gate before moving instantly a long ways ahead. Happy to be off the Honda, Coots crept like a rag on wasp's legs. It would be best to let Barnes see that there was nothing at the graves, then return to him. On the other hand, deeper into the burial grounds — vast — he noticed cross-paths and cul-de-sacs. He might get lost out here, celebrating this fool's errand by his own tragedy. This place at night was a sullen metropolis, its high monuments like a blind skyscape. The roll of it had its own charm, but not now.

He called ahead to Barnes. There was no answer. Coots was at the bottom of a very dark, long hill. He should stop, but he couldn't.

"Not yet, friends. Three or four more books I've got in me, I think," he announced to the brothering tombstones around him. No limit to the elevated vanity of some of them. Who the hell did they think they were, these fat-cat dead? No doubt with hordes of progeny scumming the Northeast. Old tennisers and polo players who should have died at birth, but giving the granite finger to the lowly and the modest who neighbored them. No worse fate than to fall and just be *discovered* out here.

Something let go a howl, canine and terrifying. It was too high for Barnes or Latouche. Too beyond, too nauseating. He stumbled down the hill toward it, however, loving the pistol when he felt it again. Ghoul, I am ready. Eat me, try. Then he heard what was plainly Barnes, near a big tree by the moon, weeping. Oh no. Oh what.

Apparently Barnes had done the howling. He sat at a plot of three stones.

Latouche had got deeply into one of the graves. His head was in it and both arms. He lay there — bloody, barefoot and dead. The name on the stone of the scratched grave was VERNA LOUISE LATOUCHE.

Coots kneeled, arm on the shoulder of the muddy Barnes, who was beating the ground with his hands, sobbing. He turned his face, changed into one hole of grief.

"Imposs— He was already coldish," said Riley Barnes.

"I think, lad, you'll find he's broken his fingers and his jaws. Poor Latouche."

"He was the finest man I've ever known."

"What was his given name?"

"Harold. Harry. I'm just a termite." Barnes was able to quit weeping, slowly. "What are you doing with that gun?"

"I . . . suppose I was going to try and woo him out of it with a piece of familiarity. It's his. He was an uncommon pistoleer."

"That was nice, Coots."

Barnes stood, filthy at the knees and palms. Then he kneeled again and pulled Latouche out of the hole; he was at the depth you'd see when an infantryman was caught out by bombs. Coots looked up at the rushing beardy clouds. He preferred not to see Latouche's face. That would be profane. Barnes, brushing the dirt from the doctor's face, seemed to agree. He would not look at him full-on. They also agreed that officials should be told — the ambulance, hurling lights, Coots could already imagine. This was enough.

There was, of course, the unspoken idea between them that Latouche should not be found like this. The gossip, the ugliness, the possibility of blemish on his life. Neither said anything for a good while until Coots, finally, spoke up.

"Really it's a better death than most. He didn't have to wait for it. More valiant, don't you think? We've got one problem. They won't believe it."

"It doesn't matter. All of him was unbelievable, when you study it."

"You go call. Can you do the Honda?"

"No problem."

"I'd like to stay and watch. A few more minutes with him."

"You're a good man, Mr. Coots. I really never knew that, by your stuff."

"I have my vagrant loyalties."

As he waited, seating himself finally in an ecstasy of relief — so tired, so worse than weary, his right hand in an agony from twisting on the motorbike — he found a Player's cigarette in his coat and lit it. Nature did nothing more, but the city became louder. Horns, screeches, a ball game, airplanes — it was all obscene.

"Oh yes I saw 'a death,' Harry. So Harry —" He stopped.

Coots' eyes became misted and blind. This was all right, this was fitting.

"But what a gap, Harry. What an awful gap you leave. And I only a watcher."

Bats Out of Hell Division

W E, IN A RAGGED bold line across their eyes, come on. Shreds of the flag leap back from the pole held by Billy, then Ira. We, you'd suspect, my posteritites, are not getting on too well. They have shot hell out of us. More properly we are merely the Bats by now. Our cause is leaking, the fragments of it left around those great burned holes, as if their general put his cigar into the document a few times. Thank you mercilessly, Great Perfecter. But we're still out there. We gain by inches, then lose by yards. But back by inches over the night, huff, flap, narg. I am on a first-name basis with five who have had their very trigger fingers blown away — *c'est rien,* mere *bagatelle.* They mutter, these Cajuns. Something about us their cannon doesn't like, to put it mildly. By now you must know that half our guns are no good, either.

Estes — as I spy around — gets on without buttocks, just hewn off one sorry cowardly night. Morton lacks hair, too close to the cannon before he decided on retreat. I have become the scribe — not voluntarily, but because all limbs are gone except my writing arm. Benedict, Ruth and the Captain say I am not unsightly, in my tent with the one armhole out of it, not counting the one for my head. I'm a draped man of some charm, says our benign crone of a nurse, Emmaline. Nobody comes forward to our rear like loyal Emmaline, the only woman to see this much this close. She comes up to the foul hospital, carrying a depth of pity. How, we wonder, does she carry on? "I've seen everything, boys! These milky old eyes have seen it all!" The only real atheist around, she carries love and helplessness forward in a bucket in either hand. We wonder, surely, whether this is the last woman we'll ever see. Maybe they use her to make us fight for home, but which way would that work? Better to think she's part of no plan at all. The best things in life, or whatever you call *this,* happen like that, even I in my old youth have learned. This marks the very thing, most momentous, I am writing about. It's over for me but I can't leave. No. I'd rather just stick here at my niggled work, undismayed by an occasional overshot bomb. I just lean over, disgusted, and think there's not much left of me to hit. Shrapnel blows through my tent-dress every now and then.

The best thing is that on retreat our boys run the rats and shocked wrens and baby rabbits back to me. Out of my tent shoots my arm. Yummy. The creatures had figured me for a goner. The smoke from the enemy's prime ribs, T-bones and basted turkeys floats over here at night sometimes, cruelly, damn the wind. In my long glass I can hardly find a human figure over there among the thick and bristling cannon, and when I do find a face, the smirk on it is killing. That is enough. I whisk back to the rear, wheel rapidly under my dress. Wind blows my tent up and I must resemble some fop's umbrella, rolling in the wheelbarrow. Some of us in that last long entrenchment, I noted, are so narrow against the wind they suffer the advantage of disappearing as targets. One man cuts and eats his own bunions. Corporal Nigg was still in his place, frozen upright, long dead but continuing as the sentry. Who can fire him? Who has time for clerical work? Nigg is present, accounted for, damn you, a soldier's soldier. So Private Ruth brings my journey in the wheelbarrow to its conclusion back at the tent, puffing. Calamity has provided me with perquisites. Some resent me, as they go off to lose an eye or ear and return to chat, lucky this time.

The charge, our old bread and butter, has withered into the final horror of the field, democracy. It is a good thing we are still grassroot-mean, or there would be no impetus left. Referendums for and against the next charge take a long time, collecting ballots down the line, out in the swamp. Every sniper has an opinion, every mule-lackey, every musician. The vote is always in favor, for we are the Bats Out of Hell Division, even if we are down to less than regiment size. These boys can still stir you. When I know something big's afoot, I shriek for Ruth, who rolls me up to jump-off with the shock troops. Nobody is disheartened by my appearance. There are men far, far worse off than I, men unblessed with the ability to write and read; men whose salivation has been taken from them by breathing in one ball of fire too many. Oh Jesus, I'd go rolling out there with them if I could. It's Ruth that holds me back. Otherwise I'd be in the fore, quill high, greeting their cannon — hub to hub they are — a row almost endless of snobs' nostrils, soon to come alive with smoke and flame: grape, canister, ball, bomb, balls and chain. They greet us even with flying glass. I'll never forget the lovely day they took nearly my all. In a way I want to revisit it; a sentimental journey, however, this war has no time for. Ruth won't budge. He has his orders. I, the scribe, have become as important as our general, who is, of no debate, criminally insane just like the rest of them.

Shot to pieces in that rehearsal excursion down to Mexico, the man was buried, but returned out of the very earth once he heard another cracking good one was on. At last, at last! The World War of his dreams. "Thought I'd never live to see it! There *is* a God, and God is *love!*" I have license to exaggerate, as I have just done, but many would be horrified to know how little. He is said to have commented on hearing the first news, "Brother against brother! In my lifetime! Can Providence be truly this good?"

He is dead-set on having these battles writ down permanently in ink and will most certainly push me on afterward, whatever befalls, into working up his own biography. There is about enough left of him to drape a horse. Once he's tied on, his voice never stops, and you can hear the wind whistling through him even in the rare interludes of quiet when he has simply blasted away his throat organs. Up and down the line, his raw nagging moans away, overcoming shot and shell; a song eternal, this bawling, in the ears of the ruined but driven. The two colonels and four captains flap around in imitation, one stout captain with a shepherd's crook in hand. He is likely to pull a malingerer out of the trench by the neck with it, and has often pulled up the dead and scolded them and their families. *Audace, avanti, allons mes frères!* Captain Haught is from everywhere. He is the one who told me our colors were inspired by the Russians in Crimea and that there is no more suave concord or color pleasing to our Lord than gray trimmed in yellow. No coward or lay-back, he walks straight up at the front of his unit into the very jaws of their hydra and returns at leisure, starched, unspotted, perfectly whole, armed only with the shepherd's staff. His only flaw is his appetite. It is rumored he has stolen biscuits from corpses right in the middle of an enfilade, and can't be hurried.

There is a man, way forward, who claims to have been shot through the very heart. He has found a hidden place out there, however, some hole in the field, so that he never retreats full and properly, but stops to burrow in like something feral. His boasts are relayed to us in the rear. Soldiers have seen him during battle and do report there is a great dark stain on the left chest of his tunic. Then they see him in the next assault *in media res.* This is what he has said to them: he doesn't want to miss a minute of it because there will never ever be anything like it again. It will set the tone for a century and will be in all the books. Great-grandchildren will still be shaking their heads, overpowered. There *can* never be any repeat of this thing. He saw the first long shadows of it at the one around that church in southern Tennessee and he has been in three worse since. So. They imagine he lives on roots and their liquid in whatever small cellar he has found or dug. Already he is practicing his posture around a stove fueled only by corncobs in an impoverished, riven home. He speaks his tales to gathered neighbors, family and children. They say he has a mirror down there, long as a tailor's, at which he practices. But he can hear our general bawling and their hub-to-hub cannon, and is never tardy for the charge. He is always already into it when his fellow soldiers catch up with him. His name is Beverly Crouch. Crouch has the distinction — whether he's truly been shot through the heart or not — of having been a *white* slave back home, right alongside the Africans with hoe and sack sometimes, but bonding out for other jobs too, wherever the weather and agriculture were better.

Our pathetic cannoneers, the remains of a proud battery of near-geniuses who could shoot the head off a chicken at a mile, speak with great accuracy still but no force, so little shot and shell are left, the main charge yet to come. The conservation they endure in the very heat of battle is almost hysterical. The salvo, that precious Italian concept, seems like some remote advantage in a historical tome. They can hope only to demoralize the other side a little, with an occasional round hitting one of their colonels amid-shoulders. I was never impressed that much by an officer's head blown off beside me, but the general declares this is a huge mournful event "over there," where they are different. The artillerymen are aided in their precision by our forward observer Jones Pierce-Hatton, who has never dressed in anything but civilian clothes, in the beau monde way — gray suit with wide Panama, and binoculars of the Swiss avant-garde. There is a lone enormous tree on a little hump of hill, into the top boughs of which he has fastened a crow's nest. Here is where he looks and rains fire on the enemy. It must be rather godly up there, calling the wrath and precision down on individuals of the indigo persuasion. They really hate him over there. His ladder's been all shot away for a long time. They brought out a line of sharpshooters forward from the ramparts; all of them blazed away upward at him. Now here was a salvo, remarkable, before they were convinced to retire by our own Kentucky experts. Some of these men were hardly anything but eyes, shoulders and trigger fingers. They slipped back gaunt and wispy into their nooks and bowers. The entire top of the tree and especially his crow's nest, all was shredded, much bark and lumber falling down. Somebody yelled up to him, seeing his wide hat come up out of the nest again, asking whether he was hit. There was a long pause.

"Why shit yes! What would you imagine!" But he did not come down and through the days, nobody asked any more questions. Spots of blood, dried, lay around the roots of the trunk where they rigged his food and coffee basket. All he insists on is the coffee, the only real stuff left anywhere over here. He has the canteen that would have gone to the general. Mr. Jones Pierce-Hatton seeks no other reward.

Our only triumph was knocking down their one competing balloon, an airship with basket for the observer underneath, and for this we can thank Granny Nature. The same ill wind that brought us those belly-churning odors of roasting prime meat increased and blew the thing off its anchor, so it wobbled over here right up alongside Jones Pierce-Hatton in his nest. You could hear the cries of dismay from the disheartened passenger as he came alongside the lone enormous tree at bright high noon. Pierce-Hatton shot into the thing with his French double quailing piece, and such a blast of burning air covered the top of this single stick of the forest we reckoned on a momentary view of hell itself (and saw, truly, it was barely a degree worse than what we had).

Somebody called up to Pierce-Hatton to ask whether he was injured. A head wearing nothing but the scorched crown of a hat arose from the hutch.

"Why shit yes! Haven't you got eyes, man?" came the reply.

Something big is afoot. The cannoneers are bringing up the last of the magazine and stacking it. We haven't seen this in weeks, seems years. The thing, our last, comes on at dawn tomorrow. New flags, last in supply, are unrolled. The band has swelled. The deserters, not that many, have returned, but most are in the band. We've never had this enormous a musical outfit before, nor so well instrumented. Fifes, drums long and short, snares, French horns, an ophicleide, banjos with new woodchuck skin, trumpets and cornets, trombone, four marching violins, and a brand-new man with huge cymbals. They rehearse very softly, but I am told it's a thing from Tchaikovsky they have in mind, a military arrangement of the Concerto for Violin in D, Opus 35. The lines are shaken out, just two fifty-yard-long vanguards. Even three of the camp dogs are with them. We have no rear. The band is right behind them. When I know thoroughly what is up, I double my shrieking at Ruth. We are going, definitely. You bastard, you think I would miss this? I know you've been having it easy. I remind him profanely of his family and tell him I will search them out and write about them badly. So, by God, we are in there too, just ahead of the band. I put my quill away and exchange it for an assault saber. They are lying about everywhere and easy to find.

Is there a better music than the eruption of a true salvo from our beleaguered cannoneers, hub to hub, those ten of them, at the first sparks of dawn in the gray mist? You die for this music. But it lasted only thirty minutes and then we move off in our ghostly ranks, Ruth cursing and whining as he lifts the barrow behind me. Their cannons have not opened yet. They are waiting, waiting, perhaps till the last cynical second, every drop of blood squeezed from their dramatic absence, wrecking us in the mind — they hope. But there is no hesitation and when you see the pitted and shell-raked field, the last quarter mile, suddenly the band up and high in the best enthusiasm, tearing and swelling the heart, we know we have seen heaven. Then their cannon erase their fortifications in serial billows, and the rare banshee music of passing shot that few are privileged to hear seems so thick we have another firmament to breathe, an ozone of the delirious. I am so happy, so happy!

Hardly anybody falls. I tell you we are gaunt! We are almost not there, and we are starting that dear, deep-down precious trot toward them. Their musketry is popping and pecking. Their men are so thick on the line the flame is solid, and it is all we see out of the cannon smoke. Now at last we run; run dear boys, run! I had a chance to look about and the flags, my godly stars and bars, my regimental white cross on blue field, were clustered, gathered to the center. Oh boys, boys! I am shrieking. Up, get it up, my brothers! To them, into them! The general ahead, squalling atop his beast, rides straight into the furnace and our lines go in, and I go in. What a *hell* of a band we've got just behind. You can tell they are committed. They are going ahead too! Oh, happy bayonets high, oh happy, happy, happy! Then we are running in sudden silence. There is mystery and miracle left in this hard century! They are not firing anymore. We are running through stone silence, the grand old yell in our throats, our gray and butternut and naked corpses hurling forward, barely finding their rail fence, their earthen works, their growling ramparts. Bayonets down! Earn heaven, lads! Murder!

But the smoke has cleared off their line and we run up to stare at silent men with their guns down. Somewhere just behind them *their* general is bawling, even over the volume of ours.

There is great confusion, but I am glad I was near the center where General Kosciusky, a Polish-Russian, was screaming at the men in blue.

"Stop it! Stop it! I can't take it anymore. The lost cause! Look at you! My holy God, gray brothers, behold yourself! Cease fire! Cease it all!"

So, you see, we were just staring at their deep and thick line, every soldier in a new blue boat, their general screaming behind them.

"By God, we surrender!" he shouted. "This can't go on. The music. The Tchaikovsky! You wretched specters coming on! It's too much. Too much."

Our general, stunned, went over to take his sword. We, all energy gone in the last run, sagged about. Nothing in history led us to believe we had not simply crossed over to paradise itself and were dead just minutes ago.

In their tent there was a conference. Then their men began stacking arms and bringing forward food to us. You wouldn't believe the victuals. I gorged on honey and oysters fresh from the shell. You could hear a long constant moan of gnawing men as we sat around with plates on our laps, sucking in venison, turkey, porterhouses, piles of fat white beans.

When their general, a splendid tall man, the very replica of the bearded Greek commander, returned to the line and chanced to look down at me in my barrow, he began weeping again, and I am sorry I had nothing but a greasy face and the eyes of a dog to greet him.

Such arms, cannon, even repeating rifles; such almost infinite caissons, so many thrilling flags and handsome plump mules; and thousands of cutlasses and musical instruments — these were all ours. We, the few of the two lines and the band, could not encircle them. We did not know how to guard this host, and just gave up and fell back on more food, whiskey and coffee.

I was, as the scribe, invited into the last conference on dispensation. Our general, held by two orderlies like a towel between them, was still too stunned to gloat. His impossible silence spoke the whole moment. But we must argue a bit on the matter of a name for this battle. There were no landmarks or creeks or churches about; only a family of Germans named Hastenburg who had lived in a house northwest of the field, long obliterated, suggested any proper noun.

It was decided then that this was the Battle of Hastenburg.

The Vision of Esther
by Clem

I F YOU WERE Clem Mestre you would look over your yard fence and see the new woman on the block, Andra, with her two-month-old black Shar-Pei dog on a red leash. You'd see Andra in a long brown medieval print dress and lizard sandals looking from their hill toward the precincts of the town, Ruggle Hampton, where the men were away and the women were left in the shops, which were wilted, going fast with no grace. She wouldn't know, Andra, that these plain women were keepers of the flame in failing shops; pockets of ardor and kindness, Clem felt, while the men, the owners, were away, embarrassed. The mall stores were killing them. The men did not want to be seen standing behind forlorn counters looking at the weather. Clem could see, he thought, the used gloom dripping from the windows — an unhappy dew, behind which kind and plain women moved quietly. Andra, probably a graduate student at the town college, was plain too. This moved Clem. He was a doctor, reading books and looking hard at forty. He felt very gentle toward plain Andra with her rare little dog, both of them looking at a new town.

Something had just happened lately to another plain woman he knew, Esther.

She had been raped, by several men. It had made television news. He could think of nothing else but Esther and the book he was reading. He had marked two lines from it just now: "Deep down, I'm in a panic all the time" and "He's a thief, a drinker... He rapes a bit." Esther had loved him. He'd ignored her. He had been short and unkind to plain women throughout his life. Now, deep down, he was in a panic, and very sorry for it. Who had he thought he was? Many of them had asked for nothing but simple communication. He was not up to it. He could not deliver himself to their moment. He thought he was a big cheese, with too much to offer; hence, they got nothing.

Clem had had an arrogance about his unusual impression on plain women. He had been unable to disregard their plainness, and wrote them off. But now he was wishing that he had caressed and cheered them all. He had missed good fevers and much easy conversation. Esther Haste was one he should have embraced. He recalled that when she declared her love, he was spending his time, almost all of it, with a self-mocking beauty named Eileen who went through a list of her flaws as if it were the only possible subject on earth. Soon it became clear that this self-assault was merely a social veneer that, when studied with the slightest effort, revealed a bottomless worship of herself, such a solo chamber as he'd never viewed before, where her attacks on her graces were the other side of a monologue through which her charms could shine all the more for being doubted. Even now he was going on in his head about Eileen more than the damaged Esther, simply because of Eileen's beauty, a thing to which he regretted so much was owed.

Esther had been used badly by several men on a houseboat. One of the men was her co-worker in the Game and Parks service — Victor Kepps — whose indicted slumping shoulders and petulant face Clem had seen on the local television news. The woman's name was not given out over the air. Appalled beyond his usual irony, Dale Shivers had whispered it to Mestre. The truth worked on Clem, creating a vision of Esther that surprised him. She became, well, yes, divine. Esther was all at once divine, a treasure that he must hurry to and shower with respect. He must honor her. This was urgent. Terrifying honor was due her because, with his chance, he had slighted her badly.

She'd said she admired and loved him, this on their third meeting. Mestre was busy with Eileen at the time and had told Esther certainly she didn't. She didn't know him well enough. But this was all to get rid of her and make the path smooth and clear to Eileen. What a vicious American blunder, everything for romance, *one* romance. Even the most horrific bands on the radio sang, all the time, one, oh oh oh one, you the only one. One woman, one life, all that. What a stupid lack of option, he felt now. Thick goonish Mestre, looking through Esther to Eileen, with her sex spread redly, her spoiled, infinitely photographed face wide-eyed with climax. He grew conscious that with a peculiar case like Eileen, he too could adore *himself* out of existence. Too appreciated, the object disappeared. But with the avid, kind Esther — doomed to plainness, by his standards — so much of her remained undiscovered, and he could see that pleasant sea of her smiling through her bangs. In injury and insult, she seemed a goddess to him now, a woman out of one of those dreams that hurl an ignored female face at you, someone ignored in your day life now calling. You answered with late passion. She held you, and you flowed into her, stunned for days afterward.

But nobody even knew where Esther was staying. Was she even in town? In other days she had divided her life between the stone house in the state park around the reservoir and her apartment on Virginia, the third story of a whitewashed chalet weathered and splotched by the boughs of an enormous maple, below which you could see her yellow Hyundai with a sap-drenched darker roof. Mestre had been up there only once, and had been too shifty to appreciate the small romance of her green and violet rooms. Years ago a writer for the town paper had destroyed himself there in an experiment with "designer" drugs, on which he was doing a series, so the place had the musk of near-authenticated artistic suicide. Esther had been proud of her cheap rent, and Mestre had nodded, not really caring, not really that delighted for her. What did it matter that a plain woman in forestry and wildlife management had colorful quarters on a shaded back street? He hated his smug, awful decisions on good plain women now. There must have been a dozen of them who had wanted to get closer to him, and he had denied their friendship; truly, even their whole unglittering lives. Esther seemed all of them in one. Why couldn't he find her forestry and wildlife interesting, and why couldn't he commiserate with her about her ridiculous salary? Why couldn't he have bought something happy and simple, like a chicken, roasted it on her grill, and had a bottle of middling wine with her? They could have talked on her balcony about the poor departed journalist, whom she'd known. The journalist was the sort of pal — a low-achieving hopeful with large ideas — that girls like Esther always had. Mestre had the sort of foxy, prosperous vanity ripe for humiliations by Eileens. He saw through others constantly to the withered ghosts they really were. Now he saw himself as among the withered ghosts, seeking membership, hoping much was forgiven.

He continued to watch a minor version of her in Andra over the fence with her little Chinese dog, both well groomed and expectant. The rest of the town would not see it, not a bit. Esther would be the used and outraged woman, hidden away for years, maybe creeping back into view somewhere else, in a place that would not know her shame. Even her name changed, maybe. This would be the common guess, the common *want*. You saw her going back to her meek people, where she remained in bed suffering for months, none of them knowing how to help her, watching gingerly for signs of lunacy. They'd get her to venture out, say to a pharmacy, and the kindly rube who filled her script would nod with thin warmth, then talk her case up with the senile drone at the cash register when she left. Much nodding again, sincere awe going around the shop like a monkey in a bow tie. Clem could not bear this. Feebleminded men at the bait and tackle hole would nod earnestly as her family car passed by, lamenting her "case." You could see them wagging and getting moony in the eyes, hundreds of them out there in the dense air of gossip, the mulling progeny — Mestre recalled the phrase from a wag — of Mortimer Snerd.

Poor, poor Esther. Radiant Esther. Clem wanted to clasp her in an endless hug and be her champion, running out for errands she barely required, in defiance of the ghastly hicks.

Clem Mestre knew one of her assailants on the houseboat. He'd met the ranger right at the lodge in Tishomingo Park where he took Eileen a year ago. Clem wanted to have her in a cabin overlooking the rock bluffs and creek near the Tennessee line. It was a nippy, fireplace January. The best part of the trip was keeping Eileen away from her society, a constant squad of swains and their envious lovelies who woke the needs of Eileen with hymns of respect and surprises for her day. Eileen was a speech pathologist who did not practice much. She'd never mentioned her clients, most likely because it entailed, oh, well, afflicted people of another dreary sphere. She was much wanted as a co-anchor on a show in Nashville, but with great flirting she kept turning them down, listing her flaws, which anybody prescient could see were actually virtues. These self-criticisms set a further glow around her, this great beauty so human and unconfident. Now Mestre could see that this obvious method had worked handsomely for her everywhere; it had baffled him — the most promising suave Mestre — perfectly. A childish bid for even more attention, an algebra of pity raising her to withering popular status. Eileen was, simply, after everything. The cabin bored her instantly. In the city of love she was a kind of Mestre-humoring mechanic, with condescending huffs of pleasure. After two days in the cabin, though, it murdered him. He saw he was not having her at all. He was not even an equal in the room. Even her diligence hurt his feelings. He began using his mouth on her, like a slave. "Oh, why don't you come back up here with the big people, Clem?" she said after a while.

He thought she didn't care for the outdoors because it challenged her total concentration on herself. The stony hills and the creek might as well have been rivals in prom gowns. Yet, finally, she admitted, "I'm not all that much. I'm shallow and I'll never ever do anything extraordinary." By God, this won him all over again, the chilly minx, smart and humble about her future like this. He wanted to eat her alive, forgiving all, nearly desperate for every part of her. All of this should have been done for Esther, he saw today. If only Esther had been there in the cabin, receiving all his study and adulation, reflecting his love, charmed by everything about him. It could still be done! What brightness in that. He saw them: "Clem, I simply adore you." And he: "Esther, you can't know. I'll begin with reverence for each of your little parts." Though he wouldn't say quite that thespianly thing. All his gestures would be put to the good, absorbed in her light, all of her, queen of disgrace and insult. She would not have been available to the horror on the houseboat had he seen her sooner, she'd not have had to suffer it at all. He was almost devout in his groin as he thought of her out there on the water.

But what had happened was, he'd gone to the lodge, where he met the ranger Victor Kepps, a lean freckled man stooping over a long cigarette at a domino table. The man was having his break, with coffee and smoke, and Mestre recalled he was one of those men — how do they do it? — who make the act of smoking a nasty, wet, almost threatening thing. The ranger had a way with his lips of grimly sucking the filter. You saw he was a fellow of low, mean hungers, too pleased with his tan ranger uniform. The man sold him two gnarled walking sticks, hooped at the end, very rugged and folksy. Clem thought this would cheer Eileen up and give them a memento of their nature walk through the woods of storied Tishomingo. He was, however, unnerved by the ranger, who acted miffed to be waiting on him, making mere change, while the large woman at the register was away in the back somewhere, averse to tobacco smoke. The man said not a word and seemed to despise Mestre on sight. Then he spoke: "Thet your girlie or your wife up to the cabin with you?"

"I don't see any reason to answer that," said Mestre instantly. The man was angered, and with his lips worse and redder than ever, he went mushy in the mouth.

"Don't let me stop you doing your duty by her. A thing like that don't give it away free."

The words, out of order, were delivered with that solemn country bemusement Mestre detested, and the bitterer thing about them was that they were absolutely true, though Mestre, a snob who had spent his time since mid-adolescence trying to obliterate his Appalachian brogue, resented the ranger's eyes and imagination near his realm. Mestre was a physician, an M.D., for starters. True, only a sports doctor, but this was by choice. He was a sporting, damned well-kept and attractive man, and expert at what he did. This leering student of Smokey the Bear couldn't even keep up the elemental courtesies of his lot, and Mestre couldn't quite believe the uniform belonged to him. Some browbeaten uncle must have got him the job. Later, with Esther's awful houseboat experience in his mind, he saw this freckled nephew led off sulking in manacles on the local news. Mestre sank as a too detailed vision of sexual assault — on poor Esther! — blew up his head. He saw the ranger's member, uncircumcised and freckled, seeking Esther, who lay bruised and cut, in shock, watching her supposed buddy throw himself on her, just another of the wild pack — maybe the leader.

Mestre had seen Esther once or twice after his weekend with Eileen in the park, and commented on the lowbred ranger who'd sold him the canes. She told him, well, that she had no trouble with Victor. He thought he was God's gift to babes, but nobody before her had bothered to joke him out of this notion. She could handle him, though, with one finger. Mestre rebuked himself for his lewd imaginings. His mind would run and stun him, despite his cool treatment of both men and women athletes. Medical school had never beaten down the prurience in him, and he wondered if there were many physicians like him. He worried that one day, somehow, somebody would shine a light through his head and expose the lascivious theater on a screen for the world to see.

When Clem was a youth in Kentucky there was a woman in the neighborhood who warned her daughters, Mestre's playmates, about "evil-minded doctors." This woman, a second grade teacher, was a very bent puritan. Even Mestre's father chuckled about her obsession in this pious town where, Mestre later heard, there were several men who had fathered six and eight children without once seeing their mate naked. The schoolteacher ignored the McCarthy Communist paranoia of the fifties, bent already by her larger obsession. So little Clem chuckled too, but he had grown up the very monster of her admonitions. Or was he simply modern and average? In the case of Esther, his imagination was unwanted. He was scum, she was a saint, with her honest spoken love of him. A graduate student with a year of eligibility left at college, Esther played volleyball for the girls' team. Nobody much cared, hardly anybody came to the games, but she'd twisted her ankle badly one afternoon. Mestre happened to be there, and his first touch of her flesh must have been the beginning of her love. My, it was rapid. And he'd blown it off. Jackass.

The last humiliation in the cabin with Eileen had to do with the walking sticks.

"What's *this* you have? A Good Shepherd's kit? Am I supposed to be Bo Peep? Really, Clem," she said when he raised the canes up with a smile at the door.

"These are for us to hike the trails." He grew downcast, trodden before he'd begun.

"Well, maybe for *you*. I'll watch *you* hike. Go ahead. I'll wait."

"You won't go?"

"You take the hike. I want to see you with this crook thing, making your way."

There were several other couples staying in Tishomingo, young and middle-aged and obviously in love. Mestre had seen them around the park. He had imagined that this simple pleasure, walking, had *created* the love, made it a deep, priceless thing. He looked slyly at Eileen, whom he had banged away at with the result of perfect indifference. It was a dreadful fact to read in her eyes. And she was so svelte, so gorgeous with her blond hair pulled back, chilly, in her black shirt! Murder.

Now Esther again. Esther had that devout plainness seen in the face of madonnas, a beauty (yes, beauty) irrelevant to college contests, pretty meat on the hoof in swimwear and formals. More abiding, with a strength that touched him liquidly.

He had set out with his staff, the third wheel at his own party of two. Nature was glum, fierce, mocking, fingers lying on him with smothering irony. Was there ever a gloomier journey? Chief Tishomingo, tall, betrayed, noble, could never have known the petty whining in this white man. He could fall down a ravine, thought Clem. He could see her incredulous, though, moved to high irritation, her arms folded while the paramedics from the ambulance scrambled around. A woman like that got out of sex without even a crease in her brow. In Esther's case, he knew he'd *have* her, truly and finally.

He asked around the college and called the park office, but nobody was sure where she'd been taken. The meek Hyundai, yellow under its brown sap-stained roof, was painful in its absence. The vacant oil-splotched drive under the great maples moved him almost too much. Each time Mestre passed, he felt more greatly the sinner. He was aware that he was becoming almost vain in his sin, all the friendly plain girls of his past around his head like a nimbus of medieval angels. Some worker in drug rehab once explained to Mestre something called grandiose guilt. The addict, in his grandiosity, assumes that the derelictions and horrors of his past are too special ever to be forgiven. He continues his substance abuse in this vain fatalism and individuality, captain of iniquity, untouchable. Mestre began asking total strangers about Esther on the sidewalks downtown. Couldn't they, wouldn't they, know something?

The houseboat came back to him. There was a shot of it on television, looking discarded, torn into silence by rape, a floating crypt of gang hunger, bottles and cans here and there. The places of crime were even grimmer-looking than their pilgrims, Mestre noticed. Grimmer than even the culprits. The place put a hard stare on you, and seemed even lewder than warranted, when you knew the outrage that had transpired there. Same with her vacant apartment window next to the grillwork balcony, ivy clutching the bricks down from it, black-green like sorrow.

He came on a cop, a young skull-shaved bullet-headed man, hat off for a break from the heat in late May. The fellow was leaning on his cruiser, probably for passersby to review his build. You could tell he spent much time on the weights, and had that prowling-gorilla bow in his arms Mestre had seen athletes of a certain class work for; a subclass of cave-era goons thrilled to be hunched meat. In fact, across the country, these sorts of boys were likely to gang up and take some woman serially and invoke scandal, wandering back to the coach, eyes on the floor, saying "We thought it was a *date,* sir, everything was all go." Mestre asked the cop if he knew Esther's whereabouts, or could tell him. The cop recognized the team doctor, and did know where Esther was. He whispered the place to Mestre.

"Doc, I've wondered. Who gets to, say, would it be *you?* — you know, *examine* them after something like that, uh, assault?"

"Who *gets to?*"

"Yeah. And *paid* for it. Paid to look into things. Now there's a life."

"I'd imagine a female doc at the hospital. You're a sick man, a fool." Mestre surprised himself. The man was a brute but had kind and sad eyes. Mestre was sorry. He half wished the man would attack him.

"No offense, I always imagined you were a man all set up with no great cares."

"No, no, I've got cares. I need to see her," said Mestre.

"She ought to be where I heard." The man seemed relieved Mestre had settled down. He was alarmed by emotional discharge and had probably never been called a fool. Briefly, he'd been reduced to a confused infant, but now he was angry.

All of Mestre's gloomy sin popped in his brain—something red and racing. For this dolt in blue he almost spat out a rapsheet of what?—perfidy, malaise, malingering, concupiscence, general time-murdering sorriness, inner pornography. He was a hangaround, a layabout. He was not a good doctor at all. Yet he maintained the false gaudy innocence that cops always elicited in him.

After medical school, which he had done merely to prove that a boy from the east Kentucky hills could do it, he was exhausted. There was a hardly a bit of medical want in him. His parents were glad, but when he did the internship and residence, he might as well have been a zombie. He did not impress his mentors. There was a wrong heaviness to his mind, not in profundity but mere mass, thick unsalient slabs, shuffling back and forth in twilight. Many days he suspected he was not very bright.

It came to him, the very picture: he was an unshucked oyster, hurtling on the winds, all air, gonad and gut. Chances seemed in a loud hurry around him, but he could do nothing—nothing—about them. Mestre yearned to be driven by some grand circumstance. Everything in his existence was too slack.

On the road thirty miles from Esther yet in his little Mazda Miata convertible—a brighter yellow than Esther's Hyundai—he thought of women again. Back to that misty weird little club that Mrs. Freeman, the schoolteacher who warned girls of "evil-minded doctors," led. She'd had a hold on small boys too. It began as a vague thing. Clem and others in her second grade class were wont to feign nausea and gag whenever kissing a girl was mentioned. There was a strange youngster in their room who grabbed and kissed girls all the time. Mestre and his mates just could not abide this and would shout and hold their stomachs. Hideously, most of the little girls were pleased when Leonard slobbered on their lips out on the playground, a thing of rough coke soil above mountain caverns. Mrs. Freeman watched the boys with narrowed eyes and much trembling glee. She favored the ones who made such faces and fuss over kissing. Mestre and his friends were in her club. She watched them with fascination and gave them special, private favors. She hated kissing too, Clem now understood. In the little movie house on the hill on Saturday mornings, she was likely to be sitting near the back row, alone. When the characters onscreen kissed, the little boys began raving in outrage. Mrs. Freeman would egg them on. They'd turn around and catch her waving to them, in league, urging the catcalls. "We don't like that stuff, do we, boys?" She'd cheer them outside in the hurting light afterward, and walk partway with them. Even then, the boys felt odd about Mrs. Freeman. They weren't that glad to hoot the onscreen kissing, and they did not want to be in a club headed by Mrs. Freeman, with her crinkled eyes and risen waves of white and black hair. Mestre thought he saw Mrs. Freeman in his yard once, looking in at him, but he never told his parents and didn't know whether to believe what he had seen. Another night he saw a lone hand rise at the back window of his house, and felt he could never discuss that either. It remained one of those many childhood incidents, awful and untellable, that haunt existence.

Something else happened one summer at his relatives' house in Virginia Beach, where his childless uncle and aunt had invited Clem's family. His uncle was in the navy. His wife was a real looker, and Clem was old enough to know this. She looked like all the brunette beauties from World War II. Through an opportune accident of door crack and a mirror somewhere, Mestre saw his uncle on his knees before a bed, his wife's raised legs around his head. Never, ever, could he confess this to anyone, but it made him wild and dizzy in the head. The sight of his uncle and aunt drove him thereafter from the room. He could still remember, and still lived, that riot of nerve ends and fast blood, childhood shut forever out or, rather, amplified in hot blood and quick heart. Somehow he connected the face of Mrs. Freeman with the sight. She was there looking too, reprimanding. Much later, Mestre heard that the song "When You Walk Through a Storm Keep Your Head Up High!" — whatever its name — was played at Mrs. Freeman's funeral. From then on, even the song was darkly sexual and forbidden — and wonderful. Mrs. Freeman nodded in music over his aunt and uncle, delirious animals. Mestre felt strange and ill thinking of this.

Esther, now that he brought these memories forward, lived in the condition of a stained glass window, purple and green, looming over the devout. His gentleness was so extended it became holy. He had never felt anything like it before. But his blood was hot and his heart very quick. He was in a trance almost liquid, the ecstasy of lust and piety upon him at once.

He had tried, weakly, to adopt the priestliness of habit in his medical ventures. This was the mode of his esteemed mentors and others in the profession he admired. But he was far, far from it. With his sporting build and smooth face, framed by cherubic black hair, he was conscious of himself as too handsome for the trade, and often found women staring at him while he examined their knees and elbows. Custom protected this subromance, but Mestre, in his weak priestliness, was always afraid he would blather out something over the line and embarrass his profession. The two snakes coiled on the staff — the caduceus — were likely to rear back and strike Mestre in the ears, routing him and the oath, at some horrible moment. Truth was Mestre often thought of being, as more native to his destiny, an alcoholic painter, with only a bicycle and two changes of clothes, wild but clean. But he could not even draw, he could not drink much, and just thinking about a bicycle led him to imagine the right kind of all-sport Reeboks to buy with it. A pair, in short, that swankier girls would pass on. Women like Esther would dream of helping him, saving him. That was the huge trouble with Mestre's life now. He needed saving from nothing. He'd achieved a smug carapace, reaching out weakly to diagnose with hairy little feelers. An M.D. not wholly a doctor was likely to be a monster of some sort, he knew, not just another citizen. He felt natural at nothing. His function could have been filled by any normally bright person with a year in nursing school. Mestre painted at three fixed canvases, wanting passion to come along — perhaps even talent — but his conceptions and executions were vile. They depressed him. He kept them in a secret room. He did not want to be known as a doctor who dabbled. He reminded himself that when he did practice medicine, he was pretty good.

The little village where Esther had retreated (to a widowed aunt with roses, a garden, and trellises behind the house) was marked by a despondent neglect. You saw the hollow lack of use in the few buildings, almost a cry — you heard — from the remaining crust of heart in them. Such was the ruin Mestre had wanted to forever avoid when he fled east Kentucky, where the air was bit with such lack of promise you presumed headless bodies trucked back and forth inside, grazing for water or bread. The aunt's wide cottage seemed at least brave in its difference.

Clem had made money too late to change the life of his parents. They were beyond wanting anything else by then, and they were frightened by "those new mods" like microwave ovens. His convertible had terrified his mother. A home on the seashore would have served merely as a booth for pale, wrinkled relics. Even the idea of the sea seemed to trouble old Mr. Mestre. Clem was quite sure that his father thought great creatures got out of it and walked around the neighborhoods. His parents would have settled into that peculiar ghastliness of old Floridians who never leave the house. Dr. Mestre's childhood friends were so far gone from his hometown, there was nobody to come back to and impress. The aunt's house, minus the garden and roses, reminded him of places back home, anchored well-deep to the grim and habitual. He circled the wide cottage — asylum of the raped, roses flocking it — and looked for signs of Esther. What would he say?

It was likely that she hated men at large now, and that Mestre might make her skin crawl. It occurred to him that he had never known of a woman confessing to a rape in her past. He had seen a group of them on television once. But they claimed to have been raped by their husbands. Mestre was uncomfortable with their going public about this matter.

He caught sight of Esther, who seemed tiny and retreating, on the back screened porch.

He felt too handsome and smooth in his yellow Miata, like a birthday cake candle, irrelevant to the moment.

Mestre had had, of course, a wife at one time. She was a lazy nurse who'd now and then have bursts of manic zeal for very eclectic things. Things of sudden, irksome importance: some new friend, the Bible; a glass frog collection; the Catholic church, with bedroom Madonna statuary. None of the enthusiasms lasted. Her equally lazy and snobbish brother would visit. They liked nobody, really. The world was in for general hell when they were together. The two of them would retire unto themselves for an afternoon of contempt and giggles. Mestre was cut off from their spite reunion. Once he announced he had seen a large dead dog, a shepherd, dragged from the road by two weeping children. Mestre had been deeply moved and needed to share it. The two of them found a clever way to giggle even about that. He never forgave them, and began thinking of them as the evil twins. It was a delight to see her brother, shed by his wife after multiple mean infidelities, become a bawling penitent in Mestre's house. Brother and sister liked to cook up a batch of chicken gizzards and devastate them, an act Mestre saw as an ugly communion with their past. The stench drove him to the front of the house. He found out he despised his wife, hating so much this filth that she ate. What he had taken for an easy, philosophic high style was merely torpor. Yet he continued living with her, and this was the thing: he began raping her. She did not know it, but he was raping her, his body in a frenzy like a shark's. His act was one of total control and disgust. In fact, it was good, and his attitude lasted the final year of their marriage.

Now in his dreams and day reveries he got a delicious chill when he thought of several men taking women sexually, the woman a thing of only slightly resisting orifices, until the animal ecstasy struck her. This was precisely the point, Mestre considered, staring at Esther, who had come out to the lawn.

Writhing orifices, the whimpering, protesting mouth — Esther, my Esther — the amazed eyes, the unbidden hunger. That is my Esther. He had to stop this quick. He had heard of a priest who resigned because the confessions of his parishioners were so dull. Bored petrified, did he dream off into his own better ones? Mestre could sympathize, too much. Remarkably, he'd achieved with time a defined contempt for the ill and a high regard for the healthy and the dead, so eloquently quiet. But he resisted the arrogance of his profession. Maybe he was not that good, simply. He was a layabout, merely heavy in the mind, with no weight. He could barely look at Esther now and he felt, out of his loud toylike car, a rolling fool and an impertinence. She was not a glow. She was a woman only five foot four, with square shoulders, ordinary as the tomatoes behind her, this mystified pinch to her face. It was a country look, little-eyed, mouth forming zero. Could this thing be real? all the rubes were asking, nationwide. Then she smiled as if she had found, say, Venus in the telescope. He was almost on her before she called his name tiredly. "Clem Mestre?"

I need, I need badly something ongoing in my life, thought Mestre. It has to be her. I can love her. I can surround her with care. Wasn't he seeing love and care in her eyes? He went up and clasped her in a great hug.

Esther had, he noticed, rather insinuating haunches, and moved with a lot of tease about her, maybe deliberately set on being girlish despite the recent horror. Trying to have her self back. She was made up with some flush on her cheekbones, and she couldn't have been preparing for him.

"I didn't even know if we were friends. I thought I'd run you off," she said.

"I've never forgotten you." A field of gray set in Mestre's mind, narrowing to the image of a kind of bowling lane with pools of despondency here and there. But he pressed on, trying to bring some honor to his route.

"You know I'm all right, physically, don't you? The doctoring is over."

"Bruises on your neck."

"Do you want to ask me things, Clem? Or should we act like nothing much has happened?"

"Tell me about your aunt. What's she like?"

Esther resembled somewhat the older Princess Margaret, and like hers, Esther's hair was swept back from the ears. He was waiting for Esther to leap into his own beatific vision of her, tresses streaming down. He stared at her rudely, as he himself had been stared at by the injured women he'd touched.

"My aunt. Well, she was fun once. Now she's religious. Golly, like the D.A. Everybody around me seems to be turning religious. What are you looking at? Don't!"

"I'm sorry."

"At my neck like a swan's, but purple and yellow?"

"Not that. Just you. Seeing you."

"Like I'm about to burst into a gas."

"You feel that, Esther?"

"The same as my aunt and the D.A. I was going on with the story and looked over at him. You knew he was waiting for me to burst into flame. The *Hindenburg*."

"Mal Little seems to be a good man. If you believe in good men anymore."

"Oh come on, please, Clem. Sure. It's me, still me. The one that had a crush on you." She placed one foot forward in its black pump, arms out, as in a statue of mercy. In truth he had expected more the mad maid twirling between the hedges in a long white gown like, say, Ophelia in *Hamlet*, the only play of the bard's he'd read. "You think you're looking at, gosh, I'll bet, Saintness Somebody."

She was clever. He didn't remember that. Mestre had once heard a comic say that beautiful women had to listen one hour per day to people calling them beautiful, whereas ugly women had the whole extra hour free to get smart. Esther wasn't ugly, but...One of the men on the houseboat, his hands around her long neck, thrusting, tongue out, eyes shut, flashed and shamed Clem.

Second one on her, enormous with waiting, chooses sodomy; another one yokes her. Please. Mestre was embarrassed and disgusted by those hip naked orgies in the seventies. But his mind would not quit flashing.

"You can't be having this much fun," he said.

"Oh Clem, there really *isn't* a way to be now, is there? It's a kind of yanked-around nonexistence I feel." Clem could see the aunt looming in the doorway to the screened porch. He wondered what the old woman thought she needed to hear. His youth was beset by hearkening interlopers—spies, really—women in windows, telephone in hand like a virus. The men had no stories. It was only the women who had a point of view and a theme: evil is breaking out. What I saw this morning. Who Jenny was with. *Another* man with Esther. "She doesn't matter." Esther knew who was behind her back on the porch. "She's got three friends in the church, even more religious than the minister."

"What about your spiritual state, Esther?"

"This is a surprise from *you.*"

"Why?"

"I assumed most doctors were atheists. Just did, since I was a little girl."

They sat on the wire drugstore chairs under a spreading pecan. Mestre was shy of his question, a little, but his eyes pressed on at her without his consent.

"It's a way of asking about you." He blinked. "Just how are you fixed in your soul?"

"Is it a preacher?" came a quack behind him. It was the aunt and he jumped. He wasn't loud. How could she have heard? What long, long ears. Esther shook her head at the aunt. He heard a movement of retreat at the porch door.

"Who changed *you?*" Esther asked.

"That kind of language made me uncomfortable for many years, I admit. Not now."

"Uncomfortable sounds very modern. Like without remote control. You mean now with the Great Victim in front of you, it's all right."

"Well, I guess. Exactly."

"You're attracted to pain? Or is it even something nastier than that?"

My word, she was Princess Margaret, but beatified in the face, thought Mestre. It collected light now, he was sure. Beautiful, not pretty, like the madonnas. It hurt your groin and made you chilly, then warm. But he could not reply immediately.

"I never had a chance with you until I became the Mother of Victims."

"You've also gotten very smart, Esther. I don't remember you this... acute."

It was three in the afternoon, a time Clem had never been fond of, but Esther drew all nature to herself, green, yellow and blue light, and threw back a calming beam from the beige of her face at him. He was sure.

"I doubt you remember *anything* of me," she said. "I've never been so looked-past in my life."

"I think it's my lousy bedside manner."

"I think you were totally uninterested."

"No. I just didn't believe anybody could say those things so quickly. You hardly knew me."

"There was no reason *not* to love you, fool. A handsome doctor wanting to paint, with black hair like a poet's, if poets look like anything anymore."

"I don't feel those things are all that good."

"Doctor False Modesty carries on."

"You can really burn down a fellow, Esther. But no wonder now."

He knew she didn't like what he'd said, though she stayed radiant. He wondered if they were going to sit here on the nice little lawn forever. The house seemed a bugged crypt inside with that aunt around hovering. They themselves seemed to be hovering, too, no real place to land. He suggested they take a ride in the Miata.

"Eee. I'm thinking the D.A. won't like this, maybe. He wanted me to be practically a plainclothes nun here until the trial. 'Deportment is most urgent,' says prosecutor Little. And a garish little thing you've got."

"But this is all innocent. It'll be practically a church picnic. I'll get the fixings to roast a chicken somewhere around here. There's a half case of New Mexico wine in the trunk. Grateful patient. I've heard it's very decent stuff. Don't you need away from this place a while?"

"Very. But you know I won't be going for any wine or chicken. That's pleasant, but I'm warning you: I'm in love with you still and I want a friend very, very badly."

She whisked around and whirled her dress, a bit calfy and athletic in the legs, from all that volleyball, he imagined, maybe a bit full at the ankles. But who do I think I am, grading her? Mestre swore at himself. All my life, who did I think I was? Grading women like cuts of rib-eye since I was a little pest with seven hairs near my pod and red acne on my chin. "I'll tell her something and get a thing or two!" Esther called back over her shoulder.

Clem heard the aunt inside, quacking out in disagreement. Even graver duck sounds came from her as she said something about it being Sunday. But he heard the lighter tone of Esther, resolute, demanding her right to play, and Mestre rolled back into his childhood, circled by stern women monitors. In his car trunk he had a rag football they could toss in some meadow. The games of youth, that was it. Games gave the better thoughts — they made one feel pure, direct, happy. Maybe he had not simply fallen into sports medicine.

He also recalled that he had once seen Esther in a bicycle helmet. She'd looked exceedingly ugly and dumb, like something on the prow of an old ship of a losing nation. Mestre tried to banish this thought. So headlong, dreary.

And at volleyball, though she had made the team, she seemed to be playing in sand. Through the years he had noted certain overachieving athletes a step behind everybody else naturally, always seeming to perform in sand while the more gifted flew around them on glass.

In the car she told him there was only one thing that bothered her about his face. It didn't seem to have any history behind it. It was almost too clean. She was measuring *him*? But that was all right, why shouldn't she? But Mestre protested — lamely, unnecessarily, he thought — that he did have history, too. Privately, he thought, I wouldn't be here if I didn't have history. I can't say this, she'd take it wrong. Esther went on anyway, pertaining to an awful thing she had to confess.

"Maybe I'm talking more about me. A thing people do most of the time, selfish us. I was horrified I didn't have any history. Who wants to look at a modern girl without any history? I mean men, especially. There's a part of me that's proud now. Can you not be repulsed, Clem? I am somebody, somebody they paid attention to that way."

"*Attention?* God help."

"You don't know at all what being ignored is like, Doctor. You walk in an office or even onto a *field,* and all eyes are on you, respect and love. Look at me. I was just honest, or stupid, enough to blab it out pretty instantly. I don't care. I'll just go ahead and tell you (you aren't a spy for the defense, after all). Yes, I liked it at first, all those men around me when the houseboat left the shore, looking at me, and me in my just slightly agitating swimsuit. I have a decent body, don't I, as you may recall from when I was in my volleyball uniform years ago." She waited.

"Yes. I noticed," he lied.

"I didn't mind being the county Cleopatra on the barge for a while there, day all sunny (the houseboat was Victor Kepps', his dream. Now you can guess what his dream included). Floating down the pretty Tennessee/Tombigbee all the way to Mobile maybe, who knew? Seemed a day not to care and let happen. They were much impressed I had a graduate education. They didn't seem bad men, and they were *witty* even, for a good long while. So I enjoyed all the stares like accidents in my direction. You blame me? I'm too old to be your smart-dumb coed unconscious of her impression on others, half naked I guess, no. I didn't even mind the accidental nudges after they'd had a few beers, but I was looking at the whiskey — so much of it! — in the cabin with a little concern. I thought *three* rough county boys might be trouble, but five of them, now that was closer to a salt-of-the-earth family with their girl mascot. Decency would exercise itself, I was sure. And it did, until Kepps started the more serious stuff. I never knew how he hated me, my education, my ways, my — whatever was *withheld,* I guess. Maybe he thought a plain girl with big teeth like in the British royal family should feel lucky giving it up. But it's him that most of it's about, and it's him that planned to kill me when they were all...done."

"There's no reason to tell it all, if it hurts," Mestre said like a physician, though he wanted to hear more, and was driving his car too seriously toward the bottom of the county for the chicken in the dingy store — priestly sexless monitor. The top was up as a tribute to her guarded role in pretrial, but the day was very warm. Also, nobody was in the fields, the houses were few, with only a porcine woman at the end of a drive challenging the afternoon. Esther went back to her plea.

Hardly had even a kiss in four years. Ignored. Could he know what that felt like? No. Friends at college were blacks and dim freaks from the college radio station. She'd felt for everybody. She felt for the blacks, not taunted but just looked-through, something like a flawed vacancy, slightly worrisome. The boys in the radio station cheered ugly garage music and science fiction like nerds everywhere. The volleyball team won but was yawned past. She felt for the gays and lesbians: I am, I am, she'd thought, in their little clubs. She even had friends on the staff of the wastebasket patrol, who saved cans. The last thing she would say, because she did not like the trembly awful pity for herself any more than he surely did, was that her aunt's place remained her last outpost. Her father ignored her too, and only wanted her out of the way. Her sister was a looker, a charmer, his, at another school, private, downstate; the father knew the aunt had gone religious, too. So she was pushed back like a nun everybody forgets forever. The D.A. wanted her to be a nun. They all wanted her pure air to look through, bolstered in some vague way by the religion of the widow. But she was an office-supply junkie, did Mestre know that? He looked over, not getting it. All my life I've liked pens and paper, even paper clips, she said. All the things around her that went to write on paper. She had a history now, she was somebody, she was finally going to write a book or a long story, she didn't know which. During that last trip to Wal-Mart she found herself among very lonely women like herself and had almost burst into tears, thinking of her future, these older sad women defining themselves among aisles of created need. She could see herself old and lonely out there, lonelier than ever after marrying somebody who was simply male and had paid attention to her. Pardon the sentimental clichés, but there was a story in that too, damn it. This is pathetic, poor-mouthing little ol' me stuff, but I tell you, Clem, I'm just beyond any irony now. Mal Little told me the trial would be long, graphic, ugly and two thirds untrue, get ready, and he had found that rape trials even got very *funny* in this state—the more humor the defense could bring in the better for them, because the public would rather agree that there was simply a *misunderstanding*, at root, ha ha ha. Sorry for this long talk but you are the first I could ever talk it truly through with, Clem. I wasn't about to give my aunt much at all, as it would set her off. Mal Little needs mainly the threat of murder—they were so drunk they thought I couldn't hear the whispers out there—and thinks one of them will "flip" for him in my behalf, be a state's witness.

Mestre went in alone and got a nice chicken, some charcoal and fixings, but he forgot the ice. He almost turned back, thinking of the hot wine in the trunk.

"Oh, no matter. I know a brook, a perfect little thing behind the post office in a ghost town. We can do it all there. Perfect. It's got those old-style gas pumps and just lizards," Esther said, putting her hand on his arm. "Chill the wine there."

Mestre had not remembered that his vision of Esther was likely to talk. A lot. There were no legends of a chattering madonna. Life was breaking in and he was a bit gloomy. Also an ass, he reminded himself. Why shouldn't she talk? Nobody had listened to her—in her whole life, maybe. There *was* much to say, and he should listen. It would all be over, and he would be glad. So they drove back toward the middle of the county where her aunt's house was, but took another road. Silence reigned. See. See. Over.

"It's a cold brook too." She broke it. "That must've been lovely having the water right behind the stores to dream over. Last time I saw it there were hordes of little purple flowers alongside and a tiny brown pebble beach. It's gone now, nothing in it, that town where my aunt was once happy and fun, with her funny drinking husband the crop duster, an airport bum. Bad for the local women too, I heard. The man would get drunk and lie down right in the road, they say. You couldn't budge him without his friend the county sheriff being called. Uncle Ulysses would get a 'high lonesome' going, he called it, and just get country drunk. But the next day he was fine, sharp. What we laughed at must've worn out my aunt. He was bad to write local women letters, too. They say he wrote a beautiful letter. He'd tell them the time he would fly over their house and dip his wings for love, and gratitude. Aunt Trudy came on with a holy vengeance once he was in the ground. She saw the post office itself as evil, and I know she's glad it's gone and dried out. Makes you wonder if women get nuts when they don't get laid. The first two, really, I didn't mind that much. We were just talking, friends in the cabin, and movements were made, it seemed no time at all. First Kepps was in me, the other one smiling and holding my hand. I can't say I loved it, but it was such a new and daffy thing. Then he came for my mouth, and it wasn't friendly anymore. At the end Kepps came again, and I was beat up. I had been saying no forever and finally just shut up. Kepps was *so* drunk and angry."

"You're telling me too much, don't you think, Esther?" Mestre interrupted, but a black excitement was on him, despite himself, the bullet-headed cop asking "Who gets to look?" I do, I do, I do.

"I can't quite figure," she said with another big breath. "Are you here as a doctor, or friend, or...I'm talking everywhere because I can't decide. This is my story for my *story,* not the court, you see.

You aren't a spy for the defense, so you can know that. There's *another* story to everything. Someday I'll write this one, I think — for whom, who knows? I've got all my supplies stacked. Those blue lines beckon. They had weapons. I saw knives in the kitchen. They wanted to kill me and dump me in the canal, with weights on my body. This is what matters, isn't it?"

"Yes," said Mestre.

She began whimpering and cried soundlessly into her hands.

"Kepps is a monster. He led them all, his cousin and all the rest. He just *has* to rot some. I don't care whether the state wants this trial or not. *I am a woman worth something!*"

"Of course you are."

All this land around them looked black and rich. Nobody was bothering to farm it. The few homes looked so *shut in,* pulled away from the rolling fields. Mestre, from coal-mining and scratch-farm country, deliberately knew nothing about either. Were folks paid to shut up and not farm, get concerned watching "Jeopardy!" over Shake 'n Bake dinners on TV trays, served up with Crystal Light? He didn't know. Some of the yards were very clean. Was that their profession? The homes struck him as lonesome morgues for passion. But then after vacant brambles and low weed-wheat acres, he sensed they were coming on a settlement. Ruins of pickup trucks held out against weeds and kudzu, as if they had almost made it to town. Now, by what he could guess, Mestre figured the real point of rural America: to have pickup trucks and run them into a rust hulk, exploring internal combustion. He saw three wild housecats hunting, then a solo dog in the act of becoming feral. Next, round a bend came the town, and it was very much a ghost. Citizens had picked up and left, a dry curse still ringing through the planks. This used to be Uncle Ulysses and Aunt Trudy's town, he understood, and there was the post office, ruined, hollow. Esther had stopped talking about herself. She was excited about something else. Passionate phrases he barely got the gist of sang from her, yes it was a song of memory about nature, nature and the brook which could not betray; it was about things from her girlhood, things standard, unchanging, and about all that dreaming by the brook as she listened to the blacks and whites exchange stories at her back, stories she could barely hear but did, and she knew then what the *real* South was, others didn't. What she dreamed of when she was a teenager! A man in a white suit, maybe a doctor. She smiled and looked over, giddy. He was happy she was happy, and the form of her, hurt but beaming anyway, came back to please him. You want to paint, paint this, she said. The brook of the soul running through destitution, soul man, she cheered.

In a trice, as the old stories say, we are here, giggled Esther. Behind the shell of the post office — just a deep booth anyway, with pigeon holes, racked with mud-dauber clods — the brook was certainly there, with its tiny beach, two big chilled frogs waiting for them until they got too close and the frogs shot off in the burbling drink like space machinery. Mestre recalled that after the two frogs surprised and scared him, his existence would never be quite the same again, as they said in the old stories. Nature could be very, very quick and odd. The creatures went out six feet, more like technology than flesh and blood, making Mestre and Esther both gasp. Then they laughed. Everything afterward seemed in rapid motion.

He had forgotten any kind of grill to put the chicken on. But right on the floor of the post office a few steps behind them lay a piece of screen and, merrily, a large hubcap with spinners, a relic from the fifties, the decade of Clem's childhood. Mestre matched them instantly and made a grill on the beach, feeling very adroit, even suave, and he was congratulated wildly out loud by Esther who said it was still the age of miracles. In that vein, he later recalled just a bit of his own talk about a miracle, one of those things unshared with anybody else since his youth. There are miracles, he thought, with Esther sitting by him, pink silk dress on the pebbles, not caring. He told her about a grotto for black Catholic priests in Virginia Beach with a freshwater pool, a most pretty little place. He and a boy had caught a burlap sack full of crabs and were walking back to Clem's uncle and aunt's with them, proud. They had, really, too many crabs. Mestre took five or six of them out and put them in the grotto. The other boy said, Why that's just cruel, they'll only die. But Clem told him the others were going to die boiling. Which was better? The next year Clem was walking by the grotto alone, and went down to look in the pool. Something fantastic hung over the place even before he saw what he saw. Where were the black priests in training, where did they go, who ever heard of black priests anyhow? Not in Kentucky. Also you never saw them *anywhere* around. Their training was secret, deep and Catholic, scary and too quiet. Then he saw a crab swim up from the fresh water, this ocean crab that shouldn't be able to live. The crab came to the surface and stared at him. Deeper in the pool Clem thought he could make out scores more of them, fading smaller in their army claws to the black depth. Then they all flashed away, having shown themselves enough. They couldn't be there, but they were, thriving. He never went back because he was afraid he wouldn't see them, and he never told anybody. There, a miracle.

But this speech faded into other matters. The chicken was cooking, lathered in sweet barbecue, the smoke around them comfortably; they were like a picture on a calendar as the words went around. You are my miracle, my friend, Esther said. He found Esther on his lap, legs out on either side. She had put on sunglasses and stared blackly at him without words for a long fast time. Fairly soon something became noticeable. Under the dress she had on hose and garter belt, but no panties. Her skirt of pink and smooth silk came up and he saw the outraged property itself. Clem had seen his wife's, of course, but it had been a good while since Clem had looked, direct, at the place itself, framed by the garters. He marveled at the original hurt, and felt very meager. Her scars were so much beyond his. He had no scars; he had gotten through smooth as a baby's butt. What did he have for pain? Tennis elbow. What a weak slick thing he was. Just enough injury to make him mewl and wimp around, unable to protect her reputation on the streets. He thought she'd gone in the house just to get a few things. A minx, her place of rage, concocted — all these flew to mind, because he was still mostly head and unprepared, here in nature.

Esther spoke: "I've always imagined Adam and Eve had the first big sin by a beautiful accident, like most great good things. It was so *easy*, so helpless. People throw up such a storm about it, but it's just so easy, just a piece of cloth away."

"Ah."

"Don't you imagine they just fell into each other, my friend? They were friends and then they were something else. It was too easy."

"It wasn't even fair. Yes," whispered Mestre, some of his Appalachian brogue spilling out.

"My friend!"

"Friends."

"I'm in a dream!" she sighed as he took the natural way. The brook seemed to shake and get loud behind him. He could hear it tearing through the weeds.

But Mestre felt he was more in a saloon, a battle of notes rising from the piano, the gamblers yelling "Har!" as her garters rubbed him, Esther on his lap in sunglasses. He looked past her shoulders into the open post office above. That's when he saw the old woman watching them.

Hair in those risen waves of black and white, she was the image of Mrs. Freeman from the second grade—her stories of "evil-minded doctors," her anti-kissing club, still having it when she was dead, "You'll Never Walk Alone" played at her funeral. The exact title came to Mestre straight out of shock.

The old woman caught his eye and huffed, he thought, before she turned and went back through the shell of the post office. Esther was up by then and saw her go. They heard the car roll away in the dust.

"That's one of my aunt's church friends," Esther said sadly.

"What was she up to?"

"God knows. It couldn't mean anything, could it? No. She's just a telephone Christian, is all. Holier than the pope. Thing is, we heard she was one of Uncle Ulysses' women. Down here..." Esther said in a flat small voice. "Down here for one of his letters? I don't know."

The chicken burned up right behind them. They must have stood watching the absent car for a while.

Clem thought he smelled men all over Esther. Her back was sweated orange against the thin pink dress. It was not a good evening. Later he could not drink enough chilled wine from the brook to make a difference. He flipped pieces of burned meat in the brook as Esther got sillier. He would paint, she would write, she kept saying. No he wouldn't.

Out of strength or weakness—he couldn't figure—he stayed loyal to her through the next months. She was depressed, then exhilarated, about the looming trial. Clem would see her face sometimes and feel the plain sorrow in it. When she didn't talk, she moved him very much. Just the face and the hurt green eyes, maybe looking sadly down her driveway, through the maple leaves, at nothing. She would remind him of Kentucky men on their porch steps, looking down another evening.

The trial was of course nasty. Every reputation was ruined, and the people of the state seemed sorry it was carrying on. Then there was no trial at all. The old woman from the post office took the stand, very voluntarily. Neither Esther's aunt nor parents were there. It was just all nastiness. No trial left at all. But people were impressed that Dr. Mestre was standing by, every day. They remarked on the fact she must be of some quality to inspire this.

Clem and Esther married at the next Christmas. Clem could not tell whether he was happy or sad, and he was wholly neither. But he was comfortable now that he had a past, and had done something for plain sorrow. He left athletics for family practice after a summer and fall of study.

Esther became friends with Andra, the grad student next door. They played with the Chinese dog, which had gotten very stout in his rolls of skin. She was extremely happy, except sometimes when she looked out the window into something like the pulse of time, it seemed to Clem—the seasons taking on leaves and putting them off, something somehow rushed and slow at the same time, and not looking back at her at all. She couldn't figure why Clem had married her.

On these few occasions, Clem loved her. He felt part of a big thing.

Allons, Mes Enfants

I BELIEVE you know me. We met at some wharf, I recall, years
ago. I'm Daniel Broyard. I live out Whelp of Dimming Way in,
well, a city.

Like old Dor Gray, I'm a laster, hardly a speck of age on me, they
say. "It's almost a scandal how you at your years don't show a thing,
not a tuck out of place, seeing what we've all been through together." Like most, they understand too quickly. But they're wrong.
Comic how people think they know you, but not. I've been at much
more than they, especially these last fifteen years, and I barely sleep,
don't have to. I "run with the big dogs" when they're on the divan,
the bed, the lounge chair, the hammock. I've even seen some of them,
those still employed, snoozing at their desks. Some of them were
doing this at forty. Mark their activity, their cries for rest, their inau-
thentic fatigue. You see, I work with street children, and I know
what work is, this work the others don't know about, because it's all
of the night and profoundly psychosocial. I'm making a difference
out there, darn it.

Now I call them children because I am ancient, no matter what
your eyes or my mirror tells me, but I am not talking about your infants, your waifs, your elementary tykes and nubs. We are talking,
say, eighteen to thirty in some cases, seriously troubled and unem-
ployed hoodlums, curb whores and a few tourists from the suburbs
trying to look earnestly bored and betrayed. You work with the
young and it keeps you what? Young. Goes the old saw. Pay attention to this: I believe that the man whose work is never done has a
goal that keeps him in shape as truly as a long-distance runner. Some
Christians look almost this young because they will never save everybody; there are the Hindus to bring over yet. Well, it's good for your
blood to be futile, though *every* drop in the ocean counts, darn it.

You could call my city Atlanta, although it's not. It hardly matters, but some approximations of Atlanta I find apt. It is one of those
cities once with character but besieged in the sixties by corporate

midwesterners, then occupied in the center by blacks and deliberate hoboes, so that old character is diffused and insulted everywhere, and you wind up with all things slick and egregious, watched by alarmed "professionals" in the suburbs. Neighborhood fiefdoms are the norm, and many of the beloved young I work with keep veritable moats of enmity between themselves and others even fractionally unlike them. The only thing they have not done to the city is set it on fire, a fact which puzzles many in an urban zone that murders, usually, unless there is a hard freeze out, ten people a night. Buildings are defaced so quickly, maybe there is an instant nostalgia for the sordid here. The papers say three murders but I know ten. Many just disappear and their proxies, for years, appear at the welfare office for their checks. The person handing over the check is likely to be drawing illegal welfare himself, and hardly anybody is questioned because everybody is apathetic and armed. Many in the city, too, age instantly, the result of a sort of "peer pressure" from their dead friends. Add the murderous specific, "crack."

Well, darn it, this doesn't look to be the kind of academy that keeps a man young, does it? But I jump into it all like a briar patch full of tar babies, starting about ten every night. Never have I even been bruised. You may think about me going along my way with great Beethoven's "Moonlight," "Appassionata" and "Pathétique" sonatas, barely heard, but straight from the sweet chambers in my head. Such has it been since I was small and busy at my games, always *accompanied,* and I would advise this thoroughly, to choose a soft music and live by it — one's "score." It cuts right through the hideous enforced public Muzak, the infantile ravings of the "concrete jungle."

I go down there without, I'll go ahead and say it, any sexual persuasion. I have no sexual persuasion. Nor do I own a gun or knife, even though I work in the Bronze Age down there. Let us have it plain: my society is comprised of metal-worshipers. They pray to metal, are owned by metal, and metal uses them; it shoots them, it stabs them. I witness its sycophants, grave zombies, moved about humorlessly as its agents. My minions are spiritually rapt as the age climaxes in gunpowder. One notes that, upon first being handed a rifle — by Burton or Speke? — a chieftain blithely shot one of his own lackeys, expressing radiant joy as the man tumbled down dead. Do not stop there, happy Klansman, but watch with me early in the morning as I come in from work: across the street here in the clean "burbs" your white policeman goes reverently to his car with a deer rifle coddled in his right arm like a precocious, beautiful child. This man lives with a pistol on his hip all week, but that is not enough, no, he is *devout* and it is the Christmas season. His own cowardice, affirmed by the use of guns, would not occur to him any more than the cowardice of God. The gun lobby, oh my peaceful friends, you may hate, but first you had better understand that it is a religion, only secondarily connected to the Bill of Rights. The thick-headed, sometimes even close to tearful, gaze you get when chatting with one of its partisans emanates from the view that they're holding a piece of God. There is no persuading them otherwise, even by a genius, because a life without guns implies the end of the known world to them. Any connection they make to our "pioneer past" is also a fraud, a wistful apology. Folks love a gun for what it can do. A murderer always thinks it was an accident, he says, as if a religious episode had passed over him.

End of sermon. It's sermons that make us old — all that presumption screws up the mouth, creases the forehead, dries up the sweet fluids of life and makes the stomach sour. If I may quote from one of my dear sources on the act of preaching: "a kind of vampirism in which mesmerizing assertions of authority drink the energy they arouse." It's adventures and journeys that keep us.

My dress is collegiate and moderately expensive, modestly expressed, with only here and there a flash of high vanity, but in small insignias, say a silver collar brace under the tie, or a watch chain across the vest. I affect, admittedly, svelte brogans, highly polished — in brown, oxblood and black — and laced to above the ankle. Hard to find, these late-Victorian boots are made by one New Jersey company, and I have watched, subtly, some of my minions begin imitating me with cheap translations from some neighborhood ethnic shop they've browbeaten. A working man needs a working shoe. Believe it or not, my wards have a nostalgia for this footwear of the sharecropper and the row-chopper, carried out in their high-topped white, black and puce sneakers. An undeniable subreligion of the young is their shoe — thanks, says your millionaire sneaker baron. Enter your throbbing social worker: "Of course, it's all they've got!" Pure drivel. They have mouths, backs and time. "They have the absentee father!" The old parental vamoose, yo? Would that my own father had left the nest two decades previous to when he did. A missing father is an invitation from the divine. I make them see that. The foul-mouthed inadvertent saints some of them have for mothers must have their due, for a while, though spoiled infantilism explains half the crowd you see on the street. You dare not mess too deeply with mothers at first, though, only suggesting more blissful territory seven blocks away. I'll get to this. In my own case, I went nearly mad with drive and creativity when my old man was at last calm in the ground, and Dad was better than most in his "dysfunction" — this cheap word usually spoken in the nasal by some whelp of compulsive hypocrisy. I drive a Saab convertible which stays, top down, right in front of the Filipino grocery on Hague, dead center of the wasteland, almost with its hand out waving to thieves, yet untouched.

Patience, and you will find me more than a braggart, I hope.

No, I go right into my "classroom," my "chambers," a room so flaked and ugly it laughs at paint. The spotted, ruined pink reminds me of something, and I dare not touch it; one flight up from the grocery store, take a left. There you will see me with my polished boots up on the chipped pecan desk my dad used in the utterly banal but sane trade of burial insurance, still the burned chocolate trenches of his cigarettes all over the edge. I am carrying on, Pa, I am putting it to them, though there is no continuity in our businesses at all, unless it be that I too speak to the almost dead rather constantly. So here I am, addressing the bottom end of the hysterical modern spectrum — Bronze Agers killing themselves — while out there at the other end the universal therapists wail for universal "co-dependency" and classes in masturbation. Let one not fall into cheap cynicism, another mark of the times, either; another feast of the narcissists; one could wind up as Gore Vidal, intercontinental bile-ist. We don't want to be sulking second-stringers on the badminton team.

I in fact address logorrhea and suicide, right off. "That you are here at all, my pitiful brothers and sisters..." Many of them simply can't quit talking. Their brains, unnourished, by some awful fluid thinness slip forward directly into their mouths, where every speculation is announced, the mouth always just behind the last message by nanoseconds. You might be looking into a row of heads slapped voluble by unseen harpies out there. But soon they're quiet. About suicide, I ask them why are you here? what's the point? why do you in your raving homicidal nursery not see the squalid end early — so ghoulishly apparent all around you — and take the ultimate pleasure of blowing your own head off with your favorite champion "piece"? You, yours, you know, hardly ever commit suicide like good white people, all gates wide to them. Is it pussy, cock, sex you're living for? (After the first meeting it is known that only I, the successful adult, can use bad language — the "Moonlight" Sonata is still in my head, though running a little jaggedly, but I'll soon slip back to dreamy ecstasies.) Your next high? Even the minor orgasm of your next *shit?* That's the end of the foul language, almost. Why not suicide? It is your narcissist who shoots himself, that's why. I mean almost always, even your frail acned "dweeb," head pounding with self-desire. You sheep don't even have enough self-worth to destroy yourselves. You wouldn't have that final religious ecstasy at all. Line up a number of successful "productive" types, all nations, creeds, and throw in a wino, a stinking offensive hunk of mobile trash, and most likely he would be the *last* to kill himself. He knows there is *no* significance, waking, sleeping, dead, or in hell. Living on, despite hilarious persecutions of body and soul. Well, what is it but brute animality? No dog kills itself, no ape, no crocodile. This makes them nervous, and you may wonder how it is I haven't been pitched out the window years ago into my gloating Saab. Because I came in quick — their hatred at neap tide: What are you trying to be, vain and stupid? This is your aspiration, the dream of those little white chickens in the sororities across town? Looking good? Looking good? Change in your pocket, my *car,* except lower and longer and fucked over (oops) by jungle bunny accessories? I see in your faces — I don't see your faces at all, I see blocks: big furry dice coming up number thirteen. I see *hood* ornaments, homeboys and little mamas in flight, solid tin. Big youth stirs out of its infantilism out there in those chairs. Shouldn't we kill him? It barely helps that I myself am "black" — Haitian. I've got them right in the eyes.

Hasn't it ever, ever occurred to you that you are in the wrong *place, mes frères, mes soeurs, mes semblables?* Did the Jews prosper in Egypt? Did they flourish bigly in Dachau? And I ask you, have the Irish ever flourished in *Ireland?* Barely. It's the wrong place for them. All Irishmen were made for *Italy,* obviously, where poverty, overpopulation and blind jabbering ignorance have a certain élan, a romance. Every arriving Irish émigré is invited over to Gore Vidal's Italian palace immediately for potluck, *upon arrival,* I swear to you, those few in the know. *Cognoscenti.*

Only a couple laugh. But they're more settled now.

It is about this time that I darken the room, having rolled down the screen, and begin my slides.

Bust a move! . . . to France! I begin.

The boulevards, the parks, the wide streets, Montmartre, l'Arc de Triomphe, *rive gauche,* Seine, bistros, Notre-Dame, la Tour Eiffel, funky hotels, Colonel Sanders, the countryside, Normandy, crashed German tanks.

But more to the point:

Josephine Baker, happy
Richard Wright, happy
James Baldwin, happy
Anonymous blacks with white beauties, happy

And the finale, the very Prince of Hip, in a rare photograph:

Miles Davis, happy in Paris.

The French love you, they worship you. You've already done most of your homework just being what you are. I would venture, my friend, that a third of the class has never heard of France. I am giving them their first, palpable, geography class, ever.

Then I remind them in another voice entirely, much quieter: every leader you ever have will betray you — in this country. The leading money- and music-maker in the history of the world, ever, has bought himself a white skin and white's hair, unable, apparently, to wait for Jehovah's Witness heaven. This bleached toy commands your millions and your idolatry — in this country.

Money, I say. The chairs come down to the floor from the stilts they were making of them, leaning backward. You can hear a pin drop. Money takes time. Usually it does. A ticket to France — let's call it an even five hundred — may take a job, a skill, but France is *there,* your goal. You can see it, you can feel it, you can touch it. France is that big liner down at the harbor seven blocks away, waiting, hoping, lights on even at night like a giant smile of welcome from this great country. You can have a skill when you get there. There are even classes on the boat. Concerning the rap sheets on a number of you, my people can present you with something on an international computer smooth as a baby's butt. No exceptions. This is new life, new you.

Then I get the tall stack of hundreds out of my briefcase and just set it there on Dad's desk. This could be, one hundred dollars each, our "investment" in them, never to be paid back, not even a postcard of thanks required. Here, some nervousness and impatience implode in them, you can feel it. Those who have been here before look away or down at the floor. Lights are back up, slides stuffed away.

Some of you will run. Some of you will go buy your "crack." Some of you will not find gainful employment. You will not dream.

You will steal for it, and some — five? — of you will be shot dead, stealing. It looks like... I pause... *this* for almost all of you. Then I go immediately into it. I have been told by some out there, now in France, that it is the most paralyzingly awful thing they have ever witnessed.

All my true years suddenly come on me. I strain, my mouth widens, I can even feel my pores widening. My jaw drops, my tongue comes out to the side, dripping what must be phlegm. It is a combination of total relaxation and herculean effort. My eyes redden, and a moist gray crepe covers my face. There is even snot involved. It is the old man, worse than death, *living death*. I am told it is so revolting, my age-hard wrinkles, my chronology in spades, my black tongue, with the beggarly snarl, the whimper, that no monster film — which they adore — even comes close. And I am right in the room. I have never watched myself in the mirror. I'm frightened to. I take a step and the chairs rattle, many of them wanting seriously *out* of there. Then I heave and stare at the ground. After a full minute I lift my face, as usual, to them. I almost don't need the lectures or slides at all.

Being shot and leaving a handsome corpse bothers half of them none at all. But this, *this*.

The visionaries, gentle bigots, who are my employers, pay me very, very well. Bills are always paid and my check is never late. About a tenth of the class actually get on board the liner and we've had touching successes over there. We've received touching postcards from them, some of whom have learned to read and write. In French.

As those say about my face, you say why isn't this a scandal? How can I sleep at night? How can I look at myself in the mirror? Your universal therapists are pouring out of their forlorn belfries like bats in protest.

Yes, I am a kind of double agent, citizens, as are most of us always. But on the other hand, this removal to France, what else have you got? Some days I think of leaving the Saab and all of it and getting on the ship with my last class. In fact, I've no doubt I will. Shuffleboard and a fast-forward class in carpentry sometimes appeal very much, until I look in the mirror again, lucky bastard.

I remain, very enthusiastically, *young*.

Evening of the Yarp:
A Report by
Roonswent Dover

DARN IT WERE BORING, wisht I were a hawk or crab. When I seen him first I leapt out of my face for glad cause nothing moving lately but only rabbit nibble and run headfirst into the bottom of the purple cane. Deacon Charles at the VT school say go a head and write like this dont change. He wants to see it quick cause I seen the Yarp. Or somebody like him. Xcuse me please for not correct but I am hard attempting to spell at least sweller it being so important. Of a mountain man/boy nineteen first that day at two forty-one o'clock afternoon on the watch I found at the road going up to Missus Skatt's house.

The sin of the old people I wondert what it was cause I dint feel it. The evil things of Roonswent Dover which is me werent felt by me like the others cause I had no feltedness of their kind of sin. I found out the Yarp did too.

He was a man hitchhiking where dont nobody come, ever, up a red ditch juncted to a road so dirty and spit out red on the paving. He was a true-looking lean man near hungery looking in a high collar white city shirt but no necktie up on it. I passed him then slapped my thigh, why not, I'm so miserable bored. Maybe this man knewn something markable or a good thing to seek, him wanting a ride up that ditch where nobody but old woman Skatt lives. Rained down to gullies, that road, but we figure she be hungery, she walk out of there, down the mountain with her crooked feet, buffalo toenails and ruint smell. I backed up and he looked in the window. I say can't you see no truck nor even tractor could get up that gullied red road? He said he would go on with me and rest and see Missus Skatt later. He sat down, no suitcase, bag, nor cane nor hat, just coming out of winter and going to near freeze this night. Thanks for the lift. You know where you are? I asked him. Yes I been here plenty time and I know your Missus Skatt very very well. It doesn't matter much when I get there sooner or later but I will go with you to the store.

I asted him how he knewn I was going to the store (and I was). He said life is simple around here and I had the look of a store visit on me. Nobody much con fused him and now he was hungery, feeling low and getting chill. He gave me a cigar for my trouble and said it was the kind governors and dictators smoked from Latin America. We lit up and I was feeling chumly. He asted me would there be music at the store. This struck me goofy, of course there were a radio at ever store and a televisioner too. And would there be food? I turned over to him saying what else would there be in a store to be a store at all, certain it has food, gas, oil, shells, bait, sardines, herrings, rat cheese, and two old geezer at a wood stove playing Risk, and Macky Vellens. He said what, I repeated, he pronounced it better, MacKeyavellea of course, the writer of the *Prince* they used as a handbook to Risk, taking on personalities, book falling depart apieces through the generations. Mr Simpson and Gene James owned it with theyr smart pet goat that makes change I swear not, only the truth alone.

Then that man, the Yarp, he said shut up. Riding aside me afortunate my charity, he said Shut Up ragely. It were glum, I werent happy, but couldnt get mad cause he seem a danger now. I dont want to hear none of your tales, boy, he kept on it, too many tales come out of these mountains and everwhere. There shouldnt be any tales.

I said well you can see the goat with his front foot, but he hissed or spat so I look out the window away from him, stopt talk.

In your mind you thinking you paying for the gas and tires hauling me. And it was true, what he said.

We had eleven mile to go and it was crooked high down to low then high again, not even a dead dog nor cat nor chicken keep you company under the overhangs of them sweaty rocks. I aint nere liked them and now, getting on dark, the mountains I feel they live and sqeeze in on you to a narrow lane when nobody's around. I nere give up that feeling sinct I was a kid. It aint Arkansas or no real place. Now come sleet specking my poor dusty glass all acracked, which, I didn't like the sun running down either.

We'll have a nice snow tonight, the Yarp adventured. The quiet I was keeping didnt make no call to break it so I remaint quiet. Nineteen or not I was frighted. But if the quiet woulder asked me I woulder said You fool, it's on too late to snow, that sleet is just a peck from some froze cloud way up there. Its April, you fool.

Yes it'll catch Missus Skatt just unfreezing from the winter. She won't have enough wood. I'm sure glad I'm going with you to the warm store, Roonswent Dover.

Yes he called my name. There aint no way of knowing my name and be a stranger cause I go by Bill Dover to everbodys knowlege. I aint got even no license plate on this truck. You can see ten mile clear out here, cant be no stranger as ever came near your house nor your daddy or mommer that you dont know about. Our part of the county can't have no stranger moren ten minutes. So it were cold quiet now, believe it, no heater in my truck only a lantern in case of a mountain accident, lucky if theyr matches in that glove apartment. I couldnt get no speed outer her neither and we aint got to the real high passes yet. We was in a holler and then a vale, pinking out to the sides. There was some sun, a bit, so sudden I got brave.

But you shunt know my name.

He nored me.

You know too many legends, boy. Everbody does. You got to lie to stay halfway interested in yourself, dont you? The imagination is what ruins it. They shouldn't never imagined heaven nor hell. They shoulder taken their years, thats all. You already know the more you think of something aforehand it isn't anything like that at all. They'll be legending though, they'll be doing wrong and doing nothing, bargaining with heaven or hell. They shoulder just taken their years and practiced being dumb, over and over. Already that school is con fusing you and hurting your mind, Roonswent Dover, son of Grady and Miriam.

I just fix small engines, I aventured.

You lie!

That last shout was good for another two mile of silents.

It snows here when there aint no snows anywhere else near. We must be higher, higher than all Arkansas and Missouri. In our county the Indian were never pushed out and we has whole fullblood Indians, but they are innocent. All the killing and stealing on tourists or policemen or sometimes a local for peculiar reasons is done not by them. Some said it were womens, womens and girls. A Indian told me that when I was seventeen. Now our Indians are Nini Indians. They fought on the Souths side and had slaves where nare white man here fought for either side, most for not knowing there were a war on and the rest, said my Uncle Rell, because they were drunk or idiots. A Ozark army might have swayed the war, says Rell. Our family wernt interbred but some Ozarkens, come to church and school too, theyr daughters get pregnant by them or theyr sons. So the Indians were defeated, and without slaves they moved up here from like Paragould near the river and sorrowed-out and become puny. Anybody can whip an Indian a head taller than him, a girl could do it. It is still a agony how many years? a thousand years after the War Between the States now the Indian is in deep sorrow even to plant a bean or tote water or feed his dog. They groan out loud all the time, feeble and they hate it, cursing Robert E. Lee who promised them slaves all the future. So theyr homes is tragic, likely to be a stricken old bus or a natural cave or sometimes what I saw, they tooken to living secret under a white man's house that they dug a hole under it. And they are in ever abandoned shack or outhouse, they are in so fast, they might be puny but they are quick, whole families can get on a squat quicker than deer fleas. (The old shacks and cabins here and there was left over from the diamond rush when my pa was a boy.) Reason Im explaining the Indians is they had legends more than us. Theyr chief drives a school bus to the VT school and will lie like a mockingbird back and forth to it. The bus dont allow nare radio so that Indian Don Suchi Nini sings to us these stories and believes he is the one who will change them back to real. They still want slaves and Don Nini says the whites better remain strong or, clunk, they be Indian slaves come nigh. When I was littler he had me making my grades and I went to the VT so I wouldnt be no slave. So we know what theyr thinking, and theyr everwhere, slunking round and creeping lenthwise in some Ozark ledge or listening from some nookery, and you cant do nothing about it. Xcept sometimes a girl will kill one, and they are set back in theyr revolution for a few week. I never treated nare Indian bad and most here dont. They might be puny but they scare me, the men dont care whether they got on a dress or overalls, and they will melt right in front of you into a line of trees. So, three mile up from the store on that last bad mountain, this Indian goes across my lights, which, wouldn't you know, is full of snow, active snow, and he was old and naked except for rubber wading boots. It just made me shake. I never seen nare like it, cracking my teeth that way. Then there were a little mountain girl coming after him with a fork hoe, what a dreadsome ancient sneer on her face. They come off the side of the mountain across the road and maintained on down the mountain where nothing but no goat should get a perch, on down to awful black night rock near the pitch of a well.

Oh! I said out. You see that? Hands bout to tear off the steering wheel.

I didnt see anything at all, lad, said him.

Everthing since he got in that truck was mocking me, minding back. Xcept maybe that speech on legends, hell and heaven.

The snow was churning and up in the road, some storm blowing down about three mile high, seemed right from the North Pole, only in our county. But it was, I knewn he was the Yarp in a way already, I bet. He was lost over there in the dark seat and maybe he didnt see that old Indian and girl. Wouldnt you know the engine quit and overheat and I had to coast down, Ive did it before, all the way to the store. Xcept the unsound got to me, in the curves and sliding on them circular threads that does as tires. The quiet was outside and inside and my poor lights was flickering. I knewn Id have already been down twict and back if the Yarp wadn't with me.

You hear about murdering thieving females in these parts, said the Yarp.

I werent going to adventure, Nat Hidey, no I werent. Was peering in the snow which, it was heavier than normal snow and it was gray not good white. A Yarp's eyes of course is suppose to be hot yellow and his skin disappeared from his throat so you can see its tongue long in it and tonsils and open voice box, it makes you sick. I werent going to look over there at all. I werent getting it yet but the Yarps smell of course would be a combination of bull spunk and road kill. Your Yarp suppose to have tiny long bird legs and big long feet too. I was on my way to the store, nailed in my windshield. A Yarp doesnt have to be none of that unless the time come on him. A Yarp has passed for a preacher, you know that. He dont know any breed and he can be an Indian or Kentuckian or live far off in a hospital. But he denominates in black garments, sudden he will lift his coat and you can see all his digestion, everthing he's eaten all chewed and gravyed-up in them tubes and holds and glands, and it makes you sicker. Thered be a baby's foot or one woman saw his stomach and there were a human brain. You can picture me as a hard looker through that windshield.

A Yarp is weak and quick like Indians in the legs, thin, but in the upper body powerful, so this thing throw through the woods and running water and pea gravel top-weighted. It can reach up with its arms and yank you down, but it aint hardly nothing underneath but coot legs and wading feet. My grandpa knewn a family of Yarps, peaceable, but nere eye has set on a whole family sinct his time which was eighty year ago when the Ozarks was founded. A Yarp really belong in Europe or Asia is what my grandpa say, he dont like it here in

Arkansas, but some fell off accidental in the boats going out and there we are, they come a Yarping with Vikes and Pilgrims, they dont know no breed. Like the Indian they would be not so scarey if they *was* strong and upright. They is twict the fear to me weak and slimy, hanging down toward the ground like a slug snail, presiding on you specially when they are in groups nearby you, glooming at you, wanting something you cant give but they have to stay after it. That feebletude and they putting hands on you, that belongs more in your nightmares than a strong evil man, it gets your back clammier, your head colder, your heart miserabler.

I coasted on down not talking at all like Im talking now, lights flickering at the snow that were like gray scales, I finally got it, like fish scales, aflapping on the glass. I wouldnt look but he started shaking with cold I guess, commenced knocking on the tin floorboard of my Ford, gruesomish. There hadnt been lights left or right the whole trip, nare cabin nor goodly shack even if there were a light to commit, you hadnt sawn it.

Hurry, lad, the store, said him. I was cold to bones too. When what you know, the engine caught on for maybe cooling down gainst the snow. This thing get a hundred mile on a gallon of water when its good. Will there be music, he asted again. Saying from my choked throat was grievous.

Even if the radio broke they have a televisioner that pull in a music channel all snowy. Out here for the mountains we cant barely get waves, but there is people moving, dancing in the speckled screen we dont know the source, but there be a tiny music at it. The people is sad-looking themselves back and fro specially when the music goes out entire, you just having loud snow and forms pitching and pulling at each other. But I didnt say this to the man I knewn certain were a Yarp, chatting and shifting with cold. I wont it were light enough to see his feet and legs so thin out the right side low of my eyeball.

If there isnt music, lad, we must ride on.

Oh no we dont said I to me.

He knewn already that at the VT school we gathered with Deacon Charles, some nine of us young hillbillies at the head of the willow creek back of the parked schoolbus, the Indian chief Don Nini with us too listening and saying and ahearkening at lunch, seemed it was wouldnt you know subject of females and some studying the old stories and some about the at large way of the world. Some of them had Satan with a fiddle, why Im assaying off again here, the music. He was known to come to a dance out of nowhere and negotiate his fiddle to warp womens and girls. But Deacon who is reasonable in the head and forty-five and run the small engine course said that was made up by jealous male hillbillies whose wives and sweethearts was taken off by a musical stranger. Any slicker could do her, even out of a flat Arkansas town. You might as well say that Satan had a good car or money, which would work better. Deacon knewn the flat delta as well as us in the hills and of course was in the arm service when we was fighting I believe India. He said there werent even half the real tales never that they claim, like youd think a standard Ozark person was going round hardly nothing but a blabbering tale, tales piling up in ever holler and cove. No, and a lots were did pure for government men and university people who wouldnt leave them alone and specially during the Deep Ression. In the Deep Ression times folks often told a tale get the government interested in you as interesting, as workable or feedable or sometimes even free money which they awarded you for not coming off the mountain and mixing in nare cities, which already had too many folks. Some had went to California and messed it up terrible. The governor of California had began a new state and he didnt want nare hillbillies on it. In California they have science that grow eggs on a tree, and them hillbillies so sloppy and shuffling, they dont know how to harvest them down and walk cracking them with their stupid Arkansas feet. Deacon Charles would hold up his banana at lunch and say Whats this? A banana. Well, more than that, friends, youre looking at California, where I shipped out to the East. You say I went west to get East, how? Well, friends, there is a line in the ocean all stormy where everything gets backwards, that's how. They worship whats little, like a stick. Back to the tales, he said when you then dropped the ones said by parents to scare theyr young into formity, you hadnt hardly no real tales left. No, your witches and your haints, there wasn't many of them and the tales told about them got them wrong, my hillbilly geese, all gaggle and tongue. Your active supernaturals aint ever going to get that *apparent,* for one thing. He live on the rim of things and dont want to be discovered. I seen exactly one Yarp and I been searching all my life.

Finally the store, but it looked dim in that rain of snow, just a quarter the light that usually come out of there from Mr Simpson and old Gene James, tall and gray-bald with a bowtie like some girl stood him up sixty years ago. The thing, the Yarp, hopped out and went on in while I gassed up and watered the truck. Ice and snow was already thick and made my truck ghosted. Oh it were freezing and I trembled scared both, not wanting in the store but too cold not to.

The Yarp was over next to the wood stove where they was sitting just staring at the Risk board, no pieces on it. Something was wrong and I were glad theyr was somebody else to share the Yarp with, even nineteen like I am.

He had said something made them stop and frown, Mr Simpson out of a old blanket over him and the smart goat next to the leg of the Yarp. That goat *could* make change for a dollar, signalled with his right foot.

Theyr not believing I am Missus Skatts man, Roonswent, said the Yarp.

Mr Simpson had a face long like a mule's, with magnifying glasses he wore making his eyes huge and swimming at you. He said, That old woman crooked and near eighty and dyes her hair red? She on them inclines like a crab been skint. Aint no young man like you be courting her. Why youd be too young for her *son.*

Before this night is over I will be with her. I have seen her many many times. I have been with her many many times.

Gene James spoke, God made the vaginer of even a plain woman so sweet that even after knucular war and it was the only thing left, the race would be continued. But she cross the line.

How could you get up there? said Mr Simpson.

You cant hardly get up there on a hard summer day, said Gene James. Hed of been the right age if nare man would court her, which, it made you sick to think about. Its froze in on top of being naught but gullies, said James, like that was the law, that was it.

Why I'll walk right up there from here, said the Yarp.

Some dimwits was released on the county about when I was ten from a buswreck down a iced incline, them that wasnt killed out-right. They come from the hatch in Little Rock to spy the Ozarks. Folks liked some of them and took them in and some of them bred, we all knewn. Gene James looked at him and then me like he might be one, this Yarp, just now showing up from torment. You couldn't tell them from normal. But I was busy looking at that mans legs and feets. The feets were long and wide all right, in Ill be hung, dirty white or gray scuffed brogans like an normous baby shoe. You never seen that brand nigh nowhere round here. I liked being clost to my home, three mile on.

Mr Simpson he would wear a gown or womens pedal-pushers, and highheel canvas sandals with bush socks, anything, so he wasnt one to pass judgment, but I was flickering with my eyes at old James wanting him to see the infant boots. Before he could two Ninis came in stomping snow off. They had on blankets and towels and you couldnt tell man or woman or two of the same. Mr Simpson spoke some Nini because he traded with them. One had on a beanie thing on its head with a rubber band under its chin, and it said something so Mr Simpson pointed and the two went back and sat on the one piano bench and the one in the beanie commenct playing the piano, Indian or bad, which was good for seventy-one out of eighty-eight keys. They took up some time from the Yarp question. You thought about the only one ever truly play that thing was away high and rich maybe on Mars by now, Len Simpson. The Yarp was closing his eyes like sweet music was alooning. I was trying to whisper *Yarp* to old James before that thing raised up his coat and made the geezer vomit and die. Gene James was a stubborn born liar, but I was the first to see the Yarp. Now someways out of my fear with four other rightly human persons, I thought I had evened with Deacon Charles. I had a true tale and would be the center of the lunch talkings for a long time. Gene James was only fifth or eighth on what he'd seen true, at eighty or more. The Yarp spoken again.

I've a great hard long love for Missus Skatt. Shes not always what she looks to you, a goat or crab scuttling down that hill of false diamonds from her house. That is a good house, built better than most in the county. And I don't look like this all the time either. Her children is what I love, the young ones. She cooks a sumptuous venison and hare, and has a wheat patch, crushes her own meal herself for larripan bread. We have roasting ears and sweet potatoes right out of the wood ash. Im going to feed myself here.

Before no man could commence his tongue he had come back with a bottle of herrings and sour cream which he put upon a saltine and sucked in, not a crumb left on his palm.

Missus Skatt can lasso a deer. But its her children most I love.

She never had no children. Married but barren or maybe too foul to touch, said Mr Simpson.

She lasso them hares too, ho? said Gene James.

She stares them till theyr hearts break, said the Yarp. That fine house was built by her husband Andrew and shortly he fell dead.

We know all that, the two geezer spoken together.

But you know only a mite. I'm going to tell you of her children and her charming history which will explain why you are sitting here poor, ignorant and stupid with bad backs. For Missus Skatt she runs a sort of charm school you would call it in a town. Unknown to you she has raised every woman in this county. And before her another woman kin to her. While the Indians play that music that I love they cant understand me and even when they stop theyll just look at a mouth moving.

That one without a hat understands American, said Mr Simpson, eyes swole in the magnifying glasses.

But that Indian wont hear a thing. This isnt Indian business.

Then he told a long weirded thing such as I cant hope to repeat only relying on my memory with my simular attempt.

He says all the girl children is drawn to Missus Skatt and sneaks over to her they cant help it, when theyr ten or like that. This was even before the founding of the Ozarks with another woman. Why even right then a girl was hauling wood to her cause she knewn it was cold and she was near out of fuel. All around the girls and the womens learnt at her knee these things: how to pleasure a man so good hed cry for it, how to coy on him, how to get inside him like a mindful tapeworm, because she anointed them with special powerful sexual parts and strong soft arms and eary soothing voices. She coached them when to begin apleading for all they want within the county because they could never go outside the county ever and their men couldnt neither. And how to nag and harangue and beat down and whup their men not raising a little finger, and how to make him worm small and stuck to his spot. You take mind, the Larp said, that this county aint forever had nothing but tired sorry men droven down like a stake to their patches. They never went off to fight a war even when the whole world needed them to fight evil. Nor none of them was athletes nor only feckless at lumbering or even executing in a automobile. And none ventured out or away and couldnt hardly catch a fish on a spring day with trouts leaping on the bank. Nor with cow nor horse nor goat (the Larp kicked the goat and Mr Simpson and Gene James seen them whitish baby shoes of a sudden) any count. That they died not only before theyr womens but passed over like sissies mewling and pouting ten years afore they ever hit dirt. You notice how they are coming down level and under the Indians. The Larp pointed over at the back of that Indian who was playing and sudden he began playing something ghostly like what were wrote by a man with a long beard in a Asian castle and sung by his beautiful daughter.

You notice too the crimes of murder and theft in the nights, all them I tell you now by her womens and girls. Not found by sheriffs nor nobody because the innocence is what she drilled in to them. Right now she is teaching that little wood-hauling girl how to be innocent and quick and steal, you bet. Its a thieves university, the womens, yes your wives too and your children-seeming girls has done it with bloody hand and prestidigitation of the fingers, theyr off with stolen goods, what theyr men dont get them. And sometimes they drop things like the watch Roonswent Dover found. He turned around and his eyes was yellow on me. I couldn't look and down at his knees I see them thin chickeny legs cutting out under his black pants. I just gulped and he was around, said Now this! and he pushed himself right up to Gene James, pulled his coat out.

Old man James took a gander and begun vomiting and then he fell off his chair dead with a whitened head. I was holding my hand over my eyes and didnt know what he was after for a long second. Mr Simpson hed seen but he survived and got up and yelled to them Indians for help but they never even turnt around.

Yes her time has come. Its over for her now. One last night of pleasure and it will be done. This Im getting xactly I think.

You wont tell none of it Simpson because theyll think youve passed to senile and take away your store.

He turned to me. I was ten feet off. The pet goat was nuzzling my legs for comfort and baaing.

And if you tell anybody this you will die, Roonswent. You are going to know whats wrong around here but you cant do nothing about it and that is your eternal curse, which is like that of many a man. But I wont have to worry. Youre of the age where a woman has already touched you and touched you deeply. You think you are being so kind to your mommer taking her a fixed sewing machine but when she takes it you look deep like you've never looked, youll see what is there.

So Im up the hills and mounts, so give me this.

He took a fold-in plastic fishing pole off the wall. It made a stout cane. He went toward the door, red spots on the floor off his infant shoes.

Theyll be out tonight, but just your littler girls. Even I have to swat them off. Youd think not, but I tell you, even Ive been womaned. I aint half the Yarp (he said it!) I used to be.

Therell be a time when the Indians will get the courage too gainst us old white bones. The Yarp went out in the cold snow and turned toward the mountains wed left. But he didnt take all his smell.

Mr Simpson looked horrible miserable.

What did he show you? I asked him.

Miz Skatt's head in his belly, cooking and hollering.

Later in the week me and two, Deacon Quarles and Chief Nini, clambered up the hill and went in the house. There was just, you couldn't believe it, piles of jewelry, watches, radios, knives and ribbons, deputies badges and wigs. Missus Skatt were in her bedroom with a old head and a young body, all laid out nude and peaceful.

So I havent said it, Ive written it and I hope this might make a difference. But I think it wont, not at all. Im got, Im doomed.

But its done for Deacon Charles and he says he will send it on to the governor. That makes me even or better than Deacon Charles, remember.

A Christmas Thought

WANDERING JEW and Methodist, the two of them, deliberately feeling alien to the Yule season, jeered and grumbled when they drove by signs of the season: the draped lines of lights, the mistletoe wreaths, the brass quintet on the corner. They were in league against the Christ Child and were having a dialogue as if the both of them were Herod.

"I shall strike the babies."

"I shall not play Captain Kangaroo with them, nay."

An old tattered half-Chinese Negro walked out of the alley, leaned against the wall of the laundromat and spat feebly, looging phlegm on his left cuff. Then it fell and brightened over the pants of his knee, like a cobweb.

"Ho!" said the Methodist, once a conscientious tenor in his church choir.

"Oh, let's dig Mister Poor-At-Christmas again," said the Jewish crew-cut man, a lapsed rabbi.

They drove the van once more around the block. In the back, stolen wreaths and cut-out reindeer swished and knocked. The smell was piney in there, and warm with their cigar smoke and eggnog breaths.

The van came by the laundromat once again, its windows rolled up securely. They stared at the foul and bleary half-breed, who peered into the laundromat window, perhaps seeking an acquaintance or easy frightened Mexican wife he could touch. The two men stared at him, the Methodist knocking on the passenger window so the fellow would turn around and give them his entire aspect again. He finally did turn. He, if his eyes were clear enough at all, could only have seen their mouths moving and heard nothing.

"Yo, Mister What-Christmas-Is-All-About," said the Jew.

"Is he not Mister Dickens himself?" said the Methodist. "'May I speak with you a moment, sir? Sir, I've had some bad luck,'" he mimicked the fellow. Then this ex-Methodist made a flatulent sound with his lips.

When they came by the third time and stopped, they were glad he was facing them fully. They were overjoyed. They were going to pitch him a wreath.

When the Methodist man, long white ascetic face on him, rolled down the window, the winey, crack-besnotted person came alive. He had ripped up a yard-long aluminum alloy track from the floor where a washing machine had been taken off for repair. He hid this piece behind his leg and when he saw the window come down, he rushed over to the van and drove the track-piece through the eye of the Methodist man with such force that it came out bent through his right ear, evicting a burst of dark blood upon the windshield.

The Jewish person at the wheel was transfixed by such horror that he was for all purposes mummified when the assailant jerked away the rod with a gruesome banging of the passenger's skull against the window ledge and flew around the vehicle, tearing open the door the Jew held.

He could not even plead before the man rammed the good end of the rod through his ear, again with such vehemence that the end curled around out of his mouth, dragging a clot of tongue and tonsils with it, and with much dark blood.

The half-breed then waited, simply, hands on hips, for the two of them to gurgle and whisper, then die.

When you read and wonder, for six seconds, about the random, pointless violence of these days, then are blissful it was not you, having, really, a better day, stop and think: Could not these felons be, really, God's children, loose, adept, so hungry and correct in our world?

Ride Westerly for Pusalina

MEX NEDD, some time ago, was perishing for a jungle, then a drink. He had ridden himself out into the Raw Barriers, which was much like making your way over a bald, bleached skull. There was hardly a pleasant or ambiguous place to hide his stash. No, it was a torture and constraint here even to hide his intent. But he knew down some miles in a little block house lived the Widow Brown and her boy Jim, who languished with the scrofula and the pube whuppers, glaring out and licking at the window, extrasensual perception of anybody within the territory, and the lad knew it was Mex Nedd, not his name, but his horse how it leapt, scraped and shambled, like a horse from a town.

The Widow Brown was commencing her chores of spying herself naked and unneeded in the brook water that ran right through the house. She hoisted her nipplements and sighed, O so lost and unreckoned with except in boy Jim's most slimy scrofula dreams, though waking he knew what she was. Lost on the parchment of this orange and white waste, *why?*, away from Detroit, behind this blanket where she dressed and had *her* dreams, wanting to be longer, for she was a tiny short woman with way-out enhooterment. Her former husband, the broken prospector John Allen Brown, overlooked her, almost forgot her, until that day, in the barrens west of the Raw Barriers. He had remembered her that once when young Jim was made.

Why, here you could not even have fly-specked, so dry was it. The flies would have been nice for company, though she would have slain them instantly, this fastidious woman of Greek or Slav extract. Flies, she thought, busy nasty little messengers, so like the other girls in her orphanage, anxious to betray. She was so pink and lonely, also more than weary of young Jim. She could do, how she wished, with a daughter for company, a fat-butted little toting and fetching freckled wench to pervert and have chats with. What she would do, Widow Pusalina Brown, she would trap a buzzard after young Jim lay on the ground for a long spell meaning to be dead. Then they would spring the trap on the buzzard, the trap which was only Widow Brown in a blanket with a piece of ham on it. They did this. She grabbed the buzzard by the leg and young Jim cold-cocked it with a roundhouse fist, his little pubescent arm about exactly up to this task. Next, when the buzzard woke up it had a message tied to its inner thigh with a bow, very sissy. Since a number of men in the territory were in the act of dying or near it, she hoped her chances the buzzard went to them were several, and the man with enough spunk and curiosity left to shoot the buzzard was her cup of tea, a natural stud carrying her little new daughter and not even knowing it yet.

Pusalina could see the freckled bubbling infant at her teat, heavenly bundle unawares and gurgling until the horrible things the widow knew were delivered into her ear. For Pusalina had been more than an orphan. Yes, she was the vampire nun of Detroit. This was not her first family. She'd had one child promptly at age fourteen, nearly on her birthday, then had taken on the false habit of a nun to protect herself, roaming the streets for a crust. The progenitor by force, an inebriate mick boasting of his conquest of the tiny orphaness to friends around the wharf tavern, perished with long spurts of his own jugular's blood. The child, a male, disappeared. And further, young Jim Brown was despised, head to toe, and only suffered by Pusalina until that day when his chores were done. Then he was in perpetual danger. It was a girl only that she could love and properly corrode. She knew Jim's moist sick dreams and she knew with his laziness (lengthening his days on this earth) he might never finish his chores. Picking up after the wild mustang horde forced by lightning to the Raw Barriers past their mud home was one. Pusalina was fastidious, mightily. But in this way her own demands for the fastidious defeated her aims.

An old clipping from the Detroit paper, still crisping in her cedar box, read:

> Downtown beggars have been targeted by businesses and shunned by residents. Now they are getting the brush-off from churches, which fear panhandlers could cut into attendance. Churchgoers have long been favorites of beggars. But now an off-duty police officer stands guard at one church, shooing away anyone asking for spare change. Clergy at other churches urge congregations not to give money to panhandlers.

Pusalina noted in some ambivalence that this was her life's only "write-up," though it did not of course mention her by name. She was one of the beggars "shooed away," as she worked the cathedral portico in her little false nun's habit. Brown was, at that point, a too tenderhearted churchgoer who had then brought her away to the West. Excepting that one time, he thought her only a bondswoman, and another mouth when the food ran low. Later, the aerial assault from below would completely surprise him.

Mex Nedd rode faster, out of the last scraps of the Barriers, thinking again of his friend, just dead at the ranch, who had brought him into the Brotherhood. He was forgetting all the scholarship, but he remembered that they had called him Hermes. Nedd pressed on after the freakish business with the vulture, not entirely comprehending his mission — which had begun before he was made a member in Detroit, where he had never been — but alas, even then he was already on it, somehow. It was a misty thing, but Nedd was good at the task anyway, before he had ridden buddies with Zeke Nestor, a former priest. Nedd laughed, although there was much trouble behind him and not far. The amazing information of the last few days had made him near daft.

There were at least two ways a person of a domicile met the oncoming long-rider at this time. There was not just one, joyful, out of one's eternal sorry loneliness. There was the other, too, depending on the day: one had accumulated maybe not much, but by the sweat of one's own palms, a thing around himself, had ruined one's horny hands and bunioned his feet on behalf of his grounds and bounty, and was also enraged, seeing a loose ambler tucking down his scarf, looking this way, wanting some of it; if he was not a thief, then at the least he would be a mandatory neighbor, code of the frontier. So yes, Pusalina was enraged when young Jim told her someone was approaching, though longing for that freckled daughter, and suspicious. You had been familiar with the weather changes and loved them, alone; in a way loved your loneliness, having the elements alone as they came from where they'd been with somebody else just lately, and you wondered carefully, who? Such as those spots of snow and then the full gale, you loving it all until it came the blizzard and then you hated it. And Pusalina now could also see the tumbleweed litter young Jim had not picked up from the floor of the barrens, so she was in rage and humiliation, lest the stranger think them "wanton."

It was, out there now at the top of the window, Mex Nedd riding into a gulch, disappearing, then his flat-crowned hat emerging, with a couple of nods of the head with the horse as it was prompted up by some change down in the gulch, because Nedd sat straighter, more vigilant as the house came on to him.

That man, she wondered, could he be holding the note from the buzzard's thigh? Something dear, or from another person's dreams, went mellowly through her mind — "...an attentive, loving husband; children; and a quiet house with a clock that chimes." Was it something she'd read? Why was this? "...sure that no one was hiding in the nooks and crannies..." She was feeling someone else's gentle domestic thoughts, or was it that man rocking on toward her, his nice posture that brought old discarded (when?) feelings to her: domestic bliss, ease, normal quiet...a big white dog, softly furred...Why, her heart seemed to be all softening up as Mex Nedd rode and stopped, surveying, readying a formula of introduction. His horse, wet red, was smoldering under a heavy load. The man, she thought, if he had the note from the buzzard, would be squaring the message with this domicile, having his first impression, for it would have been a surprising thing to find this message with its directions out here in a piece of space so harsh and unwomanlike — fixed with only a nickel-eyed child with his tongue out troubling in the window.

Something the size of a barrel sat under the tarpaulin on the back of the horse. Young Jim imagined it greedily, because there had been nothing for Christmas these last eight years. Far away over the Raw Barriers there was a city, full of shops for boy things, he had heard — tormented by his mother — machines with rolling parts, whistles and traps, a true boyland, where he would never go. Why, that barrel could be a store-boughten great trap for something. Young Jim admired traps violently. Like for a lion. He could *have* a lion. They would be friends.

The widow had gone outside where the south wind had whipped up. She saw the man was off his beast. He was all in faded tan corduroy, except for his hat, black and wet, outlined in dust. The boots, the boots were the single item that heralded him most. They were tall military lace-ups, very fine and about her size, for she had long feet. Three pairs of socks and they might have been made for her — she could feel them push around her heels and long toes. About the stranger's face: his hat was down, and he was coughing out the trail dust now before speaking. He had a wooden formality to him at first. But generally about any stranger's face: the yardstick for beauty out here had been lost so long you could not rightly tell much and it hardly mattered. Enormously ugly people married true belles out here; there were so few people aesthetics had gone out the window. Adonises, too, coupled with troll-women, having forgotten the civilized norm. This reflection came boomeranging in Pusalina's case: she wondered as the light grew darker if she was of medium or great attraction.

"I am," Nedd said, "a liberal man. But there has been a misunderstanding and that red cloud you see coming down the near side of the Barriers is a spiteful mob. One of us is dead already, and your thick mud home seems my natural fortress, there being naught else redoubtable on this plain. So excuse me deeply."

He walked past her — he was high, two heads above her — into the rectangular room of the place, splashing through the meager brook and interested particularly in the windows east and west, where young Jim still dreamed about the bundle on the horse and had not turned from his covetousness yet.

She was right behind the man, feeling almost overlooked all over again.

"Quite a nice speech for a dusty throat. You can see there's nothing much but me and the boy and the windows. Would your innocence be causing us any danger?"

"It depends on the humane delicacy of those there."

"There's aught of a buzzard concerned in this?" she hoped.

The man looked at her negligently. Was he handsome? Well, maybe ordinary, but the high threaded boots brought off a sheen to him. Maybe his nose was long, but it had a policeman's suasion to it. His stride toward the boy was confident.

"Here now, ladly. You like that horse? We'll be bringing her in, against them as would take my transport from me entirely with their first bullets. One of them already gutshot my packer the other day."

"I was looking at the hump on her," said young Jim.

"Have a care, mister. We are woman and child," said Pusalina.

"I'm counting on that," said Mex Nedd.

"Is that a toy sack, you are the peddler?" asked the awed Jim when the horse came ducking into their very home, his mother's hung dressing room blanket waved aside by its withers.

"Well, I've got bright serious implements for the both of you, if you were my friends," said the stranger.

"For keepers?" Jim was too delighted.

"Keepers if you can shoot enemies of mine," chuckled Nedd. Was he going to die this lighthearted? Pusalina wondered. "And true, little woman" — his eyes fled to and past her prominent breasts in the muslin, then up to the round Greek mouth — "there was a buzzard the other vultures was persecuting for its sissiness, familiar as a schoolyard scene in Fort Worth. I ran off the bullies, blew its head off, and there was, damned and darned if there wasn't, a lady's bow tied round its leg with a note scrolled on it, and your map. Isn't that right? Thank you."

He was acting as if there were ample time for the oblique.

"Even dead horses come in handy. Yes, my packer went down, if you catch my drift, lady. I didn't know then I'd *need* this fort. It was before the final episode at the Knuckle Ranch."

"We cotched that one ourseln," said the boy, happy there was a trade and honest. Then he flew to the window. "There's specks of men and horse in the gulch, mister!"

He cut the ropes on the bundle and it fell with a huge metallic sound, little nicks plunking on the hardened mud floor. Those would be bullets, young Jim cried, hurrying to pick them up for the man.

"Hold there!" Nedd cried ominously. "I'll do the fetching of them." He drew out two nickel-plated vine-engraved .44 Colt handguns. The boy gasped. Such elegant guns he had never seen. He had, truly, seen only two guns, one of them the loose-stocked .30-.30 single standing in the corner, so gnarly on the butt. The stranger gave him a loaded revolver and Pusalina the other.

"Just fire these rapidly. It's nigh dark anyway. I'll be taking on the individual marks myself."

"— you hear?" called a voice, tenor and dusty, from far outside. "Is there woman and child in there, Nedd?"

"Yes!" Nedd called out. "With a long rifle built for your buff at a quarter mile away."

"You'll be releasing them, I know, Nedd, before this rain of lead, unless you're coming out too, seeing it's hopeless."

"Last time 'twas hopeless I nipped your throat as I'm recalling, Smitty!"

The man was lighthearted still, Pusalina divined. The gun in her hand was enormous and she could have shot him, he was so loose, but there seemed no profit in it, and her girl was in those thighs, above those nice boots, she knew.

"Fire away!" he shouted and jacked in a cartridge.

"Well, if you're not a cavalier!" shouted the voice outside. She could hear a number of them muttering from that ditch that coiled out of the gulch toward the house and drove north.

"Well," somebody else out there said weakly.

"Please, you'll stand at the forward window, and you, ladly, at the back one." Hand on her shoulder, the stranger pushed Pusalina to the sill where only her head was visible outside. The boy, ready with his new grand pistol, moved to the east window.

"A nice piggery in this," Pusalina huffed, almost as if she had once known high society. She looked out on seven shadowy hats at the top of the ditch, the last one near their chicken pen. The lone cow wandered beyond them, eating at a gaunt tree.

"This here's heinous, Nedd!" called the dusty tenor again. Other grumblings rose and fell. "Not a pleasant man!" "No civilization at all!"

"Commence firing," said Nedd. He was still lighthearted, even daffy. The little woman spat on the ground. But the lad's gun roared to life, and he did not give it up until all six blasts were gone. "That's the fellow!" praised Nedd.

Pusalina would not shoot and sulked grimly, a bull's-eye for all outdoors with her head and tresses, some gray at the scalp.

Mex Nedd went out the door in silhouette, catching them unawares, the long rifle speaking like a Kentucky senator, an old man of thunder. You could hear the yelps and scrambling when toward the end of the magazine he took more care and danced and feinted to the few awkward replies from weapons in the ditch. Pusalina, unable to contain her zeal for man-killing, began shooting. Though she hit nothing, the live ones were stunned by this horrible betrayal of etiquette, and largely discouraged. They crept back up the ditch to the gulch and their horses. Mex Nedd had stolen from them, but they agreed it was not really that much, and they were tired and very hungry, agreeing this wasn't a good place to eat as night fell with its unhappily bright and wide moon. You couldn't burn mud here, either. The discourteous woman had thoroughly demoralized them. They knew some things about her and had seen prospector Brown drive his buckboard into their ranch road, yearning for help, his throat ripped all but out, only half an artery left to him. He had meant to tell them she was a fantastic thing, but this was muddled, and then he perished. A messenger was sent over but was spooked or bored, and just left the area entirely. It was so far away that only every now and then would a lone rider hunting a lion for his sweetheart see the line of smoke from her chimney. The harder fact was she never came looking, nor sent the boy. Now, in a riot of the perverse, rain fell on them out of an open full moon.

A man who'd lost what Mex Nedd had in an old Fort Worth atrocity, but not the concomitant desire, might indeed feel daffy or bulletproof. He enjoined one burst of memory flush with another, each of lust nailed on lust: a saloon woman, a former wife, another saloon woman, Tuesday her name. He had later played both saloon women like goats, for they had, in league, betrayed him into the hands of Dark Melvin the cutter. The women had grown tired of Nedd cheating on them both. Down the hall he staggered, blood on his thighs. He had, when all was over, a consuming desire and hatred for women. His own money, finagled, had paid off Dark Melvin, and he was penniless, some valve of rage with desire left open in him, so that Mex Nedd moved westward like a reamer. The eunuchs, they say, were handsomer than others, a glow and vapid pronouncement of features marked them. Mex Nedd, half eunuch, had a testy sharpness to his look coincident with any excitement whatsoever. Since Fort Worth, he adored gunfire and he had seriously hurt three women. He was without the caution of a whole man.

"Nicked a couple at least. Thanking you allies," he said, back in the door again, chuckling. To Pusalina he seemed almost on fire. She forgot her indignation, lost to confusion.

"I'll be helping you with the rest of your machines, mister," said young Jim.

"Hold back!" warned Nedd.

He went to the hidden kit and, drawing two rifles out of it, wrapped the rest back up with his back to them. Pusalina couldn't help but notice his concern with his covered burden — another fiery thing. When he rose, the fine silver flower- and vine-engraved guns lay on a cavalry blanket.

Looking down between his fine boots, Pusalina saw an infant daughter among crib rails of silver scrollwork. Nedd's thighs, rising from the boot leather, were full and proud as a grape to her. Though her comprehension of the man was fading, her dreams were growing, and the old want, like hatched fry, poured into her blood. She had sparkles of nerves at her crown and in the soles of her feet.

Only now did he take off his hat again. His brow was creased but dry. Nedd threw out a forelock and then tossed it back flat to the back with a snap of his neck.

" 'Mex' Nedd, my troops. As you can see, I'm not Spanish. Name comes from a long story in the Yucatan. You've seen those gargoyles on the ground there, ma'am? No, no, they say that's how I looked

coming down the stairs after a certain piece of trouble. Some upstairs was sorry they had jumped me."

"Why are people always jumping you, Mister Nedd?" asked
young Jim, warm gun in his fingers, happy.

"Something about my face, ladly," he smiled. "Too, they resent
my imagination."

In her peculiar trance, Pusalina went to the iron stove and began
knocking something together. Nedd brought two cans of bully from
his hoard to add. She did not thank him. He also had a candle, a
large Christmas thing, which he placed on the table. It cast a sweet
luminescence about, so that the evening was becoming an event,
guns glistening on the floor. The man's horse was still inside, but it
was a funny thing, lying in a corner like a goat and becoming a small
matter.

Pusalina spoke not a word for an hour, through the supper and
after. Nedd was not surprised. He knew all their tricks, how women
bullied by their silence. The candle was half down, so that as he
worked the last bully and grits from his molars with tongue and
pick, he was staring, through accidental fatigue, straight at her neck
and hooters, pouting there in the muslin.

"You ever been night hunting?" he turned and asked the boy.
"With a new lantern, magnified? Up-to-date one I got's a regular
hand moon."

"You'd let me use one of those rifers?" Young Jim was startled.

"After a rain like that everything comes out to eat the little things
has been drowned. You could shoot your ma a nice fur coat: coyote,
lion or wolf. I did that when I was a chap in Durango County. Got a
goodly long knife too for it."

"Ma, Ma?"

She nodded. Nedd pushed cartridges in for young Jim, counting
all fifteen. The lantern was no myth, fitted with magnifying glass;
then the knife, out of the kit delicately. It was a great razor-sharp-
ened Bowie in its own belt and beaded scabbard, which Jim wore,
extra hole in the belt for him, like a smitten knight. When the boy
was gone, Nedd wondered if she'd speak. Supper in him, now how
he wanted and hated her.

"Give me that girling, hot Nedd. Give me that girling!"

She rubbed the long flaccid conduit of Mex Nedd in her palms,
eyes glistening.

Nedd laughed, sprawled on her country bunk, raised and nailed on sawhorses.

"I'll bet it's been a long time for ya, hot big Nedd. A long, long, long one." She agitated and rubbed him, like biscuit dough.

"You ain't showing *me* nothing, I believe is the trouble," he advised her. She was in an urgent, pleading dark space, his face nothing but a blur.

"L'l darling."

So she set her dress off her shoulders, and he pulled it down to her waist, revealing a most glad hourglass of flesh, fetched down and neat into her navel, so it seemed. The nipples on her, plump out to suckle, might make a steer moan, thought Nedd. Why she's a lode, better than they'd said. "Why, you're such a sanitary woman. I don't smell nothing at all," he told her.

"Touch them, touch them, hot Nedd!" she cried.

Nedd laughed, toiling and having, with his palms.

"Looks like my big chief's still sad, my dove." But he continued chuckling, again daffy and loose.

"It's time. The moon is fine. It's my time. What's the matter?"

"Can't seem to find the magic."

Yet she drew him inside her and he pretended, giving a howl of success at the end. She drew away, despising him but happy with seed, she imagined. He was an odd one, even now chuckling. He went over to the smaller hump of tarp.

"You'll be forever getting something from your kit, you funny one," she said.

"A man like me loves his little treasures." He dug and moiled. "Got a frightening picture or two, my Pusalina."

"You have a whole town in there, seems."

How she detested this man. He had not even held or caressed her, lap to buttocks afterwards, like the other fool. He had not even removed his marine boots. She could feel them on her legs. A woman and a little freckled daughter could go far in boots like that. Her breasts already ached for the infant, dearly. Cubby dear bundle at her hips. There would be little delicacies for her, as never for the boy. She could barely even remember that one's name, only his motions doing his chores and much of the womanwork around the place. There would be a nice stash in that bundle, serving mother and daughter come nigh. You didn't have gunfire as a few hours ago over a few guns and a lantern.

"See now. The gargoyles I was speaking of."

They were the great-mouthed Mayan things, fallen to earth out of somebody's dreams. Gnashing creatures, guarding something. Pusalina felt a thickening in herself. She was conceiving right now, that was what. She sucked in her abdomen and rolled over to have the minutes privately. She was not sorry she and her egg had seen the gargoyles. Now she wouldn't say anything else for a while because the sleep of conception was on her and she closed her eyes, blissful in this labor. Soon she was in the shadowy nooks of a jungle with fluttering things around her.

When she woke the Christmas candle was down too, so that Nedd was only a form in the corner, hat on, seemingly asleep with his face in his chest.

She could hardly see a time when it would be any better, and she crept toward him, all alive and feeling thick in her muscles, her jaws warm and her teeth sharp, her lips like cracked glass. Men die best from the least expected thing. She would always have that advantage. Already she saw him, bootless, riding off on that red paint, holding his throat, seeking help. Funny how they traveled like that when they saw there was no help near them. A man in Detroit had staggered blocks and blocks. With a smile she recalled the last thing she had said to Brown when he was holding his neck, staring incredulously at her, all bloody. "Now who's going to clean all this mess up, I ask you?" She had heard that in the old days the blood was drunk, but she didn't like men that well. That Old World business was another thing entirely, and too entirely messy, like old Greece itself.

The horse (how could she have forgotten the horse was still in the house?) gave a rustle of its lips and piped nervously from its nose. Pusalina was right on Nedd, reaching out, when he lifted his head and asked, "Ain't satisfied, my dove? Mrs. Brown need another tumble? I'll bet the pictures stirred you all up."

"Yes," she lied. Was anything worse than mimicking beggarliness when what you meant was hate? So demeaned, but caught, nearing him for a closer chance, she reached into his loins to stroke his ballocks. It flashed in her that all whores were horribly underpaid. She felt a stiff big thing already, but brought her hand away quickly with a yelp. When she put her fingers to her eyes in the dim lamp she saw it was her own blood on them. Her fingers were sliced and pouring.

"What's cut me, you thieving piece of trash?"

He was rising, blanket falling away, coming near. "Alas, it's the duty of the Brotherhood. And you might call me our Hermes, him of the little dingus and strong limbs. But it's my pleasure as elected me. There ain't nothing happier than a man takes joy in his work."

He rattled as he came on and she could now see the implausible instrument, an octagonal harpoon-bladed protuberance fastened on his groin with what looked to be the top part of chaps. Eight blades, bristling and serrated, were in a cluster some eight inches long. This machine of grim surgery fascinated her at first — its antisepsis blazing, its gruesome medical usage, what? Then she saw how ridiculous the man was. She could not hope, ever, to reduce another man so foolish and diminished. She was mesmerized in joy.

"I never give you none of my spunk yet, Mrs. Brown," said Nedd. He crouched. Not yet did one see the terrible way he could use this preposterous device.

But maddened by this late joy, she leapt at his throat, a real ascension, feet off the ground, her arms locking around the back of his neck. Her teeth went pumping over his jugular, found a purchase, and she was right at biting down on the moving thing when she felt the awful tearing in her thigh, with his mad hunching.

Hurling herself back with a shriek, and beholding only the flow from the smaller vessels of his neck, she felt down into her ripped dress. When she put that hand back up, she saw it almost black with gore.

"A palp'ble hit, Mrs. Brown, I believe. My Pusalina!" he shouted, spying the blood on his own hands from the neck wound.

"Nothing. I can go all night with you. I'll outlast you, man. You can't keep it up."

She flew over the table and fastened on him again. This truly shocked him, and he hunched in the empty air feebly a few seconds, the last light of the place reeling around. She was a strong terror to divest. He was diminished, busy with his arms. Her teeth went down deeply into the long rolling muscle of his shoulder. Though she'd missed the mark, he felt the sinews rip in great agony, and he roared. She was off, laughing at him. This was also a withering thing. You'd never expect that sound from her, and nobody ever much heard it in a lifetime.

"But we in the Brotherhood know the 'Cry of Dolores' from Hidalgo the Creole, you blasted bitch!" Nedd set up a moan that rattled from deep Mexico. He ignored the pain in his shoulder and crouched, making toward her at the window with tentative hunches, knocking the furnishings away to clear an arena, leaping sideways across the little brook.

Ten minutes later, it was all over.

He drove the spike back and forth into the oral canal and nearly out the rear of her skull. The giant heaves of his midsection, thighs to kidneys, became weaker as he realized she was done in. He had to push her face from the cruel harpoon to liberate himself. This was his last effort. Dragged a ways, her body fell down and released him to his long huffs. Nedd was dazed and sickened by a feebleness never endured before. He sat, unable to even begin unfastening the loin harness.

The door had been ajar, with the great moon shining into the chamber. Young Jim had been at the door watching, holding the rifle, very tall, with its butt on the ground, his lantern exhausted.

"Sorry you had to see that, young Jim," Nedd managed.

"It's all right," came the surprisingly steady voice, a cracking bass in it now as late pubescence was settling in. "I've seen worse."

"Great God, son, you have?"

"I was just a tyke when she bit my pa's throat out. Never let on I knew anything. But I knew what she was. But, mister..."

"What?"

"Did you have to enjoy it so much?"

"Alas, ladly, alas. I'm really not a very good man."

The child motioned to the outside. He had been greatly struggling himself. There was not much spark left to him.

He'd dragged in a massive lion, inch by improbable inch. It had taken the whole seeming century of Nedd's fight to do it.

It seemed the boy was waxing now as the philosopher.

"Well, Mister Nedd. Out here we don't get to choose each other very much. This here lion was the first real choice of my whole life. Just seems like the rules just puts things in our way, and we have to live on with them for a piece."

"That's mighty wise. That lion coat'll look good on you. I'll help you with it, but not just now. Its head'll come right over yours, and you'll be a warm snazzy little brave."

Both of them went in and slept without another word. And they slept long into the morning.

The boy first heard some movements outside the door before he knew it was another day. The big chamber of the home, meager but extremely neat before, was not sightly. The sun sprayed into walls brown-red with splashed gore. The two chairs and table were drenched and still wet with it. He recalled no voice had bellowed him awake, ordering him to the cow or chicken pen or telling him to be fast with her coffee. At the end of the table he saw the bent form of her under a blanket, dark and wet around the head. Now the night lit up for him again. Most soothing, though, was that the coffee was already made, without a screech or complaint. He'd begun tasting it just lately and found it good and rousing, especially too to think of Galveston or New Orleans, where it said it came from on the bag, towns he had understood as both across the ocean on a continent where things tasted good. He had not thought of Mex Nedd until he saw the bottle with elegant black scripting on its label. From his scrofula, worse in the mornings, he coughed but held the quart and tried to read about this whiskey. It was a most enervating but sweet occupation of five minutes for him. *Tennessee.* On the bottom of the cork was a pungent dew, which he licked. This sort of taste would put another whole bite on the day. Something mournfully wrong then happened, and happened again. Young Jim stumbled out of the house and clawed toward Nedd, on his knees before the carcass of the lion.

"It's not dead. It's talking," he told Nedd. The man looked at him blankly and then rose to go back in with him.

He told the boy to stand away, then pulled the blanket off the head, horrible and bloated with green and black bruises on its cheeks. The head spoke and shocked him. It seemed to be demanding something of him, but in a ruined English, as if growled out by a person with stroke. Nedd pulled up the shoulders and with some trouble set the torso in a chair at the table, where it fell back, looking with one eye out the window. Then the eye went around the room, over the filthy walls and down to the bloody table it was leaning on.

"This is a right miserable thing, ladly. Don't even watch."

"Ain't you going to shoot it?"

The mouth moved and again the demands, just blown through her mess of cords and tongue, came on again, sort of an imperious mooing.

"What's it want? Stop it, Mister Nedd!" cried young Jim.

"No. This thing is just beyond me. I'm sorry. We'll just get out. Except for the lion I was ready to go anyway."

The head was louder, trying to shriek but there was nothing in that register left. The boy was transfixed.

"I know what she wants. She says don't dare leave until we've straightened up this mess in the house."

"I don't seem able to finish her off. I'm very sorry."

When they were outside the moaning demands were even stronger. Nedd busied himself with the lion, and did not have so good a coat for Jim as he would have wished. When they rode away, the boy riding in Nedd's lap, items falling off the load behind them, never even acknowledged, they could hear the thing inside, raised to a bass squawl, dragging at their ears and sickening their bellies.

When they were rid of it, the boy asked where they were going.

Nedd spoke of going south. He was tired of the West. There were, he said, cities of Cortés stacked with gold and treasure, most likely underground, far underground. You wouldn't see a woman there. It would not be good for him to see women again. He spoke out of a high defeated whisper nothing like the Nedd of yesterday. It unsettled the boy, though he was excited.

"You mean we will be rich and in Mexico all at the same time?"

"Probably not, Jim. Best a man like me can hope for from now on is just to blur out and have a few good days. Same with you. You won't ever be the same. Lads shouldn't ever see what you have. You can't tell any of this, never. We'll just do some long blurring out together."

The horse stopped a mile away. They were sure they heard it, the imperious demand on the little wind from back home.

"She won't hardly let this story be over, will she, Mister Nedd?" said the boy.

Dear Awful Diary

M EG AND MARGE were happy but below them Nick, in the downstairs apartment, was very sad.

"Oh, dear long and wide Lord," cried Nick into his hands, with Meg having Marge upstairs and no longer caring for his love. "What can I do, how can this wretched thing be?"

The phone rang. It was Meg from upstairs.

"We are in ecstasy now as I speak, Nick. How could it get any better?"

"Please," pled Nick. "Is this truth necessary. Why?"

"So you can go on and make your pathetic adjustments."

"It's so . . . *awful*."

"Our ecstasy increases with knowledge of your sadness. It is sublime, I tell you."

"Gasp. How can I, Meg . . . carry on?"

"I don't know. It's delicious. Don't change, please. I beg you."

The Spy of Loog Root

THE OUTCAST NEPHEW was farhearinged. As with *farsightedness,* his ear could not register sounds up close, only those far away, up to a quarter mile, a distance of course at which the rest of us townsmen can hear little at all except explosions and aircraft. Only when voices were soft enough, and faint enough, could they penetrate his tympana. How did sound waves travel in his case? I don't know, but imagine the tenderness of his ears, bent by the incredible bawling of noise he must have sensed up close. He'd run away then, holding both ears in agony, dispossessed of normal human intercourse.

He was one of those exceptional children, ghostly with long blond hair, to whom none of his family out at Loog Root Pass felt kin, except the mother. We never got, because of his affliction, a definite reckoning on his intelligence before he ran off, alone, into the hills.

He had bought with his duck money a marvelous Zeiss, I think, telescope, which he wore on a plaited necklace made of leather shoelaces. The family lived out where nobody went, and we did not know when they decided he was not one of their kin or whether the parting was mutual, loud, passionate, untoward, with him the initiator. We did not know, simply. He was too elusive then for any truant officer, or now, at his age of roughly twenty-three, too innocent for a country deputy to have any interest in. Nobody paced the floor thinking about him, anyway, except his mother. And myself, knowing he was not so innocent, either.

A local college fraternity saved all its beer cans for him — a vast heap of aluminum weekly — in piles thrown out near a defunct railroad track. Notable, since fraternities never are for the individual loser, only the wide "charity" that reduces their guilt. Likely one of the members may have been kin to the nephew and agreed on this punishment suitable to their pledges. He lived on the proceeds, bringing the cans to the recycling depot on Saturday afternoons, and that was the only look we got of him. Nobody, I should point out again, paced the floor worrying over him. Why should they? He seemed healthy and perfectly harmless. That he lived like a shadow and inhabited the class of, say, a hobo, was only a curiosity. When you run a tramp down and lay scrutiny, the truth of his existence is usually not very interesting anyway.

Only I have ever done this. I love to surprise them in their lairs and persecute them, using good old-fashioned kerosene on their hut and bed garments. I cannot bear lice and I cannot bear, truly, those who are seriously different. The ecstasy of flame we sometimes forget and reduce to anachronism, but most assuredly not in my instance. Like the shadows and tramps, I am everywhere at hazy times. The thieves in the projects must be attacked directly and stolen from. It's the only way of flushing them without pathetic law and busy red ink, a trunk's worth of formal papers. For the homeless, too, one must act to keep them so, lest our happy clean village wind up molested and newsworthy. If the citizens knew my work, I've no doubt most would approve, in that calm inner voice that has nothing to do with speech, always corrupted immediately by our "law-abiding" audience.

The boy is nosy, I know that. He's been a hard one to catch, and I've had to employ my own telescope, one just like his, if he had that Zeiss from the same sporting goods that I did. You saw him in the round eye, poised on a hill with his own round eye and farhearingness, searching into the lives of others, hearing the talk from his safe distance, while you can only see their images. I've traveled just quarter miles behind him over field and hill, careful in my camouflage suit to avoid discovery. I've even worn waders, crossing through streams to follow him. He does have something there, with his "life," granted: the lives of others are more interesting than our own, much more. And why watch the strutting dead on television while we have the real thing, occasionally jumping, heaving, tumescent window-operas in rural homes. Rural people don't use curtains much, and neither do those in the subdivisions farther out, as the two of us have found. But I can't suffer it that he can also hear them, while I peep discontentedly at my silent movies, afraid to move lest his freakish ears pick up my steps and thrashing and rout the spoor.

If I were a murderer, sure, I could have had him any number of times. The telescope, cross hairs fastened on, a .30-06 speaks and smack, out goes his throat or heart or wretched driven brain. But, juicier and saner, a confrontation was all I wanted. He is *always* red-handed, showing his prurient interest in civilization, then flying off, long hair streaming behind, to wherever he sleeps. And has his things. Everybody has his place and things, but I couldn't find his. He got sly when he neared it. The boy was educated, I mean he can write, you could see he'd been to some forlorn county school at one time. He wrote down what people said in and around those homes. I had to get the book I saw through the scope, his hand restless, working in his lap. He knew he was uncanny, I imagined, and was keeping his own record — this eavesdropping tramp, forever on the move.

One of these days he will move in and steal something. Eventually, always, a tramp will see something he can't resist, wait for the occupants to vacate and move in on it. He gets tired of his rags and meditations, you can't gainsay me. Even our Savior did not linger in the desert forever. No, he came in and took someone else's corn on the Sabbath, then was attacked not for stealing but for working on the Sabbath, as I recall. Rural people — read the local paper, please — often miss goods, meat from their freezers, fowl, whole calves, in the hills around here. Where does the boy get those new clothes, for example? He has a different change every two weeks or so. He's certain to have raided some clothesline.

The book of his he writes in — through the telescope I see him scratching avidly, an act from this distance very disagreeable like self-abuse, his hair falling down forward to his groin, a blond tent around his face, hidden but excited, you can see. This act is so antisocial it throws me into a fever of imagined prosecution, but I must, in my agitation, keep still as I move within range, never to spook him. He was quicker than a field mouse. All you saw is folds in a field of green corn, tall heads of it shaking as he scampers off, hoarding his visions and dialogues.

I waited across the parking lot for his arrival on Saturday mornings, low in my old giant station wagon the color of hard rain, ghosted, with the ropes and handcuffs in the back — just an encouraging dream really. Nobody paid much attention to him anymore, but they didn't know what I did. By this time he was causing me outright sorrow. There would come a time when an act would be necessary. I rode my indoor bicycle and lifted my fifty-pound bar repeatedly in preparation for the designated day when I would stalk and strike.

The family showed no interest in him after he left, and except for pejorative interest, had had none anyway. He was near beautiful, in that feminine way of the moon child, and the adultery he represented must have worn out his mother's welcome, though she remained. It was hard to tell which was her husband out there. At their place, a settlement of several decaying buildings, its own hamlet, really, Loog Root, I spied the woman, haggard and reed-thin, going back and forth between each squalid estate to service the men, four generations, each to its separate hovel. The ancient great-grandfather still lived in a small hutch of iron-gray boards fitted with an entire rubber-tiled roof they had torn from a motel unit, hauling it over on one of those filthy blond-clayed flatbeds, the operating one. A grandmother lived in the bed of another, not so fortunate in her roofing: tarpaulin several wars old. Sometimes the mother of the boy looked in on this shade, but not often. She'd take a bucket up the step (a stump), look in, and howling was indicated. These people were so numb unto themselves, I could get close enough with my telescope to hear voices, yet not so close as to be included in the boy's telescope eye myself. You saw all the history you needed to convict down there: men, women, and even a baby they kept in a discarded freezer. What they had not pilfered, they surely stole. Especially obvious was the headgear worn by several of the men, the sort of bicycle helmets reminiscent of magnified sperm in full motility that were certainly plundered from one place at one time. It was the illusion of space aliens they gave, waddling here and there on their tasks, grunting at each other.

What *was* the woman doing besides feeding and watering them? She was not such a hunched primate as the others, and very nearly too poised for their league, stepping lightly and dreamily about (remember the whole-faced capability of my fifty-power telescope at two hundred yards) with a look of long regret on her. Tallish and nervous, she went through a group of them who were toiling at the carcass of a golf cart, holding up her skirt from the ubiquitous oil and rain pools — a skirt harking back to modest hillfolk, those of the quilts, harmonicas and dulcimers. These were the junk-hillers, congenital junk themselves, making junk on a hillside. What they did was scour the county for cast-off machines, then correct and sell them. Their bit of farming and goats — with some other low animals — was running scattered down the hill above and to the east of them, and could not have produced more than dreary snacks for this clan.

The woman was a creature of airs to them, if my instrument caught their shy faces accurately, as she brought them constant "baits" — a billy's term for lunch — and was cooking perpetually. They never quit eating. Three of them were tremendous, wrapped in smeared quilts from their kinder ancestors, vast rubber boots on, scowling under voluptuous orange beach umbrellas (stolen from a road crew, I'd suppose). The woman was almost a smoked meat herself, smoke boiling not only out of two chimneys from the main cabin but from out the kitchen windows and fogging the filthy crawl space under the house, where three urchins tormented a duck. Crows and buzzards blackened the sky above them, and what was cooked did smell deadly. But the woman went to a well house — actually the best-constructed building on campus, with a high-peaked roof and lattice-work lathing like a gazebo; the hand of an artisan in all this muck and fuss. She would sneak away to it, a hundred yards or so out of their sight, behind a hackberry screen, and get *in* the well, head lowering, then gone. She stayed an hour as I watched around at the boy's people. The great-grandfather would poke out of his hutch, wanting something. They had him hooked up to an amplifier, and his voice carried through the idle factory grounds in perpetual complaint. It was loud and punctuated by screeches of doomed equipment. I don't believe it was English he was violating, it was simply some horrid idiom of pain, the very tongue of morbid distress.

It bothered me from these hundreds of yards, but none of the clan was disturbed, neither the goats nor ducks, habituated to it as to oxygen. The old man played a guitar, also amplified — another speaker box in the fork of a dogwood — and it was loud too, but, incredibly, accomplished: something between banjo and the regular guitar, I'd say.

He was very ill. You could hear him screaming for drugs, especially codeine. This must have been part of the woman's duty also. The men paid no attention at all, even as he listed in great volume all his diseases, a litany past comprehension in a surviving organism. He was culture, history and disease all at once, an antique font of it, to which they paid not the slightest heed, stoned on the miracle of metal and wires broken into parts.

I saw the boy up on his perch above the farm plot. I had scoped back to him often while trying to survey the family. He was in a cam-ouflage suit, much like mine, which I highly resented as I bore down on him unseen with my telescope. He was looking at the well, I thought, for his mother or sister, whoever the woman was (I didn't know which then), waiting for her to emerge. He looked anxious and sad, beautiful wretch, sweating and moody beneath his chopped bangs, his lean body cocked over as in an attack of heavy grief. How could he ever know how I planned for him?

The two of us had seen into a number of homes in the upper county, he as an unwitting forward scout. To track him on days other than Saturday it was necessary only to appear on any chosen weekday and he'd most likely be there at his perch, telescoping the family. Or if he wasn't, I simply went home and became ill. I looked around that perch, at first thinking it might be his regular lair, but there was nothing about, only his impressions on the grass after rocking and sprawling this way and that for his vantages. What cursing and whimpers I heard from myself, another version of myself beside me. That was the day — after I went home and became ill — I became more resolute. I began reading books about famous expert trackers and scouts, how exactly they did their work — Carson, Horn, Crockett, Sacajawea, Ronald Limestone — and was paid high in romance but low in practical skills. I was just killing time at my tobacco and magazine shop, biding hours until Saturday and his appearance at the recycling dump. If he did not appear I faced madness. The few who came in the shop to buy (smoking and reading falling more into disfavor in Montana, I never expected a living; good grief, I have money from an old land sale in Oregon) would have seen me jittery and gruff, a bit short in the dialogues we regularly had about old values. They could not know I was their calm inner voice and soul, naming truths and prepared to act, defending the health and decorum of a town too often molested by new chaos. Remember the "Rainbow People" — those vile grubs. They almost never left! I've forgotten my drift here, recalling how I languished and repeating it emotionally. To return: the boy had led me to houses in the country where we saw domestic things we should not have seen, suffice it to say. I'd followed him to a tent once at which a mauling took place right in the eye of our instruments. This camper, I believe, killed his partner, but I had to go away. The boy walked in when the mauler packed and left, but I didn't — I didn't want to know this sordid thing. It had been done with a trenching tool and entailed a long, loud scrape, fuss and run. I let the more veteran interloper have it, but you can believe I went home frantic and ill, having seen the boy's hair shine as he drooped down toward something in the weeds.

The sun on that hair made me angry and ill, the way it fell and draped sparkling, hardly of this world. I still had the goading image of it on my ceiling when at last sleep took me. This was not just a country man, coonskin cap and black socks still on, taming his woman; this was illicit, shot with dread and pleasure, especially in the way it caught his hair, he concerned, dropping his book...

Fonder Remus, that was his name — the county ghost, villain, peeping Tom free to fly anywhere at his vision's call. I said his name over and over. Do we really want people like that loose and free in the county? No official could touch him. How could I call him down without accusing myself? I was in, in, *in* it! I read the papers, listened for news, dumbed up by circumstance. You see, you *see,* don't you? I stuck my tongue out at the ceiling before Morpheus reigned and slept a lengthy one until half the next morning, when I awoke with blisters on my palm and red welts on my face.

That day, next to come out of the well house — which surely was no real well — after that hour, was not the woman but a man, a lean strange man with hair like the boy's, but thinning and dirtier blond, simply older and used, as if he'd been turned upside down and used as an eraser on a page: such is the face of many in their sad forties here on the range — wind, smoke, snowburns, carbon monoxide, or their own narrow melancholia pinched into creases. The woman finally emerged, obviously from a stepladder down there, looking fresher but uncheerful, red in the face and yanking the lap of her long skirt down. They were already bawling at her for grub and a bucket of "root," some kind of home beer they cooked in the kitchen. The racket over the loudspeakers never let up. The ancient invalid musician either crowed for relief or twanged his instrument, continuously, or sometimes hove forth on electrified fiddle, a devastating spiteful attack on folk music. A long schoolbus arrived, no seats and its back end hacked out for commerce — otherwise a billy's version of a wheeled "vacation" home, I suppose. New relatives would arrive in it every month or so, I discovered.

A man trying to seem cowboy drove the dirty blue monstrosity; he of the class (millions) who buy loud and cheap in imitation of some sparkling goon on television, never coming near a horse except perhaps in lust. Heaving mattresses out of the way, they bore and threw in their "repaired" junk for him to sell somewhere. These people come from a backward state down South, probably Arkansas, and were expelled even from there, you hear. It is true that Montana was settled in part by runaway Confederates after the war, but the news got to these rebels late, and here they are still trickling in, bane of a fresh Montana hillside, more than a century late, and one suspects their heritage has always been tending and arranging the junk of others. I've read about their class. They did not fight for either side, but trailed armies like jackals, raiding battlefields and corpses for salable equipment. They are the kind who, if you asked them direction to a place more than five miles away, would reply, if at all: "Eh? Never heard of it."

But the woman, the boy — these were the only true mysteries left. When you "understand" these people, after all, you've not gone very far and feel sorry for the effort. The boy could not leave them alone with his eyes. He was up there pining and spying, pariah, note-taker, scamperer, mountain hind, eavesdropping hawk. He was the only peripatetic representative of their awful kind, free and threatening the town. I intended to oppose him. What was this? I saw him suddenly in the lens, hangdog and shaking with grief I supposed, but he was gone next time I looked. What was the sudden regret in him? He was always up there, calluses on his behind, surveying them. Why now the sobs? I could not let him get out of sight. I got in my wagon and drove around to the other side of the hill, watching him descend in a field of lodge pine and buttercups, a gorgeous towhead in the dying western sunlight. Was he still blue, my blond hillbilly? Fonder Remus.

I recalled that a Japanese man, found with a telescope near the home of a logger and his woman hereabouts, was severely beaten and kicked. No, some folks do not take kindly, though the man pled innocence, interested only in Montana astronomy. His attacker was never charged with anything: privacy of the frontier. The boy was leading me on a dangerous path, out of my citizenhood altogether.

That night I spoke to the wooden Indian in my shop, as I do when forced by special loneliness and the hardship of being the only actionist enrolled, attending to the voice of others' secret demands. The thing should talk back. It cost me thirty-five hundred dollars, old woodcutter inflating with the times. It should dance and serve me dinner. My long bachelorhood sometimes has occasion to want a friend, though not, please, that woman I tried in marriage ages ago; a demanding witch, near vulgar, wanting coitus four to seven times a year. What did they have in the well? And how was the woman a part of it? There are still live silver mines still struck. You read about them in the papers. Indians hereabouts are known to keep a few hidden. The lone prospector still roams, though mainly broken eccentrics you'd not want near your town, along with that curse of ponytailed backpackers lined with highway filth, tipping nobody in diners and expecting handouts as their birthright. The hills scream for revenge on these smug, happy traffickers, defiling our gaze of big-sky country. Your towns have spat them out. Your decent restaurants don't want them. I once drove one — blasted loneliness! — the whole state across, and he never offered to buy gas or a meal. He told me vitamins were a "scam" like most everything else. Oh, he had it figured. Tobacco was a horror inflicted on us by the Indians, like our drink and smallpox on them, etc. He didn't even believe newspapers, any of them. Feebleminded when not cynical, he stood to be choked, which a less contemplative man would have done.

Outcast nephew! Which was the uncle? Where was the father? Nephew of the hills, rain and snow and wind will beat his beauty, it cannot last, I thought. One day he would have to do more than look, and smear himself on something, just smear himself. There and there! Touch it, touch it! I twisted and fretted.

Those men in their sperm helmets noodling over the gutted arcade games, the motors of three-wheelers, half a miniature golf course, an enormous clock off a skyscraper (how?), a money machine from a bank — they wandered here and there, calling for food and "root!," the woman sweeping past busy as a row of ducks in a shooting gallery. Playing my round great eye on each to each, you can imagine my distaste. I lingered though, looking for the secret. Why didn't I just go over and ask? Because I didn't want to be seen by the boy. The pieces of his history I had fastened together were hard won from town denizens: the can man, the railroad man, a forest ranger who thought he lived in the park, but so? That was some half million acres. Besides, I could not be too interested or too to the point. There was some stealth required for the thing to go correctly.

The thief. Now he was stealing all my time, all, nearly, my life. Orphan gazer, interloper, weird eyeness of my life. I was there that last Saturday. Fall had come with cold drizzling rain and I was in it, invisible. Rain the color of my car, color of those old haunted movies dear to me, never seen again in our town: is there anything like good rain in an old movie? It was I then, the stare, peering across the tracks at him as he eased in with his sacks filled with cans for the recycling depot. For the first time I was going to see what he did with his money, what were his necessaries. He walked out and up a steep hill, hair down long and arrogant, drenched. Curious not to see him rushing at last. I marked the crease of his buttocks, where he'd sat in loam. He wore cheap serge pants, snagged and run. Power in his step, loins floating, back straight like a shaft, then sloping over, ready to scamper. He did not have his telescope in view, while I had mine full on him as I eased the car up the hill, patient but charging inwardly. He could be mine, yet not here in the town itself. He walked past the police station and I thought he was going in, stopping there — the perhaps dead camper flashed in my head and nauseated again—but finally he decided nothing, his feet in moccasins scuffing on despite his conscience, whatever he had left, this compulsive voyeur.

He paid no attention to me as I followed in my gray auto through the rain. Careless fundament, whither? He went to the last café in town, but would he sit down in it? Yes. His coat flared and I saw the round instrument in the waist of his trousers. An old man's coat was on him, flat and brown, which hardly did for a rain jacket. He was one wet puppy, slicked down and vagabonded by the rain. Allow me my phrases: there is a strange and deep thing coming, like a mouth, at the end of this. You can't know how I was drunk, sucking on my detective's flask in the car, getting the will to go inside with him and study him as never before.

I went in, blind and paralyzed by my casual air, and could not have seen a walrus when I sat down and ordered coffee. I looked over and saw that was what he was having too, only he was relishing his cup, while mine was like copper in my mouth. By now I had a gun, only a little .22 revolver I kept to discourage loiterers around my shop, of which there had been none since 1975, but one did hear of the national homeless breeding—more and more the subject has taken over the papers. So let them try loitering around my work. I wished he would loiter around my work. In the old clean days, the law, I heard, would drive them to the town limits if they had less than fourteen cents in their pockets. Vagrancy used to be an actual charge, before Marlon Brando and others made it into a national pastime. He was there head forward into pleasure, righteously, rightfully, with his can money, though then out came the book and he began marking in it with a missile-shaped pen, seemed stolen from one of those holders at the post office or bank, with a chain on it. Under the booth, his moccasins were staining the floor with streaks of mud. I could see he was in to stay until he was dry, granted that by the coffee. It is awful what a mere cup of coffee entitles the filth of the nation to do. The sky was lowering, nearly a night outside. No way to humanly expel him until he was good and dry. Can't you see the worthless, the derelict of this sad, once sturdily pioneering country, having their smug booths and coffee for endless hours all over, everywhere? It is the God-given right—they have it—of any bankrupt fiend to squat and claim, having purchased an existence for a few cents until his rump tires, while the seats are made, of course, for working townsmen and your good village philosopher, such as me.

I watched his hair dry, goldening, loosening off his scalp. He sipped and scratched. I was forced to swill more of the coffee and buy a paper. My casual air was making my back hurt. My face was pained by nonchalance, eye on the storm outside, then him, detailing his crimes in the notebook. It was labor, looking on his beauty. He was not handsome but pretty. Somehow this made me even angrier. There is a kind of pretty boy, accident among the red plain faces around here, their western bovinity, that calls up my wrath. It doesn't go with the country, it's loathsome, like a logger with a diamond necklace, or one of those odd collisions of genes that make a bluebird claim kin in a group of sparrows. Eyebrows too long, skin too fair, eyes too glassy blue, something almost rouged like an old matinee idol. The feigning and peeping was hard and long, but I knew what I would do, quite all at once. In the book now he was not writing but drawing. He left for the restroom and I spied at the page. It was full of small human torsos, male and female, executed nude and shamelessly, as done by a glib child prodigy. The minuteness of them—hundreds covered a page—interested me. You could not tell whether he was just saving paper or indeed meant something by the tiny mass of them. I went out to my car and waited for the rain to quit.

He shuffled by the grocery and came out with a sack of goods after ten minutes, then he headed back down to the tracks, where he soon hit raw nature and got himself up one of our beige rolling bare hills, aiming for the forest and the park, parallel—it would be in five miles—to that dreary settlement that used to be his homeplace. I drove straight on the highway and into the park road, where I arranged for an old cabin I knew of at the edge of a stream that formed a boundary of the government lands. It was deep back on the western side, so not many campers wanted it; it had been neglected, shuttered and dusty, but it was prosperous to my aim. One trip back to town and I procured my livables, then bartered for a window mannequin I'd had my eye on, lying that my niece (nonexistent) was a dressmaker and could use it on weekends she visited from Missoula. The owner, whose store was going under quickly anyway, did not mind parting with it at all. At another store I bought the clothes, recalling what that curious obsessive woman I'd been married to would want, in the camping and sleeping vein. The minx surely did run through "sleepwear" she thought would fetch me. On to college and criminology, angry with that quick snapping thing under her navel. The clothes made me a little warm and bilious, or maybe it was the awful amount of coffee I'd drunk watching him. Nobody but a hardened slut would sleep in what I bought. Maybe I bought too much. I was surprised, suspicious. You prepare too much and usually nothing happens, my general rule.

So I was out there warming the place sincerely that very night, though I'd not start anything telegenic until the next afternoon in clear light. Right on my wishes, the last of the storm blew out and by midnight the stars were out over the narrow field beyond the stream. The place lit up off a generator. Yes, we were remotely all made for the true "rustic," off from the other cabiners, with their conveniences, even microwaves. Hardy us. As with the Indian, I was already in conversation with the plaster bitch, and had purchased a large range hat that made me into quite the savage cattleman. It does not hurt to change the wardrobe of our soul now and then. I, without a mirror, was having a good time rehearsing myself around the merry fireplace, pounding the boards back to the kitchen and bunks. Reader, not often do we discover the grand old monologues in us, in our noisy crowded age, where conversation, especially out here, comes down nearly to "yup" and "nope." What would you say if given the advantage to talk importantly out loud for hours? Isn't there a grasping actor in all of us, another vocal and dramatic self that accompanies our social necessary person less real, that drives through the day saying little, as if that were the law? Our age is too comfortable and too mute. Look at the violence, cholera of our times. Thirty thousand dead of firearms every year. I fingered my weapon, but called forth private beauties from my long-still tongue, such as I can't share in this close-kept humiliated age. With the hours I got better and better, closer to the bone and heart; unlike the divorced one, who talked endlessly, the wench, about "love" and "closeness" when all she meant was rude blank crotch. Criminalized by the boy as I was, I also developed a character strange and iniquitous in light of the plastic woman, who lay there forked up on the bunk.

I would wear my hat and stand smoldering, shouting original phrases of cursing at her that would make a sailor blush. One can really loosen and oil the mind, let go like that. One splits off in two, eventually, no deep psychological fuss to it, as the woman talks back in falsetto and develops her own antagonism. Truth and high rhetoric boomed and shrilled out into the lodge pines on through the wee hours. I thought it might go better tight, and so at midnight I gripped the flask and, done with it, used it as a prop. I was good, good. Overwhelming. All shot, I fell asleep around four in the morning and did not wake until one the next day, when I ate some beans and canned meat. The woman lay there hands-up on the other bunk and I did not at first know what she was. I suspected I had done evil on a woman and here she was all rigid.

For three days I rose and dramatized, large gestures and voice, taking the dummy to the porch and crowing to the magpies. I'd keep it beside me for a while, then hurl it away as the tempting fiend. I did not remember the plays very well, that is, of Shakespeare. It had been a long time and no doubt I confused character and situation, bellowing Lear and Hamlet and Caesar, barely scraped together against vague queens and daughters.

It was my last noon at the rented cabin when I saw him. I'd snuck to the crack in the door with my telescope; he could not see me. At last, at last. You would not believe my heart. By this time I couldn't make myself eat and I was hoarse and bearded, weak at the shoulders and knees from roaring and plunging. But he was there a long city block away in some undergrowth, and I spoke up, knowing he could hear my words. What would get him in?

The window was wide open above the bunk. I stood the woman up in her flattering wrapper, then tore it off her to her brassiere and black briefs. Then lay on her, yelling I know not what at Mother Nature to announce my astounded pleasure as I hunched and waved my ranger hat in the air. Then I cried out in a voice that could be hers, a falsetto, rooting me on, as I recalled from domestic services in old times. When I went up to the crack I saw that he had come closer and was beaming, solemnly awaiting the next act.

Well, I dragged the woman to the edge of the door, so her legs raised out and her whole reality could not be perceived. Though requested perennially by that wife, I had never submitted to this disgrace, and so now I wailed to her as I bent and sopped. Deplorable and odious, but necessary. Back to my crack in the door, I saw he was transfixed, so I slipped out the front, leaving her feet outside the door, and circled with rope, cuffs and gun. I walked straight through a short herd of tame elk nursing their ferns — elegant querulous beasts. As to my purpose, it was firm even in my extreme weariness. You could not know how fat and cracking my footsteps seemed to me, flushing my plans and future — "sweating him under the light" — for which I had hoarsely researched and driven.

This was an old Tom Mix (how this dates me) trick and might be the final grand strategem of my existence, for I wanted a multitude of penitences and explanations from him: something that might seize a day in glory. Set me up in heroism. Then they would see their secret voices actualized and perfected. I become a solid figure of conscience, a true ranger of the country. In my shop, humble and straight, behind the counter, I'd be that rugged Montanan who does things simply and righteously. The boy must be catalogued and convicted — he had seen and not reported a murder. And he had seen much else. Splendid that I trap him by his own prurience. Snared finally at his doings and towed to some foreign quietness, as he was destined.

These thoughts lightened my excruciating steps and when I met the remains of a path on his side of the stream, I was the light fantastic personified. Those ears, those ears, I never forgot, thinking of a cur who hears his master's tread a furlong away.

The cur, exactly, beautiful thing though, was busy drawing and I must have been stealthy beyond myself, because he never noticed anything until the gun was in his ear. Up, my squalid Leonardo. I spoke loudly and he grabbed his ears in pain. The smell of wet Montana was all over him, as of a truck of onions some feet away. On his lap the prodigal nudes, tiny, thrown this way and that; and his dangling telescope, scratched by his furtive usages against decency.

"Up and at 'em, Peeper Man!"

He staggered up and lowered the icy blue eyes at the weapon and cuffs, rope over my shoulder, ranger hat secured by leather chin strap. For a moment I must have looked extremely official.

"Rat, oo, zar?" he voiced. The hearing, the voice. I might have known.

"I am privy to your route and your doings. We've been after you some time. Now get these on."

He cuffed himself with no protest. The cuffs were tied to the rope, me holding it there, having forgotten what must be those powerful hill-gaining legs as a danger, yet the firearm seemed to settle him.

In the cabin I told him to shower and change into the vestments I had brought — a loose utility suit much like what a convict should wear, all international orange for easy spotting. He was speaking a bit more clearly now, though it cost him a pitiable effort. I had to whisper for him to bear the volume at all.

Then he sat on the bunk, tied closely to the refrigerator's handle, so that if he sprang, he would have to bring this square little onus with him — unadvisable, I with my pepperbox; I waved it now away from him and, really, I had not steadily looked at his face. Perhaps I was afraid I would find him junk-ugly, after all, and shoot him. Much of that is done in the wilds of Montana, let me caution the reader. *Nota bene*: the previous murder our eyes had beheld, but he knew it more criminally, while I but half knew the finality of it.

"So there's much you'll want to tell us now, isn't there?"

"Ah done nawthin'."

"But yes, yes, you'll want food soon. Best get along with your confessions."

Still, I was gazing away at the log wall, waving my pepperbox for commas and periods.

"Ah not ar criminuh."

"At least you don't stink like one now. But first, who is the woman? The one in the long skirt who goes into the well for long spells. Rather lingers there, ho, with a man. Have I guessed? Are they your *parents*?" Happy.

He was horrified, almost barked from his eyes. The shower was evaporating from his hair. It was out glossy like a drape of old hay in morning light. He was pigeon-toed in his anguish.

"You can't know her way!" he said almost that clearly.

"Her way? Come ahead? Tell me. I know plenty, anyway."

"She has to be with them. She has to make her keep. She couldn't keep me."

I asked him what he meant, even prodded him with the childish peacemaker. Then I told him, by kinder hints, there might be a scholarship to art school, fame and money for him, if he spilled the beans on the whole set-up.

I forgot to whisper and he was in an agony, unable to reach one ear with his cuffed hands. Asking his pardon, I went back to the role of the kinder dick.

"I'd imagine the clatter they keep up at Loog Root really pains you — the loudspeakers, the old fellow on guitar always beseeching."

"Mister, I can't help just being *around*."

"One wonders where . . . you settle. Your hole, your digs, your lair. What do you call home?"

"A good piece of the time, one of these."

"You mean a cabin?"

"Where nobody's there."

"What does your mother do in the well?"

"A man that acts like you with that dummy shouldn't ought to know."

"Ah, that was all for you. And you're certainly *here,* aren't you?" I got sterner. "Come ahead. Spill it. They have silver there?" I brought up the gun, a sad afterthought.

"No. Babies. She has babies and sells them."

"Not from a well?"

"They heard about 'underground operation.' So they made a place down there for them so they could have an 'underground operation.'"

"She and the man make babies down in there?"

"Yes. But I wasn't made there. I was aboveground, usual. But I, me, blond hair, brought it up. They wanted to sell me. A man came along, Kansas, where I was borned, and wanted to buy me. But she wouldn't sell me. So they made her have some more, three, and they sold them out. They brought that blond man back, my real pa, and made them have babies. And sell them."

It cost him to continue. Speech was a trial for him, anyway. What did I feel besides overwhelming disgust? You might think pity, but no. Not the barest. Drying out, and clucking this brute tale, he had moved into a candescence. He glowed. Having mentioned school for him, I could truly see him as a handsome savant on campus, his past treasured by an aesthetical crone of the Art Department, the weak bohemians enthralled. But he was mine, this Fonder Remus.

"So repairing junk is just a cover?"

"They make hardly no money selling junk."

"What would they get for a baby?"

"Ten thousand. She ain't getting pregnant quick enough again now, though. They mad at her. They send her down that well too many times. But she ain't took seed."

"The babies look like you?"

"Yes, mister. But I'm the onliest one is farhearinged."

"You love her, I guess."

"Yes, sir. She's my ma. She wouldn't let me go till I was big."

My interest was getting flat. When someone tells his story, and you have it there in your ears and mind, is there much left of him? Hasn't he decided, for you, that something serious should be done with the shell that remains? Why, there was hardly much to him any-more but his freakish beauty, a mutation from those people, and, really, it was rather an annoyance up close. My imagination had given him stature, supplied him, enlarged him. Now he seemed much like a cracked old record from an era of bad taste and excess, hurled out to the garbage. I wanted to be passionate again. He, tied and cuffed there, the absurd popper in my hand, it all seemed as gloomy

as the weeded patch behind a mechanic's garage, which beckons suicide. I believe I was just tired, daunted by the nullity of adventure,
humiliation of the spirit: worn, worn. I fell asleep right in front of
him.

I awoke with a start, then was ravenous for the last of the beans
and canned meat. He watched me but would not admit to being hungry. I told him, for lack of more direction, to take another shower. I
untied him from the refrigerator and indicated, with the popper, the
scissors I had put out. I wanted to see him without all that hair. He
didn't seem to care particularly. I heard him whacking it off (without
a mirror) and truly liked him armed, something of a threat. My spirits had come up. I heard him lay the scissors down. When he appeared, chopped like an old friar in front and less shaggy in back, I
liked what I saw: here was our star student; "Pomp and Circumstance" might have poured from the bathroom behind him.

"What is it you want most?" I asked, whispering of course.
"Mama?"

"I'm too old. I come to know too much. I can't be her baby boy no
more. That's why they thrown me out."

"Because you would tell about the babies?"

"No. About the world and how it's made."

"What, pray God, would you know about that?"

"It's in the book. I couldn't help but know it. It came to me."

I picked up the book and leafed through it. Here and there were
scrawled words: "man," "woman on earth," "woman in sky," "man
on hill," "man in tree," "people in schoolbus," "dead man with
frown," "woman with root beer," "baby with duck," "mother with
goat."

"You have nothing but these tiny naked men and women, and, I
guess, babies, for everything. Just nudes, turned this way and that."

"That was given to me. It is the selfs that is the world."

"The selfs."

"Part on it, I learned at school in Kansas. The bology and the
skyunts."

"What the hell, *skyunts*?"

"Skyunts of everything that moves or don't."

It was at last clear that he meant *science*. What must have been the
infirm den of night where he went to school? Of course, he couldn't
have brought much to it.

I gave him the last of the chili and beans, then sat beside him. He
smelled of Lifebuoy and was younger in the face, wondering with

those glassy eyes out of his schoolboy bangs. Pained angel, back row in the one-room school on the Kansas prairie, hands over his ears; brute horn-rimmed primitivist whacking him over the shoulders with the pointer: "Listen up, hands down!" He plunges out into the tumbleweeds; first inklings of his mobile home of roving feet, forever. Home to bawling amplified great-grandfather, men screaming "root!" and banging on metal. Mother pressed to sell him. Then ordered to mate and bring more like him to market.

"These figures, what do they signify?"

"It tis the inner order of everything, selfs. How they're fixed to be the bigger thing and make it be."

"Are you meaning *cells*?" I whispered.

"Yes, selfs, is it."

"All these naked things moving against each other this way and that is their biology?"

"Gene told them to do it."

"Ah yes, Gene."

"Every second they could change up and act different. Gene changes the signals. Of the whole world, move and don't."

We inside are a horde of tiny naked men and women in combat, as his drawings showed clearly now, always changing positions and sometimes ascendant, sometimes routed by the others. I looked more closely. The babies, sexless, were among them too, somehow swaying the balance. All was in constant flux and push.

Why not? I thought. Seems I had once seen a medieval thing not far off the substance of this. It could do as well as any, as we creep along with our baggage, dunces in fury, down the long ditch and into the passionate night.

There was a man I saw frequently at the post office and sometimes along the roads. Inevitably he wore sunglasses, a pith helmet, a pack on his back, and held two plastic bags, one on either side. He trudged everywhere. Never saw him near an auto. Never spoke a word. Yet he seemed to be mailing reports. I assumed he was a naturalist or scientific collector of some sort. Then Peck, the grocer, told me he was stark mad. He was brilliantly on schedule, with the same apparatus every day, zealous on the byways and through paths of the realm known only to him. I thought of him just now, too deeply.

I was all at once enormously despondent. My foot was out in front, veteran trafficker of sixty years, all hoofed and leathered to walk another route. But to where and why? My foot seemed exorbitantly lonesome and melancholy in its boot and rubber heel — the better to bounce hither and yon? *Quo vadis, quo vadis?* Then to be covered by something else entirely in its casket: the miles, the globe-trotting I had done behind the counter of my shop, attempting my dialogues with the wooden Indian and the rare customers; none of them, it seemed to me now, amounting to a significant paragraph. Unwatched, unheeded, unlistened to: years, eras, eons.

Then, after all, there seemed not much to know. The boy had said a few things about his people, and they were flat there, the dusty record in the garbage. My interest was exhausted entirely. Many people sold babies now, one way or the other. There was no great hopping revelation here.

My foot seemed so lonely, so doomed, I insist.

So I shot it.

The pop, just a pop, drove the boy wild. He wagged his head and tugged the little refrigerator off the counter, trying to run out the door. His cuffed hands pressed one ear and then the other, and I was sorry and took great pity on him. The pain in my foot was at first agreeable, but straightaway, as I sat there, it was not. Blood began to soak up into the top and onto the floor. I suppose I had shot it through. Poor lad, his lunging around the room, pounded into the midbrain by the shock. When he looked at the floor he was amazed, fearful, one would guess, that the next blast was for him. You readers who have been seriously punctured may allow me not to acquit myself of these minutes at all.

My eyes stayed on Fonder Remus throughout. Gad, how he wanted back to his wilderness and aluminum cans. That life, rather complicated really, must have seemed simple to him now. But he must have known it would bring him to something different. I began smiling at him, because I pretty much had it all in my head then.

"I'll need help here, my boy. All kinds of help."

I was a good week in healing back at home, and we began getting on finely, he and I. There was the matter of the unreported murder I held over him, easing him out of the cuffs and showing such food as I'm sure he never saw before, even the famous Montana elk steak, got off Peck at too high a price.

But the principal of it, the persuaded good servitude and penance — how he would begin his new trade, duty, outposting — was the watching, the constant watching that he did for me in the next months. Yes, I had not felt observed, had not felt *beheld* as a man of the town such as I should have been. I was exceeding lonely and unknown as the rose that blushes unseen on the ocean floor.

"You have your freedom, relative, for a while. I would just like you to watch *me,* you unseen, as I go through the day in my shop. You can set yourself where you wish — nook, corner, rooftop. But I need the sense — you have it, boy? — that I am watched."

So it was that I went about my days, speaking dialogues that he could hear, with my thespian limp. Acting old and new thoughts out, while the microscopic men, women and babies fought it out inside me for my soul.

Mother Mouth

T ODAY, VERNON, I noticed Elvis was getting hairy. Finding that, my tongue got hot all the way down to my heart to which it was attached. There was no keeping off the temperature or the *rump rump* noise of my want in my person. We don't go to church hardly anymore except to learn good English. Their music ain't ourn. Ourselves, we suck the air out the radio when it plays the Memphis beam with Negroes, shouts, moans and *rumps* in it. Between ourselves we conceive a sound like a worried panther having lots of mama and baby words. It can't be in a church. We take the airwaves out of our little Philco and spit them back with the mama panther in them. The Philco is all we could afford after you wrote the extra zero on that check and left us for three years in jail.

From now on you are such a disgrace, you understand, that you have absolutely no sway in anything and will only hang in the back or at the rear side to us in disrespect. I, with my dark inset eyes, him and his rustling eyes, we have made a vow, Elvis and I: that we will remain slim and elegant and catlike in our movements until the day he has captured his child bride, who will dye her hair jet black like mine. Then I, then he, will get fat together in blurring of each other toward the end, and we have impacted ourselves so. We like pills when we can get them but our beauty we know can't never last, that's a part of the glory. We can't *be* forty years old. Romance don't really allow forty years of life to what we are. Oh, we might go on as *something*, some shape or mass, but we're not even there anymore, it's burnt up, panther and all.

He will sing about the Teddy Bear, how he wants to be it, and millions of little ears will hear something like never they heard before, down to their feet, and wealth untold will unfold. Every song will be about me, it won't be no real girl, and that is what they will hear and gasp upon and find so magic all to their toes. In pictures you will see him with women, all kinds of gorgeous girls and cute like what ignored him when he was poor and baby-pretty, but you will never

ever see love in Elvis's eye for any of them, because it will only be me, and our music together. He'll be looking away like into a mirror all his life but it's me he's looking at. You won't be able to imagine Elvis *ever* looking directly at anybody, it will *always* be off to the side at guess who, the mirror maybe? but more me.

Then I will die and the source will dry up for him. The famous will visit him at some mansion right on Memphis's Main Street, and he will tell these people, in maybe English, "Mama ain't out there no more feeding them chickens in the back." The tears and the crack in his voice will always be there from then on, Vernon — jail trash, you'll be back venaling around like a rodent with an evangelist hairdo, but the money will be *bad,* Vernon, always bad, like that extra zero you wrote on that check — and my boy will get coiled and wrapped and weird inside and out, leaping in flight wild with Tupelo space clothes on him, doing movements that are trying to climb the ladder to heaven where his mama is, and the music gift will still be there, only there ain't nothing worthy to sing no more, and he is making those thrown-out grabbing postures and sweating like with my fluid all over him, becoming a mass, just a groping mass, on the rope — up, up, me waiting for him.

Because there ain't anything like Mama Nooky. Ask all them soldiers that lay dying on the fields of that great war you weren't in.

Rat-faced Auntie

EDGAR PLAYED the trombone and for eight years he was a most requested boy. Based in Chicago, he did a lot of studio work and homed in the fine, lusty Peets Lambert band. He could step into a serious club and be hailed and dragged onstage by any good band. Even back when, in Georgia at age seventeen, he was more than accomplished on both slide and valve. He favored the copper and silver Bachs. He'd come out of Athens roaring, skipping his high school senior year because he was such a prodigy. Edgar had then got the ear of a jazz fanatic on the university faculty who contracted for his audition in Nashville with Peets Lambert's old big band. It was turning electric and throwing out, ruthlessly, the old players. Lambert had a new sound — jazz/swing, jazz/reggae, jazz/classic, jazz/blues, jazz/country, even. This was simply desperation to survive. The band had not recorded in seven years. Now even the manager was only twenty.

Lambert, a disguised sixty-six, had not made enough to be comfortable from constant tours. He was wearing down, had emphysema, and it was hoped the new Lambert Big Thunder Hounds would get hip and record again. Edgar was approved immediately. He found himself in Chicago with two suitcases, two horns, and ten thousand dollars from Lambert. The band members came from everywhere and almost all were near-adolescent. Edgar loved them. He'd been on the horn so thoroughly since age ten that he'd never been to a scout or church camp or had even played in a high school band, having bypassed them for the Atlanta Symphony at age fourteen. So this was a grand society for him. He loved it, lived it, inhaled it. Immediately he began cigarettes — what the heck? — and staying out late with the guys: hipsters from Los Angeles, nerds from Juilliard, a gal bassist from Jackson, Mississippi — his crush — who hardly spoke except relentlessly and in exquisite taste with her Ampeg fretless. Edgar was in love from their first meeting. He too was shy and awkward, except on his horn, and it took him a year to ask her out, though he watched her religiously during his breaks —

how she stood, short and blond, but somehow with long, heart-breaking legs in black hose as she called on her strings to provide the hard bottom gut of the band. When they *did* record, *did* make money, back down in Muscle Shoals, Alabama, he listened and was caused to tremble by the wanton bass authority that poured from the modest, yes, woman. "All woman," he repeated to himself.

Lambert threatened to throw them out if they took drugs or even drank much. The parents at home loved that about Lambert. He'd returned in fame from a beloved, almost persecuted era in music, and seemed a practical saint to them, a saint of cool when he appeared on television in a turtleneck with his still thick salt and pepper hair, beret, and those long genius piano fingers, announcing against drugs nationally. He was one of the first celebrities to do it in the seventies. A victim of cigarettes, he gently pled for the young to avoid his error, though everybody noticed the good man lighting one up in the wings or bathroom every now and then. He looked guilty, though, and nobody said a word. Edgar, with no prior use or education in drugs at all, learned something alarming: Parton Peavey, the black boy on guitar, came into the band daily on heroin and never stopped in the years that Edgar knew him. (He was a fabulous crowd-pleaser in a herd of twenty-six crowd-pleasers — flat-out celestial on an old Fender clawed to pieces, maybe dug out of a burned-down nightclub in the Mississippi delta, the great bad taste of the fifties left in its remaining blue — Parton Peavey was a star and everybody knew it.) Parton was from east Texas, like the Winters, Stevie Ray and, later, Robert Cray. He would vacation in Beaumont once a month and return with a literal bag of heroin (China White in a one-pound burlap sugar bag). Edgar, drop-jawed, saw him fix himself in a Milwaukee hotel room, calm as putting on a Band-Aid. Didn't he know Lambert would can him instantly? The band was heaven come real to Edgar and he couldn't understand why Parton would do this. But Parton didn't care, it seemed. He played brilliantly, though, and gigged out far more than any of them. The truth was that he was close on being a celebrity at his rail-thin age of twenty-one.

He was so good, or so wanted (guitars owned the world), the suspicion was Peets Lambert couldn't get rid of him, even if he did know. When he let out, peerless amid the stage-packed Big Thunder Hounds, it was a sound such as not heard *any*where. Maybe he was addicted to that, too. Come another year he could fire *Lambert* and buy the band himself. He already had four records. Really, after three years and all that money, it was a miracle he remained with the band at all. He was an imitation of nobody, seemed unconscious of anybody before him, and had his own cult. All this with heroin. Edgar constantly expected him to fall over or go raving, taken off by ambulances and the police, but Parton didn't.

Parton was docile, not sullen or conceited, uneasy with women, and in ways more boyish than Edgar. He was not stupid, but he didn't know one state capital, and when they were headed to a city, he'd only ask, "Up North? Down South?" He seemed barely to have known an ocean, though Beaumont was on the Gulf of Mexico itself. The Pacific off Los Angeles–Venice rather frightened him. He believed, Edgar figured, that the United States didn't end, ever. There was a lot in the world most of them didn't know, some of them near-infantile despite their prodigy, but Peavey took the ticket. Even during his molelike existence in Athens Edgar had never approached this insulation, practicing upward of twelve hours a day. The thing was, this made Parton Peavey likable, in a strangely hip way, and he began a fad of willful ignorance in the band. People would claim they knew nothing, had never heard of spearmint gum or a pocket calculator. He and Peavey became good friends. Everybody wanted to be close to him. There was a good, young quiet warmth about him, an endless politeness, too. And he was shot full of the world's worst bad, all the time.

The band rose. Edgar had two cars — a Volvo coupe in Chicago and an old vintage Caddy convertible back home in Athens where he got the G.E.D. one idle summer at his parents' insistence. He was a minor star down there. Nobody cared much for the trombone, but they respected him as an eccentric phenomenon, and the local paper kept up with him. He affected, newly, an old Harley Davidson motorcycle and a pet weasel that clung to his neck when he dashed around Chicago and Athens. Edgar had a plain, narrow, long-nosed face. He let his hair grow down to mid-back, sometimes braiding it twice. He had the necessary headband — chartreuse — and he had a tattoo of an upside-down American flag right at the bottom of his throat where a tie-knot would have been. (His parents gasped when they saw it and he did, too, thirteen years later.) Edgar had always felt behind on his personality. It was near the end of the Vietnam War, so he had to get in fast on his outrage, and a bit louder. He'd gotten tattooed, sober, by the best in a New Orleans parlor, although the old mulatto was an ex-marine and hated the job — "Strictly for money, boy, you got the American right, you got the American right.

Play your horn and sport while they dies for you." Somebody gave Edgar books by Kerouac, Bukowski, Brautigan, Hemingway and Burroughs; also the poetry of Anne Sexton, which he liked especially and reread. He was coming on strongly to the bass-playing woman, Snooky, and barely knew that he was capturing her with his new vocabulary stolen from Ms. Sexton. With her and the others his library stopped. He could not conceive needing anything else, ever.

Edgar could afford to get a sitter for his apartment in Chicago, a jazz-smitten female student at the University of Chicago who was just a friend. She took care of his weasel, his Harley and Volvo, his books, his stereo equipment, and his collection of trombone recordings, which dated from the twenties on. Living the trombone had paid off in spades. He could buy and sell most college graduates his age. He had the leisure — holy smoke, he was *playing* all the time already — to take Caribbean vacations, playing trombone with West Indian steel bands (what a sound!) and drummers in Rio (salsa, salsa). The girl, from Louisiana, would boil crawfish for him on his return. He pretended to like them, but it was really Parton they delighted, by the potful, his chin shining with juice. What wonderful friends Edgar had then! Paradise, and Snooky slowly falling in love with him. She had a wild side, of course, especially liking midnight and later on the Harley, whipping around Lake Michigan on the back, hands under his armpits, in a dress with a bare twat underneath, her legs spread, the wind slipping around her joyful "womanity," she said, confessing shyly to him after several rides. That, and the fact she was quietly but increasingly jealous of his house-sitter, sitting closer to him and nailing down his thigh with her little hand, were the signals she was going for him in a long way, Edgar thought.

The band went by chartered plane. Snooky was flirted with by everybody, even Parton, but inevitably she'd sit by Edgar, trembling, and he would nurse her fear of flying. Her outfits became sexier and more garish as she was brought out front more and more to riot the house. It was a beloved thing to him that she remained shy and girlish as she aged. They were growing up together, a very privileged American jazz adolescence. In a way, though, to the crowd, Peets Lambert was her pimp. He went *wow* and stroked his chin at the piano when she came out nearly nude in her brief gaudy dress and stiletto heels, hamming with the happy lech smashed by her naughty rig, avuncular (old Peets had seen the wimmens in his time!). The public loved it, the Hollywood Bowl howled. Could it get any better? They did nine encores one night. Edgar played so well some nights that he knew he'd lucked into another whole planet of jazz, just a few of the greats nodding wisely around him. Somebody told Edgar that jazz was the only original American art form. He felt safe in history then.

Most of these nights he was secretly drunk. Edgar, still abhorring Parton's habit, was becoming alcoholic, having never touched drink before age twenty-four. There was no great reason for it. The band was chaster and soberer by a long shot than any of their contemporaries. Some of them, get this, *Rolling Stone* noted, played dominoes and *Scrabble* at the hotels, enormous bars flowing around them, themselves oblivious, like a bunch of Mormons in the lobby.

Only Edgar and another man, a middle-aged survivor from the last band, a relative of Lambert, hid out in a dark rear booth, drinking, playing nothing but boozy arias back and forth, in prep for the gig. The older man was a veteran. Only vodka would do, maybe a dex on a tired trip, then Listerine and a quick Visine to the eyes before stage time. (Lambert *would* throw you out.) Woodrow, the saxman, assured him that liquor, when controlled, was a friend of music. It was no mystery then that Edgar was playing better. Woodrow argued that he should know, he himself wasn't worth shit, never had been, and had plenty of time to listen, since Lambert rarely used him unless in a loud ensemble. But he knew music and Edgar, you cooking infant, you are away, man. You make other grown trombonists cry. Edgar rejected Woodrow's claim: you're the wise one, the dad, he said. You're the tradition, the years, the true center. Holy smoke, man, you're *football,* or a *church.*

Rolling Stone, concentrating on Parton, Snooky, the maniacal drummer Smith, Edgar and Lambert, had them in a big article called "Revenge of Big Jazz." *Life* did about the same in huge pictures. Parton Peavey had never heard of either magazine. What a gas. He led both features, quoted in his wonderful innocence, drug-thin and solemn in nothing but boxer shorts backstage with a bottle of Geritol in his hand. The following spring their new record, *Quiet Pages from Little Lives* — the loudest thing they'd ever done — went Gold. What jazz had done *that* lately?

Edgar let out an unusual, drunken obscenity of approval as they looked at the articles. Snooky was shocked. She accused the house-sitter of pushing drinks on Edgar and maybe the black cigarillos, too, cutting into his breath, his life, and so on. The house-sitter began crying. Though Edgar denied it, the upshot was that Snooky told the girl to leave. Nasty, but *her* man. This was the final signal. They soon married in her city, Jackson, with Parton and Lambert in attendance. Afterward, Edgar and Snooky began to make love clumsily. They had a long honeymoon in the apartment with only the heavenly gigs to interrupt it. Edgar would look up at the cold black Chicago sky and say, "Thank you." Snooky loved this. She did not notice his drinking. He was such a perfect, gentle, vigorous husband. Nothing could be wrong. On the plane they were treated like two people "going steady" on a high school bus trip. He could swallow nearly a half pint of vodka at once in the jet's restroom.

Lambert got cancer, but he could live with it. For a while the band's celebrity increased because this fact was known. He never missed a show, even during chemotherapy. His piano playing became quieter, more wistful, more classical, his contemporaries noticed, adoring him further, if that were possible.

Then, pop, America forgot them almost wholesale, down to bargain basement at the stores. The band held a two-year discussion about this fact, but nobody could find a reason. Did *Life* kill people? They hated, in all their musicianship, and with saintly Lambert's genius, to have been some vagrant novelty. The jet trips stopped instantly and the hotel rooms were poorer. They ganged up in rooms to make the budget. They traveled in a bus. None of them except Woodrow had saved much. Their foot had been in the door, they were about to step in as permanent guests, then...But they had youth and were extremely loyal to each other and to the music. Edgar, who could barely read music, if truth be known, began trying to write for the band with a computer, but he wasn't any good.

Two more records, then studio time became too expensive to make them — that kind of sales. So it was all over America, slowly and much more than anybody wanted. Lambert would fly ahead. Sick and more irritable lately, he'd greet them cheerfully, but his heart was down. All the kids were down. The halls became very thin, half deserted, echoing. Cocaine, more cigarettes, even cough syrup for its codeine became usual. Edgar stayed with the vodka. He'd tried Parton's heroin once, over his protests, but it made him very sick. Snooky and most of them still took nothing.

One night out of Oklahoma City, Edgar had a sort of fit, insanely unlike him. He shouted another withering obscenity, grabbed the steering wheel away from the driver, and raced them off from the rest stop, screaming "I'll take us somewhere! I'll take us somewhere!"

He turned the bus over on a curve, laying it down very fast in a long ditch. Everybody was shaken badly. Some had cracked ribs and terrible bruises. But there were no serious injuries except to Parton Peavey. His left hand would never be the same even after three surgeries. Also, something was wrong with the bus insurance — not a dime, and they didn't have enough to get the bus fixed. The band canceled and laid up a month, leaking money.

The third week Lambert called for a band meeting in his small hot room in the motel. He began calmly. Then he insisted Edgar come up front. The general feeling was that Lambert would forgive him. Lambert was that kind of man. But then he saw Edgar was drunk. Edgar and the band had never heard that kind of profanity and hollering from him. Lambert kicked Edgar out and screamed at those, like Smith and Parton, who stood up for him. It was a bitterly sad thing. The worst, thought Edgar. But he was wrong.

Snooky left him. The pets, who'd been disturbed by his behavior, went with her — weasel Ralph and dachshund Funderbird. The house-sitter came back. Edgar slept with her mournfully.

Parton, who'd left the band — several others had too — and gone on to solo celebrity (loved by the knowing for his crippled left hand; he was a real vet at twenty-nine now, a dues-payer) came by for a last visit. He didn't blame Edgar at all. Further, he was tearful about Edgar's breakup with Snooky, who remained with the little-attended Big Thunder Hounds. He had no solutions, no black Beaumont wisdom, except, "Up to now, Edguh, we been lucky. Don't rush it."

Edgar looked at him through fuzz: a child. He felt much older than Parton. He didn't think he could live at peace like that. He was often breathless and felt dirty around the neck, sweaty, where his tattoo was. An old Dylan thing chased around in his head: "boiled seaweed and a dirty hot dog." Most of the time, he could not even eat *that* down, but it was what he deserved.

He'd made a lot of friends, however, gigging around Chicago, and for a long time he was known as a classy drinking man, an aristocrat of the 'bone, my man. Then he became a student at Northwestern where they had a fine music program and worshiped pros. He'd heard Snooky was there, studying double bass, but he saw her only twice. Edgar was an uncommon freshman. He'd thought college was the thing to keep him straight, but it wasn't. He felt elderly in the classroom, the reverse of his band experience. He did not know what the rest of them did. Against the odds, he played the clubs till five in the morning, around Rush and out in the burbs where jazz was a discreet rage with the young rich. His appearance in class — blasted, orange, looking thirty — was a miracle. But he pushed on through classes where he was not valued, making poor grades, keeping his mouth shut, and memorizing desperately. He fell down more than once, smashing his head on a desk. A mere pint a day was a masterpiece when he wanted the bar. The house-sitter left. There went any order at home. He developed separate dumps of classwork. His refrigerator became green inside with uneaten food as the money got low. By the time he graduated at twenty-seven, thin and trembling, with a sociology major, he was a bum. He had no more time to fool around.

He crashed his old Harley into a pier post after a graduation party he gave himself and the fellow bums on the South Side, where he now lived with his few remaining possessions, a small dusty transistor radio and shower shoes. A lot of his clothes he simply lost. He was thinking an old thought about Snooky when he hit the post, his motorcycle flying out into the water of Lake Michigan. The yachtsmen were highly irritated. When the ambulance came, he still knew nothing. But he remembered what one paramedic said when they were lifting him in, looking at his tattoo: "Look at this piece of shit's throat. Drive slow. He comes out of the booze, he'll scream when to hurry."

His sternum was cracked. For a month afterwards he did not drink. The Dilaudid was pretty good, though. When they wouldn't give him any more he had three specially lonely, agonized days. He wrote — why not? — an old aunt who was rich, and lied to her that he was in graduate school and poor. From La Grange came a note and money almost by return mail. What a mystic boon. He drank a great deal on it.

He would retell the story of how he'd had all the clubs going for a while with his "new" sound, but he was a sick-drunk by then, the spitty and flat noise duplicating him. Even the avant-garde had found out he was merely drunk, and given him the door. But now his chest hurt too much to play. Plus, both instruments needed fixing.

He liked to travel light anyway, he told the fellows on the corner. Those cases were *heavy*, guys. One of them took him at his word and stole both horns. He knew who'd done it, but he was in such a world now that he just stared with his mouth open at the man and asked him, please, for a slug of port. The man refused. Edgar, forgetting the trombones, said he'd remember this. He wrote his aunt about his graduate studies and here came another money order from La

Grange. Guilty, he began making notes on the bums. He used the back of his classwork pages. Some of the bums were long and vibrant narrators. Two of them spoke to Edgar in Russian. He kept scrawling on the page. As payment for their stories he would buy them drinks (sometimes the fellows cleaned up enough to get in a bar, hair combed in a bathroom). They thought he was very classy. The trombone stealer died. One of the narrators kindly took him to the pawn shop and he got his horns back.

He was thirty-four when he finally got treatment and afterwards, why not, he headed back down to Georgia on an Amtrak which went through Jackson, where he looked stupidly around for any sign of Snooky. He kept clothes and toiletries in his horn cases. He wanted, he thought, never to play the horns again. He could smell alcohol in them and they made him sick. But he wanted them near to remember.

Edgar's sobriety did curious things to him. For one thing, he had not realized he was tall. His posture was still poor, though, having been curved over in search of the pavement all those years. He had blood and air in him again, and was still a bit high on withdrawal. His face was plumper, unblotched, his hearing and eyesight better. However, he had the impression he looked suddenly older, thrown forward into his forties at thirty-four. He had intimations that he would die soon, and must hurry. He also felt exceedingly and cheerfully dumb, as a saint or child might feel. He greatly enjoyed not knowing vast lots of things. He could remember nothing from his college "education." Going back to school now under the patronage of his aunt (under the lie that Chicago, foul and windy, made his studies there impossible), he found he could barely write, and did it with his tongue out, counting the letters and misspelling like a fresh rube trying to explain Mars to somebody back home. Women, though his desire was wild from lack, frightened him. He withdrew from music. It hurt him even in restaurants. He discovered himself asleep, eyes wide open, for long periods of time. He guessed he'd nightmared himself haggard with liquor and his body was still catching up, sly fox. He became agoraphobic and would often walk straight out of a room with more than three people in it. Attending class was hard. Then there was one last thing: he was certain that he would do something large, significant and permanent. Yet his imagination was gone, and he supposed it would be a deeply ordinary thing he'd do, after all.

At the little college in La Grange where he pursued his master's degree, depression hit him and he could barely stutter his name. One day he stopped in the hallway of his department in flowing traffic and for several minutes had no real idea where he was. The voices and moving legs around him were suddenly the most poisonous nonsense, but there was nowhere else to go. He was older than everybody again. Later he remembered that with seventeen years in Georgia and seventeen in Chicago he was torn between languages, even whole modes. He hadn't heard Southern spoken by a large group in ages, and it sounded dead wrong, just as the crepe myrtle and warm sun seemed dead wrong. Somebody passed with a Walkman on. He awoke, sickened by the tiny overflow from the earphones. A winsome girl was shaking him by the arm. They were classmates. She, astoundingly, seemed concerned, though she made him afraid.

Next was the matter of his aunt, whose patronage he had never quite understood. He was into her for many thousands already and did not dare count it up until he was a well man. Neither could he face his parents, who had lost him during the years he was a bum. Athens was not far, but it was a century away. They were old people now. The sight of him might kill them.

Long, long ago, his father, who rarely drank, had got loaded on beer to level with the famous hipster his son had become. Edgar was touched. His father, who wrote innocuous historical features for the local paper, seemed bound to drill at the truth about his wealthy older sister, Hadley.

Hadley was rat-faced. She resembled other animals, too, depending on her anger. It was a shame she was so homely and bellicose. A low, crook-backed and turtled thing, her typical expression was the scowl, her typical comment, derision. She scratched the air with snorts and protests. Edgar got it after he'd moved in: "You keep your room like a doghouse!" Edgar thinking it near clinical in classified piles. Nobody could remember her being pleasant to anybody for very long. When she was young she had considerable breasts. Two husbands comforted themselves briefly with them. The husbands may have become husbands mainly for such comfort. But the harshness of her face reasserted itself and the mean gruesomeness of her voice knocked out, in a few months, her breastly charms, and the long rut of acrimony got its habit, driving the last husband pure deaf and happy of it. The old lady had retired from formal religion long ago, blaming the perfume and powder of her contemporaries, widows like her, who gave her "a snarling snootful." Now she listened to the pastor on the radio, but only to keep up a mutter of assault against him. He was too meek and liberal for her. Hadley was a loner first, but not finally. Curiously, she'd had three handsome daughters. She wanted an ear, she demanded an audience, but something that nodded and remained fairly mute. She had worn out her daughters years ago. Her iron-jawed homeliness depressed them. They avoided her except at Christmas and Mother's Day, which she always ruined. They wondered why there was such a long mystery of dispute with her as she was wealthy, safe, air-conditioned, pampered by a forgiving black maid, and hardly threatened by the music, newspapers, widespread fools and widow-harmers she so reviled. Paying for anything especially disgusted her and there was always a furor about some bill. The habits, hairdos, and clothing of her daughters' husbands moved her tongue to little acidic lashes, as if they weren't there, only their shells. The old woman, though, was smart and not just an ignorant blowhard. It seemed she had educated herself to the point of contempt for close to everything; further knowledge was frivolous. She dusted it off with a snarl.

Edgar numbed himself early on. His own rages and countermeasures had cost him soul and ground in the past. He was still a wreck easing himself slowly back into the waters of hope, and with caution he might repair some of the mournful holes. He was dutifully hacking away in sociology in exchange for his roof, the use of her car, even money for postage. Edgar, on the advice of his counselor, was writing letters of amends to Snooky, Parton, Lambert — still alive! — and delaying the long one to his parents. The old woman knew he'd been a drunk. Said she could smell it in his letters. Hadley relished it, she had him. Edgar would rally up a blank nod and she could scratch away at will. He hid his smoking from her. The day she smelled smoke in her Chrysler would be a loud, nasty one, he reckoned. His elegant garret in the Tudor mansion hid cartons of Larks and ephedrine bottles. The horn cases, necessary, made him sad.

Auntie Hadley had no bad habits. Her enormous love for chocolate was controlled. The single Manhattan she poured herself at six-thirty, correctly just preceding dinner, was all she ever had. He wondered why she bothered. He could have had twelve to establish his thirst. She looked in his eyes for the suspected thirst. He stared down at her legs and was shocked to see them smooth, pretty enough to flirt by themselves. Here she was seventy or more. Her back was slightly humped, her chest low and heavy. The young legs were an anomaly, tight in their hose.

She dressed well. Much better than he, though he did not care.

She'd put him in designer dungarees. He had several too expensive turtlenecks from Atlanta because of his tattoo. He wore a better coat than he'd ever had at the height of his money. Maybe clothes were her bad habit. She dressed way above the town, her blouses in warm hues like the breasts of birds. Her pumps were girlishly simple. The girl who'd held his arm in the hall saw Hadley in the Chrysler once and said she looked stamped by Vassar or Smith. But Edgar knew she'd had only three years at a women's college as undistinguished as the one he now attended — private, small, arrogant, and mediocre. From Northwestern to here was a damned other free-fall of its own. Still, three years of college for a woman in the Depression wasn't bad. His aunt had a certain sneering polish to her. As for himself, he had flogged into the "program" with minimal credits and letters of recommendation from three drug/alcohol counselors who almost had to approve of him. The big letter, though, he'd touched from a senile prof who had been a high horse in urban ethnic studies. The quality of his dementia was that he cheered thunderously everybody he came in contact with. A hoary, religiously approving idiot in atonement for all the years he'd sternly drawn the line, perhaps. Edgar sucked up to the emeritus, who favored the phrase "my poor children!" He'd never even taught Edgar. But he had a letter from the famous old man and could have had his clothes and car. The faculty here were impressed to the point of envy.

Edgar looked bent, used and ill. In short, perfect, "one of ours" among the faculty, young and old. Even his former "rough time" with drugs and drink worked for him, and his jazz name was never forgotten. Those narcoleptic from two glasses of wine could hardly believe he was alive and were glad he'd got through to bring forth more good things. They trusted him more than he did.

Gradually, though, Edgar did get better. He took to running on the track in the hot sun and at night he slept like a babe. His cough disappeared and his ulcer was cured — he became near lotused-out by well-being. The people around him were good and nothing was ruined by irony, except for Auntie Hadley. He could shake hands and mean it. Little beautiful things. But watch your pious little disease, Edgar, the counselor's voice had warned. It'll leap in good times.

Edgar unearthed his notes on the bums. With an appalling gloom he found them well written, though barely legible. They were dangerous, like his horns. He was another man, then, in his whiskey insight. How long could he go on being a mute fraud among these good people? Well, he'd practically whispered to the chairman that he was going to write about bums for his thesis — whether Chicagoan, Russian, or Southern, he didn't know yet. But were bums all right as a subject? The chairman thought it excellent. Think of the therapy for Edgar, too. This was his life's inevitable opus, wasting nothing. Hardly any of the profs had experience with a big city. The man was so happy, Edgar felt even more guilty. He did not want to write about bums any more than he wanted to play trombone. This was not how he would be significant.

In the spring the social sciences party was held on the ground floor of a Victorian bed-and-breakfast hotel made over by two bored doctors' wives who became livelier in the role of perennial hostesses. Both of the wives were flirts, sexually attractive but chaste, fired by their Perdido Bay suntans. They danced their narrow waists, merry calves, and clapping sandals over the swank oak-plank hallways and up to the "boudoirs" above. There Edgar dreamed he might surprise them with the salty fluids of his mouth: desire was grinding awfully on him now, the gates thrown open by his health. He'd have to watch it. The wives served wine and cheese on silver trays worth more than the annual salaries of most La Grange faculty. One wife when asked about her husband shouted, "Oh, that dumb old bum!" Edgar hoped the man would die soon from overwork so she could kneel in front of him with money in hand, dragging on his jeans — holy smoke. Quit. She would find Edgar "darned alive!" He'd show her deep, rare animal need.

Could he awaken her senses, perhaps in a shack by the railroad, with only a naked light bulb and a soiled mattress on which she struggled rump up? Bum's dream, sot's hope. He was waylaid, beyond himself. The faculty men around Sally had looks of civilized attraction, he noticed. She seemed nothing but a pleasant ornament of a rousing spring day, something to break up shop talk. Oh, Snooky, Snooky.

Edgar's aunt was at the party, too, hopefully lost in a blockade of deaf people. She'd insisted on coming. He did not know what she expected from the event. Maybe to spy on him, the fraud.

Great hell — Auntie Hadley was six feet away, under the archway, staring straight at him. For how long? He'd been caught in point-blank lust for married Sally. The old woman bored into him with distaste. In his hand he held a glass of nothing, a lemon-lime drink at which he now sipped, mortified. He pretended an aesthetic view of the premises. Whom did she expect, Plato? Since she was not mixing, not having a good time, what exactly did she want? To stalk the territory until she found something appreciably awful, like him?

He slouched away to the cheese. What she liked best, he thought, was fools in authority. Maybe she'd find a dean and nail his moronism for Edgar later. While he was tracking décolletage and secondarily a man who could be a chum like Parton or Smith, anybody but another recovering chemical fraud stuffed with sincerity, their happiness right from the manual, he glanced over the crowd toward Hadley. She was holding her wine glass like a hatchet. Some old cowboy bum wisdom he'd once heard — "Small-breasted women are mean" — could not apply to her with her low great ones. No fury like a woman scorned: by her own parents, seeing their ugly duckling have no reprieve over time; by boys and men making rude comments; beaten back into her shell, sad little ducky, left to suffer among the natural beauties of Savannah; sad in the playroom with her gorgeous dolls, maybe beheading them, and her toy villages, setting them on fire. He was trying to achieve sympathy.

"You saw that lady?" came a girl's voice below. It was the grad student who had touched him in the hall. He liked her looks, all fresh-faced in her green party chemise, above the mode of faculty wives and her peers, who were deliberately nondescript. "She dresses so well. Must be somebody. An older Jackie Kennedy, except for the hump and the dog-ugly face."

The girl was naughty but risking it, touching Edgar's arm again for the first time in months, eyes bubbling, needing discipline.

"Ow, I'm sorry. Real rude. I'm half drunk."

"It's my aunt. My landlady, too. She's making things easier for me here."

"Truly sorry. Let me tell you something better. My friend knows two deaf-mutes who were looking at Pres Reagan one day on television. They began laughing like crazy. Friend asked them what it was. 'He's lying!' they signaled. They knew."

As for décolletage, this girl Emma Dean was well fixed. Either that or boosted. Her cleavage practically spoke to him and he was positive she knew it. It made him happy.

"I work with the deaf. Lifelong dissertation there, Edgar boy. They know many secret things we don't."

"I believe you."

"I know some of your secrets, too. I'm a busybody, probably *bound* for sociology, and I can see that you're not too happy here, believing it's beneath you and not Northwestern. You know too much about music and life, and worst of all, poor you, fame. You've got an honest, seasoned face. But with your slump and the hair in your face, you're so...morose. Like you're expecting defeat any second...Hate me, then. I've been improving the world since I was a little tapper."

"No. You seem kind." He straightened up and pulled back his forelock. "I've hardly seen you," he lied, spying her every other day, wishing.

"You looked drunk. That's why I came over and embarrassed myself. I'm drunk. My glasses are all fogged up, too." She was even more friendly when she took them off. "Do you expect a lot from yourself?"

"Maybe just the rote stuff, for a while."

"My parents were nothing. Daddy at the dry cleaners his whole life, and mother had to work — white domestic help. Imagine that in La Grange. We'd drive past all the great white mansions and spreading magnolias. I wanted to be somebody. Even now, I'm not going to be just...sociology. They're not going to be able to study me, class me. Hey, I was a virgin till I was twenty-five. You heard of that lately? Not because I was any holy-roly, either. I knew I'd enjoy sexual intercourse with the right person. My orgasms come very easy and I cry out like a panther. But..."

Her lips were dry and she stopped. She licked them and took a breath. Edgar noticed her eyes were moist. She was almost crying.

"Get me some more wine, please."

He got it posthaste, hoping she wouldn't use up her drunkenness on somebody else. He hadn't been near a woman in five years.

"I'm all ears."

"See," she wept a little. "We lived in a brick bunker on a bare yard at the edge of town. There were eight of us with about the money and room for two. I wore my brother's awful brown shoes in ninth grade when it really, really mattered."

Edgar guided her to the big front porch. Good, nobody else was around. It was a wonderful bluish-yellow and green here in mid-spring. They sat on the steps facing east. She wouldn't say anything. He was afraid she would go off in a sick fog.

"What about those doctors' wives that run this place?" he asked.

"Society cows looking for an audience anywhere. I'm so direct today."

"I don't mind. I like you. You look good."

"How did *you* fail? Were you poor?"

"Fail?"

"You're here, I mean. You don't have any money. Nobody really means to be in sociology, do they? You're older. You look *delayed* or off track—I can tell. I can spot true success a mile off."

"Fail, really..."

"See, if my mother and father hadn't had to, if they hadn't...they got married when she was *fourteen*. My mother was beautiful and at forty she looks as old as your aunt. But they just had to...couple, see, they're blind as swamp rabbits. Two of my brothers are deaf, but they kept on keeping on. I was sick one day at school my senior year and walked home. We hardly ever had a working car. I walked in and tried to get on my pallet before I threw up again, and from their room I suddenly heard this ruckus. I couldn't bear it. It was noon and he was home from the cleaners. They were in there mating, cursing each other, awful curses. I went out to the front yard and vomited, all dizzy, then looked up. Right on the road in front drove these rich boys in my class who were out for a restaurant lunch. They were hanging out the windows laughing at me. I never told that to anybody, Edgar."

"Oh, no. Awful. You poor girl."

Edgar took her hand. She had long fragile fingers with a class ring from Emory on one. It was still a teenager's hand.

"Nine months from then I had a new baby sister. Mama all crumpled up and thin and lined. But I had a bright inner life and I went away on scholarship. Made A's in almost everything, and Atlanta hardened me up."

The party inside seemed a dim fraud, with Emma and her featherlight hands out here.

"I won't tell you his name, but I had an affair with a married man—a wealthy important senator in Atlanta. The upshot was it ruined my life. He and his wife 'reconciled' and they named me a call girl he'd only seen a couple times during their marital stress. He'd promised me marriage, of course, but I never asked for it or wanted it. I took some money and shut up. My pop cursed me. My mother just died. They had principles, you know. But I gave him all the money for the four kids still at home."

"Rough."

"You might ask somebody in Atlanta who the senator was. Not me."

"I believe you."

"The man would put me naked in a silver Norwegian fox coat and work me over good, half a day at a time. He took poppers. We frolicked up where you could see all Atlanta. I liked him. We played backgammon. He cried when he lost me."

"Were you 'somebody' then?"

"No. You know what I was—mainly dumb."

"You don't hear many people being truly 'ruined' anymore."

Now there was another voice behind them and above. Edgar quailed.

"That was very nice, Edgar. Perfectly stranded, and I barely knew a soul." His aunt stood peeved, he guessed, though her voice had some teasing in it, maybe in deference to Emma. He and Emma rose.

"Aunt Hadley, this is Emma Dean, one of my...colleagues in the department."

"Can anyone tell me, please, what sociology *is*? I've asked four or five times and got the silliest stares."

Clearly she did not want an answer. Emma smiled, blinking her eyes dry.

"You've a lovely suit!" said Emma.

The old woman did not acknowledge the comment.

"I guess I've had enough 'higher education' for a day. Are you done?"

"Yes, ma'am. We'll go then?"

Edgar was forlorn and felt infantile. The old woman demoted everyone, he knew. Suddenly he wished that he had vast wealth.

"I'll ride home with you. My home, I mean," said Emma. "I don't even have a car, Edgar. Can you believe it?"

"Oh, the poverty-stricken bohemian student is rather a tradition, isn't it?" Hadley said, bright with scorn.

"Then I'm very traditional, ma'am."

"But you go to honky-tonks."

"Ma'am?"

"Your dress. Those see-through shoes."

"Would these be like what the 'flappers' wore in your day?" Emma remained kind, without strain.

" 'In my day'? I'm not dead, young lady. Surprisingly, I believe I'm still alive enough to pay all the bills."

They were quiet going to the car, calmly elegant like the old lady. Edgar noticed with some horror that Emma promptly opened the front door and sat down. Auntie Hadley just stood there, flaming.

Edgar froze, with gloom and awkwardness. She knocked his hand away when he tried to help her in. They rode a piece in hard silence until Emma instructed him as to where she lived, sounding drunk. It was way out south of town on a tarry country road, Edgar found out slowly. When he finally got there and drove into the "park" it became clear she lived in a long redwood mobile home in a group of pines. There was a man sitting barefoot on wooden steps at the front door.

"That's Michael the Math Monster. He's deaf," laughed Emma.

"You have a husband?" asked Hadley.

"No, just a friend. Another grad goob. Shares the rent."

"And all the fun, I'd imagine."

Edgar was vilely impotent. Emma did not seem so attractive and remarkable anymore as she hit her leg ("Ow! Gee!") getting out. She was common and messy. He winced when she stumbled in the pine straw. His aunt would not be missing a stroke. Emma had become the thing Hadley knew her to be. But it was not Emma. He wasn't himself either around this poison. A gutless lackey at thirty-five, losing worth by the minute.

How many people become what they seem to be to harridans and wags? He was furious as he drove. Then he recalled his aunt was still in the back seat.

"Wouldn't you like to ride up front?"

"Might as well continue on back here. They'll think I'm domestic help or some retarded person not let near the wheel."

"I'd be taken more for the chauffeur. Here I am with tie and suit."

"Eyes on the road. You drive like an old man from Nester Switch. Slow, but dangerous."

"Don't want to ruffle you."

"You and those mummies I saw at the party couldn't ruffle me if you tried. You tell me what sociology is and why it is necessary they draw salary."

"It is the study of people in groups — money, trends, codes, idols, taboos." With his rage still hot, he wanted to focus on *her* case, but subtly, subtly. "Class distinction, or sometimes just ordinary meanness."

She was quiet until they almost got to her big shaded Tudor redoubt. He wanted two quarts of Manhattans just for starters.

"In other words, nosy parasites without a life of their own," she said.

"All kinds, great and low like anywhere. Could I ask you" — Edgar flipped by money, the room, the car, the stamps, clothes — "has there been anything...unusually *terrible* in your life?"

"What? Why no!" He noticed in the rearview mirror that when she scowled she was twice as ugly. "You're not using me to study. You stick with the bums."

A man twelve years in prison wouldn't take a rim job from you, he thought.

But he tried to set things back to the ordinary, crabbed as it was. He parked out front. He'd run for supper. Hadley liked Chinese food, Mexican, or something from the deli. She liked cream and pickled herring best, curious for an old Protestant woman. Edgar wondered if some Jew in Savannah had given her a kind word once, maybe he'd even loved her. Auntie's wild loss.

"Well phooey," she said, out before he could help. "You were supposed to drive into the garage. There should be something in there for you by now. It's something that looked good for you. I had some advice."

Edgar walked to the garage. What would need a garage — lawnmower, weed-eater, leaf-blower? Something meek and janitorial.

When he nicked on the light, he could hardly reckon on it. It was a showroom-new, cream-colored BMW motorcycle. He was knocked dumber when he recalled what they cost. The keys were in it and he had to get on and drive, ho neighbors! But first he must see his aunt.

She was at her Manhattan, watching the television news.

"Thank you. What does it...mean?" That she projects I'll kill myself. But a new one wasn't required. He'd almost done it on that piece of rolling bones an era ago.

"I thought about you lumbering in to park that Chrysler on campus. Not really fit. I'm told these motorcycles are 'hot' with your young professionals."

"I'm staggered. Thanks again."

"Get *on* the thing. Drive it, Edgar."

"Yes, I will."

"It must be a great fight, staying sober."

He was trying to see something of his father's face in Auntie Hadley's: a long-nosed projection of the nostrils, a gathering of the lips into a plump rabbit-bite. Another animal was present, too, in the forehead and eyes: a monkey. Some breed rarefied by spite and terror, squawling from a nook in a rain forest. But his father's face was pleasantly usual, as in one of those old ads of a bus driver inviting you aboard, happy hills and vales ahead.

"Frankly, boy, I wish you were more interesting." She studied him back. "Your father really didn't give you much to shoot for, did he?"

Could the troll guess he was thinking of his father? His regular face. His father was deferential, almost unctuous, and uncritical. He was all right, was his father, Oliver. He should see him soon.

His father was a newspaperman — no, that was too strong a word — whose regular column in the local paper was, essentially, one timid paragraph of introduction to a reprinted item of obscure history. The articles illustrated that people of the past were much like ourselves. He had little money, few other interests except choir, and viewed himself as a meek servant of the Big Picture. His only small vanity was in seeing his articles reprinted elsewhere every now and then. Edgar knew that outside the small-town antiquarian South, a larger newspaper would have pulled the trapdoor on his father and his monkish library work. His father had wanted to be a history teacher but could not face the classroom. In the forties, in fact, a huge bully of a student, smelling out his fear, beat him up. Hadley had dutifully reported this to Edgar when he was newly in the house. He was also informed that Sue, Edgar's mother, had always made more than her husband, doing the books of shops around town. She was a C.P.A. They were faithful moderate Methodists. His father — he hated this — sang in the church choir. He did not like him forming the big prayerful O's with his mouth, his eyes on the director, a sissy. The BMW was coming with a great tax. He felt murderous. He should have known.

"When men were realler, they drank for good reasons. Look at Grant and Churchill with their great wars. Look at Poe and Faulkner and Jack London and their masterpieces. Now you've got a national curse of drugs and drink, millions of nobodies who never once had a great day or a fine thought. This puny *selfism*, uff! It seems to me you became a drunkard just for lack of something to do. Just a miserable fad. No direction, no strong legs under you." She was building.

"Don't you want to add 'no intestinal fortitude'?" Edgar said helpfully, blazing inside.

"Now your proposed treatise or whatever, *Bums of*. Name your poison. Why, Lord, that's less a topic than a confession of *kin*. You want to go to school and still wallow with the wretched? Where's the merit? With your history, it seems you'd seek something higher for your interest. You'd have got a snootful of bums in the Depression. It took a Roosevelt and a world war to get them off the streets."

"I suppose" — this was the limit — "you labored greatly for your fortune and all was perfect with your marriages." Her first husband, by what Edgar knew, amassed his wealth in lumber and chickens by deliberate long hours away from her. The second, before he went willfully deaf, was something of a bonds genius. He built this vast house — for her, why? — then fled to a single basement room where he did woodwork with loud tools.

"You're a spiteful young person. And not very young. I was not idle. I guided their affairs, if you want to know. I had *presence* and spirit. Both your uncles had weak hearts and not very much will. I don't know why God matched me with such invalids, but that was what I got. I'm not the prettiest thing on the block."

Her voice had quieted to something like a lament. He wondered how deeply she believed herself. What was the truth? Maybe he was the last of her invalids. Maybe she must have them. When was she going to die?

"Well, about supper."

"I'm no good for supper now, thank you. Go ride your present. Ride it, please, with one thing in mind: your talent. I've read your letters, of course, and I saw your notes, scrambled as they are. You can write. You have seen trouble. You have conquered a great flaw. Now, Edgar, nobody has known it, but I have diaries. I have jotted histories of my time. I believe there would be a discerning audience for it. And you can write it."

"Write what?"

"My life. My life and times."

He turned and went to the motorcycle, still in his suit, drenched with perspiration and stinking of acrimony. The BMW seemed a nasty, irrelevant toy. A mighty vision shot to hell. But when he got it going down the streets, big beam out front, sweet cut grass smells flowing by, the wind whipping, he began to giggle. There it was: her patronage, her life as done by Edgar who could write no more at all. He drove on to Emma's. Why not?

He felt rangy, and much better. In the summer his work in the classroom went well. He knew many of the answers and seemed to have the good questions too. His more rural peers gave him some reverence. Some of them were hardly more cosmopolitan than the rube who sang about Kansas City in the musical *Oklahoma!*

Even better, Emma Dean seemed to be going for him. He recalled Snooky and tracked the difference. This time he had to do almost nothing. It was a rapid impassioning with young Emma — was she twenty-seven? But there was an unhappy strangeness to it on her part. She wanted him near, but it seemed she wanted him mournfully. The affair was making her sad. But Emma persisted: she bought him things, and slyly hinted at the times when Michael the Math Monster, who was deaf, would be out of the mobile home. She told him mysteries about the deaf and what they knew. What that permanent silence gave them — some claimed to hear music from heaven, or right from the brain.

One night in mid-June she was impatient and gloomy, yet suddenly she pulled off her dress. This "courting" could not go on forever — they weren't infants. She did cry out like a panther, bless her. Edgar was very happy, but she wept. She wouldn't tell him why, and he could only tenderly guess, remembering her history. He knew things would get better, more natural. Most stunning, though, was the certain knowledge she would be his last woman. The truth banged him with an enormous bright weight — at last things were in motion. He was very lucky to have her. And this time he would not destroy.

For Emma he improved *his* history, sometimes believing it. After the collapse of the band he said he'd become a long meditator. It did not necessarily mean failure. It was a long wait with a nobler design. He had shed material wants willingly and sought different, wholer, more authentic company. These phases were not unknown to many great men, not that he was great. But he felt a mission, and had for a long time.

The term *mission,* in regard to Auntie Hadley's request, still made him giggle, then snarl. He began writing even worse at school. He had never answered her. This was a petty and vile act, but it bought him his first taste of power in her petty and vile world. The only token in her land was cowardly muteness. Wasn't it cowardly, after all, to nag and bite like she did? Wasn't it the life choice of a nit? He pretended to be hurt by her comments against him and his family for much longer than he actually was. She was watching him cautiously now, and keeping her mouth shut more. It wouldn't do to offend the *author,* for nit's sake. Giggle. But he was not rotten enough to tell Emma about it. All in all, he couldn't get away from pity for his aunt.

"Let's go riding on the bike, you behind, Emma."

"But I'm afraid."

"You won't be. And let me suggest something — take off your underpants and wear a dress instead."

"Excuse me."

"Please do it. Women find a whole new world, I hear."

"Well, I'm all for that."

She was game, and by Lake Tornado, she was hugging him with delight, bountiful sighs going in his ear. He was sly. Nature was with him. She liked that he'd had a wife and was experienced. She told him he was a new man, all bronzed and straight, on the motorcycle. They would have times, good times. Yelling back, he assured her — *the* best time, he shouted. Ah, he was all gone for her now.

They'd told him at the ward, just hang on, hang on. Good things would come, eternal things. It was a law of recovery, tested millions of times.

Take it at the flood, then, Edgar Alien Po' Boy, which is what Emma now called him. Her love name. Oh, the wimmens, the wimmens. Their world — holy smoke! — and how he'd missed the light hands, the sly codes in the whole little city — its own language — they set up around you. The unexpected, priceless gifts, good nowhere but the city of love. "Give me some sugar," she said. How long since he'd heard that. Despite her Emory degree, summa cum laude, Emma stayed more the congenial truck-stop waitress, the charity that most got near him. Maybe because of her many brothers she understood the good-natured cuffing that men did and the brawny highway troubles behind them. She was a pal, a corker, a skit, handed to him. Pale fire burning through it all. With her, Edgar found, in some discomfort, that he could write better, he could wax forth. But she was always a bit sad, though she worked diligently with her deaf people in the institution south of Atlanta. It was not an unworthy mission — here we were — to alleviate suffering: find its cause, cut it off, and kill it, as General Powell said he'd intended with the Iraqi army in Kuwait. Emma was a great cheerleader of the war. Her patriotism was caught up. Democracy, freedom! Protection of our sand brothers. The tattoo on his throat — Emma'd never seen it, they made love with her glasses off — caused him no end of grief. For he felt Southern now: proud and brave with no irony or cynicism. Leave that to the hag in the Tudor dungeon.

Yet Emma stayed sad.

There was something in her he could not yet touch.

Nobody had said of this mission that the good things wouldn't be tough to get. He was with her a great deal. Good Michael the Math Monster, attuned quickly in his deafness, stayed out of the mobile home for long tracts of time. Edgar halfway moved in, while he worried about the feelings (and money) of his aunt.

After, at last, the long honest letter to his parents, Edgar shook with relief. They would go to Athens. It was time, and Emma agreed.

He was gratified by her presence. He still did not feel worthy to meet them alone. Emma, a prize, would tell them he stood tall. A weak and dim man could not have her. A dim and weak man could not handle the BMW with this intelligent brunette frightened on the back seat. Deliberately he drove right into the racing ring-road fury of Atlanta traffic, cocky and weaving at seventy-five plus, envied. Emma almost died, a happy leech on his back. It was the city of her "ruin," but she laughed at it, another whole venue. A woman's shouts of pleasure could knock down buildings.

Athens had grown, of course. The university took in forty-five thousand now. Edgar got solemn when they rode into his block. He hadn't remembered his house as this unprosperous. It was stained from tree sap. The yard was shaggy. All this dereliction was unlike his father in the old times. Inside it smelled like used lives — corpus smells in the homes of the meek, hard to believe of one's people. His own smell was in there somewhere, he reckoned. But the chicory coffee his mother drank constantly — a special blend from the French Market in New Orleans — was sweet nostalgia. She'd cooked a raisin-apple pie for them, too.

For his advent, Edgar's folks — Oliver and Sue — had dressed up. His father wore a tie and the gray strands of his hair were nursed back. His mother had on a blue churchy dress. She had a lot of hair, but it was white, a grief to Edgar. What did he expect though? Athens was out there, doing better than they were, that was all. His dad moved slowly with arthritis of the feet. His mother seemed resolute on showing off her younger health, bouncing a little with her coffee cup.

It went much better than he'd hoped. A taste of the coffee — like a swat — filled him with a glow. They said he looked wonderful, all grown and mature, maybe taller. He almost forgot Emma. Out back with his father, they laughed about his aunt. Edgar played her as a more minor crank than she was and spoke of "paying her off when I head out on my own." On horn or in academe, his father wanted to know. Not the horn, Edgar said. His dad didn't understand: why couldn't Edgar recover it all? He was still young. What a gift, what years! Edgar turned and saw Emma with her coffee, not glad, eavesdropping from behind the kitchen door. The back yard was bleak, rutted with water drainage.

When he left, despite the small melancholy, Edgar felt fixed and relieved.

Emma did not. She didn't speak on the motorcycle all the way back. In Atlanta, he thought he heard her crying through the wind.

He was attentive and wanted to help. But it was a cruel night for Emma. She claimed her back hurt and he could tell she wanted him to go. She'd been hurt and made sad all over again; she didn't even try to smile. There was maybe even something like hate in her eyes. Well, Edgar Alien Po' Boy's out of here, he said. This got nothing from her. The mobile home looked glum, newly desperate, not the lake cabin it had seemed before.

At his aunt's he sat unbending from his trip snags. After a while he felt there was something different about his plush garret. Then he saw — how could he have missed them? Stacked neat and high on his desk were handsome purplish leather-bound books. There were two stacks, each two feet up — her diaries and "jottings." They made him angry. They were arrogantly under lock and key, but with the keys out for him to jump in and have a go. Hadley was away somewhere. He let go an uncommon obscenity. Then he went straight to bed.

At breakfast she was on him before he could dart to class an hour early. Quietly, more like a human being, she began.

"Edgar, one thing I notice about your graduate studies: you don't really do that much. You've time for all kinds of things. I've seen your motorcycle at Emma Dean's... place, more than a few times."

He resented this, and braced. But she wasn't her old self. He frankly liked her pleading.

"You, if you could just do a *bit* of work every day, say two hours, on our book. You could make your own notes and start the outline, almost idly. Do the readings. I'm offering you treasured, secret views of a heart and mind that has been through crucial times. You never knew, for instance, that *I* had my day with music, did you? Not your noisy success, not your... bubble. My time was milder and private as girls were taught. Why, I'd play an afternoon triumph of Chopin, there would be Father, sneaking in to listen in the hall. He'd have tears running down his cheeks. Too, I did dollwork, their porcelain faces showing history and nationality when there was no world-consciousness in Georgia at all. They're still in the attic for you to see. And I will be constantly available for you to consult. I've bought a new tape recorder, which is of course yours after our interviews are done. I've completed an outline. We can compare outlines once —"

The horror! as Edgar Alien Po' Boy might have written, grabbed him.

"I was no mean student, nephew, but in composition I couldn't quite express myself, though I was excellent in elocution. Ethical elocution — I was the star there. My first husband dragged me from college. There was heartbreak. Big moments in the sun were probably waiting for me! But love, love, was the order of the day. Edgar, I'm not going to live forever, I wouldn't think."

Was that a frightened giggle, a voice from a little girl in her horse-drawn carriage?

"Academic people, I've noticed, will delay things *forever*. Why, I sent some things to the press at Athens years ago. It took a year to get them back, and with a *beastly* note, beastly."

Edgar became, though sickened, interested in the long confession. Here was a sick glee, close to a great pop of vodka in a rushing airplane.

"In Savannah, old Savannah!, there were gay times. Homosexuals *won't* steal that term! There were lanterns on the levee indeed. I was good with horses. What a picture, I on my roan Sweetheart on the way to third grade in the city! Horses were thought elegant, a whole culture gone with the wind! Stephen Crane wrote *The Red Badge of Courage* in ten days, I believe. Not that you, with all our source material — seventy-three years! But Edgar, you are falling *behind*. I won't watch you do that again! You've a degree from one of our great universities."

"I'll read and form an opinion," said Edgar flatly with ire.

"Further, it would be all right, I would allow, to have Miss Dean stay here with you. You can have a larger room — Hank's, with his special woodwork, and a television, too, and his Victrola, unused since his deafness. I'm no prude. I can modernize. I don't want you at that trailer. A man needs pleasure, but in the right place. I'll put in the large couch with a fold-out. We'll get right to it. Shelley had *his* muse."

"Didn't she write *Frankenstein?*"

You couldn't get to the old thing anymore. She just faded away.

That night, Emma still in grief, he sat his horn cases on his desk next to the books. He didn't know quite what he was doing. Both things made him sick. He stared a long time, judging the contest.

At the end of the summer after two major exams, essay-type, the chairman called him in. Edgar liked him. No great achiever either in the classroom or in research (though there was a rumored thin book, *When God Was a Boy*, they said), Schmidt cheered the worthy and had no envy. He said Edgar looked good, but there was a problem.

"Your prose style. Your writing. We don't see that kind much. I agree academe needs shaking, but there is a sort of...grunt-talk, a primitive getting-there. Seems almost to cause you...pain. And some to the reader. Now I am a Hemingway fan, a Raymond Carver *zealot*, but are you trying something *new*, dimensional, I don't know, would this fit the bums' world, is that what?"

"No, sir. I'm not trying anything that I'm aware of."

"This is your best?"

"I'm looking for an awakening, I guess. In the old days at Northwestern, though, I could write better."

"Then we'll just root for you. I appreciate your honesty. We want to get life and expression together. Isn't that the whole point?"

"Sure."

"The example of pain into flowers, ho?"

Edgar nodded.

"Because very soon it's thesis time for you. There are outside readers."

Peets Lambert and his band came into town, out from seeming nowhere. Lambert was still alive. Someone called Edgar from the college and said Lambert had left tickets for him in the chapel where they'd play. The student coordinator later said Lambert was very cordial and, whoa, eighty-five years old. It had been almost twenty years since Edgar first played with the band. Lambert remembered him well and wanted to chat after the concert. The student, who knew Edgar, said Lambert wanted to know everything about him and had even driven by his aunt's house, but had found nobody home the previous afternoon.

Edgar, Emma and Auntie Hadley went together. Emma thought it would be cruel not to invite her. She'd love big band swing. This would be quite the sentimental evening for everybody! Obscurely, Emma had gotten happy again.

And swing it was. Snooky wasn't there, nor anybody near her age. Lambert had brought back some of his old friends including Woodrow and settled for what he could get on the nostalgia circuit — hence La Grange. By far he was the leading ancient, but several in the band were close. They had a bad singer, and no one looked particularly happy in their black suits. The playing was sloppy and sometimes verged on the funereal. But Lambert hammed and was hip, very, like a confident ghost pawing at the band. Surprisingly, Edgar sat through it calmly. It *was* a sort of music, and he did not hate it, he was not made ill. To his left, he saw his aunt looked very pleased. Her eyes seemed to be swooning back in her biography. The band played a Charleston, capping with the bad singer, the only leaping youth in the band. The students who were there — not many — liked it, they were charmed.

So when the band was breaking up, Edgar and Emma went backstage, which barely existed. There was Lambert, alone, unmobbed, smoking a cigarette but looking guilty, same as years ago. The old cancer thinness was on him, his face speckled and translucent on its skull. He lit up when he saw Edgar.

"I know you, my 'boner. Oops, sorry little lady!" His naughty hipness was imperishable, sealed with him. He wasn't missing a thing with those eyes. Edgar wondered if his hearing, however, had dimmed.

He drew Edgar in, slipped into an undervoice — old collaborators — a few feet away from Emma, who was not really shut out. Lambert smiled over Edgar's shoulders, always a dog for the wimmens. He told Edgar about Snooky, mother of two in Dallas. Parton Peavey had cleaned up and as everybody knew was a "rich old man, nearing the big four-oh." Edgar was downed a little by how much they had aged.

"You guys didn't know, but I invested for all of you, us, the cats, way back then. Young people, all they thought of was their axes. So there's a piece of your salary you never saw. So, beautiful, it's come to, da-dum, something big and tidy."

Edgar jumped, very alert. He planned suddenly: cash in one bundle back to his aunt. A made man, he'd get his own place and fix up his parents' house. He would buy an island, where? Emma would continue to work among the native deaf and he, what? He'd come out with a large thing from his meditative years.

"After what I did for you, I know you'll sign it back to me. Parton Peavey, Smith, Snooky, no problem, they all did. You can see that I and the band, we needs the bread. Verily."

Edgar, first raised, now bumped the wretched bum's pavement.

"How much was it?"

"Near sixty thousand apiece. A hundred, near, for our legend Peavey. Isn't that great? I brought the pen. You know what I did for you?"

Edgar signed three lines as Lambert held out the stock transfer.

"The band goes on. I can afford a casket." Lambert winked. "Good young people making the band go on. Woodrow takes it when I'm planted. Your funds, Big Thunder Hounds Foundation, huh? Not even really for me, get it? Look at me."

"Yes, sir."

"And I saw that house where you live yesterday. Not gone with the wind, ho? The wind has come back and put you in a castle. Edgar, Edgar, I'm hating this, but could you spare me a little? A couple thou. What I did for you when you were a baby, remember. Times are rough. You can see. I'd never have seen you, chicken and peas La Grange, man —"

"I don't have any money."

"House-poor, huh? But a little scratch — the things I did for you — you cost me, the bus..."

Edgar moved away. Lambert was in a fit of his own virtue. Stooped and angry, Edgar caught Emma's arm and they ran to where his aunt was waiting in the foyer, caught in the act of giving the snoot to a couple of leather punkers who'd come to (Edgar wished) spit at Lambert's Wall Street Crash music.

"What's this rushing?" his aunt wanted to know. They were in the car before Emma told her.

"Edgar has just lost a great deal of money he didn't know he had."

Emma's work with the deaf must have given her some kind of ears, Edgar grieved.

"Oh, yes. The music's wonderful for a while. But your musicians are notorious bankrupts," said his aunt.

"They're just 'bubbles,' aren't they?" He smashed at her.

"Exactly what I said. My generation always knew that."

By Christmas break, things had changed only for Emma. She had blitzed through her work and was taking the master's. Her thesis on the deaf was heralded and would be published, with the help of her major professor, her major herald. Edgar didn't know she was this good. She even got a small advance — one thousand — from publishers in New York, and was hounded instantly for it by her father, from the school of You Owe. All eight of his children owed him for their lifelong hard times. Emma gave him seven hundred.

They remained passionate, but she would not move to Hadley's house. Edgar was glad. They did make love, though, on the sofa a few times. She opened his horn cases one morning and peered at the freckled and scarred instruments a long time. They seemed to make her angry. Without a word, she left the house and drove away in the Japanese wreck she'd bought.

He was baffled by her sadness, which was turning more into anger nowadays. She would clam up and sometimes beat her fists on whatever was near, including once, his thighs. She had a television and watched the war news through January. She liked to turn up the speech of the generals and said she had a crush on Powell.

The terrible day he went into the trailer, February was ending with a big blow that made the pines *whoo* and shiver, spooky, warning the homes on wheels beneath them. There had been, during the morning, a burst water main up the road, catching the whole trailer park without water. Emma had been busy cleaning with Lysol, and was outraged by the stoppage. She was in a torrent when he entered, with good news, he thought. Inspired by her, he was well into a book about Chicago bums. He could write again, and what he had was so good that the chairman was trying to get him a large grant to revisit his old haunts. It would be enough to take Emma with him. It was not a bad city at all. Away from the South, she might be happier — holy smoke, why shouldn't she? She'd never left it. There was her depression, itself.

Edgar sat on the sprung bunk she slept on, petting her. He told her about bums.

For many years, he and female drunks had simply wound up together. He had a place. They just appeared in it, no memory of having got there, isolated by the blazing nimbus of alcohol. The woman might even be sober, some pitying angel on the spoor of a heartbroken man. You could not be awful enough for some women: they were stirred by emaciation, destitution, whiskey whiskers, bus fumes. For other women you could not get foreign enough. Witness Clem, the acned Iranian sot, always with a beauty queen. Some black women were greatly attracted to downed white men. What wild loyalties he'd seen when he'd been sober enough to notice. You had Commies, capitalists (ruined, but adhering), even monarchists, in bumhood. Take away the sickness, he had loved a good deal of the life. He even missed being insane, sometimes. The world matched his dreams some days. Something, a small good thing, almost always turned up. He missed making the nut of drink every day. He missed the raddled adventures. There always was a focus: securing the next high, defending the hoard of liquor money, but with chivalry; getting through the day without murder; being a world citizen, voting and passionate, about the headlines off some fatcat's newspaper. What about the exploratory raptures of one's own liquored mind? The drunkard, or bum, was not wasting his mind all the time. He was going deeper in than others: great lore, buzzing insights. The conversation frequently was above the university. Some few bums were *renuncios.* They had given up the regular world on purpose, and could explain why in long wonderful stories, each one distinct, bravely of no category or school. He'd also met deaf bums, of course. He knew more about them than she'd thought. He knew the blind, too — what stories he could tell about Rasta Paul!

Emma listened closely, having stopped her tears long ago. She seemed avidly sympathetic, her pretty mouth open, her dress falling off her shoulders like a flushed senorita's, carelessly revealing those breasts that shot warmth through his manhood. Her eyes met his, and it was off with her spectacles and dress, on the bunk in a minute.

Hang in, all good things will come, Edgar remembered. Even his reverie about Sally, the doctor's wife, lived out long and more on that dirty mattress, a single light bulb shaking over it. Never had Emma been this carnal. She threw herself into long rituals of defilement, yes. Begged him to take her back there, as never before, and then she was on him with her mouth lest he finish without her tasting it all. She hurled back and forth, then out with her legs, voracious. The panther cry came, rose and fell, rose again. Then she suddenly cast him off, screaming no, no, no, no, no! Immediately she began to cry. She reached and put her spectacles back on, peering first at his naked chest, then at his throat.

"What the *hell* does that tattoo mean? I never saw that! There's a war on. Are you for that monster we're fighting?! Our generals, our airmen — they're men, and you, you don't have...*moxie, moxie* — that's it! Your aunt keeps you! Peets Lambert kept you! You ungrateful *bitch!* You're *gothic,* Edgar!"

This was terror. She wouldn't quit.

"You won't even play the horns — your natural God-given ticket! No, crowds get to you, weak bitch! Memory gets you! You drag me to your pitiful parents, and I saw the nowhere, the awful never, of you all. But I had to be there to prop you up! Your significant thing, your meditated thing, I've screwed, sucked, let you... You've even got gray, waiting, on somebody else's motorcycle!"

And, before the dish came at him,

"Now your bums, your magical romantic bums. The deaf don't

have a choice, Mister Chicago. And let me tell you something else. After this book, the deaf aren't going to *be* my life. I've done them, I'm tired. I'm too *selfish,* if you've got to know! It's *my* time. I can't help it. I want healthy people, and rich, traveling people, happy *doing* kings and princes. But I had to love *you.* Love you, I *know,* more than you do me! How could you?"

She kneeled and brought up a bowl of Lysol and threw it in Edgar's face. The pain was so horrible, the act so sudden, that he simply laid out his arms and rocked, before his hands came up on their own and dragged at his eyes. He was conscious of her running back and forth in the trailer. But there was no water, not there or in any trailer around them. It was a long, long time before she had him, naked, in her Toyota wreck. Something went wrong with it, though, and it stopped. He was blind. He was probably good and blind before she, having raced around desperately for ditch water, opened the radiator for its fluid and came to him with a few drops of it, sprinkling some on his eyes. It tasted like antifreeze.

When he left the hospital ten days later, he had only a speck of vision, low in his left eye.

Emma had never left him, and implied her remaining life in this act.

"I'll never leave you, Edgar," she crooned, over and over.

She never discussed anything with Auntie Hadley or him. She would be there at the house with him forever, or wherever, she said. Emma had real power in her guilt. The aunt might be flabbergasted, but Edgar couldn't see things like that now. He never heard an incautious opinion from his aunt anymore. Emma said, indeed, that the woman was being sweet, real sweet. He could hear them in conference. They seemed to be agreeing about almost everything. Emma allowed the aunt to buy her clothes. She described them to Edgar, meekly delighted. All he could see were the new Paris shoes.

Her love for him, he felt, went on past the penitential, which he, manly, protested many times. She swore it was not so, not in the least. Horrible as it was, throwing Lysol at him had been an act that told her where she belonged. He could not know how much she loved him. That thing about kings and princes was just the last of her daydreamy youth shouting itself out.

Edgar asked for his valved Bach trombone. It didn't really taste like whiskey at all. He practiced it awhile. Blind men had come forth beautifully in jazz. His aunt's hand was on his shoulder, appreciative.

One day his parents came with a present of Lambert's latest swing record, a minor hit. They said it brought back memories. Edgar loved them desperately, and he could hear the kind Emma celebrating his progress as they left, meaning to visit often. It was all delightful, but the horn itself was no go. It was as if he'd never touched one. There was weakness in his chest, not from the healed sternum, but something more. He just couldn't. He cried a little. It was mainly for Emma, anyway. He didn't want her to see him cry. In fact, he was glad he was no good.

He'd gotten the grant. Emma was ready to lead him in Chicago, back to the old haunts, anywhere. Handicaps very often increased being, she said. Such people were called the "differently abled" nowadays.

Edgar had never wanted to go back to Chicago. That wasn't his item, his thing.

Once, a month blind and just sitting there, seeing if he could read a long speck in one of Hadley's diaries, he came across something from 1931: "I...am...made...all...different...I...can't...enjoy...anything...God...you...my...husband...pokes...at...me...I... am...angry...feel...there...is...a...dangerous...snake... down...there...not...him...me...before...he...got...there... God...help...me."

Hadley made a movement. She was next to him, on a wooden chair. Emma was away. Auntie Hadley started whispering about Milton and that "Argentina man," and Helen Keller's triumphant books.

"Milton was years preparing for his life's work — what a paradise regained for us all, Edgar. His daughters served him and took his dictation. I can have all this *brailled* for you. You could then dictate and Emma would surely help. She is *all* you. You are luckier than your ugly aunt, in many ways."

"Actually, the blind can write," said Edgar suddenly.

"A whole new world. 'They also serve who stand and wait.' But you wouldn't have to wait anymore."

Edgar grinned. They'd not seen him grin. He knew something deep and merry, the exact ticket.

"Your physical needs are all covered. Then there's my will, after I...and a big sum for the book. And all the instruments, of course, for composition."

"Do something for me, Auntie. Would you put Lambert's record on the Victrola so we can listen together? The past, swing, times forgotten."

She played it and sat, not a squeak.

God, the band was wretched, and yet they'd come round again with a hit. You never knew.

He screwed up his mouth when it was done, tongue against his teeth, watching Hadley's foot bounce to this *merde,* holy smoke!

He told her there would be a declaration when Emma came back. He wanted a gathering. This was a big moment for him.

Emma sat, a Manhattan like Hadley's in her hand, at six-thirty that evening. They told him it was snowing out even though it was early April — so very rare and lovely and ghostly quiet. The town was filling up and mute. A beloved merchants' calamity thrilling the young at heart.

"All right, let's get started. A real book knows everything. Let's clear the air in two ways. First, Auntie Hadley, to get modern, when did you first know you were a *shit?* Was it a sudden revelation, what? When did it arrive that you were and would be, *awful?* Next, we of the addicted *must* write letters of amends to everybody alive. Maybe even to the dead. I want to hear that pen scratching near me while I'm at my work, sweetie. This needn't take forever, though the sheer amount of paper will be staggering."

There was silence before she acquiesced. Did he hear something moist and flowing from her?

"Emma, dear." He himself began crying. "I release you body and soul. Don't need no cellmate, not even no lovin', till the old opus is done. Think it over then. Have at the kings and princes."

Why was he so happy, so profoundly, almost, delirious?

Loud and bright and full of jazz, *Rat-Face Confesses* — that would be the title of their book.

Scandale d'Estime

THEY WERE DESTROYING a theater in Kosciusko, and my father bought the bricks. He had made a good deal. He asked me and a buddy of mine to live there a while in a hotel to stack the unbroken bricks for him and load them on a truck.

We were, my buddy and I, probably seventeen. We read *Downbeat* magazine and knew a few Dylan Thomas poems, which seemed to us as good as poetry could get. Horace was the better reader and memorized poems whole. There was a small college in our town, and we knew some of the younger faculty who had left in despair and irony over the puritan expectations of it. As they had been able to talk about upwards of three books, we considered them great poetic souls. I wish there were a good term for the zeal we felt for these older hip brethren, which included one stylish lady named Annibell: *cats* almost got it, when the Beats and jazzers established themselves. Those who got the joke and continued on with their private music. A personal groove.

Now and then there was a question of what we should do with the new women in our heads. You might go out with some local girl, but she was not really there, she was not the real faraway city woman in your cat head. You might kiss her and moil around—but she was, you knew, fifth string, a drear substitute for the musical woman in a black long-sleeve sweater you had in your mind on the seashore of the East—the gray, head-hurting East, very European to my mind, where you thought so much and the culture labored so heavy on you your head hurt. The beauty and the wisdom of this woman—uttered along the seashore in weary sighs—was a steady dream, and I woke with it, pathetically, to attack a world fouled by the gloomy usual. I yearned to talk and grope with a woman who was exhausted by the world and would find me a "droll" challenge. She would be somewhat older. She either sighed, or mumbled pure music. I had no interest in the young freshness of girls at all.

Every brick I unearthed from the dust and chalky mortar, cleaning it

off with a steel brush and wet flannel rag — which made my hands red
and sliced with little lines all over — became part of the house I was
building in my mind for this woman. New York Slim they would call
her. The house would be on the seashore, where you could look out
the window and sigh in a big way. For her, even a special sighing room.

The old hotel we stayed in had rail balconies on the inside floors
where you could lean and look down into not much of a lobby, your
feet on a gone tan carpet.

It felt good to be tired and cut up at the end of the day, just showered and looking down at the lobby with your hair slick. You felt
you were a working man. I had a red kerchief tied around my neck
like a European working man, all shot with working blood. A whole
new energy came through you. This was before I began to drink and
smoke, and I would not feel like this, clean and worthy and nicely
used in the bones, for many more times, for a great long while. The
only problem was that there was absolutely nothing to do. The town
might have been named for a Polish patriot who led American
troops in the Revolutionary War, but the glory just mocked you in a
town where shops slammed shut at five to prevent any history whatsoever beyond twilight. We had no car and had read all the magazines backward. There was a bare courtesy light bulb at the bus station, and we actually went to stand beneath it, hoping to invite life.
But nothing. A man who hated to move ran a restaurant up the way
and we soon got tired of his distress. Nobody even played checkers
there. Gloomy John Birch literature would fall off the checkout
counter, and there were flags bleached to pink and purple in a bottle
on it too, seeming to represent a whole other nasty little country.

I leaned and watched the lobby for New York Slim to walk in, lost
in Kosciusko, Miss., and looking for me. I would look at my watch
and curse fate, giving her just a few more minutes. Then I would
curse her and tell her I was through. Natalie Wood, or more probably her cousin from the South, Lee Wood, would come instead. I had
seen *West Side Story* that year, and Natalie was slowly replacing
New York Slim. When New York Slim did finally get here, there
would be hard words, tears, and it would be tough to tell her she had
lost everything — the brick house on the seashore, the sighing room,
my drollness, everything — and that I was giving it all over to one of
the Miss Woods. There was nothing I could do about it I'd say, it was
an *affaire de coeur,* sorry. The fact is I was going mildly insane. I
peered harder into the lobby. All you saw was a solitary whiskered
gruff man, probably retired, not even reading a magazine, but look-

ing straight ahead in a sort of shocked anger that put some fear into you. He was not the denizen of an interesting passionate play by T. Williams, as you might hope, but a horrified sufferer of age bound to a colorless tunnel, as if his stare were tied in a knot at the end of it. His face was spotted red, from waiting, I thought. Someday he would just disappear into the wallpaper, which also had red spots in it. Though he'd been without applicants for a long time, in my mind I made him into a smoldering corrupter of the young. We never said a word to him.

In my own town a man named Harold, old enough to be a teacher, was attending the college. Harold, who lived in an attic apartment, was balding and already a man with a heavy if not lengthy past. He had been drafted during the Korean War but had not gone over there with the army until the truce was signed, so that his adventures in the East, for which he had made a lurid album he showed me, were all done in peacetime. The photographs showed a bunch of men in fatigues hanging around in squads, the usual thing, but then there was a whole woman section too. Harold was still in love with these Asian women—I believe they were Japanese—from around where he was stationed. But I had never met a man in love this way, this very meticulous strange way. One of the women had her legs open, and Harold had pasted a straw flat on the photograph running off the picture to the margin and a small photo of his own face. The straw went from her private parts into his very mouth. He had written *More, More, More!* in the margin. I had seen a few pictures of naked women, but this one drew me back again and again, especially when Harold was out of the room, because I had never seen a woman so seriously and happily showing herself. A dark riot of nerves came over me when I saw her face, so agreeable to the camera. Harold was a very thin man with white hairy forearms, just weak sticks, and narrow in the chest, also hairy above his shirt opening. It must have been a time when American GIs were overwhelmingly popular over there. Harold did not seem like a man who could support this weird Asiatic "love," yet there were other women—none of them whores, he pointed out—who had loved him, and were also photographed coiled around Harold. Some were full naked or not, and some were playing with each other, happy. Their eyes were all for Harold, who gleamed brightly into the camera, younger and more prosperous than now, a bitter student on the GI Bill.

Harold was a smoker of those short cork-tipped but unfiltered Kools. He wore black hightop sneakers, decades before they were necessary, with irony, for artistics everywhere. The startling denominator in Harold was that he was capable of great passions high and low. I saw him stare at the woman on the street below his place, an abandoned woman I found out later, who walked the bricks smoking a long cigarette in a holder. I've never seen so much smoke come out of a person. She would walk slowly along in the regular fog of a ghostly cinema, staring ruefully at the brick streets. She was the daughter of a town scion, a remarkable chemistry prof who was also the mayor, and lived with him on the other side of the block. But her lot was lonesome and bereft. She was one of those women who'd had a single lifetime catastrophe and never recovered, beautiful for the tragedies of T. Williams but now almost unheard of, when everybody joins something and gets well.

"She needs me," Harold spoke, watching her with deep concern. "That woman needs my love, and here I am selfishly withholding it from her." But Harold, I thought, she's the *mother* of one of my classmates — she's very, very old. Harold went on condemning himself for not stepping out to the curb and offering his "love" to her. Her son, my elder contemporary, was a person of almost toxic brilliance, scowling and reviling any collection of people in every room I ever saw him in. Another friend later explained that the woman died of a heart attack in that same house, with her son, then an M.D., attending. Or rather, more just technically witnessing, as my friend had it, using chilly terms like *infarction* and *fibrillate*. Then she was gone — *bam,* he had said, as he struck his palm with a fist. I saw the wide and high Victorian house as a place of almost epic coldness, a hint of sulphur in the rooms. Harold stayed at the sill, hanging in the window between thought and act, the shadow on a film always in my head, like a ghost on a negative.

Harold found most learning at the college "morbid" and would declaim hotly how desperately much he did not want to know zoology, Old Testament and history. But he was here exploring the "possibles and necessaries," vaguely of the arts, "doomed to Southern history." "Oh God, yes I must *read* it, the obituaries of everybody I despise." He had a personal contempt for anybody who had ever made a public dent in anything. Fame and battles bored him — all species of dementia. Harold despised so much, you felt very lucky for his friendship. What he liked best were small, troubled people. His passion for the Asian women seemed conditional, almost, on the enormous trouble they had known. Harold attended every play, concert, reading, art opening, and recital at the college and in the adjoin-

ing capital city, and found almost everything "unbearably poignant."
He was all for the arts, the more obscure the better. His friends, besides me and two other pals with their "maturity of vision," he'd call
it, were all girls of forlorn mark. Too fat, too nervous, too skinny, too
scattered for talk in this world's language. These he would play bridge
with in the college grill. If your back was to them and you didn't
know, you'd have thought they were all girls. Harold loved low gossip and considered scandal the only evidence of true existence on this
morbid plain. His voice would go girlish too, more girlish sometimes
than that frequent effeminacy you heard from mama- and maid-
raised boys. The college was a harbor for great sissies. You'd turn
around and see all the hair on his pale, skinny arms and think, well
golly, that's Harold, old veteran Harold. The full Harold to me,
though, would be him looking down at that abandoned wife, on the
old brick street, afternoon after afternoon, hating himself for all his
"wretched hesitations," saying she needed him, and that he was a cad
not to "venture unto her, take her hand." Wretched hesitation,
Harold said, is what embalms our lives, and that was what age demanded of you more and more, to get less and less life. But he was
passionately involved in all the troubles of the odd girls he escorted to
the grill, and they had a clique around him. It never occurred to me
that Harold was sleeping with them, but an older guy much later told
me that most assuredly he was. I could think of Harold then, a
teacher of history, with another album of his women, and I could see
these troubled girls, naked and happy — Harold's harem, holding out
against this "morbid waterless plain," as he called the environs.

A few scandals at the college made Harold beam and emerge from
his habitual state, which was, I think I can say, a kind of expectant
gloom. A luster came on him when it was clear the speech and drama
teacher — who had kept one of his male protégés, a prominent sissy,
in lust bondage — had gone down to scandal, and packed up, leaving
in the night. Harold's pale hairy arms flailed out and back, delighted,
up to the neck in it. "Oh, the truth and beauty of a wrecked life,
nothing touches it!" he went, imagining the moment-by-moment ex-
cruciations of the discovered pederast. The drama master, driving
lonely and flushed in his car back to North Carolina. Then there was
the milder, but somehow more "evocative" disclosure regarding the
tall Ichabodish French teacher, a curiously removed (how! they
learned) man, who drove a giant old blue Cadillac that seemed even
larger than Detroit intended. This timid man oozed about in something between a hearse and a cigarette boat. His exposure came

about when his landlord opened his rooms one holiday. Everywhere in the room were Kleenexes and castaway plastic bags from the cleaners. He would touch nothing in the room without a Kleenex. He had his socks and underwear dry cleaned, and wore them straight from the bags. Unused clothes were stacked in their bags in the corner. Kleenex was all over the bedsheets. He could not touch the telephone, doorknob, faucet, or even his own toothbrush without them. Kleenex boxes towered in all nooks and closets. In his diary, there was a last sobbing entry: "Night and day, I detect moistures around my body. Must act." He was, this French prof, comprehensively germophobic, and the strange order of his disorder howled from the room. Probably this was not even a scandal, but in this small Baptist town with the landlord so loud about it, the professor too was reduced, and soon prowled away in shame. Harold relished this. The perfection of it almost silenced him, a silly eye-shut dream on his face. "The perfection, the perfection, of this." Every worthy life would have a scandal, Harold said. There was a central public catastrophe in the life of every person of value. The dead sheep, the masses, who lived fearful of scandal (though feeding off it in nasty little ecstasies) were their own death verdict. "Prepare, prepare, little man, for your own explosion," he told me sincerely. "I am trying to be worth a scandal myself." Oscar Wilde enchanted him, and Fatty Arbuckle, but not Mae West, who had worn scandal like a gown and made a teasing whole career of it.

I once was sent over to the college by my English teacher to pick up a tape recorder, and was making as long a trip out of it as I could, when I passed a class and saw Harold in the back row, looking down at his desk in silent rage, not as if baffled but as if understanding too much, and personally offended. But this was less noticeable than what he wore. I had simply caught him out of his house in the act of being Harold, gritting his teeth, twirling his pencil, hissing. He had on an old-fashioned ribbed undershirt, some floppy gray-green pants, and some sort of executive shoes, I think banker's wingtips, with white tube workman's socks. His hair curled out everywhere from his pale skin. At this college they were stern on dress code. But they left Harold alone, I saw. He did look piercing and untouchable, his Korean near-veteranship a class of its own. They did love the Christian soldier, which he was not, but he had absolute freedom nonetheless as a lance corporal of Section 8. I was very happy for him. He had real dignity in his undershirt of the kind big-city Italians and serious white trash wore. The best thing was that he was unconscious of being out of line at all. It was hard to imagine Harold charging in the vanguard, or even hiding in a frozen hole, against the Communists in Korea, with his ascetic thinness, his hairy arms and chest, thrown against some garlicky horde and their bugles. Harold was not a coward, I'm sure, but I saw another thing suddenly about him, this partisan of Wilde and Errol Flynn: Harold was maybe doomed to no scandal of his own at all. He was too open, too egregious (a word I assure you I didn't know then) to have one, especially there in his undershirt in the fifties. But he wanted one so badly, and one for all his friends like me. He fed wistfully on the few scraps thrown his way in our dull society.

When the symphony director and several doctors and lawyers were tracked down and filmed by city police in the old city auditorium — usually a venue for wrestling — preening in women's underwear and swapping spit, Harold howled "Impeccable!" He hoped, he wanted so, for them all to be driven to the city limits sign and hurled out in shame down a notch of high weeds, their red panties up between their white buttocks. An M.D. was exposed in a zealous ring of coprophiliacs, sharing photographs at parties centering on soiled diapers. "There is a god! God is red!" In Harold's senior year, here came a lawyer exposed for teen pornography, hauling girls over state lines. Again Harold trembled, but there was always a bit of sadness that he himself was not cut down and hauled off — he loved most the phrase "spirited away" — for some dreadful irredeemable disclosure.

Harold never worried himself about the life *after* scandal. He indicated that he was, in fact, carrying on lugubriously after a lurid bomb in his past (not *the* bomb, but a bomb), but I think he was playing me false, for the first time. He wanted it so much, and lived from one minor scandal to the next, but as I say, I never expected him to be blindsided by disclosure, after I saw him that day when I was seventeen. I got the sudden sense of Harold as finished, even though he was shy of thirty, too transparent and happy in his sins. He would never get the *scandale d'estime* he so wanted. I had even thought that Harold wanted badly to be gay — queer, we said then — but could not bring it off. He was a theater queer around me sometimes, but you knew he couldn't cross over the line, it wasn't made for him, or he for it.

Harold was one of the few around who knew about the existence of Samuel Beckett, and he hailed the man, perfectly ordered in his obliquity for Harold — an Irishman close to Joyce, veteran of the

French underground, who lived in Paris, wrote in French, and had absolutely no hope. Drama couldn't get any better than *Waiting for Godot,* whose French title he would call out now and then like a charm, appropriate to nothing at hand I could see. Harold felt *Godot* was written in "direct spiritual telepathy" to veterans of Korea. He skipped nicely over the fact he never fought the war and I could agree that he was a telepathic cousin to them, because Harold was not, whatsoever, a phony. I was always struck by the fact he felt so sore and deep about particular people, and I felt dwarfish in my humanity, compared with him. Harold had seen *Godot* in Cambridge, and when it began playing in the South he drove his squat-rocket, mange-spotted ocher Studebaker far and wide to cities and college campuses to view it again. He would do the same for *West Side Story,* which he regarded as the highest achievement in musicals, ever. He saw the movie a number of times. Sometimes he'd take one or more of the odd girls with him, and once he asked me. He intended to drive all the way to Shreveport to see it again. He said I would see the kind of girl I wanted to marry in Natalie Wood and would hear the music of one of America's few uncontested geniuses, Leonard Bernstein. Then we would dip back to see a production of *Godot* in Baton Rouge, which, he warned, I was not really old enough for but needed because even a dunce could tell it was "necessary" for any sensate member of the twentieth century.

My mother was not enchanted. She was not happy about my trip with Harold, and much unhappier when she saw him, balding and with one of those cork-tipped Kools in the side of his mouth, behind the wheel of that car. I was a little embarrassed myself, because my folks put high stock in a nice car, and Mother was very sincere about appearances. I had told her Harold had ulcers, though I don't know how it came up. But when she said "He shouldn't smoke with those ulcers," I could tell she was much concerned by more than that. Neither was Harold throwing any charm her way. He never had the automatic smarm and gush in the kit of most Southern men at introduction. I knew he was too experienced for that, but Mother didn't like that he was a Korean near-vet, this old, just now going to college, and my friend. I waited for him to light up with just a bit of the rote charm, but he wouldn't. He looked bored and impatient, thinking probably she owed him thanks for taking this probationary brat off her hands for a weekend. I was conscious that she thought he might be queer, so I just told her outright he wasn't.

"Harold has *many* women," I said, picking up my bag. She looked at me more suspiciously than ever. I just piled in, we left, and I was unsettled five ways as this rolling mutant of the V-2 went off simpering with its weak engine. Harold said nothing to cheer me up. Then he finally spoke, across the bridge after Vicksburg.

"Your father's a very lucky man."

"You know him?"

"No, fool. Your mother's fine, A-plus fine. I'd die for her. A woman like that loved me, I'd cut off an arm."

Again, Harold seemed to be talking way beyond his years, and I believe now he must have thought of himself as extremely old. But it was the first time I realized my mother was a well-dressed, finely put together woman, and I began looking at her anew after that. Harold sat so wordlessly in silhouette in the car—I wondered if he was stunned and *putting the make on her*. With my *mother*. What impeccable depravity, as he might have said.

I had a little dance combo at the high school. Harold had come to see us, and he bragged on my trumpet playing, many notes and very fast, but, unfortunately, no soul. Soul might come to me if I was patient, he said. It could happen to Southern boys, look at Elvis, and he went on to call Roy Orbison much better than Elvis. You must hear *that* voice, he said, but he failed to get it on the lousy scratching radio. What came in almost solid was a special kind of Studebaker music, mournful like somebody calling over another lost radio. He predicted men like that were going to make horns obsolete shortly, and Harold was dead right. By the time I finished college, nobody wanted to hear anything but guitar and voice. Even pianos were lucky to get a chip in here and there. I was destroyed by the absolute triumph of the greasers, the very class I and my cronies pointedly abhorred. Maybe there is no class hatred like the small towner with airs against unabashed white trash.

He was right about Natalie Wood. I had seen her once in *Rebel Without a Cause* but ignored her in favor of Dean. In *West Side Story*, though, as she was dancing and singing, and especially when she performed "Somewhere" amidst the gang horror of New York, I teared up and wanted her more than anything before in my life. She was *it,* tripled. Please wouldn't she wait until I got famous and rich, and got some more height? Harold stood there, forever, as the credits rolled at the end. He seemed to be memorizing the name of every member who'd even carried a mop in the studio. I was smitten, looking down at the floor I was so charged, and still riding on that New York music.

We went to Baton Rouge to sleep at a Holiday Inn—very new and seeming swankier then—but on the way down Harold said maybe he should tell me this was a Negro production of *Godot* we were going to the next night.

"You're kidding. This Beckett wrote for Negroes?"

"Grow up. He wrote for *man,* little man."

"Oh. Well, sure."

You would not believe how condescending and polite I was in that audience of Negroes in suits. The play was riveting and strange to me, and I thought maybe I was one of the few not getting it, just here and there a dose of sense. Nobody laughed, and I don't know at all about the quality of the production. But it was a quiet smiling scandal that we were here at all, and I was glad to hear Harold's earnest sighs now and again when a point of confusion and futility—I got that—was made. I felt very allied to the culture-hip scene. We were not going to put up with any racists once we were outside the theater either, me and my Negro friends, hearkening in our suits—goddammit, *let* there be trouble. Our very class and righteousness would blow them away.

Out in the foyer, digging the crowd with Harold, I felt very promoted in my suit and Ivy League haircut, only I wanted a goatee very badly. Harold had pulled off to a wall for a smoke. I also wanted to say something on the mark.

"Way out, very. But really, how many of them you think really got it, Hare?"

He was disgusted, eyes closed in smoke.

"You tit. You little tits go right from blind ignorance to cynicism, never feeling a damned thing."

"No, no, I feel. Miles Davis is my man."

I was rescued by the appearance of the first great public faggot I'd ever witnessed. This black thing, tall and skinny as a drum major, was leading a trio of admirers out of the auditorium, hands curling and thrown out from his chest, squealing like a mule on fire, and dressed in something mauve and body-fit with a red necktie on it.

I smiled across the way at Harold, who had distanced himself, checked the near-empty theater, and began doing the pantomime I had learned off Ray Wiley, a worldly child of the army base who claimed to have encountered many queers. I wet both forefingers, smoothed my eyebrows with them, and formed my mouth in an O with my lips covering the hole, then held my arms out as if in a flying tackle. We conceived of queers as sort of helpless roving linebackers apt to dive on you and bury their faces in your loins. Wiley told many happy stories about how these men were discovered in their act in army lounges and stomped senseless. You could also use burning naphtha to rout them.

"What in hell?" Harold hissed, flicking eyes around the precincts like a spy.

He came over and grabbed my arm very strongly for such a skinny creature. Harold wore a formless blue serge suit with a clip-on green tie on his flat collar like a salesman at a funeral. I don't believe he owned a button-down. He had on those heavy black executive shoes too. I noticed him red-eyed. He'd been crying quietly about *Godot.* Just as I'd wept tinnily for Natalie Wood.

"Behave, fool. You're not in your own pathetic little country. Something wonderful has happened here, and you're totally unmarked by it."

"No. I'm *marked,* Hare. Truly marked, I swear. It was all there, man, straight on."

"That and *Our Town* are the dramas of the century. Now you've seen both of them, thanks to me. What do you get from them? Zero. Out here queer-baiting. My God, you remind me of all those wry husbands dragged to the theater by their wives. Not a snowball's chance in hell."

"Look, man, I *got* something from it, all right? I only wish Natalie Wood was in it."

Harold had pushed too far and I went sullen, out to his hopelessly square car, which looked even more like the grounded rocket of a very confused small nation. I thought about how stern old Harold was a great hypocrite, really, him with his album and glue-on straw from mouth to girl. The Studebaker left the campus with its weak hissing. He wouldn't let it go.

"You're not even up to sophomoric yet, is your trouble, cat. Cats *know* things, they *sense* things. Young men like Elvis have left you light years behind."

I got a thicker skin of the sullen around me. Oh yeah? What about your Asian women, the trolls you cultivate now? I wanted to say. What great sense was in that? And, and. Harold did not wear his heart on his sleeve. He wore it on his forehead, throbbing away at you. I had a mother to scold me already, thank you.

"If you were worthy, I'd take you out for a drink, a liqueur. That's what your mother *expects* me to do, teach you to drink," he suddenly said, picking up on the very mother thought in my head, flicking me, chums again, on the suitsleeve. "I'm sorry for growling, cat. Really."

"Likoor? Liquor?"

On Harold's patient directions, the amused bartender at the Holiday Inn made us a sort of booze snow cone with crème de menthe. I guess I was so healthy and unpolluted, I felt it immediately, my first drink, or suck. I lit up like a pink sponge. All the world seemed at my feet, and I could barely stand the joy of *Godot*, Natalie Wood, and Harold in it at the same time. Even the city name, Baton Rouge, was vastly hip. Red stick, red stick. Very way out. Life was a long wonderful thing. It was so good you expected some official to show up and cancel it.

I tried to impress Harold with scandals I knew of myself, and told him about a shooting on a town square down south. A man had killed two policemen with a shotgun and gone home to threaten his own family, whereupon his oldest son ran him against a house with a truck and killed his own father with a .22, nine shots, the father yelling "Oh my God!" over and over. At the end, the son threw the pistol on the ground and said, "Daddy, why'd you make me do it? You knew I loved you."

"No, no. That's...just baroque misery. So beastly obvious. Nothing but low, mean, stunned feelings result. Nothing is left but the mourners. It's the province of our bard up at Oxford. Nobody throbs in shame, derided worldwide. Scandal *pierces,* is *poignant, piquant, resonant.* If I could reorder that sad thing they call a state fair...You see, scandal is obsession, essence! Instead of the freak show, I'd have the heroes of scandal caged up while folks filed by to review them."

"Review them? Then what?"

"Why, throw rotten fruit, eggs and excrement at them!" Harold gave that long girlish neigh that grabbed his throat after some of his insights, and too many heads turned in the Holiday Inn bar. He didn't care.

"Scandal is *delicious,* little man. All we are is obsession and pain. That is *all* humans are. And when these wild things go public, and are met with howls, they ring out the only honest history we have! They are *unbearable!* Magnificent! Wicked! You read where the pathetic object goes off to psychiatric care or some phony drinking hospital, or a dull jail, but that's only for the public, slamming the door shut on them. What they really are is raving on the heath, little man, in their honest unbearable humanity!"

So, in months afterwards, I tried to achieve soul, or stand in the path of it so it would come to me. And I thought deeply about what I could do, what I had, who I was, to possibly rave on the heath someday. I wanted very much a rare, perhaps even dark, thing with a woman — Natalie Wood or her cousin, after I'd sent New York Slim off begging. My imagination could do nothing else for me, otherwise.

Harold sort of faded at the little college. I got tired of him, and at midyear a real Korean vet appeared as a late student on campus. He was much *like* Harold, they said, and Harold was very annoyed at being somewhat displaced and duplicated. The other fellow went crackers in a motel over in Jackson one night. Harold was called over by a local pastor to help minister to him. He didn't like this role at all, although he did what he could. The man had true awful memories of Chosin Reservoir and was not poetic at all in his breakdown, also very real. Harold, you could tell, was fairly sorry to help him get back on his feet, and considered his insanity banal. I'd never seen Harold this ungenerous before, but I guess he was threatened by this man at the tiny college, where he used to hold forth among his desperate harem in the grill. He began giving "all of his entity" to a new large buxom girl with red cheeks who played clarinet in the orchestra, and I quit seeing much of him. He swore she was the one, an honest life's passion. He was glad the waiting was over. I saw them at the drugstore together once. Harold was even paler and thinner and a good deal shorter than the girl. Drained by love, I guess. She had big calves and a very long lap, and seemed completely conquered by him. He was soon to graduate and become a high school teacher in a town north in the state that I didn't think held much promise for scandal. He went off with no goodbye, the girl with him.

I just remembered that before he left I at last hit the mark on scandal for him, and he saw I was coming around.

"Okay, give me a worthy scandal, little man." I was taller than Harold.

"This way. General MacArthur is discovered hunching a sheep just minutes after his 'Old Soldiers Never Die, They Just Fade Away' speech to a grateful Congress."

"Finally. Perfect. Discovered by one of Truman's aides, some nervous square from Missouri."

The wild horsey shout.

• • •

My parents were much relieved, I detected, when Harold was finally away. The age, the dress, his bewildering pull, never set right for them, and my mother was disturbed when I told her he had found her attractive.

Now I was being a fine lad with my pal Horace, but not too fine, pulling out the bricks from the theater razement by honest sweat and toil, bored insane and almost to bed in Kosciusko. I looked down at the lobby desk from the balcony a long long time, but nobody came. It was just the old man sitting the night in the same chair, full speed ahead with his tangled stare, a silent movie of *Godot* even further gone into real life. Just to get a rise from him I spoke out the French title, like Harold loved to: "*In Attendant Godot!*" a little above normal speaking voice.

This worried the man, and he turned his head slowly around, then cocked it back at me, whose face denied anything had made a noise at all. He seemed very worried, even alarmed. Then for no good cause at all, I did my queer pantomime, slicking my eyebrows, running my tongue back and forth, my eyes big and avid, arms out as if to dive down on him. I was suddenly very angry at him for not being a woman. He was looking backward straight up at me. His arms began moving and a low rush of language I did not understand muttered from him.

I felt so good and healthy and showered, but I was using up all my potential here. My manhood was being sucked away by a dead town. My pal Horace opened the door of our room. He'd taken a nap to prepare himself for a real sleep in a minute, and gave a grogged palsy smile, feeling good too, with his body worked. I kept up the queer routine, which he always thought was a howl. He mimicked drop-kicking a homo in the groin. Horace was a bass player and quite a scholar, much better at books than I was. We passed much time mimicking the stone-dumb and depraved creatures of our state, especially the governor, who had recently suggested setting off large nuclear devices to blow open a canal way from the Tennessee River to Mobile.

"Come here. I want you to listen," he said.

"Listen?"

"Come here."

He took me to the window, which was open to the lukewarm Kosciusko evening, and told me not to look down, just listen.

At first I heard what I took to be just somebody mumbling on the sidewalk beneath us. Then a harmonica started up, very softly, lonely as a midnight highway dog. It was the blues, with no audience, for no money. For all my musical life, I'd never heard the blues erupt solitary and isolated like this. When the harmonica stopped, the voice went very high and strained in its grief—you couldn't really tell whether it was a man or a woman.

"Let's..."

"Don't look down," said Horace.

"What? Why not?"

"Let's don't find out who it is. You don't want to know, do you?"

I saw his point. Horace had a copy of *Swann's Way* on the bed beside where he was sleeping and he was deep.

Kosciusko was a better town than we thought, if it afforded this tune at ten in the night. Maybe it was a man just released from jail, or maybe a woman just off a bus somewhere. Horace was right on, it was best not to know the source of this eerie, moaning thing. You couldn't quite make out the words, but it had the blackstrap moan in it all right. The harmonica trailed in again, sweet and with a bit of terror in it. I grabbed the song. It was all mine. I heard something when the voice started and I could tell Horace had not caught it. *Buddy, could you spare a future? This can't be life.* Then it just stopped and did not come back, like something swallowed up in a storm drain. I didn't hear any steps going away. I looked over to shake my head, smiling, but Horace had already gone back to sleep.

I went out, closed the door, to see what more I could get from the balcony rail. Sometimes you see something that seems made for you, like a good fishing hole, and you won't leave it although the hours prove there's nothing there. The old man was still at his post, along with the gone tan carpet, the gone desk clerk, serried cubbyholes in a rack behind. But then, I could hardly believe it, feet in ladies' sandals appeared, and a stretch of nice tan leg, black short-cut hair in bangs with a few strands of gray in it, and I could not question: a black long-sleeve slightly unseasonal sweater, bosoms small but prominent, and like great lamps in this stag-dark tedium. It was New York Slim, about ten years older than I had guessed her. I was back to New York Slim, instantly unfaithful to Natalie Wood, Natalie was nothing, this woman and I already having had two years of history in the head, you can't deny old lovers. I couldn't see all her face, but from the cut to the profile you knew she was at least summer chicken going into fall maybe. She talked to the old man, but he did not rise like an Old South gent should. Then she came up the stairs and saw me, kept going but slower, and the age in her face wasn't too much—not quite in my mother's era — with the muscles in her face making lines that matched those in her legs, drawing tight in strands as she took the last two steps. She did not look of this place at all. Then she smiled but at the same time shook her head, as if she knew something about me besides the fact I was nothing but a boy and felt that very much as I looked into her eyes — what color? — and sensed deep events decades long. Also, she was easy here, maybe she lived here, because without checking in she opened the door two away from ours and went in. I was so happy and tormented I looked at the last of her foot going in the closing door many times over, gathered to the rail like a great sinner at the bar.

I checked quickly, very quietly, to see if Horace was still asleep. Ever since the music out on the street I knew something was being made for me, only me, unsharable. It might have been her singing, though already I knew it wasn't, no, but the singer could be an agent of telepathy as Harold believed in. Sure. The set of her was foreign here, I was certain of that. I had nothing to say. But Harold, now Harold would just go up to somebody and talk if he wanted to. With women he told me he just went right up and said I think we should be friends and probably sleep together, and it worked, he was right in with them. I went to her door and knocked, an enormous chill all over my body. It took a while. I thought I heard her say inside *not yet*. I knocked again. She opened the door barefooted with a bottle in her hand, a little clear one not for booze, and she was about to say something but I wasn't who she thought.

"I feel I ought to know you," I said. "You ring a bell."

"You don't know me. And I don't want to know anybody else now, especially not anybody decent and young." She took a pull on the bottle, and she seemed a little drunk.

"I'm not so decent as all that."

"He thinks you are a Communist. He forgot to say you're only a boy. Why'd you scare him?"

"That old man down there? I was just clearing my throat. Stretching."

"He said you had symbolic gestures."

"Oh. He's a sick one, you know."

"Yes he is. A very sick one."

"Could we just talk? We've been working bricks and it gets lonesome. We've been at it now a week."

She pulled from the bottle again and I could smell something familiar from it, not booze, something we'd had in the house. The label had microscopic print.

"Come in, oh Mister Communist Police. Arrest me if you must, but I will never break. I will never tell."

"I'm no Communist. Don't kid. Say, you've been living here."

"I doubt it," she said. Not only was she blurred in speech but the speech wasn't quite American. I knew it.

"I go away, I come back. I go away, I come back," she continued.

Besides some domestic things on the dresser, there was a bicycle raised on a jack to its axle. You could pedal and go nowhere. I pointed this out, asking if something was wrong with it. You never, also, saw a woman her age on a bike where I come from.

"I go nowhere on that one." Beside the bike were tall black laced boots, looking serious and military, but they seemed her size. She sat and slumped to one arm on the bed, pulling from the tiny bottle again.

"What's that?"

"Happy medicine for nervous bad women." I saw it was paregoric, the stuff prescribed on ice for nausea. I didn't know about the opium in it then.

"Your voice."

"Canadian. Quebec. World citizen. You all sound like the nickras down here. Who taught who to talk? This man I paid out of jail today down over Lexington, he hates the nickras too, but I ask him why does he talk like them then?"

"What was he in for?"

"Throwing things in the night. Fireworks."

"Disturbing the peace?"

"More keeping. Believes. Depends on what you believe. But dumb to get caught. More of the white trash. *Lumpen.*"

On the dresser were several long steely pins. I went over and picked one up. They were too long for hairdos. It was extremely sharp on the end.

"Medical," she said. "Look but don't touch, if you please. Acupuncture, for relief. Go ahead. The man out of jail didn't believe in them either."

I wondered if she was practicing some kind of voodoo surgery. Those signs you see along the road in the country, on the outskirts of town. SISTER GRACE, PALMS. You sometimes feel your blood go darker, and I was feeling it here, more excited than disapproving.

This world was fetched in fresh just for me, but I could never tell Horace. I was greedy for all her details. She was European, ageless, a brunette Marlene Dietrich with those long legs.

It was then I saw a Klan robe, a green rounded cross on the left breast, all white otherwise. It had a small ladies' hood, cut to fashion for her, or so it seemed. The closet door was half open and she didn't mind my seeing. It all was like stumbling into an alien person's attic. My people hated the Klan, and I did too, I thought. But there is an undeniable romance, maybe adventure, to hating a whole race of people: it had its sway. Recently in Bay St. Louis, I had left a beautiful girlfriend to go to New Orleans. I did not get much of anywhere with her, but she'd talked affectionately with me. As I was leaving, she said, truly caring for me, I thought, "Oh George, do watch out for the nigguhs in New Orleans. They're all loose and free over there and they'll just do anything." She had seemed lovely in her need to be protected from the dark hordes. I was taken very warmly by this problem, and went off like a knight of the streets, full of romantic charge, with something to prove. I'd been at the closet door overlong. The hanger next over held a great length of dog chain with bracelets at both ends. I supposed she wore this around her waist, like medieval women in the "Prince Valiant" comic strip.

When I turned to her, she could see my face was different, even though her eyes were blurred and she looked ready to sleep.

"I told you thas too bad. You're decent. I'm not, young boy."

"But not really—"

"Don't tell me. I know decent from the other look. I can sort them. You've got that decent polish on you. You are decent, and you will just go to sleep with fairy plums in your head, not like me."

"That's not a church choir gown. I know that. Still—"

"You have to go. Somebody is coming. You don't want to see him."

"The man from jail? What's he...It's late. Why's he coming?"

"Why to frig me, I'd imagine. Out of here, Tom Sawyer with your neckerchief. Put all those nice muscles to bed."

She was right that I didn't want to see the man. I closed the door with my head flaming, confused. But I was not disgusted. I wanted to save her. You could see she was too good for anybody around here. Forces were martialed against her.

I couldn't go into my room. I put my hand on the knob of the room next to hers. It was unlocked. The room inside was made up, unused. I crept in and waited, dark in my head, forcing myself toward love of her. Even the muscle lines in her face would go away if I loved her right.

I lay on the bed without moving a spring. Then I crept to check for a hole in the wall. There was none. But I edged up the window so as to listen around.

Not five minutes passed before there were steps on the stairs, very slow and dramatic, you knew it in the rickety floor. He went over the carpet and opened her door without saying anything. She knew him all too well. Nothing, not even muffled, came through then. I lay half sick waiting for sounds of protest and struggle, and when they failed to occur, I knew the drug was used to smother her will. Mute things were proceeding as in a film so bad I might have written it myself.

But through the window I heard the clink of, yes, it had to be that dog chain, and then soon with it, at first unaccountable, but there was no mistaking it, the whir of the bicycle being pumped and clanking just a little. This went on a long, severe time. Through the window this was quite clear. I was thinking of creeping out there, but then the man's voice said short things, low and anxious, while the bicycle kept up. It was moaning, pathetic, but fearful at the same time. At first I thought it was the woman. Only her voice, in a dismayed faint gasp was heard then, and this was unbearable. It seemed as though she was afraid that he would hit her. He moaned shortly again, but not in sex: it sounded like encouragement in another language. The whirring slowed, and I heard his big steps, the knocks going through the carpet in my room. I waited and waited, waiting for bedsprings and weeping, but I never heard them. The silence became deader than quiet, and then *Now here it is!* the man said very plainly. But there had passed an enormous amount of time. Only my head was racing, flushed, ahead of the seconds.

Then I heard nothing for so long I fell off asleep very deep into the night, close to dawn, I think. I woke when the light came in gray and went back to our room. I stared at the ceiling, and that day at the bricks, a moron's job, I was worthless. Horace wanted to know what had me all blown. We'd eaten in the hotel dining room, but we were the only ones there. He wanted to know what I was watching for, what was ailing. I kept going back to the hotel all day, telling him I had a bad stomach. I was really letting him down on the work. The old man still sat there, but once, for the first time, he was gone. I couldn't tell if anybody else was around. So I knocked on her door, worn out and shucking my labor.

She was having a nap and was fresher than last night, no blur to her, and in a homey wrap. She didn't mind at all I was there. I asked if I could get her anything. She said well indeed I could get her two Coca-Colas with ice. I was so fast at this, down to the dining room, troubling the one harried fat lady — though she was doing nothing else — and back, it had to be a record for service. She'd brushed her hair (I mattered, she cared) and her face was not so tired.

"I have the feeling you could use a friend, miss." I had rehearsed that all day.

She put her head down, then sat. I was sure she was crying. Her eyes blinked pink at the rims when she lifted up, and I was gone for her, out of my depth. The other Coke wasn't for me, though. She poured from a new paregoric bottle on the dresser into one glass and added Coke, storing the other one. Then she drank.

"Much better. It gets hard alone. This is a clean drink. All this is very clean. With your Tennessee whiskey it gets sloppy and all ragged. This is dry-cleaned magic. Not so bad."

"I guess the nerves never leave you."

"Never. I had a husband and you aren't like him at all. But it's the youth, the age we met, nearly the same. You get to me, neighbor. It's clean, the look. Washed and pure in the blood, that lucky color. I've had it." For the first time, she smiled. Her teeth were not that bad, a maturer gold was all. My dentist could brighten them right up.

"Tell me, George. Why did you yell *waiting* down to him last night? He thought you knew all about him. He was very disturbed."

"That old man." I was struck cold and wretched. "*Him?* You waited for *him* last night? I don't believe it."

Not only that but the man was her father-in-law, and French. Her husband had been killed with the French Legion at Dien Bien Phu in 1954. The Communists did it. The father had lived in Saigon, wanting to be close to his son with the war on. She was Canadian French, going to school there. It was ballroom and ballet dancing, her whole life, until the war went bad. She'd not been married very long when Edouard was killed. His father had lost twice now from the "other side." He had been Vichy, was imprisoned after the war, but got out still vocal against Communists and Jews. France was inhospitable to him, so he went to Indochina, and made much money in rubber and tires. After the death of her husband she was lost and absolutely poor. Her parents had left for Canada. She did not think of the old man at all. She began dancing naked in a special club, full of opium and not knowing whether she liked it or not. The old man came in with some friends, he too in awful despair. He did not know where she was, nor did he know it was "Baby Doll" — her husband's nickname for her — dancing. He watched her on the stage and she soothed his grief long before he knew who she was. He'd only seen her a few times. He went up to her afterwards, she in her silk cape and big shoes, stage-dancing whore shoes. They fell into each other weeping. But he was gone for her in no father-in-law way, and she had nothing. So he took her to Quebec where her parents guessed what was going on; she would not marry him nor did he seem to want it. Her parents told her to die in hell and never speak their name. The way he was about Communists and Jews and now *nickras,* the way he sent out very angry and offensive literature, got him shunned again but noticed by a visitor from the South in the States. There was much work to be done here after the *Brown* decision, integration, the last order breaking down in the last great power, and he would be most welcome down here, he and his money and organization. People were listening up. The public was for them, only the forms against. She did nothing but be his and run as a bagwoman here and there at a necessary point. She could not stand the trash at the Klan rallies, and she never wore the gown or hood outside the room. As for the *nickras,* they were fine primitives and she felt sorry for them; some of the men were beautiful with their smiles and shoulders, and they were happy until the Jews and Communists *ageetated theem.* She had never met a Jew, but the *Communeests,* without a god they both could not bear a healthy white race, it was an abomination to them, and they owned entertainment, much of government, bragging always about how smart they were because they did not have hearts. Or guts. I mustn't think too badly of the old man. Everything was wrong with him. Bowels, liver, arthritis, skin cancers, ulcers, psoriasis, piles. There was always a good room for her. This is the worst one she'd ever had. It was she I should think badly about. She was telling me all this because I was young, something was going to happen soon, and she had no church, nor any friends. Witness Albert, the father-in-law, he had all *theeeese tings eell* and he took no pain medicine, compared to weak her, Felice, who had nothing really wrong and did not do much but whore for her kin. He was so unhealthy it didn't take but once a month or so now. It took him that long to recover. It took him forever to . . . befit himself, a longer riding of the bicycle naked in the robe with the hood on, wearing the black boots, and racing with the skirt of it tied up, the chain from her wrist to his wrist on the bed, his face buried in half a watermelon, but peeping like a child at her pumping nether parts. She giggled. Something from his youth, she couldn't know. I was not a man yet and I shouldn't smile. One day odd things might overcome me in my despair, if I ever had despair. Sometimes she thought he was doing it to his own youth, or his son, or he and his son together, at the end long long long silence, his having got with her but demanding her to ride still until it was finished and he a dead ruin. It had crossed her mind he might die, and in ingratitude she had driven the bike faster and faster, hoping to bring on the classic champion's death to him, but she didn't know if his will was in order, she'd gotten that mean. But really there was a way of not even being there and responding that a man couldn't know. Women got married and lived their whole lives doing that, absent and wild and pleasing all at once.

She'd finished two Cokes and the blur was on again. At one point I thought she was breaking down and crying, but I cannot remember at what point. There was sweat on her forehead, and her lips moving, I could swear she'd become younger and younger as her cheeks stretched, then got older at the end, the paregoric driving a hotter, duller black to her eyes.

"I need a bath. Sometimes seven or eight a day," she said dully. "Don't forget to be my friend, boy. I think I've done something to your youth. You don't look so decent now." She waved for me to go.

This had taken a long while, and when I went by the room, Horace was in it, asking what in hell was going on, the day was done.

I told him a person down the way had some medicine for me and that we had chatted while I got better.

At breakfast the next day, Horace and I were still the only ones in the dining room, and feeling obliged for detaining the help, I claimed stomach distress that was not completely a lie. I was too excited and too heavy in her story, like a walking boy museum, hebephrenic and bitten at the scalp and loins. I was up the stairs before I realized I had passed the old man, who was back in the chair, with a black suit on. I knocked and she met me in the door on her way out. She drew me in and shut the door.

"He's down there, isn't he?"

"Yes," I said, all nerves.

"Albert is very jealous. You have to watch it. It's the worst thing about him. We're going out to see my dog in the country. A man gave me a weimaraner dog, a real lovey. When Albert gets bad he threatens to kill it."

"No. He's a monster."

"In jealousy, yes."

She was dressed in an innocent-looking country outfit, printed skirt and baby blue blouse. The little bow in her hair turned my heart around. Next she put on a raincoat I thought marked for French espionage. I was simply riveted to my stuttering place in awe.

"Visit me when you can, but be careful. Tonight he's away."

"Oh yes. I'm your friend. I'm hanging tough."

That afternoon I worked twice as hard, owing it to Horace from yesterday. I was in the bricks so smoothly I might have been made for them. The sweat was pouring off me. I stood up and untied the kerchief to swab off. Horace was looking across the street.

"That old man, he's watching you."

He stood in front of the Baptist church across the road, hat in hand, and not looking at me as meanly as I had expected. He was standing just in front of the bricked marquee, with its message or sermon of the week: JESUS WEPT. COME AND GATHER. He was simply studying me mildly, almost kind in his face of red spots and raked-down short gray hair. He was younger too, up and about on the pavements, the chair a whole other life dismissed with some strength. I mopped through to my eyes and peeked. *His face buried in half a watermelon but peeking every now and then,* I thought. My shirt was off and I felt small, a grimy peon.

"I believe he's looking at your mighty build," said Horace. "Must be the village queer. Let's set him on fire."

It is quite mature, I thought, to know everything and say nothing. I had not practiced this much in my life, and felt myself almost plump with rough wisdom, as the old man walked on.

I told Horace I was not wanting any supper that night, stomach knotted and butterflied. But I was her prized friend, heavy on the aftershave, the shave itself a ludicrous solemn wipe of the blade through foam. He went down to the John Birch diner with his *Swann's Way* in hand, to give the shiftless owner more grief.

She was not right. Something had happened. There were five new bottles of paregoric on the dresser next to the long needles, the brush and the hand mirror. She stared at me with her mouth pinched and her eyes wary with fear and sadness. What is it? I wanted to know. You can tell me, in my last clean shirt, a blue one to match her blouse, telepathy.

"He took me to the field, the fence, and the dog was not there anymore. But he wanted me to look at the vacant field where it had been, I know it. The man in the house wasn't our friend anymore, either, Albert told me, angry. He was a busybody, a turncoat, maybe a fellow traveler or a Jew."

"You think he killed them both?"

"I don't know. We go on a while and then there's always some kind of rage or treachery."

"Why don't I take that Klan outfit and shove it up his ass for him?"

"No," she said quickly, head swung up to glare and then dissolve, back into her bewildered tortured beauty.

"But you have no real home and an awful life. I could get money. My father is well off. By the end of this week I'll have two hundred."

"Very, very sweet. Hand me my dream bottle."

I did, and went and fetched her two Cokes, lightning across the face of the piggish, unknowing woman alone in the dining room.

"You're Peter Pan," she smiled. "I think you remind Albert of his son."

"Your husband."

"He wasn't so much older when we met. He liked my legs, even my poverty."

"So do I, Felice." It was rich and almost too heavy on my tongue.

"All I can do is drag youth down to indecentness."

"No. You care. You're in a trap. There's a whole other world. There's movies, and music, and poems, and fishing in a private place with cypresses in the water. You with me. You can't tell. Time—"

"Oh, please shut up. I told you I didn't need to know anybody else. I'm just sailing along the current in the rain gutter, a piece of nothing, nobody can touch me without drowning."

I thought that was the most beautiful thing I'd ever heard.

I was just on the edge of breaking into song with that great anthem of blind Christian affirmation of the fifties, "I Believe." All jazz, Beatism, cattism had fallen away. By God, I was in Harold's world, women with troubles, a spell of swooning charity on me.

"You've forgotten I'm your friend," I told her.

"Well, that's something. To know you're not alone. A part of me must have that."

I knew she was about to say a thing so sincere and poignant, from that bleak experienced face of hers, that it would be a sign for our parting, and she did.

"Even in hell the real part of me can carry that young face of you with me, friend George."

I left the room all moist and on the verge of going ugly in the face with sorrow and joy.

I was wanting to be a broader man when next we met, so I picked up Horace's Proust and began reading it that night while he went down to the bus station to see if the magazines had changed. The great champion of sensitivity and time, in his cork-lined room, allergic to noise, claimed my pal. This thicket of nerves I could not broach, however, most likely because I had my own, clawing over the pages in competition. But it was still of great use in the room, because it was French, I thought as I tossed it away.

Horace came in with a great smile. I was on the bed dreaming high and valiant stuff. He looked behind him down the hall.

"Well, *somebody's* having a good time here. Did you know there was a *woman* down the way? And she must be *all* woman. They hadn't shut the transom. She couldn't get enough from some guy. Oh Bertie, Bertie, deeper, deeper!" I changed from the smile of my good dreams to a face that must have been stone fury.

"You couldn't have heard that. That's from a dirty comic book."

"I tell you. And get this, what she was moaning when I left: *Churn butter churn! churn butter churn!* Old Bertie whamming away."

He couldn't have made this up.

"Your kind go from blind ignorance straight to cynicism. You don't feel, you don't know."

"Hey, George, you quoting Marcel? I'm not cynical at all. She was having a hell of a time."

Her language, an image from French dairy cow country — my good horror. How could this thing be? Albert was using the dog against her. He was forcing the paregoric down her, making her sick and blabbering.

"Now, man. You ought to see your face. What's eating you?"

Horace was tall, too wise, knowing nothing. I hated him.

I couldn't go see her that night. It was a bitter, bitter evening. Horace wanted to go down to the lobby and lie in wait so we could check out the woman when she came by. I told him that was a horrible sophomoric idea. Why? he asked, getting fed up with me. He said we might have found a lady with a profession here. He was ready to do a Chinese dwarf.

"Let's leave it like the harmonica player," I said, stonily.

"That isn't the same at all."

"Leave it."

"You don't tell me, all right? you're not the duke of Kosciusko."

He went down and I was happy he came back without seeing her.

The next morning was Sunday. Horace called himself a freethinking Baptist. He'd brought a suit and he went out to that church down the way. I was apostate, but very glad he wasn't. I checked the rail, being stealthy. That bastard Albert was in the chair, staring tiredly, having forced her twice this week. I was praying for an artery to snap in his face and vowed direct revenge if it didn't. The man must be stomped and dragged off in a net. I could see venom popped up in his cheeks, spotting them red.

"Hey you," I called, not very loud.

He twisted his head back, trying to find me.

"En Attendant Godot? En Attendant?"

He got up, shaken, and I watched the top of his head, gray hair brushed forward Roman, leave for the street.

When I knocked on the door and waited, I heard something clink inside. She came to the door in nothing but a housewrap, wet from the bath.

"Friend George." Her eyes were very dull. She was on the stuff, her conscience awful.

When I went in she'd already gone back to the tub. I sat on the bed and heard her stir the water. Then I heard the clink again. For the longest time she said nothing.

"You ought to watch your transom. My friend heard you really having a good time last night."

There was no reply at all.

"I thought wrong. You don't need a friend so much as ... somebody to betray."

Nothing. You heard water sounds, just a little.

I studied the bed and carpet and dresser — all she had and was, as far as I knew. A hotel was a stupid and desperate place to live, I suddenly thought. And rotation from one to another, having her bicycle and robe and boots and chain everywhere, up the stairs dutifully with them again and again, setting up like carnival gypsies except with less dignity and no good at all even to yokels with a quarter. But I was being unfair to her, and caught myself up again. Because I cherished her, nothing could budge me.

"I so need a friend now. It's the end of things," she said in a little, faint voice. "Come in here and sit. There's a curtain between us. Oh!" I thought she gasped and I hurried in, face blushing and dying to help. The curtain was closed, all right, the brown shadow of her behind it sitting in the water. "Oh!" I thought she said again.

Around the front gathered edge of the curtain near the faucets the dog chain lay out on the floor with one of its bracelets open, the rest of the chain in the tub with Felice.

"Put it on your wrist, my pal," she said tinnily, almost sighing it.

So I did and snapped it on. I would be a gypsy too. I'd be the panting boy in the wings, waiting until her act was over and the others had had their fill of her. Until we made our move. This charity and long-suffering had never even nearly come near me before. *I'm just sailing along the current in the rain gutter, a piece of nothing, nobody can touch me without drowning.* The steel of the cuff was very serious and required a key for release, I noticed.

"You will be with me down down down oh! There's a way to do it in the liver they said brings it there quick but oh! no no no." This was all so faint and not recollected until a long while afterwards.

"Felice! Are you okay? I'm buckled on the chain with you."

"Something's not right, and I've used the last one." Her voice was faint, dimming like a small girl going to sleep, her breath wet on the pillow.

"Everything will be all right. Everything. I know you're under horrible pressure. I'm reading Proust, drawing closer to your world. The *French* Proust."

There would be no way for me not to view a lot of her with the chain binding us, I reckoned. This would be an unearthly familiarity. The die would be cast. The new world would begin right then, and I felt actual waves of a kind of happy nausea.

"Oh oh oh oh ohh! Not right."

This voice did not rise in friendship or passion. She was very sick and I knew something was wrong, unpretended and real.

"I'm not dying the right way, George."

I got up, thinking, and pulled the chain to the door. I couldn't look at what I wanted without pulling her a little, with a splash from the tub. I finally had my eyes just past the jamb and looked on the dresser. The paregoric bottles were there, three empty, but where the long acupuncture needles always were was empty space. It was too catastrophic a thing to even consider, but I knew she had them.

"Felice, I'm opening the curtain!"

She was lying over with her head forward, drugged, on the shower plunger between the faucets. Her hands were down on her stomach. The tub water was pink around it with three streams of blood. She'd pushed them in the right side where the liver was, I found out. *Ori-*

ental, Oriental, I remember thinking over and over, trying to call the dread something.

I got in the tub with her and lifted her. You think you are one muscled champion until you try to lift a wet naked woman dead-haul. It can barely be done, and I thought she was already dead, so that in this fear I finally did it and we both fell over together, confused in the chain, off the tiles into the carpet of the room. My nose was flat in it and it smelled like the dusty feet of a horde. She was whimpering. When I saw the head of the needles, puffed out with blue and darker skin, with a near-black blood dripping out like spread fingers, I almost went under.

I looked for a phone, but we had no phone in these rooms. Her legs began moving although her face looked dead. I drew up and whirled my head around looking. I reached the robe on the hanger and dragged it off, then threw it over her and put my arms under hers, tugging and pleading with her.

With as much ease as I could I got her out on the stoop and she began walking a little, saying *oh oh oh*. We went down the stairs very slowly. When we got toward the bottom, I raised up and there Albert was staring at us from his black suit, his eyes seeming beyond a known emotion. I gasped at him to phone help, she was dying. Some others behind Albert stood there, but I barely noticed even their shoes. I settled her on the last stair then sat myself, unwrapping the chain around us both and getting some free length to my wrist. Then I saw she was revealed and I pulled the robe together on her.

She had a great deal of blood in her lap and on the side of the robe, up level with the circled cross of the Klan.

"This is *my* affair," said Albert. "Let her go."

"It is *not*. I'm with her now. Can't you see? *I'm* her future now!"

"No you ain't, son," said my father, who'd come up with Horace, the both of them in suits.

He'd come up to bring us some treats from Mother and had intercepted Horace coming in from church. My father had a cigarette in his mouth, but it had almost fallen out of his sidelips and hung there while he stared with an open mouth at the bloody woman in the Klan robe. He looked so damned distinguished and in charge I felt dimmed out and pushed back to about age ten, staring at the handcuff of the dog chain on my wrist. Horace was holding the sack of goodies and seemed exactly the son he deserved.

. . .

I didn't see Harold again until almost twenty years later. I was in a very bad band playing at cocktail hour for peanuts and for a convention of educators in San Antonio, Texas. I had been fired from my regular job for drinking, and before that I had been jailed and nuthoused for setting fire to my estranged wife's lawn, which blew up her lawnmower. In the band I was desperate and would have been throbbing in shame but I was still drunk enough to ignore it and was majoring on the theme Whim of Fortune, and I believe trying to attach myself to a woman of such low estate that the two of us would destroy ourselves in spontaneous combustion at an impossible diving speed. But I had clarity enough to see Harold walk out of the milling pack of cocktailers in the ballroom and come right up to the bandstand, natty in a good slim blazer, and stare at me with an even brotherly smile.

He had heard about my troubles, and commiserated, seeming the picture of sobriety and successful wisdom to me. His hair was all gray, but his posture had improved, and his baldness was distinguished, even at the ears all around. Something terribly healthy was going on in his life and I envied him. I hadn't felt decent in three years.

"Oh, no. I'm *not* nice, my friend, not at all. I'm just *ordinary* as potatoes."

"Aw Harold. I doubt it."

"That was the last gasp of riot, in school when you knew me. That was the whole wad."

"You didn't reach your juicy scandal, the great one?"

"Never. My head simply turned around and I got old. I just wasn't even looking that way anymore. All I had was divorce — very usual — and my memories. It's like I knew you'd be here. C'mon up to the room. I'll show you something. Pathetic, and I can't leave it alone."

"Telepathy, Harold. Remember?"

I dragged my horn case along with him to the elevator. Harold began attacking the stupefying hopelessness of his students. I had grown enough to know only a good teacher could assault them this meticulously, and that he adored them. He was reading a paper on mild innovations in the classroom here at the convention. Many of his students had won national honors. He was still at the same obscure little school.

In the room he pulled out his albums — the one with the Asian women, and then another one with photographs of all his college girls in total surrender, bare, and all of them very happy about it, Harold beaming among them. The effect was more of an arcane archeological find where a race of drab and ungainly women were frozen in postures of ritual fulfillment. How could he get them to be so glad about it, *all* of them? I wondered. Only the last album was very sexy. There were pictures of that big woman he married, from clothed to very unclothed, to inside her, many angles. In these the woman seemed cruel and proud, with threatening smiles, dominating the photographer himself, and triumphant in a near-fascist way.

"See, I'm not nice. I've got to keep them. Look again, caress them."

Given the times, none of this was very scandalous, and you had to reimagine the fifties to get very disturbed. They were curios, and Harold did seem pathetic, hanging on to them, and having them along to assist his biography, which nobody was ever going to write.

"I'm a sad old man," he smiled.

"I had a great scandal, I think," I told him.

"Well. Word gets around. It must have been rough."

I stared at him. It must have been blankly.

"Not those. Those are nothing. Those were mere absolutely typical drunkenness, right on schedule," I at last admitted to somebody.

Then I tried, and failed, with boorish pauses and needless lies, to tell him about Felice.

She lived, but just barely. All three needles had found the liver, and others had died with a third of the same wounds. I understand she was yellow and even black all over for weeks. A newsman called our home. I had been identified as "a youth" in their local small paper. My father took the call and politely told him that I really had nothing further to add and was trying to get on with my life. The newsman himself was very understanding and polite. My father wasn't, not to me. He had a name in town. Above all things, he despised scandal.

My love for Felice went on belligerently, sullenly, for a month. It was all I had that was undiscussable and untouchable, and it pulled me through, wondering about her and the difference I might have made in her life. I would see her in other hotels, and there she behaved much like a nun of the old tales, looking out a drab window with a bar of light on her face, and you saw a tear under her eye for remembrance of wholesome youth and true love and what could have been. I tried to rave on the heath but was too conscious of the real fact that I was just bawling like a brat.

"But Harold, Harold!" I took the sleeve of his blazer, shaking it. "I was real then. I throbbed, buddy. I did throb."

Harold was stunned.

"That woman got *you*. But she needed *me*," he said.

Death of a Bitch

I'LL COME OVER and do nothing. Watch her, be near, read parts of the paper to her at most, cook an egg, help her bid farewell to it all by reminding her of the dreary repetition of it: putting on, taking off clothes, brushing teeth, feedings, throwing out the newspaper, rotation of governors, death of salesmen, birth of a fresh new fanatic, mid-life of a rector, early mornings at the animal shelter. See, all that, I'd whisper, one was in it only a few hours in the first place. You go out, still, she'd say. You go out there, into others, between others, looking around, up, down, with hope. But I've cut down my rounds, I explained. Why now only a hundred and forty beers a week fill the ticket, I've got nothing of the midnight prowl left in me.

As was hers to nag, complain, whine, attack — what was it a bitch wanted? — to empower herself over and over as if just knocked off a stage, but waddling back, holding the broken ankle, the swollen foot, hand-, arm-crawling back up the stairs, worming across the crusty boards under the proscenium, until finally at center stage again, occupied by some ghost of hers or an actual other sputtering bitch or fiend, shrieking this thing down again, settling into the old place, empowered again for a few seconds, straightening her lips, tongue around the dry scar of them, at it again: "furthermore!" Your bona fide bitch has always just been in some accident where some designed order was lost: *order's* what a bitch wants, her in the nesty warmth of her regular place, where her carping gets milder and more humorous.

Well, off to see ancient Mookie and Spot and the others a while, I'll say. What do you get from them? she wants to know, just sighs left to her now, exhalation trying to deny the catarrh, as they used to call it; heart, liver and lungs have agreed not to support anymore that old blistered rut of her throat where the words want to run out, having hell with generations backward and forward. Your bitch is most godly, you will find, it's God they delude unto themselves, filling up the absence of God most malingering, they must take his

{ 227 }

place, and get their due of eager self-worship from him most, almost, dead, *someone* must be in charge, every bitch needs but prevents her throng of worshipers at the same time, just like your god, cunt with barbed wire round it.

True, Mookie or Spot aren't of much interest, I lie, but they're always there in the tavern, my world. I'll be sure and bring any news of the tavern. Piece of killer gossip passed by the other day but I don't remember it. I'll try and come back with a good piece for your lash, dear, but let's not think I'm obligated, nope. I may have married you once, who knows?, but please you can't believe there's anything left of that paper after this century of yarbing you've provided our grim chambers, dear, that certificate was beaten back into trees long ago, wooden around this heart. Yes the whine and mope of narcissism, mrs. jehovahness, Christ do I hate you, but so long anyway, may you rust.

In the tavern Mookie, Spot, the young boy tending, everything right, no fresh sub-bitch, young, lubricating into a major one by midnight on your far stool, just the guys, the males, the boys, though over the centuries your body turns into a sort of sick woman, just an exit maze for beer, a talking ranch gone bankrupt, depression dust whipping down the holes, nothing left to repossess, only old memories humping each other come night, snakes hauling dried bellies toward a spot of cool, no warm chick to dream of now going on months.

Other purposely lonely men come in scratching the last night from themselves, athletes well done, wreckage of the body attesting to what might have been life. Why would they wear cowboy boots, never a horse or cow in their lives, a space age from Texas, but country memories like their chromosomes putting on those boots every morning. They are helpless, and haven't got much to do with it. Even hats, but this would what? keep the barlight off their scalp, or maybe one has lifted a log for a dollar just now breathing the sigh of honest labor felt necessary before twenty beers.

It's Mookie I'm keeping my eye on, betting on him. The songs and the television for Mookie are for reasons of argument, he's a player still, he'd not given up, always aiming for what's right. He is elaborately, like searching for holy grails, saving what is right, what is straight on the beam. I have been Mookie but given up. Mookie's older but still has the stuff, maybe the fear after all the damage his brain, his memory, his logic, his cerebration have suffered, but he heaves it around constantly all the time to deny, to exercise it, the way older guys in a gym I suppose are more driven by their exercises. Mookie would try to hold up a boy's fresh muscular brain despite the assault of the long foe on it as he drinks another, and he still likes his stuff hard. He too, thank God, in his head if he's like me, is all lost to women, barely thinking of them anymore, just a flash of percolation when the muscle girls do their training on the television in the morning, but nothing serious, no journey to that thrashing womb would be worth it, think of the lost vodka-and-Seven time, the loss of insight when that one dusty long hand on the clock face clicks forward three minutes. They've got our special drinkers' clock hired for us, a lovely thing, none of your slow invisible attrition built for sissies. Why Mookie's the son of a college president reduced by scandal, one of your good old-fashioned scandals that took down the whole family, even great-nephews, to their ruin. He's still got it.

See, I was right, after all, he'd tell Spot, jubilant but not gloating, this could be days and days of research and footnoting back to back although documents are not allowed, only the majority attestation of a crowd. I sometimes think Spot was hired to always be wrong or half right, that's the nature of their friendship, Spot disremembering a song or a singer or a television star's second marriage, or a rule in Iowa eight-ball. Mookie would never concede, he would go on and on, and true, he was almost never ever wrong. The year of a new beer ad and the point in a most hideous death of some comedian in the fifties. "See there, see there, I was *right,* after all." I liked the way, however, there was no brag, his drunkenness did not erupt in the swaggering boast, the thing that was right most patricianly was announced in modesty, just a sweet glow in Mookie's eyes, almost a light across his smooth brow so lately writhen. Humility was his middle name. They say he got it from his pop, he was never ever an "I told you so" man, as far from gloating as from Venus.

That day, after months in witness to his skills of memory, I took my fate in the tavern in my hands. Why he could roam in arts, sciences, athletics, finance, this stuff was just a pip in his head, a university under wraps, never even brought out to humiliate others or scorn. The tavern had its rules, a certain sternness. Let me illustrate the case of Ben, now gone with cancer of the esophagus, who was a stricken man, a poor helpless homo. He once messed with a black boy in the restroom and the tender found out about it and told Ben he could never come back in here again, but Ben telephoned after two days, weeping, saying he couldn't stand it, this was his only Society, this was his whole World, so they let him back on condition he sit on that one stool at the east end of the bar and never ever bother anybody again. So Ben was back, and right off said he wished he was Mookie's father and Spot's brother. Ben was Mookie's great admirer. Why that day I took my fate, etc., I can't explain, except I wanted to take something home to the bitch after all. I must have hit some odd hops or malt in the brew as I was feeling sentimental. Mookie, I said, why is it that *good* to be right? Weren't entire successful happy lives led by those in the wrong? Did it matter if there was a permanent system of right? Where was your deeper lifetime import in constant rightness?

Mookie may have gotten a little angry, as Spot fell out hoping with me, I believe, on my side. Why it's all we've got of salvation, fool, Mookie said. You let in sloppiness and sloth on points of fact and where are you? It is your Empire State Building, your Chinese Wall, your Underwater Diving Bell. And he turned, supremely annoyed as I've never seen him.

I come back to the house, the bed, where she's so little and brittle and swollen and yellow she's not even the boss of the bed anymore. She says, ninetieth time, You know I got cirrhosis in sympathy with you, you know I never drank much. But I didn't catch it, dear, says I. It passed over to me, I took it for you, like a chihuahua taking off a person's asthma. Yes, dear, but then I told her about Mookie. What he had said.

Oh, he's got problems, problems, that old pedant, he never got out to see what's real, and he's not been a thing since the scandal of his father, I remember him pitifully. Getting out, he would've seen it is never what's right but the style of what *is*, the fool.

No, right is our salvation.

Style.

Right.

Style.

Right.

Do something for me, I'm going.

She really was. I remembered this story of a Frenchman who was perishing on his deathbed with awful cancer and they asked what they could do. Get me a toothpick, he said. The things to fetch to a deathbed before the bitch went over the line, her new society, hell, to tame—I thought and came up almost blank. Then I said, What if I take this brush and do your hair, my dear.

No, you'd just get it wrong, she said.

That redheaded woodpecker—you ever heard this?—sometimes of a morning will begin knocking his beak on that tin drain outside my window, and I think of her.

Slow Times
in a Long School

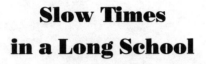

S URE, HEARING FATS DOMINO they were reminded of that ugly girl who went to high school with them. She lifted her right lip at the corners and smacked it with a liquid clicking noise—a gruesome lifetime tic. Even in high school she had dark circles under her eyes and a stoop in her spine as if going ahead to engage people before the rest of her caught up. Yo, hearing old Domino, who'd come out with his collected best just lately, they thought of their high school—pale green walls and old oak plank floors polished every weekend, oily, keen and waxy in the snort on Monday mornings; and the hot tuna fish odor blown around by the enormous fan in the small room where state history was taught. Funny about that state history. They'd read from a book and heard from a teacher that, absolutely, everything in their state was fine and correct and nothing bad or unfair had happened, ever. It was the "paper curtain" as Professor Silver later described it. In Mississippi white and black people were served up a brainwashed revisionism of their history competitive with that of the Soviet Union. Fats Domino, for example—well, listen to him: he sounded happy, didn't he? He was fat, black, and happy. Some were vaguely sad when they had heard he was dead of throat cancer, a false rumor likely started by the mean child of a Klansman, just out of spite. Their ilk did not like white kids listening to black jump music.

But about that girl, the stooped homely "buddy" of the popular girls and very popular herself because of her goofy mannish jokes. She was a "skit," she was a "nugget," that Lorna. *That* was her name, of course, a hag apotheosis, one of them said—Wilson, Dane, Foster—of the crashing blind date, set up for her "great personality." She was remembered at summer church and scouting camps as "sincere and caring" and had won awards for this, given at the end of the camping term. She won—didn't she?—the "citizenship" award in school. This was given, they remembered, to somebody with adequate grades, membership in a number of grim clubs (Forensic Club, etc.) and for being "sincere"—that it, sedulously giving a shit, revealed in the eyes and general busybodiness. Thing was, though, that she was a "hoot," the girls said, dearly loving her because she was homely, no threat.

It was a very clean school. Out of the student body of some four hundred, only seven girls were known to "put out" and they were soon married: two majorettes, three country girls, and two of those girls who by growth and fix of face were already "women"—maturing early through horror of home life. You could fool with these women and get results but a declaration of lifelong dedicated love was necessary. Looking back, the men saw these early-developed girls out in the Boulevard area as pathetic idealistic clingers, and not the withering, serious madonnas as they were viewed by frightened boys, as they themselves were. Such girls were likely to go deeply "steady" with a pre-developed football player once each year. There was always a sobbing breakup enduring a month or two. The girl had given herself. She missed much school. She might even be pregnant—rumor, rumor—and she was *so* grave, appearing white-faced and ill finally, seen as the used and much traveled, almost visibly a joint still lying betwixt her very serious loins: beaver heaven but frowning. It was easy to digress, trying to call up the career of Lorna, whose participation in the yelping hotness of teen passion was nil—but they were convinced even so that the dark circles under her eyes betrayed savage and constant masturbation. Poor Lorna, sighed the three serious hypocrites. In fact, a number of traits were certain to reveal vile personal habits among girls. Their hoodlum acquaintance, Olen, assured them that two big-breasted girls, best friends, were absolutely "sucking each other off." That's how they got that way, plain to anybody but the blind.

But what had happened to Lorna and all her awards, what did these high school triumphs mean? They recalled her receiving them at the head of the assembled student body—bent over, her eyes a dull gray, eyelids going down, trying to hide her "bad notorious self" while squeals from the popular and pretty girls advocated her unanimously, so glad for her. Yet at home, what must have been her sorrow when no guys called, or only somebody like Weejun, that guy who didn't even know he was queer yet (one didn't dare in those days), or Sparky Narpsome, so huge and happy, gregarious, later to kill himself in a rowboat in the lake near where the spring senior party was held twenty years ago almost to the day. Old regrets about his funny and enormous self in a swimsuit? They never knew. He'd made a lot of money and had a nice family by that time, and he'd become handsome and thin. Sparky's suicide had gotten them all to thinking. It was right up there on the front page of the capital paper, because Sparky was a state representative. They thought about what high school had meant, was it bad or good, or much like any place else in the fifties? It had occurred to a couple of them — Wilson and Dane — that actually it was not a bad place. Compared to the current wretched wastelands, theirs was not a bad school at all. They had felt backward, very outside the national mainstream, but they'd seen movies since that proved they were regularly hip, even down deep in Dixie. Wilson and Dane and Foster had wanted to be beatniks and had worn black shirts and filthy low-top sneakers. Not that anything ever happened. Only the small-caliber but vicious society of adolescence. Strangely, at their tenth reunion, on asking *everybody* how they'd felt about the place, not one person said he'd felt a part of the mainstream: not the class president, or the former hood (now of course the straightest of all, the *organizer* of their tenth, who'd sent a corny letter in which every other word was capitalized and afterburnt with three exclamation points). Sparky, the future suicide, was there, honest about his niggling sense that he was an outsider at the school. Dane, further, had seen the football coach Larue at his father's funeral. This bastard was mean, an insane nag, sullen and tragic about the players under him, a near Hitlerite in his elementary science class. But Larue had told Dane that the school almost killed him. He had never felt at home either, though they'd named the damned football stadium after him and his winning teams.

Of Lorna, well, did anybody ask how it went with *her* back in the fifties? Nobody seemed to have bothered. She seemed made for the place and had great success, defying every process of natural selection. My God, it was her stomping ground, she *owned* the place. She'd shown up gamely at the tenth even though she wasn't married, about the only one, very chipper and still giving "Indian burns" to girls' forearms, quite unconscious that they were turned ill — Wilson, Dane, Foster — by her presence. That she was happy seemed a monstrosity almost unbearable. Wilson and Foster were sadly married: all the dinks and flab had appeared in marriage, and they themselves now had dark circles and permanent waists and gloom.

They were more taken up with Cootie Bainbridge, totally unchanged and snapping out general disrespect. Now in faraway California with a job of clouded prosperity, he seemed to have come back only to assure himself that the "roaches," "warts," and "simps" were still maintaining. Once judged by Bainbridge, a person's worth was final. No allowance for any sort of progress was made at all. Bainbridge had a way of nailing somebody by simply making you think of their image long enough until you collapsed, weak, into laughter. Especially did he love to catch earnestness and overachievement in the act, as performed by some ungifted hopeful. He was talking optimum life at age eighteen. Natural athletes, musicians and lookers were fine, that was the real world. But trying to better oneself by any effort was grievously gauche. Anybody caught really trying by Bainbridge — a phony himself, sure, who rubbed on Man Tan and wore three pairs of socks to make his calves look bigger — he would assault this way: "Hey, consider: *Peden.*" Just the guy's name. Soon you'd be bursting with spasms. Considered long enough, *everybody* was a "grub," of course. Peden, a country boy from a bad home who ate health grain mixes, had trained himself with dawn runs of twelve miles — he'd taken the state in the mile run, which he was never supposed to do. But you could not forget the hawk-nosed angle of his face, his thick black-rimmed spectacles, his awesome, well, seriousness. He was an ugly little rube loser caught in the act of being grim. Excepting Cootie, they were more philosophical and admitted they'd been so damned laughably serious through those years at the old school. They flinched with embarrassment recalling the fights, romances, and athletic ventures. For some, the *religion,* too, holy God. The sincerity of church and scout camps. God, again. Couldn't you just go back and kick yourself in the butt?

But Cootie Bainbridge — later to slay *himself,* like Sparky, but in a bathtub somewhere in San Francisco — acknowledged no gain, no success, beyond the original granted form. Peden, now a Dr., was at the tenth, too. He had not only an M.D. but a Ph.D., and had donated a light plane to a missionary friend in Indonesia. Saintly, good Dr. Peden, all calm and composed and humble, had been since college a dedicated Christian, accepting no praise, all plain guy in a modest suit, with a perky wife. Cootie drew Wilson, Dane, Foster, and another man aside, and said noting the Dr., "Consider: *Peden.*" Once they looked, Peden seemed again the awkward hawk-nosed country boy, too correct by far, too Boy Scoutish. Everything was wrong. He should still be lost in sorrow and helplessness at his bad home on the farm. They couldn't help laughing, all of them at once with the same vision, and when Peden, with his big nostrils and black glasses turned to find the source, they had to fall out, disperse, and gag. Such was Cootie, even more ruthless than fate. Unsatisfied still, he went on to stalk more ridiculous game, more lacking and afflicted. They saw he'd been brought up short by Lorna, some ten feet from her. She was at the center of a giggling punch bowl gaggle, most of them the decade-older popular beauties she had schmoozed and chorused with way back then. It was as if they had never skipped a day. She was back with her mannish jibes and wonderful self-mockeries, smacking her rear right lips in the tic, dressed smartly and stooped into their faces, she big-shouldered and near breathless, hawing with her gray incisors. She smoked now and drew her whole face, eyes closed, around the butt, much like a wrinkled crone on a city curb. She drank amply too, and sloshed the cubes like a pro. Not many people drank back in high school, and no girls, except a couple of deliberate tramps, ever smoked. Wilson, Dane, and Foster were the wildest, and they were hardly anything, though two of them were already made alcoholics. The drinks in their hands were not idle props. Early alcoholism, actually, made them glow and verge on possession of a dark rakish charm. Their wives, both of them, were out-of-state girls with a bit more polish than the local belles (going to matrons, ding-dong like clappers in their skirts). Dane's wife, a woman of the theater, during the wedding ceremony had pronounced *Aye Dooo!* very thespianly, stunning the yokels of her church. Wilson's, of some Texas money, was forever lamenting her failure as a horsewoman in hunter-jumper competition: "I had tournament nerves — bad ones, darn it! — and they transferred to the horse." The gleam was off the local belles, sadly. Wilson and the others wondered at that *kind* of beauty, now passé, which had kept them in such agonies. Cootie Bainbridge, too. These women had made Cootie cold in the head and lumpy in the chest with desire. But he would have revenge later, attacking some flaw, when they were away: a lisp, a shuffle, a type of laugh. Then everybody could see how horribly put-on they were. What a relief. When Cootie saw Lorna having her sway, without pausing more than a slow beat, he moved right into the middle of the old society facing her. The old beatniks were out on the edge, waiting on him. They noted that Cootie was dressed very hiply in California style. He'd always put great stock in clothes, and in fact had stolen the clothes of others at the state university.

"Lorna!" said Cootie. She turned, interrupting her popularity. Cootie seemed in some anguish. "I heard that you were *dead!*"

In the old days Cootie had succeeded brilliantly because the girls and boys often just didn't understand him, and could be unknowingly assaulted to their core. Looking back to the tenth and the moment: Cootie would slay himself in twenty years, a true decade later than Sparky in the rowboat at Roosevelt State Park. The tens were ominous to these classmen. Very, very strange. With Cootie it was debts, booze, and a father who refused to help him even after he'd helped the father a great deal. Some suspected cocaine. Cootie was always hip, very *mise en scène*. They also suspected, somewhere, theft.

But they were ten years older. Lorna had attended the same state university as Cootie. She knew his joke instantly and was quieted by it. Then, looking at Cootie feigning innocence beautifully as he had always, cutting your throat while he handed over a puzzling compliment, Lorna became really ugly and crooked. Her mouth clicked, her breastless chest sank even more inwardly. The more pronounced circles under her eyes deepened morbidly. Her gray eyes became liquid. She seemed all at once very drunk or actually dying. She shivered — all of this in just a stalled, mute moment — and even Cootie was taken aback at the success of his harpoon. They saw her then as she really was, her social success dropped away. She was quite miserable, uncomfortable, this...this...freak.

"I...no...I...no, I'm *not* dead, Cootie. You know I'm not... dead." Then she thrust out of the gaggle and went down the hall into the bathroom.

The other women didn't understand at all.

But they, the old fascinated beatniks, did. Lorna did. She was revealed as the true raw meat she was, stark, heaved into the spotlight. It was so uncomfortable then, that the old beatniks feigned innocence. They turned to their solemn bourbons as if nothing had ever happened. Cootie was soon beside them, a little shaken. The point of Cootie had always been that the victim never knew what hit him. This was something else again. But you could not apologize, never. You had to press on. Still the same rules for Cootie, who, looking back, may have been the tormenting high school years themselves, in one man: the hideous beckoning mirror they ran in fear of, culprits with small acne and bad hair and wounded souls, spilling out of eyes the wrong color, with heads the wrong shape.

In the room they noted Quadberry, back from flying jets, F-4s, in Vietnam for the navy. He was classy and at ease with his Annapolis diploma, and currently a chess bum in Europe, unashamed. Even the old beatniks liked the Quad, and knew he was getting a lot, the best, and envied him, one of the few unmarried there. The paradox of Quad lingered around the room. Known as a disordered slob, personally, yet he had been an Eagle Scout, the star quarterback, and adequate on the cornet. Taking wild risks never bothered him, and he was comfortable in any group, wilder than anybody in it, really. He could hypnotize people, had read the poet James Merrill (whom he'd met) and all the volumes of Proust by now, but without brag. The Swiss girl with him was her own category of beauty, never seen in these parts, maybe only on the screen. Not normally pretty, with a raised lip over frosty canines, she was a sexual item frank and clear who made the other women ill at ease. She and the Quad had been everywhere together — skiing, chess tournaments, rare hot springs in Alpine idylls, but she seemed much the stronger partner and was no bimbo. Later, the Quad would tell her, regarding her remarkable high and prominent bosom: "You know, if you didn't have those, you couldn't get away with so much. I can't even think what would be left of your personality" — a thing it would require at least five drinks for the old beatniks to say to a woman. That was the Quad, not even wondering about his courage and leaving her flat, in somewhere like Pamplona. The wives liked the Quad, and like the old beatniks, wished they were unmarried, too.

When Lorna came out, she was fixed, but still hurt. It was better not to go over there. It was better to drink and rattle on in new friendship with the guy who'd become a heart surgeon; the Mormon ex-halfback who had *never* changed his high crew cut; and the ex-basketball star, gone neckless with fat, a big man in the church, gaunt high school sweetheart wife beside him, visibly shaken by his constant adulteries, but holding in and on like somebody in a prison waiting for the allies.

"You've got to slam a dyke every chance you get," said Cootie to Wilson.

"A dyke? Lorna?"

"Sure. She was big in the sorority at school. Everybody knew. Look at her. Who'd want that in a sorority? Those girls in her sisterhood were cute, gorgeous, smooth. Hell, they had two Miss Americas in sequential years. Yeah, she came down as one of those 'legacies' — meaning her aunt or granny was a big thing and they had to take her. Practically a bought thing, one of the token roaches they let in. Well known that some of your sororo sweeties are *lez*. Muff divers, rug munchers, they let 'em in to graze, to break in the younger ones. A quarter of your girls in every sororo are lez, didn't you know? Just spy that. Doesn't she look like every girl's P.E. coach; give her a neck-whistle. Or a camp leader. Yeah. She gets off on munching the cuties, no two ways. They'll just get bored and call in old Lorna, down on the knees, for a quick graze."

"Oh." The old beatniks, having gone to the town college, didn't feel very with it. Somewhere deep inside them it had hurt not to be university frat men. There were no fraternities where they went; they were religiously discouraged. In this state, you could stand no higher as a college man than with a mug of bourbon, in a madras coat, Weejuns without socks, on the front porch of your frat house, big blue and yellow Game Day around you, boss chicks spilling out of smoky Impalas and Furies, thighs rubbing nylons together, everywhere. What a good thing it would be to have a nickname like "Cootie" and just hang; the old word *swell* came to mind. To be a swell of Sigma Chi, a prime country club like that. The facts they hadn't heard, however, were that Cootie had been thrown out of his frat for stealing watches from a football locker room. And the truth about Lorna was more complex, they'd find. But for now, on the tenth reunion, in the whispering times when homosexuality was an outright crime, it was quite beautiful to hear Lorna done for — a coup de grace — and the sororities thoroughly damaged. They drank to this lovely truth, Cootie insisting. Outdoors the moon was up, whole, in total agreement. Christ, were they men! Could drink all night and drive their wives, tipsy off two cocktails, home, and plunder their randiness, imaginations showing the whole nude life story of Quad's woman on a screen in their minds.

But they heard that Lorna was having her success — if you'd call it that — and it looked to be a lifetime's worth. After some dim stint of "professional training" — a master's degree in Guidance at another state college (could you ever count the nonentities with this piece of paper on their wall? Wilson the lawyer asked), she was back at her own beloved state university as dean of women. Right in the mold! they roared. The Queen Bee of all the merry wet hive! "All right, girls, everybody out on the spiral stairway! It's fanny-spanking time!" A vampire of beauty and its liquid graces with a lifetime sinecure of fresh little eighteen-year-old butts to educate every fall, right on time, better than cotton in the delta.

Vietnam and the general sieges on authority had cleared their minds. It was good, after all, that they weren't frat men. These systems, frozen in and never without loud alumni advocates during the years of hippie disdain, were nothing but old racist lodges, festering Nixonites and mediocre glad-handers, old-boy nurseries where the dumb and the proud earnestly, cowardly entwined, just this side of faggotry. It was a wonderful thing they were never a part of it and they imagined they'd always hated them. Those sorority girls were horribly out of fashion now, too, the ones they'd wanted: mascaraed little pigs from Yazoo and Memphis, dead as dummies in an old ventriloquist's act. The vision of Lorna driven batshit as society changed pleased them very much. Cootie's joke would be more on the mark every day. After some muddled announcement like Nixon's, she would resign in disgrace and waddle back to her rock, her place marked for her by an arrow.

A couple of them began making money. You did not need all that much in this state to seem rich. Wilson, drunk and recently divorced, bought a Corvette, long a dream, but was promptly told by the first woman he "dated," a lawyer out of the sorority system, svelte and horny like a mod girl should be, that it was a redneck car and it embarrassed her. The loveless fornication she engaged in so vigorously broke Wilson's heart, finally. She insisted on telling him she didn't love him at all, that she was in love with a much older "self-made man." But she cried out almost dangerously when they were in the act. He was hurt. It meant nothing to her, this grinding. She reminded him that Oriental men were better, known for their foreplay. She'd never even "date" him really, only fornicate, loudly, then fix up her clothes and leave, as if just having used the restroom at a ball game. Wilson, every adolescent dream of shove and run realized, surprised himself by being devastated she didn't adore him. (He'd gotten rid of the Corvette for her.) She was more a man than he was. Yet he put it to her good, with some vengeance for her slick sorority past, which she now laughed at and satirized. Nevertheless, she'd been one of them, those preening wards of Lorna's, permanently on view, hugging each other with shrieks. But, my God, he was a man nearing forty now. He'd written a legal thriller and quit the law. She called his book "bourgeois trash. No wonder it sold."

Dane, a gifted pianist, the only old beatnik faithful to the now ancient North Beach and Village scenes, was not doing badly at the piano bars around the state capital. Graying, he even jumped in the whole nostalgic way and wore a goatee and a black beret. He wanted badly to go to New Orleans but was never invited. They made him do Billy Joel tunes at the Sundowner and George Street Grocery. He didn't mind doing Fats Domino, but Joel's piety made him gag. His own stuff was benignly ignored by the second-rate professionals (many old frat men) of the city, glib and flushed by marti-

nis. Sometimes Dane drank too much and got angry. He had an out-
burst against the whole city one night, dead with its "indecision in
the water supply, God damn it!" Dane's fragile career was in some
jeopardy. He, lamentably, had to lead a church choir for income. It
was for a denomination he particularly hated, and the minister's arrogant homilies did murder to his hangovers. At home, his wife grew
enormous. More deeply Baptist than any of them, after all, he hung
in with love and fidelity. His kids loved him. He was, drunkenly, an
exquisite father, taking them everywhere and loving them more than
normal, careful and tender — he, the beatest of the old beatniks.

Once, out of a window in late evening, he watched, in the parking
lot behind the church after choir rehearsal, a mother with two children in the back seat of her car talking to a man in another car that
had pulled alongside. She screamed at her children to shut up, then
continued talking. With more screams and threats, she left her car
and joined the man in the back seat of his. Soon the two were humping avidly, only her hair and bare shoulders occasionally popping up
from below the window. In the middle of it, the kids began raising
hell. The woman screamed over, still pumping. Dane seethed, somehow just now understanding they were committing adultery in a
church parking lot. It was a vision of sorriness and home wreckage
that aroused a cold spit on his tongue — it was something bad forever, everything he despised. Didn't marriage, children, mean anything anymore? He'd had teenage romances and lust, yes, and had
written poems to the loved girl, but he'd properly waltzed and
wooed. His love seemed pure and elegant. The woman got out and,
holding her brassiere up with one hand, slapped one child through
the window of her own car. She then climbed back in the other to finish. Dane began bunching in anger. It was all he could do to hold
himself back from killing both of them. This trailer-trash mother, no
doubt on welfare but driving this Infiniti — he could take no more.
When he left the church and walked to the cars, he saw the kids
watch him and quieten, filthy faces, red-eyed, something elderly and
vicious in their little faces already, like adults. Dane strode up to the
man's car and just before he yanked the door open and dressed them
down, it flew open almost in his face. Out came a small man, black
hair flying up like a greased broom, naked from the waist down. He
would remember permanently that the man had an enormous erect
member waving out of black fur. Dane never saw the knife, but
heard the shouting, passing strange:

"Yes sir, you got into it, dint ya? You got into it, dint ya?" the man was yelling as with high pain each time he stabbed Dane; that was an awful keeper too, his voice going *hunn! hunn!* as if struck *himself*.

When he was through stabbing Dane, well, that was all Dane recalled. He lay in the parking lot, coming to in a smell of crankcase oil and greasy water, very nearly dead. The knife had just missed his liver, or *kaput,* said the doc later at St. Dominic's.

The upshot was that the tone — a calm certitude about the town and his future — left his head, that happy constant tone that assured him all was well, something he'd had since birth, something that had made him the beloved old beatnik back in high school. He hated white trash and all its emblems, a number in fraction about a third of the state's population, it seemed, when you watched carefully enough. He hated white trash on the spot. The man who stabbed him was never caught, and it was as if Dane were staring a hole through a number of people in his way to finding him. He could never forget that afternoon and its pictures, and never understood the rage that had cut him to pieces. He carried a gun in the car, cruising and drinking from quart bottles of beer. He was not cheery and loose in the bars anymore and people did not mess with him. Occasionally he would look up with hopeful steel in his eyes when somebody called out a request for a truck-stop tune, wanting to see the man himself at the end of the voice.

Dane grew very large — almost a circus thing — and now when he sat across from his wife at dinner, their concern for each other seemed the last flicker of pure domestic joy in a poisonous night. Their largeness amplified things chaste, noble and good. Food was good to their good hearts, big hearts. It might be true that an extra dimension of decency and devotion was available to the large. Without that old tone in his head, Dane believed in this. They went to movies together and held hands, unashamed.

It was there in a specialty movie house (same one where he, Wilson and Foster saw *The Subterraneans* and *La Dolce Vita* and became beatniks), that Dane saw a film called *Sisters,* about a sorority "rush" process, featuring their very own state university, the paradigm. He called Wilson as soon as he got home. They'd not spoken in a year, Wilson's bachelorhood having made them a bit foreign to one another, for no good reason. Lorna had been in the movie, right in the middle of it, organizing and fetching around backstage, strident and squawky, a hovering nuisance and foghorn, mother figure to the rushettes. The film was one of those cinema verité jobs, sworn to no comment, but the effect on Dane was sickening revulsion that sororities could thrive at all still, with their piggish exclusions and elections of eighteen-year-olds, shrill and so dewy it made one vomit. One chubby girl who was invited nowhere wept alone. Elected mascaraed piglets ran shrieking in approval of each other. It was a devastating attack on a floridly sick thing, and the wonder was that it was allowed to be filmed. Queen Lorna, writhing in her element, seemed unconscious that she came off a monster, so busy and useful was she, so many things to order, so many little bosoms to heed. For Dane it approached something like actors filmed unawares grabbing sheep and fucking them. Speaking quickly to Wilson, Dane said, "Or an old Nazi film, or Nixon's tapes." Dane was appalled and angry at the university where his "tax dollars went" and where his young daughter was thinking of going. "Most of all the vision of Lorna, headlong in it, not a second thought, crazed and happy."

"Really grisly, I'll bet," said Wilson, angry at most women since his lawyer woman had ditched him for a young oncologist, telling Wilson straight out that the doctor was "longer lasting" and was "really doing something."

"Cootie ought to see it," said Dane.

"I didn't tell you. Cootie's dead."

"Cootie's dead?"

Wilson told him what he knew. "He won't be making the thirtieth they're getting up. Will you?"

"I don't know. If you and Foster go. Cootie. *Thirty* years."

"Seems almost nasty with time, eh? But Lorna, of course."

"We'll most definitely see Lorna."

"I heard you were fat, Dane."

"Sure am. Heard you were a drunk."

"Sure am. You?"

"Sort of."

"But better than Lorna, huh? Nationwide. A star, 'jes' bein' herse'f.'"

Foster was at the reunion, gray but still lanky, pessimistic. Foster always seemed out of work and lost, though he ran a middling-prosperous pharmacy. Lorna was not there for a while, but then she entered. You could hear the mannish voice and the snort, the clack of her right back lips, before she came in the mansion from the porch. There were only about twenty-five old students who cared to come. It became clear to them that the primary motive behind the thirtieth was a view of the mansion, in the north part of the city near the big reservoir named for a pious fraud and buffoon who had governed the state into flamboyant misery when they were in college. The great home was owned by Brew Massey, the old fullback. He was wealthier even than the heart surgeon, by way of selling plumbing parts. Foster thought it noteworthy that Massey (who was quiet, either dumb, shy or always outraged, they couldn't tell which) as a fullback was described by Quad, the quarterback (the Quad wasn't at the thirtieth), this way: "You needed two yards, Massey would get exactly two yards. No more, no less. Five and a half for a first down, he'd get exactly five and a half. I once saw the whole field open up for him. He could have walked for a touchdown. But he rammed into the ground for two yards — what we needed for the first — and came back to the huddle smiling." Such was their millionaire now, Foster told the old beatniks. "That's your plumbing baron."

Massey had married late and had two small children. The house was almost grotesquely huge and appointed. There seemed to be a quadraphonic speaker system in every room, with those "subwoofers" moving the parquet strips and carpet under your feet. Eventually Fats Domino came on — "Walkin' to New Orleans" and the songs of their era, taped by somebody (Massey, whose personality nobody could remember?), came on one at a time, bringing a burst of now almost ancient events and moods to their minds, the almost twenty-five out of the sixty in their class.

"Nah. Too good, too thick, too 'mastered.' You had to hear it over a bad Chevy radio," said Wilson, who had come sober. "And your parents had to hate it. The preacher and the Klan had to hate it too. Your Sunday school teacher had to inveigh."

"Then later in college you had some English prof wanting you to know he was groovy. He liked what you did, but more," said Foster.

Dane, grown so wide and large the others did not want to bring up the subject, went off from them, sniffing and spying at the furbishments, working on his half case of beer.

The conversation was around Sparky and now just lately Cootie. Wilson thought he saw Lorna (her mouth open, now something new: actually breathing from it, was she? tongue slightly hung over her bottom teeth, a gray dead thing, arrgh) smile (really?) when Cootie's death was mentioned. He could now hear her talking to two drained beauties, a piece of her "old crowd." She had switched to a nasal and precise tone, that of her "profession."

"Oh, there were early trouble spots with Cootie. Anybody could tell. Then that stealing business at the U. Cootie just couldn't ever get on in the world, he had that chip on his shoulder. Just couldn't put his shoulder to the wheel, couldn't get with the program."

Wilson was red, and Foster, beside him, actually made a spitting noise at the end of Lorna's assessment. The women were rapt. Nobody had really ever understood Cootie. He had spoken with a Chicago accent, and they had some notion he was cruel, but he had remained a sort of UFO to them.

"He just couldn't 'fit in,' eh, Lorna?" said Wilson sourly. The women turned. Lorna brought her tongue back in her mouth, opening that rear gap in her right lip that she seemed to breathe through. She could bring those wide shoulders forward to make her face pop into you.

"Cootie had a very big mouth, nobody can deny. His thing was envy and covetousness, not to get biblical," she said, then sucked her drink.

Dane moved up behind Wilson. You could feel the big man in the boards of a solid mansion. The women around her, voluntarily developed into unopining rather breathless helpmates, offered Lorna no support. Wilson did not feel good about all three of the men lined up against Lorna. It overkilled the moment.

"Well, I found Cootie to be a very... very astute puncturer of balloons," he said.

"Nobody said he wasn't the class clown."

"I meant more than 'class clown,' which lets too many people off the hook."

"What hook? What hooks were we supposed to be on?"

"*Are,*" said Wilson rapidly.

"I read your books. You're pretty vicious, Wilson. I guess that'll always sell. The cheap and the vicious. Although I heard the second one bombed. People got on to you."

Wilson had promised himself not to drink, but here he was fixing himself one. It didn't seem he could go more than two days straight without it anymore.

"We see you took your act on the road. Aren't you something of a star, 'best supporting' something or other?" he shouted, almost.

Nobody but Dane had seen the movie, which was "small" and shown at the "art theater," where none of them went. The women looked even blanker. Wilson felt the heat and lumber of Dane shuffle behind him.

With liquor nowadays, the first touch of it, Wilson was thrown into a narration immediately, almost as with a starting gun. This was how he wrote his books. Of necessity, he was back at law practice, miserable at it and miserable in it, his tales bottled up.

"Lorna and her duckies, duckie season every year. She guides them into all the hoops. First there's Pouting and Ignorance, next there is Superficiality, next there is Charm for Pigs, next there is...oh—"

"Your *books* are nothing but surface!" Lorna shouted. "There's sex, then image, with some music playing over it. There's nothing real like fellowship or the big picture!"

"Whoa!" Wilson shuddered, dramatic. "Fellowship, the big picture. Like you're *in* it? Like you *know*?"

"The things that last don't need explanation. Never complain. Never explain. Mister."

"Come on, come on, gang. I want to show you something beautiful. It's our thirtieth." A hand was on Wilson's shoulder. He thought it was Dane, but it was big Brew Massey, owner of the house. He'd never heard his voice.

They, all of them, went down a long hall, long as a hotel's nearly. The carpet under them was peach. They could smell a fireplace ahead. It was three days after Christmas, and they began noticing very elegant *designer* ornaments fixed onto the lamps of the hall, things perhaps British and expensive from a catalogue. They were entering a family living area, where a smart jutting fireplace snapped and glowed, and children's videos were stacked thick as a library over an enormous television screen. Next to a grand piano a woman was standing in a red and green chemise, nicely off her shoulders, between the two Massey children, ages two and three, probably. They were just standing there waiting on the crowd like a photograph, a Christmas card tableau. Rather postured and queer, Wilson thought, but he noticed Massey was beaming and felt good for him. The kids were in black velvet Fauntleroy suits. The woman had a big smile, nice teeth, very pleasing, though Wilson noticed she had the face of...well, say, a strained beautician, with that wolfish pointed-eyed aspect that women of a certain class, unaccountably, just get.

"Meba, my wife, and children Russet and Dawn," said Massey. This was only the second time anybody remembered hearing Massey speak. "What it's all about. The 'big picture.'"

The woman, twenty years younger than Massey—but with that hard face—unbent to shake hands.

"Now Dane, we know you played a little piano before—" Massey went on. The group laughed. Even in high school he was fabulous. "I believe my family would love for you to accompany them on a wee number." Massey whispered in Dane's ear. Dane was in beret and with goatee, and seemed perfect for the jolly jazzman, all that girth. He sat staring at Massey's wife, then tinkled out an intro to "Auld Lang Syne."

The woman began singing with the children. They apparently had rehearsed this a good deal. The kids had that desperate harmony that many find touching in carols of the season. Dane was weaving and sweated from all the beer. He looked up again at the woman and suddenly bolted up, hand out, pointing at her.

"You're that woman in the parking lot. These are the kids you were just, just . . . just fucking in front of! That man that stabbed me!"

The woman shook her head, eyes popping, and gathered the girls in both hands. Dane reeled out, shocked again by the same children, all dolled up.

"No!" Massey shouted. The woman and children fled, panicked, to the long hall.

"Oh yeah? Well look, you look at this!" cried Dane. He brought up his shirt from his pants and pulled it open, cracking buttons over his vast white belly. The wounds were horrible, like great bellies of worms all over his stomach. Dane thrust them out to the hall, yelling, "Where is that bastard?! Where is that little bastard?! You, stop! I tell you, Massey, that woman . . . *adulterated* you in a car right beside your children!"

Brew Massey, tall as Dane and in just a little better shape, threw himself at the big pianist. He was simply fuming, pouted up in the face like an injured small boy, making long *hooo* noises. It was a dreadful equal to Dane's ravaged stomach, horrible to watch. Then Dane experienced, impossibly again, the same travesty as when he was stabbed. Massey began clubbing his face awkwardly, *hoooing* out as if *he* were struck each time.

"This is terrible, terrible!" Dane cried.

Massey began nodding with him, hating him, clubbing away.

There was not much left of the gathering after that. Host and hostess were away somewhere, buried in a house that gave up no indication where they were, nor the children.

Back at the drinks in the more informal parlor, the serious and stunned trickled past, some knocking expensive liquor from what surely had to be the last of Massey's fine hoard into their glasses with ice. Wilson and Foster, having got Dane in hand but not quite curbed, only tucked in, found themselves dashing to their toddies right in front of Lorna. To their side, Dane had discovered another member of their class to appeal to. She was a city councilwoman now, greatly respected.

"You've got to *do* something, Marsha," urged Dane. "This city, these people, what can be done?"

Dane's big wife, finding no proper way to act at all, was draped on her frantic husband. The horror was seeping in, and there were no emergency numbers to call, absolutely nothing to do but wade around in it. Who should be comforted? It was not quite known when everybody began despising Dane. Though nobody but Dane had seen Lorna in the *Sisters* movie, almost everybody knew about the stabbing episode and Dane. It had been on the front page of the capital paper; another gruesome, foul mark on the spirit of their place, but this one touching closer to home. Dane had been pitied and celebrated for minor heroism, then forgotten. But even the drained unopining women began murmuring against him. He had destroyed Brew Massey's home, perhaps. Lorna, huffing and clacking, threw her professionalism in.

"There just had to be another way, Dane. You're a drunk, mister. That was shameful. This lovely family. What horrid, horrid selfishness."

Wilson was too gravely into his bourbon to respond, but he was livid, thinking, Dane *is* a drunk, by God. Me, I'm merely alcoholic. But I wasn't stabbed. Finally, he got his mouth out of the glass.

"You weren't stabbed, Lorna."

For a while that calmed the accusations. Incredibly, Lorna tried to hustle the women back into small talk. Wilson was not sure at all of any real zone of reality. Where could it be? Shouldn't they leave? Dane had gone outside and come in pronouncing that one of the cars in the garage was definitely the Infiniti, the very one she'd been in. White trash in an Infiniti.

"Poor Massey. Waited all of his life, and then went just over the river to *Rankin County* for his bride. No horizon, man," said Foster.

Wilson went penetrating with his ears. Was he hearing this? Lorna, asked about her movie, was holding forth, trying to whisper but unable. "Oh yes, she and I are on a first-name basis." She was talking about some incredibly minor Southern comedienne, sometimes a creature in a sitcom. "Yes, they may put it down, but you take a lonely, homesick little girl from Nowheresville, give her a place and a family where she can be something...Well, I'll tell *you,* many look back and don't find it depraved at all, not at all. What *are* we except *society?* I want to know. These young women, why from Pelahatchie to Wall Street, some of them. I've just seen the beauty of this over and over. Who was *I*, I ask you? Who was I? just a rinky-dink little scrapper."

Wilson was so truly ill that he found no direction in which to press at all. He, Foster, Dane and his wife simply left, out into the ragged cold, right past the Infiniti. "The very car, the very car!" Dane maintained, barely controlled still, his beret knocked from him by Massey and lying under the piano in the family room, crumpled, lewd, European, very Beat, the black anathema of the next day.

Having ruined Massey's home, Dane found that his own city was intolerable, yea rotten. No tone in his head, just the old wrath and funk, he realized that he must go to New Orleans, even if he had to walk. He and Fats Domino, "Walkin' to New Orleans," hear it, it could be done, oh my brethren Foster and Wilson. He never got to tell Foster personally, however, because the lanky man fell dead in his own pharmacy of a heart attack. Wilson and he were just too sad. My God, their city, their times, what was it? The funeral somehow just made sorrow rapid, urgent, steaming.

Wilson set upon him. "You're taking your family to a city that's second in murder in the nation? It's hard to talk to anybody who hasn't been *mugged* down there, Dano. It's not the soulful easy old town we loved anymore, my man. You go on Friday afternoons and every town faggot in south Mississippi is finishing work at the florist's and hopping into his car to sneak into N.O. anonymous. Friend of mine walked around a corner in the Quarter and there his *barber* was, on his knees giving head to a black man with a pistol. They had *Duke,* man, as a serious contender. Bumper stickers said, 'Vote for the Crook.' So."

"Yeah, but I stay here and I'm afraid *I'll* kill somebody. You've seen me work. I'm a good home-wrecker." Dane had quit drinking entirely. Wilson wondered how that was possible. Surely, at night… "I never pushed myself. Too beat, man, all my life. It's late, but this fat man got to learn to force his bad se'f on de public. Sure now. I got an *act,* I got the image, music can't deny me."

Utterly bereft almost, Wilson signed his new book at Lemuria, the fine local bookstore. Except for a few friends and family, almost nobody came. Wilson did not understand the lack of sales and interest after the blockbusting first one, near a movie contract, all that. Couldn't they see he was continuing the old Beat attack on the phony, the greedy, the flesh-merchants, and our dangerous pussy government, pussy lawyers, *vaginae dentatae* of your new woman, but even better? There was a phone call for him, and although she described herself as an old friend from school he could not remember her. She meant high school, thirty years and more ago. She said she had never married and lived with her mother. No, she'd not been to the reunions. She knew it wasn't her "crowd." There would be people all successful and rich, like him. But she (now giggling; he tried to see her in the halls — there were only sixty in their class: who could she be?) had always had a secret crush on him. This confession seemed to be causing a world of anguish to her. In the background he thought he heard her mother making a protesting sound. She lived out in the Rabbitville community in her same old house, "Darn it!" (giggling). She would love to see him. She'd kept up with his career and his books, of course, which were on her shelf and much thumbed, "specially in the good parts." They could meet somewhere and have a cup "for old times' sake?" But then Wilson, wanting to be a good man, a gentleman, asked what she drank, he could bring it over to Rabbitville right now, he hadn't seen Rabbitville in a long time. (Thirty years ago he had fished near this hamlet. He and some country blacks had bought beer marked up four hundred percent at a local grocery. Nothing else around but a garage that looked like a sort of morgue for cars and a post office with a hand-printed sign propped up on a barrel.) Well, she drank sloe gin, sometimes a lot. Wilson, having been through all varieties, he thought, could barely remember this one. It was that pink stuff, wasn't it? Like Pepto-Bismol liqueur. Then, asking forgiveness, Wilson had to ask her what her name was again. Victoria Lister. There were all kinds of Listers out in Rabbitville, she said.

He needed a drink first at the nearby saloon, then bought himself a quart of vodka and the sloe gin down the way.

Out in the county, pavement cracking up and potholed, Wilson wondered: even Peden and Wrabb had gotten out of Rabbitville. Wrabb, parlaying a good farm-worked body into Eastern-rich angulations, taught karate to housewives in Mobile and had his own television show. Wrabb was *with* it, country hip in some way, Wilson recalled. After he'd been scolded publicly by the gym coach in high school, Wrabb snuck early the next morning into the gym and fixed himself up on a rope from a beam so he'd look not only disgraced but hanging when the coach opened the place for class. There Wrabb was, dead, of shame. But not. The coach ran trembling out of the building crying "What have I *done!*," damaged in the profession (they hoped) forever. Wrabb also had a precocious sexual history, which he'd flatly tell you about as if he'd only milked a few cows once. Wilson wondered if Wrabb had had any of Vicky Lister, now a nurse. Nurses were a horny, head-hunting lot, he remembered, having at it willy-nilly but aiming religiously at doctors.

The house was nicer than he'd expected, brick, but built on bare open ground. Country folks, some of them, didn't like trees at all. She was at the door and told him almost immediately that her mother had Alzheimer's, now going on twenty years, and that he should just ignore her. Victoria's hair was completely white. This was a shocker. The hair was pretty, though, and thick, but Wilson felt nearly visited by a ghost. He still barely remembered Vicky. She had a pleasant squarish face, and could have been Average Nurse in a television show. It was near night. She had an idea, she'd been waiting a long time. They wouldn't "visit" in the house. Come with her, it was better out "there."

One room in the little barn, used only as a garage, was fixed, heated by an open gas space unit with clay grids. Still, it was dark (chimney swifts racing around in a mini-tornado outside) before she lit a Coleman lantern. There was a couch here, a chair, many books in a small case (Wilson noticed their high school annual among them), and a lazy enormous tortoiseshell cat in her own bed in the corner.

"Reading here is what I like best. It's so quiet. And I feel I'm in the nineteenth century, with Mark Twain and Emily Dickinson and those people we read in our class together. Listen —"

Wilson thought he was supposed to listen to something bucolic outside the door, creatures in an early spring night.

"Can we be friends, until we die? Could we be, I mean, like brother and sister? This is the bravest thing I've ever said in my life, Fletcher."

"Sure. Friends." Things seemed maybe dangerous, perverse here. Wilson caught himself. No they didn't. He was grown. The shriek and the exit from anything even marginally different, that was the purview of little social snots in adolescence. She pulled his new book from the case and offered him a fountain pen, big-barreled and elegant, mottled green.

"Sign something personal, could you?" Wilson did, straining to remember any speck of personality, then opting for the generic salutation about old high school, mighty high school.

"I've never been read to. Would you mind reading a few pages of this new one to me?" She sat in the chair and pointed to the couch. Wilson was touched. He opened the new pages and focused under the glow of the Coleman. This was very new, a very fresh thing, the lantern, the avid trembling white-haired woman waiting with pure Victorian bosom, so willing to be moved. He'd never read aloud any of his work.

After three pages, Wilson stopped. He was authentically sad.

"It's not any good, is it?" he said.

"It's classic." Victoria had tears in her eyes. "And *you, you,* right here. I'm just going to" — she put her hands, long and blunt at the fingernails, up to her eyes, then down again — "*not* going to cry." She gave that giggle again, the girlish one over the phone. "Darn it!" She patched herself up with a handkerchief she was carrying. Wilson hadn't noticed. She was like an old-timey woman with that handkerchief, always ready for tears, with her heaving bosom and maybe even the "vapors."

She had kept up with everybody possible in the yearbook. She knew that Cootie had done himself in, very terrible. And Sparky, too. He told her about Foster's heart attack. She began crying for real then. He went over to hold her and took her back to the couch with him.

"But you didn't really... *know* Foster much, did you?" he said.

"I *watched* all of you. I knew all of you were going to 'make it.' That school was full of wonderful people."

"Nursing, Victoria is... good. Nursing is a very high good."

"Yes it is, for me. You and Foster were so close — you, Foster and Dane. You just loved one another, and all so interesting!"

"Did you stay out here in Rabbitville on purpose?" Wilson asked.

"Well, yes. People like me. And Emily Dickinson. I'm the Emily Dickinson with no poems. Early on I knew I wasn't any good for out there." She indicated the world. "Remember Lorna? Don't you dare tell anybody, but Lorna had Tourette's syndrome, that snorting she did. I knew it but nobody else did. We were the two of us alone in the school bus one afternoon and I mentioned to her I bet I knew what she had, and I named it, to be kind. But Lorna got awfully, awfully mad. She warned me about ever saying this again. Then she told me that my type didn't 'have the goods' and I would never 'have the goods' to make a mark on society. She told me I was lucky — there wouldn't be many choices for me to make, nowhere to go, nobody complex to 'get over.' Lorna, you may never have known, Lorna knew things others didn't. She was very analytical and brilliant. Look at how she succeeded, even with her affliction. She's really what America's all about. What she said was true."

"You mean you quit, just didn't move, change, after what she said?"

"It was just fate talking through Lorna. I knew it. I had it in my head to be a nurse already at eleven years old. There wasn't all that much to do about it."

"Goddamn."

"That's one thing — can I say it? — I don't like about your work. Well, I like it *less,* Fletcher. The profanity. With all that vocabulary of yours."

By the time he left he was full drunk, and without another thought pulled out and aimed north for the university. Dane had given him his gun, a .38 cowboy thing, and at a rest stop he tossed it in the weeds, then urinated on it. He bought a bottle of Mellow Yellow up the road and was stretching the dilutions to make the remainder of the vodka last.

"I've done nothing about war, famine, disease, race relations, poverty or understanding queers in my time, and I'm no good. But when a thing is put right in front of you, when it is just staring at you," he chatted to himself on the three-hour ride to the university town. When he got there he hit a bar or two, angry at the casual well-dressed frat and sorority people around him "rehearsing for life," playing at youth as in movies, their rotten hollow ardor for one another rising with every beer.

Then he went up to the administration building, which was locked, and decided to wait until opening. She would be in there at her desk, arranging other lives. In his hand was the only thing he could find in his trunk, a handsaw. He had cut his own Christmas tree and tried to bring something back to his apartment, but it didn't work, and the woman sharing the bottle with him was allergic to cedar, for heaven's sake. She was a mean dumb girl who blistered everything around her with cursing. Everything everywhere and everybody was phony and pretentious, and he was pretty sure she included him. Sometimes in the night, having barely performed with the minx and leaving her cursing in the bedclothes, he knew he had brought a magnified and slightly more awful version of himself in here to party.

He was mumbling about it loudly on the steps of the building, then repeating "But when a thing's right in front of you!" in incoherent punctuation, when the security guard shone the light in his face.

"You're, if you're not Fletcher Wilson, writer. I went to school with you. Do you need help, Fletcher. What's up?"

"WhomamI spikking wiff?"

"Graham Goodlet, Fletcher. Don't you remember me? Our high school. We had industrial arts together in eighth grade."

"Can't be. Sa tiny school. You can't be here. You musta been the Unknown Student. World is full."

"Look at me. This state's got only a million whites. Pretty soon you run into everybody. Seen it happen. When you work in certain fields, the world comes to you."

"If a thing is right in front of you, you move and destroy it. You could help. R'member Lorna? You know you hate her. C'mon, be honess."

"Lorna Montgomery? Why she's a well-respected administrator. She's everybody's friend."

"Must be stopped. I'm not budging. You have the keys. Could get me in now to wait."

"What's the saw for?"

"Thing right in front of you. Saw her desk in haf. Attack her power base right on. You got the keys. Then we go public, say she got Tourette's syndrome, bona fide. Her day is over."

"Fletcher, you need help. I'm smelling it on you now. Can you understand. I never went to college, but at that high school, I just loved being around the guys and gals. So my dream came true, like Lorna's, we just couldn't ever leave school. I'm watching the gals and guys. Modern youth, Fletcher. Keeps you forever young. Just like Lorna. Man, keeping them safe, straightening them out. That's us."

"Lorna's a monster at the gate of beauty. Ya see them everywhere. Helen Gurley Brown, *Cosmopolitan,* Miss Manners, Dear Abby, Dr. Ruth, the hag behind every beauty contest. They can't get in, you know, so they keep others out."

"Fletcher. Look at us. Put down that saw, give her over. You're drunk and you're not young. That's an awful thing. Let it go."

"Must destroy. Never meant to be."

Graham Goodlet sat on the steps beside him.

"You've got to *love* something, Fletcher. More than you hate yourself or anybody, you've got to love something big."

Driven by his last big hatred, Wilson put his face in Graham's chest, sobbing, ill, looking at a desert.

Revealed: Rock Swoon
Has No Past

"**P**A. IS IT REALLY TRUE the old eat their young?"

Gives pause.

"Couldn't rightly say, son. I'm a mid-man. Feels like I'm walking on ice meself. Go on down to the barn, ask Gramps."

Gramps is down in the back shadows, some loose bales around his old brogies. Seems to be humming and eating, pulling a nail out of a rotten piece of board with a pair of pliers.

"Is it true, Gramps?"

"Wyoming's not my home..."

"Yer nuts, Gramps."

Sings, "Ate ol' granny in a choo-choo car!"

Kid goes back to the hut to see Gramps's father. Withered beyond longevity, a tiny man in dwarf's overalls, deeply addicted to codeine and Valium; fears colored people; occasionally makes scratching protests on his old violin, which has become too large for him. Every disease has had its success with him. Now he's barely a scab demanding infrequent nutrients. Bald as a beige croquet ball, he rolls his own.

They've fixed him up a mike with a cord into an ancient Silvertone amplifying box. Even his snores can be heard, slightly, out in the yard.

"Double Gramps, is it true the old eat their young?"

"Goddamn, I'm old!" blasts over the kid, feedback piercing too. The old man faints, recovers, goes into a codeine wither.

"But my question. Please, Double Gramps."

Almost accidentally, the old man fits bow to fiddle and scrawls out the grand trio of "Stars and Stripes Forever." Endlessly. It goes on the entire afternoon, amplifier picking up a prouder stroke here and there, screeching.

The kid grows up, a rock star, aging at twenty-three. He's already eating the young by the thousands when the second thought hits him.

Upstairs, Mona Bayed for Dong

OR GIVE IT another try, like a hot Hollywood novelist.

Ms. Vaught Stewart-Poore she is, my wife, cold as her father's money in bed, etc., etc. This would crack the whip, but I've already lied. I am working up to, as they say, the burning mystery, and I'm too much the coward, almost, to write it down real, which is plenty.

Face in expensive cobalt mud, she is horrified as I walk in on her masturbating, looking in the mirror *with her face like that*; knees up, head sideways to the long mirror by the bed, face in blue mud; she moved and bucked with her hand down there, naked except for her Las Vegas floorshow heels. *What could she mean by this, she so recently a mother for the first time, at forty?* Horrified, but she was too far into it, she couldn't stop the last little bucks. Was as if I were a little boy unprepared, inadvertently, who had seen happening to his mother from his pop, etc., where you think she's being hurt, gravely. It was like that an instant. I felt little, diminished into fear before the adult part came back, but was I sorry that I had seen it or was I wildly set off as I closed the door and went away saying nothing, nothing, then the both of us acting as if nothing had happened, though the image roared in my inner theater, maybe to roar forever? With the whole horny sky and her sister, maybe, in it too.

Her sister lives with us. I've never known whether she likes me or not. She is the sort who carries her catbird seat around with her. I don't think she ever had anywhere at any time any idea but that she was thoroughly wanted and adored. She is slightly better looking than my wife, more elegant in the shoulders, though I believe my wife's legs are better. In conversation and inner decision she and my wife Vaughtie are replicates. They awake with a hard schedule and set about accomplishing it with stern, almost angry, punctuality. Their practiced only slight tardiness to everything — they do nothing, really — you could set your clock by. The scheduling of the day is something they picked up from their father, whom they mocked, but who insisted on a structure for the day, which is what he had instead of theology or hope, I believe, as if pure form answered for the eternal. But this man had actual things to do and made a great deal of money selling — seems almost antiquarian now — "Let us meditate" spots to radio and television stations. His sincere belief in his "product," his small beauties, his preferred squareness in merchandising "thoughts" of Swedenborg, Pascal, Voltaire, Carlyle, Emerson, and Wilde (anything pithy and in the public domain, really), they hailed with derision, as if he had failed goofily at something and they were not using his money every hour, until it ran out and Vaughtie, at thirty, found me, forty. Vaughtie was not doing well poor, I can tell you that. I've always had a tiny messiah complex concerning her and her sis.

Vaughtie, besides her beauty, had an expensively and leisurely acquired knowledge of cultures, almost encyclopedic, although nothing at all in it had touched her much. She simply was familiar with an untold number of beautiful and true things, but was one of those women who would allow them no profundity. I was very attracted to this, and I am not, trust me, attacking women of a certain spoiled type who lie in the bed jaded and cold as their father's money, etc., etc. I *lovéd* this about her. When I was in college I learned a few deep and permanent things in the arts and sciences, but they all made me sad. I have never been more miserable than at school, knowing these urgent truths, and stalking the campus with them, fat with them as a man in the old freak tents, and as morbid. I truly think it is not right for some people to know about the life of van Gogh, and I was one of them. He was filled with intensity and mania, that clasping at life, and yet his life was not wholly his own, belonging rather to posterity, where it breathes and is adored, comfortable. Say like Christ, too. If you took him seriously, could you even have a tennis game without guilt? Space, creation, the atom — how can a man think soberly of these things, knowing that everything is having at each other constantly, nothing at peace, and persist in his merry clod-like way? So she was my queen, Vaughtie, the one who knew but "would not give it the honor of taking it seriously." I saw that quoted somewhere in regards to the requirements of "reality." I also knew she couldn't truly love, three evenings after I met her, and liked the way this shut out, after all, all the competition for her heart. You would only get her hand and the attached parts — permanently arousing, like a nice river. I know what most men want is the quality of Old Shep, waiting at a Montana train station twelve years for his master who's been taken off dead in a coffin to the East, but there are other qualities of marriage, rather strangely enjoyed.

The small tolerant smirk she showed during our lovemaking was about the most I got out of her. Experimenting in bed, I worked for the closed eyes and tight, near-release of a full smile that would signal she had crossed over into warmer abandon, into something near van Gogh and all that. Nothing surprised her, hardly anything got her there, though she spread and bent willingly into every attitude of desire. But those rare real smiles, or near them, with her mouth suddenly open, that is what I strove for and delighted in. She, without censoring herself, would aim for her convulsions. It is all the rise I ever see from her. She was forever being chased for these brief moments, and for a goodly while her coolness, generally, was my treasure. It was what we had. We had made something from nothing, as they say about dance. But I couldn't have this for long, or very often.

Between the makers and the critics, I'm afraid Vaughtie would be your critic of life and the world. These people, many of them well-off, say they never asked to be born. They refuse to live fully in what they did not choose. If the world wants to be a sort of nursery with toys in it for them, then they are slightly pleased. Something else far more important was happening far away from wherever Vaughtie was, you sensed, but you never found out what that thing was. Her sister was, if I saw it right, the only person who could commiserate on these points with her.

Why is the sister even here with us, harboring under our roof, if she annoys me? Number one, Vaughtie and Deborah have always been a pair. A matter beyond argument, a matter of something like birthright. If the subject was raised, Vaughtie might gaze at you as if you had asked, "Are your lungs going to live here too?" She would not have seen your point. They've always been inseparable except on a few occasions like our honeymoon. I can't remember the others. Number two, they could talk and measure the world with nobody else. It was as if nothing were real, nothing going on, until the other had attested to it. Yes, the water's cold. Isn't this delicious? Yummy. Wasn't the music dreadful? I couldn't believe the music. Don't you like Nick's haircut? It's perfect.

I am Nick Poore.

Then they will each comment on what the other is wearing that day. It is as if they are looking in a dresser mirror at another outfit they would have worn but for no good reason didn't. Both of them dress well, of course. They wear a style I would peg, even though no couturier, as owing some allegiance to the chic thirties, a decade prominent in knees and cheeks. They seem sculpted, with square bangs and long necks, one blonder than the other.

But now we all have grown older. Since Vaughtie turned forty, they've decided to *do* something, definitely. They grew quieter in their alliance, more serious. I found a sentence underlined, printed on a card that fell out of Vaughtie's purse: *Why do I pretend?* I looked in her purse frequently for signs of personality and passions. This is what I found once when she was in the tub: "Nothing that happens after we are twelve matters very much." — Sir James Matthew Barrie. Never had I noticed her remarking on a particular assertion by any-body. This was the author of *Peter Pan,* and didn't he plead with the audience once that they *must, must* believe in fairies? Yes, I looked it up, the same man. From all cultures, she had written down this sin-gle observation. So, out there on the porch, or in the gazebo, or in the lounge chairs next to our small pool, the two of them were out there adoring their *youth,* that was it. They couldn't get over their youth. They were looking for it in each other. They were inseparable because they had such a high estimation of their youth. I noticed how they boasted about the other, how the other was entirely better at, say, sports, and a singular cause of envy. Then the other would protest about her *own* envy of the other in art, imagination, room decor. But no, the other was *so* much more advanced in ideas. Still, no, what about the other's singing voice, couldn't she just thrill you like a bird having at it outside the window? Then sometimes, when I approached, coming home from work or Mass, they muffled their talk but kept up winks and codes so they could carry on the contest, this duet of mutual admiration and envy, while I was there — payer of the mortgage, utilities; owner of the cars, provider of food, yard help, billee of every salon and tennis club they visited; patron of their very slimness and suntans and pedicures — trying to make ordinary chatter. Soon I'd give up and dress for my range in the cellar, where I practiced the bullwhip on cigarettes and shot exotic small-caliber pistols. I would give a show of being slightly wounded by their obliv-iousness. I had tried to support them in their decision to *do* some-thing worthy, and here I was patronized, shunned. This show, only partly felt, would bring me sympathy and restitution from Vaughtie later when we were alone.

Charity and pity brought on a kind of solicitous eroticism in her. Above all things, Vaughtie adored being viewed from all angles. The languid eroticist, waiting to be enjoyed, was her best pose. She'd have made an exquisite model. I sometimes wondered about her at the doctor's, to whom she was always going, even though by all I could tell she was in perfect health. Vaughtie was faithful to me, by the way. Infidelity was not one of her electives, I believe. Yet the sacred chambers at the doc's could have been another kind of sanctioned narcissism, as hypochondria has been described.

Now, you see, here we are back at college again. These thoughts, what are they good for? What is the worth of knowing these items, that she and her sister were forever worshiping their youth, that they were talking mirrors, that feigning hurt brought payment almost instantly in gratifying my lust; that Vaughtie insisted on being viewed; that she was a dedicated narcissist even to the point of hypochondria; that it was ridiculous for me to be fiscally responsible for two inconsequential nattering women in my back yard or on couches. These are miserable things to know, and make good books, I guess. But there's no profit in this smartness, this comprehension, and having described them, what have you done? Simply taken another photograph, of which the world has etc., etc.

Great collections of things — in libraries, museums, bookstores, repositories, even car lots — make me sad. The plenitude of culture, words and artifacts, everywhere you look, brings on a tightness in my chest. I am wishing, always, more people had shut up and stayed still or just run off. Now what about J. M. Barrie, re Vaughtie: "Nothing that happens after we are twelve matters very much." So what? Are Vaughtie and Deborah sad old children, gabbing away out there, and are we all alas just obsolete children, as said by another describer, another smart boy? Do we shake our heads, another blooming truth attached to the long snarling list in our brains?

Give me tunnel vision, I say. Thought is very overrated, no? I have had more joy and gain from things I did not know, straight ahead. You pick the right tunnel, pals, and there is a lot in there, more than you can handle. Shut up, get what you can, carry on, like Vaughtie maybe, a woman saddened by her inconsequence now, but a thing for which she had been preparing lifelong. She is a figment, a joyful thing to think about, a statue with blood in it.

There is always something going on that has nothing to do with our precious insights, usually much better; the insights stand like an old spiteful bum at the back door, nose on the glass. Life throws open the door, stomps over his back making for the pool, the polished sunsets we have out there. Another Vaughtie, a real one, has wit, grace, charm, and a certain deferential reverence for things completely unlike her — my going to church and being a brigadier general in the Guard, for instance. It was fun listening to her and her sister banter, a kind lightness, a soothing music, as in the way she walked. She stressed appearance and was resigned to her own surfaces. But some surfaces are deep, positively refreshing. I have never found her monotonous. I think of Jacqueline Kennedy Onassis, who has no real personality so far as I can tell; you wouldn't put her on a list of those with soul. But she continues to fascinate, and any demonstration of mere common sense on her part is viewed as damned near sacred. She arouses perpetual salivation in any number of gasping busybodies. The cameras eat her up. Vaughtie has probably long ago absorbed Jackie. Almost all easy rhythm, the way she moves; that sort of fresh caution, like a deer on a golf course, can make you gasp, even now that she's forty. Her sister, without quite the moves, shadows her — a woman less developed, prettier, but with a set of shoulders that would launch a boat or two.

Down in my cellar there is a plaster head on a pedestal. Into the hole in its mouth I put a filtered cigarette and stand back various distances up to fifteen feet, the length of the bullwhip. I hardly ever miss the cigarette. The explosion of paper and tobacco still causes rare happiness in me. I have had a friend shoot this in slow motion, without me in the frame. You see the whip's end fall out of a curl and the fiber of the nylon kiss the tube, whereupon the thing leaps apart in shreds of white and brown. I am no freak for videoing anything that moves. I loathe the world of compulsive videoers and the zealous scum it invites, a whole new class of idiots. This reverence for the moving image seems even more frantic the less there is to our country, what with the public fools who stagger around trying to shape our hearts and minds. Nevertheless, I have *one* video of Vaughtie, almost by accident. My friend Amos left his machine at my house when the slow-motion of the cigarette was done, and I picked it up, tried it idly around the range, then went upstairs where I knew Vaughtie and Deborah were dressing to go out. There was a two-edged new excitement in the house. Vaughtie had come up pregnant. And I was about to go off with my unit to Desert Storm. I knew she feared for my life, with missiles and gas and so on. I acted solemn, but I was hugely excited. Back to this in a while. Could I get Vaughtie on the rest of this tape, right at the beginning of the long downward curve into age? She was frightened being forty. I could tell. There's a gloss that goes off, no matter how well you keep yourself.

The bloom simply goes away, on women and all of us, and it is instantly detectable. No surgery for it, no vitamins, no exercise. You will have that look of usage on you. You see some people change just about overnight. But I found the new fear in her eyes very beautiful. Now with her concern about *doing* something, she was another woman. Her anxiety for me was showing up. Flat in the middle of everything here in lovely San Diego we had us a war. I'd never been near real "action." Well, in my youth as a National Guardsman I'd helped integrate a university back down South. I was the same age as some of the students throwing brickbats into our windshield. Those weekends and the summer exercises where I'd become good with tanks marked me, as later in the San Francisco earthquake, but I did an enormous amount of sitting and wasting your money, and had rehearsed at war only about a twentieth of my whole time in the Guard. Presently, though, we were going over with the French Foreign Legion, who had a good deal to prove, as did we, since Vietnam. My job would be a boring pussy job in supply, but nevertheless I was beaming inside, like a Christmas child. Vaughtie and I needed the separation. Now I could take something of her with me.

With no plan, just lucky, I walked in and saw her leaning in front of the bathroom mirror before she knew I was around. She was in a half-slip with her nude back to me, looking at herself. Then she said something aloud:

"Everybody's dying. Everybody. It's something they have to do."

So I was there, camera raised, catching her voice and movement when her head went down, her hands on either side of the sink as she stared into the drain, where, when you thought about it, a great deal of her self had perished. But let me tell this: when she said what she said, the tone of her voice implied that she was not including herself. Everybody *else* is what she meant; as if everybody but her were going to some wretched ball, and only because they should. She seemed to be in the act of deciding whether to go herself or not. There I was, another creep with a camera, hearing this and spying into her privacy with it. But when she turned around, bare nipples almost pathetic, she looked so vulnerable, I had the camera down and acted as if I'd just come in.

"What's this? Isn't that Amos's?" She smiled.

"Memories to carry into the Persian Gulf. Memories of you, Vaughtie."

I lifted the camera and began shooting. She was teased but she liked it and held a few attitudes for me: the vagrant, chaste, or shocked wife; well, have your way. She was a long lovely woman and probably could have made a decent screen "presence." She didn't mind being seen at all. In fact, that might be her occupation, though some would view this as a nasty enslavement. I wondered if she did.

It was not definite to me whether she wanted the child. I did, very much. I had never learned truly to relax, a great flaw. I could have done the same I've done and more and had a better time of it. I wanted to teach my child how to relax and achieve that sweet ease of soul that better men have. I'd always worried and missed much life because I was forever away somewhere else in my head. This is a horrible thing — to have missed half your life, worrying it away. Baby, don't fret, the mother says to the little one. They should keep up the message: never forget. I've been instructed that great work emerges when our inklings of disaster meet against the flow of hopeful tranquillity, which the brain also provides. That's what Amos, essentially a lifetime bum with a camera, says.

The worst dilettante, but a fine man, Amos told me that Vaughtie, unlike many beauties he'd known, was, at least, not mean. Women who were told they were beautiful over and over grew to resent the world because it did not automatically give great rewards to them, so that everything began sounding like derision and cheap talk. When the compliments stopped, they tended to explode in revenge. America was worst at this, said Amos. In that way, I figure, it would be dangerous to laud a child too much. The entrance to the outer world would be the birth trauma all over again. I was already getting a loose program ready for the little one. But what about Vaughtie?

Pregnant at forty, she was likely to be physically torn down further by this late arrival, an accident. I'd heard somewhere, too, that women's brains were "softened" by birth and they were never intellectually the same afterwards. Did she sense this? She would be let out to the democratic pasture of "breeders," never a real individual again. Maybe I shouldn't have listened to Colonel Mario — a secret gay in our unit — so much. But the man is brilliant and does the better headwork for our division. He could run the show easily if I dropped dead of poison gas, etc. Some days it frightens me that I'm third in command in California, until I think of Mario and other good vets like Nimrod under me. My good service in the San Francisco tragedy, the very thing that thrust me up to brigadier, amounted to little more than releasing Mario and Nimrod to work their best, which was always swift and clicking.

Vaughtie's pregnancy had caused not a great, but slight, distance from her sister. I'd noticed Deborah looking at her sister with a baffled, even scared, expression on her face, and she was more likely to listen to Vaughtie and quieten herself. She was not so forthcoming anymore. They didn't talk of old times in their rare ecstatic youth so much. Mario said that on the positive side, pregnancy gave a woman her first taste of true power and independence. She felt, deep in her soul, that there was nobody else like her and her child. This made her happy in her work, the only distinctive work you got from merely being. A man had nothing like it. *Labor* was a woman's term, *delivery* a man's, said Mario. Among women, an unstated aristocracy of the pregnant woman existed, felt and respected by all.

Another ponderable was the happy accident, a thing that seemed to know and relish fate, that she became pregnant while the war was threatening and knew about it the day I got my summons. This made me feel very special. We had inadvertently prepared for my death, had we not? A change had come over me. At my most content, having done some work and been as composed as I ever get, I felt so good I wouldn't mind death. This was nothing like that chummy bravado, but secret fear, I had in my youth. This was a soothing, low-burning indifference to my fate, almost a chemical high. Death appeared as simply another interesting possibility, as appropriate as, say, suddenly taking up bird watching. My mother was very composed the last year of her life, a thing that mere tiredness did not account for. I wondered if there was a beautiful surge from within that prepared you for death when you reached a certain age. Am I vain, am I clutching at miracles and crutches, when I'm enjoying the appearance of new life in Vaughtie as mine is soon passing? I wondered. I wasn't tired at all. With the best ease I surrendered myself to my heir and infant.

The tyranny of the visual.

Amos talks about this; Amos, a man who lives by the eye, but calls his work ashes. He got this from a book and here I am back at college again. He has to take nitroglycerin tablets for a heart condition. Maybe it's Amos that reminds Vaughtie of death coming on to others. The war too, and I am the next carrier of it. Amos has a sort of Old Testament smile on him, a doomed twinkle in his eye: all is vanity. Most of what we do is vanity. But Vaughtie stopped his heart, as did Deborah. The two of them froze vision, made you happy in the chest. They made you feel rough and vulgar, some hauler of coal, smeared with grease, muttering and bumping into glassware. We knew that to the holy hermit in rough cloth — a man somewhere in most of us, no? — they meant nothing, that they were idle and vain, but the eye was overjoyed and sent old hairy judgment out the door.

I went to war and as everybody knows, it went handsomely for our side. I was busy and proud, more alert than frightened, eye on the sky every now and then. Young captains were smarter than I was, and better looking. Most of them had startling bodies and nimble minds, and they looked incredibly young. They could handle tanks much better than I. I mourned the justice of my position, an old man with no history signing orders out of twenty warehouses. I sat down once, outside, with a cigarette and envied a French private all sunburned, about six-two, lithe, needing no cigarette, with the deathly joy of the pro in his eyes. His eyes were a bright powerful gray. I got into the Guard, I recalled, from seeing men like him in a couple of movies. I believe I even started smoking because one of them smoked, and smoked very bravely, this actor. That, and music: Sousa, Tchaikovsky, Beethoven I'd heard — the grand, the martial, the fascistic, I guess. Even Copland's *Fanfare for the Common Man* made me want to pick up a rifle and move rapidly somewhere, anywhere, given a direction, given a cause. Is there any better feeling than standing out of the hatch with a tank under you all-out? A tank is just about it as the great land bully of our time. Be tall and want it. I chuckled, remembering how they put little Dukakis in one of those things for a photo op and just about ruined him, he seemed such a dufus.

When I called home, with still a month to go over there, I got what you might call a slow shock. Vaughtie's voice — nothing wrong with the reception — didn't sound right. She seemed short, maybe bitter. I couldn't get to it.

"Look," I said, "are you ashamed of me being over here?"

"I guess I am, husband." This was Vaughtie's familiar term with me. I think it indicated some mirth — marriage, etc. — and seriousness — I mean loyalty — at the same time. "It just seems like a long Guard weekend with war games. You ground up those people like a kid writing a movie."

"You'd prefer more casualties?"

"There *were* casualties, plenty, husband. But you just seem silly and stupid and mean, on that desert over there."

"Well, I'll be damned."

Vaughtie began crying, a thing she hardly ever did.

"No. I've been terrified for you. Those awful dumb missiles. But you're *grown*, Nick. You're not a kid. I swear, they're calling him a genius, but Schwarzkopf, on television, he seems like this puffy cartoon person in his camos, and—"

"Now wait."

"I'm not right, either. Something's happening to me. I'm so *dumb*. And I really am sorry about this phone call. I love you so. Part of me's just ecstatic about us and you. But it seems so selfish."

"Well, you're pregnant, Vaughtie."

She laughed. "I'm scared, and that seems selfish."

The word *selfish* hasn't ever occurred much in our marriage. Nor has *love*, for that matter, though I think we had it from time to time. Since we were no more selfish than our friends, I had stopped thinking of it and California, which I thought was composed entirely of selfish and asinine babies when we first got there. But this thought had sunk into the relative obscurity everybody keeps in their drawer, and I liked it in California.

I walked out into the back lot to have a smoke and think, which I'd promised myself not to do and been much happier for. That same French private, back from triumph and glory, was lazing around with some others. He had on earphones with a Walkman. He was looking very pleased, eyes closed, a little away from the other soldiers. I got really nosy, an act I hate usually. I asked him what music made him smile so. He handed me the headphones, kid's glee in his expression. He told me it was "Jane's Addiction."

"How can you stand that shit?" I joked, but the music was just paralyzingly awful to me. The rest of them laughed. They were all fans of "Jane's Addiction," and seemed no worse for it. It was very strange to know they had driven into war with that stuff in their ears, very strange. This must have showed on my face. The soldiers got soberer and nervous suddenly, wanting me to leave, I know. So I did, and my smile was phony. Those long echoing guitar chords, loud surly nonsense, went out into the desert from my mind and nearly made me puke. In it I heard the scream of Vaughtie, the scream of many women, protesting. Demons and banshees shrieked down the wind. Seemed there was only one possible music for the times—awful.

I did an awful thing when I got back to San Diego, with a hard and tan body. I began carrying on with a Chinese-Hawaiian girl who played flute in the orchestra at the marine base. It was very calculated, too, and begun in spite, right as the baby had just a month to arrive. She was a "clean" woman who said she'd had things twice before with "clean" married men who were mildly alluring to her. A clumsy, airless predicament is what it became: two people staring past each other's shoulders at something limping. She was in her midtwenties, very striking, I thought, although it is surprising how her face changed toward the lines of a vampire, even as I boasted inside about my conquest. This wasn't her fault. I knew she was lovely and that my eyes were deranging her. Corporal Ho was intelligent, and tender in her memories, calm music in her voice. But you wind up one afternoon gasping, snarled in the chest. I had come up a flight of stairs into the apartment and let myself in. She wasn't there. This California sunlight, falling in from late afternoon through the sliding glass doors, this sunlight that exonerates everybody out here, was working the exact opposite on me. I was simply a gaudy, strutting worm revealed, with a tape of a cigarette exploding at the end of a bullwhip in my hand, like a million video monsters crawling around the land with their special captured moments to reveal. I sat on the couch, like a ruined, sensitive old man in a gray European movie, watching another movie. Probably I knew the girl wasn't going to be home. After the cigarette exploded, Vaughtie came on, bare-shouldered in the bathroom, her trim back to me, then put her hands down on the lavatory sink.

"Everybody's dying. Everybody. It's something they have to do."

Now I heard it as a description of me, off dying in this low arrangement with the flutist, while my wife was back at the house preparing life.

Once I was visiting a movie lot at the invitation of an assistant director friend of mine. We stood silently on the set and watched the pet director of another technical thriller — a tall man, very stern, who had once been a doctor. A young beauty walked over to him and gave him a long cigarette, which he took without acknowledging her. I sighed and whispered my appreciation of the woman to my friend. "Oh yes. One of his. And he has many, many." This tall, current "genius" moving about the Los Angeles precincts from one woman to another struck me as a really nauseating exercise in power. I was surprised I didn't envy him. When the movie came out it was dreary, just like him, I moralized, and generally ignored, which I enjoyed: a series of computer screens and multiple whiz-kid gimmicks involved in the deaths of a bunch of women, not a hint of character anywhere, and employing that special American monster, the hip aging man, James Coburn, with the moves of a Nebraska lizard. Clinching my teeth, I recalled the looming pomposity of the director on the set. I wrote a note and left the girl, everything a bad choice, myself sadder and dumber for it all.

Vaughtie and Deborah were in the big room when I got in. Vaughtie was imminent in her pregnancy, draped in something simple and chic, soft, with mild flowers designed on it. Deborah was in a girlish shift and her tan was dark, warm on the slopes of her shoulders. They were gluing together the slats of a crib that had held both of them as infants and they were very serious about mending it. Their ignorance of the Chinese-Hawaiian girl made them seem unbearably virtuous, especially Vaughtie. When I smiled at her I couldn't focus on her face. She had been away in her realm a long time. Even though she made rote apologies, it was clear I was a redundant culprit growing hazier to her. Given any moment, she could turn indifference or pity on me. The scraps of me left to her regard seemed incapable of arousing anything larger.

Colonel Mario, after our parade, had told me to "really hump" Corporal Ho, the flutist; "Don't hold back, if you're going to cheat. Do it thoroughly. It'll only destroy life if you do it halfway." Well, here again I'd missed — an old man in supply, a miserable half-fucker. I eased down to my cellar range, put the tragic Roy Orbison in my CD player, shot my pistols, and became wet in the eyes. We were going to have a girl. Father of a girl at fifty years old.

Throughout my life an imperative had run in my head, maybe from some old movie or play I can't remember. It was simply a part of my memory, strangled under some burning bridge. There had never, not through the years of work with employees, nor the decades of my arrival to the brigadiership, been an occasion to bring it out. No moment offered itself as propitious, no dramatic swell provided for it. It was the line "Get out. Get out now." No, I had been surrounded by competence and sweet cooperation. But then, down on the range, wet-eyed over Orbison with my pistol spitting, I suppose I grew bold and nuts. There might never be an opportunity. My discontent swirled all around Deborah. I could imagine her whispering in Vaughtie's ear all these years, and especially during the war and through her pregnancy. She was the snake, the poison, the perverter of everything. How weak of me to be afraid of her beauty, as I'd been. Up the stairs I went, already hot and wet around the collar, dabbing a handkerchief on my eyes. I took a posture at the door of the big room. Both their heads were down, working over the last slat.

"All right, Deborah. Get out. Get out now."

The sisters looked up, neutral in their faces. The tenor of Roy Orbison was pining from the basement. I had made an occasional joking command, parodying my brigadiership. I suppose they thought it was this odd humor from me, and they froze to suffer it. But then they understood my face.

"Nick, whatever do you think you're doing?" asked Vaughtie.

"Deborah must go. We are poor now. Things have changed. We need a dog," I improvised.

"We are *not* poor. Stop this. You were bragging just the other day about your business."

"Just bravado. Hard times are on."

Deborah spoke. "Did you really say 'Get out. Get out now'?" She seemed near laughing.

"I did." I wished that Orbison were not singing so high, so desperately now behind me.

"What should I do, Vaughtie?" Deborah said, getting nervous with her comely limbs. She shouldn't have asked Vaughtie. She should still be looking at me.

"What have you ever done," I said, "but conspire? Bump around and gab?"

"You're a lunatic, Nick. You're going through some awful lunacy in yourself," Deborah said. "A dog, for heaven's sake."

"Dogs go with babies. A big old hairy mutt."

"Don't aunts go with babies too?" asked Deborah. Incredulous, she was beginning to cry, or wanted Vaughtie to think she was.

"Dogs don't poison the mother against me."

"I never —"

"Shut up. You need a board across your ass and a cup to beg your fucking supper with."

"Nick, God!" Vaughtie pleaded.

"What do you think, we're *aristocrats?*"

I had exploded myself. I backed down to the range, wishing Orbison would also shut up. He did. There I stayed for a long, long time.

Good soldierly coward, I got into the Black Jack, and glowered at the walls of the range. I cut up a carrot from the fridge and ate along with the bourbon. You can't hear much upstairs from here — built that way. I was glad they couldn't hear me roar. Not from the mouth. There seemed to be a loud noise in my head as I plunged around trying to find something greatly worthy in myself.

The thick door opened at the top of the stairs. Slowly, her hand on the rail, and in that stricken waddle she was forced into — a thing that brought on immense sympathy in me — Vaughtie came down with her big stomach ahead of her. I was ready for the worst. You can't have it out with a woman that pregnant. She was wearing, of all things, a near-smile, as if something miraculous had not quite been explained to her yet, and she was waiting.

"Deborah's gone, Nick. Why, husband, have you waited all this time with that on your chest?"

"It's just...the time. Husbands get to help make nests too, don't they? They have to prepare the way. Don't wolf fathers help?"

"I don't know. I've been too dumb to learn anything for several months now. You saw that on television?"

"I believe so. Yes."

"I've not let you into this very much, have I, General?"

"I don't seem to have much to do with it. No."

She looked down the range, then at the targets and the pedestal with the head and the cigarette stuck in its lips. She smiled fully all of a sudden, the miracle having been explained, all wild bliss — or insanity.

"Are you still good with that whip?"

"Yeah. The last of somebody. Not much call for your whippist."

"Do me."

"You don't mean —"

"Take the cigarette out of my mouth with your whip."

She waddled past the gun counter and over to the head, removed the cigarette, put it in her mouth, and stood in front of the plaster head on the pedestal, in profile.

"See if you're any good, General."

It wasn't me, my being any good. The bigger question was this smiling surrender of Vaughtie, this loony adventure. She was waiting on the miracle from me, but it was she who was passing over into a very, very unusual arena of will. I'd been drinking. She was stone sober, her hands behind her back, steady, like a martyr. Two of them, she and the baby girl, in two profiles.

You can believe I measured this one, but not very long. My hand went up past my ear, my arm flashing back. I don't think I ever hit a better one. The air was white with paper, the leather drawn back, coiled in my palm, and I looked through the haze at her lips, where the filter stub was still in her pout.

"Very *good*, husband! I can't say that doesn't hurt a little, though."

She turned toward me, her hand going up to her mouth to take the stub out. Some tiny fragment must have blown out and cut her in the explosion. A thin stream of blood was coming off her lip. She didn't even know it. I've never loved anything more or been more ashamed than here, just then.

"Vaughtie! Oh, my Vaughtie!" I raced to her with my handkerchief and covered her with my arms. She was surprised and some saner when she saw the blood on the white cloth. She just put her head down and let me moan out my apologies. But she didn't make much of the little cut, and we became very close.

Our baby girl came the next week, in much joy after a short labor. Now I felt thrilled, almost hot with love, really *in* love with both of them. The big hairy dog was waiting for us at home, with Colonel Mario. On the phone he said Deborah had come by, very timidly, to look at the dog, and they had chatted. He liked Deborah. He could talk to her. He almost wouldn't let her go home.

My joy was so big I began to get guilty, and I did feel selfish, finally. Me, to love this wife, especially that wife with the trickling blood on her chin, and this baby girl, born with full, neat hair, almost a wig. Just a couple months ago I was in the thick of the desks, providing for the death of all those poor Iraqis. It was true, what Hussein said. We cared more about our pets than we did the Iraqis. But the further scandal was that we cared more for our pets — old Barney — than we did our own neighbors and certainly our sisters-in-law. It did seem a sin to have all this now, but of course I flexed this right out of my conscience pretty soon.

I got the phone one afternoon when mother and daughter were sleeping. It was Deborah. She said she wanted to speak to me, not Vaughtie.

"Nick, you know our famous zoo."

"Yes. Yes. The San Diego Zoo. Where do I belong, Deborah?"

No, no, it wasn't that at all. She said she had a job there. She was guiding children on field trips around the zoo, and she loved it. She wanted to thank me for doing what I had, the best thing that ever happened to her. I had set her free of a long, not wholly healthy, confusion about themselves and their dependency. She was very loose and happy and maybe even, just a little bit, in love. She wanted to thank me for having a friend like Mario. They were just, just, getting on...swimmingly. She found Mario's loyalty to me very touching. I was lucky. And so was she. She was all ready to be a good, loving... but (she giggled) miles-away aunt.

You get this rarely and it even feels dangerous, all this warming neat happiness in a bundle, like sleep at the end of a Shakespeare play that "knits up the raveled sleeve of care," isn't it? Then there will come something, and pretty soon, something going back to Vaughtie's statement about everybody dying, they have to; then on to that wild trance she seemed in down in the basement, and the trickle of blood; then on, pow, to I walk in on her six weeks later in the bed with her face in blue mud, having at it with her aerial lover, bucking involuntarily, having at herself, only those Las Vegas floorshow heels on, silver; and I shut the door, bump. There is no possible way to ever discuss this. It is not an uncommon male dream, is it? These things are filmed. These things are thrown out of your night musings. But she was enjoying it so, better than ever with me—beyond the full released smile I worked for, beyond everything. When you see your own wife, well. I was holding the baby. I was thinking baby things these weeks, while she was going on into another change. I am aroused. That blue mud, though, that blue mud. And you thought of some blue huge man, bigger than me, better in all ways, laughing over her as he thrusts. You can't stop it. It was almost holy.

Without any explanation, she began going down in the basement. I could hear her cracking the whip, feebly at first, but then the full crack. Something hit the floor and broke. I'm holding the baby, I tell you. She seems older, but deeper in beauty, and almost angry with lust. I'm holding the baby up here, hoping I won't hear it, her call to me. I think even her voice is a little deeper.

"Husband. Come down here, would you? Bring your cigarette."

The title of this story comes from Tom McGuane, quoting the first line of a projected nonexistent novel.

Herman Is
in Another State

I WAS SOMEWHERE I shouldn't have been, she tells me. But I was at the place I've been so many times, where the vegetation and the armadillos come up close but die because of the smoke and gunfire and the grease dumped out of the house.

The gays Monty and Julian were there too. They were older now, middle-aged like the rest of us liars and vicious gossips, and not so hysterical about their place on the pier. A certain kind of rage was gone from us, as when I had set their car on fire in 1975. I'd immediately put it out, though, with my expensive coat and my girlfriend's best Irish plaid blanket.

Herman was there this time, at Eagle Lake, and the place was so changed, with the "clubhouse" and its smoke and grease around the masonite blocks. What has happened to you guys? I wanted to know. I thought just boys and old men played checkers and dominoes.

Feeling like he was about to die, Herman had brought his Polaroid 620 Sun Camera out to the old pier to collect pictures before he perished of cancer next year, as he told us, at age seventy-eight. The rest of us were wanting to be his age and as handsome, but he did have a serious cancer around the spleen, and he just asked us if we would listen to one more thing. He lit up a long Pall Mall and threw his match out in the water. The water was still good, it was nice to see. A big bream came up and bit the match in two.

"When my wife, who never made a mistake, died of the Parkinson's disease, I was pretty sad for a while, boys."

Everybody in the entire world was a boy or a girl to Herman. What a nice position of height to attain in life.

"I had the prostate cancer myself but it was taken care of. What the hell is that you're holding, lad?"

He was asking about the pocket calculator I held in my hand. I told him what it was. He was interested for about half a minute. He'd thought it was my heart-pacer or a beeper to the ambulances.

It was late in the evening. As I saw the big bass popping around the cypress stumps, chasing the big and little bream, I did a special thing for Herman. I turned the calculator on and put a bass hook on the bottom of it with Krazy Glue. Then, when the glue was set, I tied my line to the lure and cast it out near the stump.

The sun was doing a lot for us tonight as it went down to heat another world.

Herman began talking again. "I haven't had any sex in twenty years. I had a lot of sex with my wife and we had a lovely time together, lads. But when she died and we buried her, my sons and daughters and I, and put up the Italian marble over her, I just didn't feel like it anymore. I've still got all her perfume bottles at home, all her gowns and underwear, all the tools she used to fix up the house. I just sit around and *have* her there, do you understand?"

One lying old fart got off the rail and said, "I'm dying too, but I ain't dying so fucking politely."

He sighed with a deep scratching noise. He's had emphysema for fifteen years. "I goddamn hate it to go ahead and end."

Herman saw what was happening as I gave him the rod. A bass had taken the pocket computer bait and was taking the line away into the deep water and under.

Herman stood back and the rest of us moved away. Monty and Julian reached to assist the old man as he was pulled away to the rail by the fish. The bass was something and it was running out deep. Herman knew how to do it. He had it on and then he hit it good. His arms were terribly thin and I thought the bass might take him over the rail. His legs were thin, too, from his cancer of the spleen, I remembered.

"She was a wonderful woman, always trying to save my life. Eh, eh, eh."

The other old man grabbed him around the chest to help him.

I thought they'd never make it, but they, together, brought the big black large-mouth bass in. It was eight pounds, heaving, with the pocket calculator still in its mouth, and the blood running out of its gums.

An hour passed. Herman had let the big mother bass go. All the big bass are females.

He was breathing heavy and he smelled like fish. We just sat on the pier and saw the moon come over Eagle Lake from the direction of Vicksburg.

"Well, lads," said Herman.

The women had come out to see the big bass and the old man. They poured out of the greasy masonite "clubhouse" with the oily table and the bait and the truculent stepson who had been fired many times but kept returning, with his stringy long hair and his tattoos.

"Well," said Herman. "I've got to get over to another state. Got to go over to Houston and have my cancer cured."

By now it was eleven and the water on the pier was rippling around with a little breeze so as to remind us of the ocean and all the water we have not yet poisoned. Three quarters of the planet just lying there and asking us calmly again.

"I've got a better idea of my death now," said Herman.

Dental

H E WAS OUT in the country with his dog when he died. He once told my father at the post office that he was "broke but happy." The dentist left us guessing, but I with my arrogant hindsight might supply this for him:

The old man hears something at the window.

He has been out here a long time now, all alone and wishing for nothing.

He has had a secret life not many know about, and those who knew wish they didn't. In his kitchen cabinet lay six manuscripts of around five hundred badly typed pages, each the product of an old Royal manual typewriter. There was enough writing done with that machine to have given his fingers — once in my mouth — a sort of miniature biceps. He was very strong in the hands from his dental work, too. The writing, neither real novels nor whole tracts, was a mixture of what? — apocalyptic pornography, angry "realism," and extremely paranoid right-wing ranting. In one book even the space aliens are Communists, led by a nude queen who stitches the hammer and sickle on the backs of helpless nude American men with a giant atomic sewing machine. He was once inspired by the success of his fellow Mississippians Tennessee Williams and William Faulkner, both odd boys from a humid nowhere, like him. Only he would have more to say. His wife was horrified by his literature, and distanced herself, leaving him finally. The editors in New York who saw the stuff considered it too bad even for office jokes. But they were Communists, too, he said, stunned by nonacceptance, white with fury.

Saying he was wishing for nothing is probably not quite right. The manuscripts were neatly stacked in the cabinet under the linoleum counter, certain that posterity might someday find and publish them.

The old man hears something at the window, something tapping, like one of the minions or Norns of the arriving nude alien Communist queen. There was a dog with him, but here the dog was, lying just under his nose. So it couldn't be the dog making noise at the window.

When the old man was fierier and younger, he had had even more politics. This was just after the demise of Joe McCarthy, but he had clung to the beliefs of McCarthy, telling one patient it was a difficult time to work in, very difficult, what with a Communist occupying the White House. The patient could not reply because that metal draining hook was siphoning the blood and dental matter from her mouth. That woman would later marry me.

The dentist was not used to being replied to. A dentist may go through life without any true conversation at all. Maybe this is why so many dentists are strange, lonely, and depressed men, often committing suicide through nitrous oxide, which they have easy access to. They know nitrous oxide is good stuff. He had never thought of doing himself in, even after he found out that McCarthy had been deemed bogus. But he had often thought of doing some of the *world* in.

In college he bought a copy of Marx's *Communist Manifesto*. He'd begun reading it but found it totally incomprehensible. He read *Mein Kampf* straight through, however, with sighs of pleasure, slapping it down with the triumph one sometimes has in reading a satisfying novel at the beach. There were tearstains around his eyes at this time, because he had drunk a pint of bourbon during the last half of Hitler's book. There was something sweetly joyful and sinful in reading it late at night, his roommate snoring stupidly away on the cot across the room. The bourbon was secretly joyful, too. This was a religious college that enforced the rule against drink on the premises very forcefully. No matter, he never forgot the thrill of that book, though he had been a dentist in the army and done his part against Adolf. At the end of the war, however, when everybody knew the Germans were in rout, he recalled how sad it was to reckon with our white men killing their white men, and a great regret came over him, especially with the Russian Matter looming up almost instantly.

With some of his money in his fifties, in fact with a large part of it, he invested in a combination swine and potato farm. This was the upshot: all his help quit one day, leaving for Detroit, and these men, these three men, deliberately left the gates of the hog ranch open — during a dry, hard season — and the pigs ate the potatoes. They ate so many that most of them died.

He could not reconcile himself with such spite.

He put no stock in psychotherapy. Look at the lone psychologists in town — a married couple, the Beeflows. They gave their only son, whom they had not wanted and called openly to his face "our drunken accident," everything that came into a teenager's mind: a

Volvo coupe with two carburetors, high-fidelity records as soon as they appeared in the stores, five-dollar haircuts. The mother was a chain-smoker with a murderous glare for the locals. She and her husband were from Chicago, and had been educated there. Our dentist friend could think of nothing worse than entrusting the life of his mind to this woman. But he had such fire within himself that he was bound to seek solace.

He went seven counties and a hundred fifty miles away for counseling. He went to Meridian, trying to understand the spite of those black men who had treated him this way. He went to a real psychiatrist, a man with an M.D.

Still, the drive down was nervous. What if anybody ever found out? What if his *wife* found out? She ran a plant nursery and was very good-looking, though sometimes out of a certain despair she leaned toward the portly. She had large warm brown eyes, and their children were beautiful mainly because she was beautiful. He almost never saw his boys. His boys were graceful and played good, hard baseball. When he was in college, a smart-aleck friend of his roommate's had called him "epicene." He had stood there and taken it and, when the fellow left, he looked up the word and was appalled.

The psychiatrist worked above a shoe store. His own offices were much better than the psychiatrist's, who was very young, wearing thick glasses, with bright red hair on his head. He was having a bad time himself, in Meridian, and about this he expatiated. His receptionist had just quit because he'd cut off her Valium.

They were meeting at straight-up two in the afternoon, and this was a significant time, almost an oddly magical time, said the young psychiatrist. You must remember, he told the dentist, psychiatry is new to Mississippi. It came in about the same time as TV, say '52 to '53, and was met with much greater hesitation than "Hopalong Cassidy" or "Our Miss Brooks." Now since it was 1959, but only 1959, there was still resistance. People were ashamed to speak of their troubles, the trouble in their minds and with their fellows, and about their lack of sleep, their night sweats. They might be just a little different from those around them, just a little, that's all, and still they were ashamed to confess that difference, especially in the South where a man was raised to barely ever confess even his physical ailments.

The dentist wanted to know what was oddly magical about two P.M.

Thousands, millions of people are deciding right now whether to finish the day and keep on living, the young man said. They are ashamed to cry out their ailments.

"I'm not ashamed," the dentist lied.

"I can see you're a different sort yourself," the psychiatrist went on. The dentist wondered if he'd looked that young when he first did his citizen practice. The man was so young, a ray of sun would come across his face and reveal (how the dentist loved that word, using it five to ten times a day) a *veritable* boy, from a tenth-grade class. His accent was Southern. Maybe he was *from* Meridian. But his language was animated and brilliant, and very soothing. The dentist wanted to ask where he had gone to school, but decided this would be unmanly. He would look at the certificates on the wall when he left.

"So what," proceeded Dr. McRae, the psychiatrist, "is on your mind?"

"The colored that were so mean to me."

"How's it going with the wife? I mean frankly the wife in bed, Doctor."

"I didn't drive all the way down here to talk about Sigmund Freud. I'm paying cash. I had this swine and potato farm —"

"How did you feel about... the 'colored'?"

The dentist didn't understand what he wanted.

"Were you cruel to them in any way, do you think?" The young man lit an Oasis cigarette. "Did you pay them well? What is your attitude toward colored people in relation to yourself?"

"I was never cruel to anybody in my life. I paid all three of them twice what they were worth."

"What do you mean by that?"

"Twenty dollars a day."

"For all of them, all three?"

"For each one."

"I've never heard of a man paying that much for farm help."

"Ten dollars a day, then. But also gasoline. God damn it, I got them free service at the emergency room."

"For what?"

"For cutting each other up after they drank. Good Lord, man. Where have you been? I also bought them cigarettes and food."

"You ever take a drink with them?"

"No."

"You ever use dental drugs — Demerol, nitrous, phenobarb, opiates?"

"Certainly not. Yes."

"Does your wife treat your body like it was magic or does she just shut her eyes and give you the usual thing?"

The dentist refused to answer.

"Do you have visions of nailing her to a cross at orgasm?"

"My nasty God."

"Are you a 'nigger-lover' or a 'nigger-hater'? Which one, would you say?"

"Middle of the road."

The dentist looked around the pathetic dusty office, with only one certificate on the wall. It smelled of cigarette smoke, and he could smell food from a discarded white bag in the wastebasket. Dr. McRae was still sitting on his desk here in the outer room. Weren't they supposed to go back and get on a couch? There was a working air conditioner in there, anyway, and it would be a much better place to be healed in. There was also some nice soft furniture in there. He must have been looking at it wistfully.

"Sure. We can go in there if you like."

They went in and the psychiatrist shut the door.

"In this state, doctor, I find there are exactly five subjects: money, Negroes, women, religion, and Elvis Presley. Add football sometimes. The rest are nothing," said Dr. McRae. "Strip off, how about it?"

"What?"

"Take your clothes... like off."

He never went back to Meridian.

He knew young Dr. McRae was not nuts or queer. The psychiatrist tried to move him ahead very rapidly toward an understanding, and he knew it, but the pace was just too frightening. He had understood that years were entailed in this therapy, and that one often became friends with the psychiatrist. This young man did not seem to care really whether the two of them were friends or enemies. He worked toward something that was so clean, pure, radiant and true, that the dentist did not want to see it and still did not.

Was it the memory of the young psychiatrist knocking at the window when he went to bed?

Now he was sixty-six years old and he wondered if that young man was still in the state, or even still alive, still as clear, radiant, and moral as he was almost thirty years ago.

During the years, he was kinder to blacks, but he could not help being terribly interested in the Atlanta child murders. The man they had arrested had spoken of the numbers of blacks that could come from one young black male, and how if you could just destroy one, you would take hundreds away from the earth. The dentist did not want to kill anybody personally, but he considered, very profoundly, how much more pleasant it would be if there were fewer people around who never paid their bills and had no two thoughts about it.

The schools integrated.

His wife left him for a gentle cattle baron whose grounds she had planted. He had barely any money left. If the blacks who owed him money for their teeth ever showed up and paid him at once, he thought, he would have another fortune.

His sons were off somewhere, ignoring him. He was not even certain what work they did now. It was all right that he was a "failure"; that was all right. He would live out here at the old family place perched at the edge of the stranded swine and potato farm. He described himself to the few acquaintances around town as "broke but happy" — the few who bothered to ask or even recognized him anymore at the village grocery store, which an Indian couple had bought.

The town had grown very much. There were tax advantages and good schools for people who worked in the nearby city, and the town was spread out in subdivisions around the old village with brick streets, the women's college, the great Baptist church. Some of the homes south of town were worth upwards of $300,000, he'd heard. He didn't know. What was sure was that the old town was grown and gone, and there was no place else to escape to.

He had run from the young psychiatrist in the fifties, the young man who held truth like a candle as in one of those old Fisk ads ("Time to Retire"), the lad with the tire around his shoulders — the heaviness of the truth of a good tire, the candle blazing in total darkness, and the little boy in his sleeping gown, cherished in his innocent beseeching expression.

Oh, he wasn't going to run away from this place, even if the colored people showed up and paid him everything suddenly. The town was almost around him, anyway. It had nearly sprawled out to the old homeplace itself.

Here he was left with his dog, an amiable long-haired cur with the fine warm brown eyes of his wife, and the growing lawn under the pines with the kudzu creeping on their trunks. Nothing ever showed in the hot drenching wet sun of mid-Mississippi beyond a few cats looking for rats and little rabbits outside. Oh, there had been a woman over at Vicksburg on the river for him, but there had come an ugly night when he refused to pay, and she had called the law on him. The police had driven over quickly and had protected the *whore*.

He was out here on the remnants of the very farm where he had the swine and potatoes, and his meals — such as he could choke down—were mainly canned meat, crackers, and the tomatoes that came from the ragged patch at the back door steps.

Still, he could swear he heard a noise, a definite noise, at the window where the air conditioner was working. It happened at night only, never during the day. He could not find a flashlight in the house, not one that worked. They were all frozen up with their oxides. There came a definite tapping, such a definite tapping that it woke him off his perch on the chair where he was sleeping.

This time he was readier. Last time he was at the village store, he'd smiled wanly at the smiling incomprehensible Indian behind the checkout counter. It was a new Ray-O-Lite flashlight, utterly trustworthy, he knew by damn, a thing in the night like that child with a candle, its eyes wondering, with the tire of truth on its shoulder.

For three weeks he's heard this tapping, tapping, tapping at night.

In the chair, breathing too hard, he saw that he was a coward. He knew, though, that he was a man born to wander, bringing back wild beasts from rare parts for others to study. In the nude and so wild that they would barely call him a man.

He got up suddenly, and raced around the house in his old bent-down tennis shoes, not even waiting to be scared further. Certainly, he wouldn't linger anymore about this issue. He wasn't going to just sit there anymore, like the other billions, and wait for the wild beast to come to him. He knew he wasn't crazy, he knew he wasn't. He had never been crazy.

He wanted to prove this.

At the air conditioner outside he saw a tall man he took for a teenager, a yellow-brown young man, tapping on his window. The young man froze and looked on as straight at the light as he could.

"Who are you?" he demanded.

"I'm Dagen Sayers," said the man. He now looked to be about twenty-five.

"Sayers. Like Dagen Sayers that worked for me here. That let my pigs—"

"His son."

"Why. What—"

"Daddy's dead. But I came back to mess with you."

"Mess with... but *mess?*" he asked.

"Confuse you, white man. Mister Dentist. Con*fuse* you."

Our friend was gone then.

So was his heart.

It would be nice to say the young man knew him and brought him to the emergency room, but it didn't go that way. The dentist made a call to one of his white neighbors, a man *nouveau riche,* and depthless in his understanding, and horrible to his mind. Me.

And this is how our dentist friend went away, leaving a handsome, lean, gray-haired corpse behind.

His hair was shot up in waves, like an evangelist's who's heard the knock on the door.

I tongue the delicious, somehow, open space of my absent tooth behind the molar where the dentist jerked it, for being rotten and unsavable, although through the years my teeth have leaned out of their normal position to compensate for it. Such with the death of others we have known slightly, here a secretive old man. No more, no less, but somehow slightly delicious after all. I don't know why.

This Happy Breed

"THIS GOOD MORNING all around the fires — excellent! — you stand waiting and wanting for word of our excursion and our aim. We left the Chinese restaurant at one, you know, meditating our future, both bellies full of green tea, which works for good thoughts and high dreams. Not until four this morning did we shut our eyes, and then hardly any success toward Morpheus. Myself, randy as glue — such brain-letting usually leads this way — roved into a hot long navel-bumper with Doris, letting me have more than a piece of her mind for a change. Ho! Thus, as in the old sermon, we have toiled the night and come through with some reapage, some harvest, for you. Men, we are going to sell our wives. I'd heard it quoted from some film star or other: 'Every time you look at a beautiful woman, remember: somebody is tired of her.'

"Now let's face it. The great narratives of a race arrive through periods of captivity and domination, yes, unto slavery. These were the great days, days of profound note, when, God bless, there *was a story,* there was actual content. We've no heart and no journey as we come upon the end of this century. No respect is given a man or wife from his children, and rightly so — don't wonder. What is there to respect in success, really? Where does it come from but our puny civilized, dominating, ruling class with every kind of freedom? Who *cares* about such success as we see around us? What does it breed except mewling and puking and good health? Well, health for what?

"But again, to the tiredness, the simple fatigue, the ennui, the bleak discouragement over one's partner: what cure can we find except — this arrived after *days* and *nights,* forty-two of them, of thought, anguish, with — heh! — an occasional thrust of loin — by the sweat, blood, yes, and *weeping,* crying for our poor well-set-up race. (This is going to obtain both ways. In some cases, the *husband* will be sold into slavery. Rethink, now. Imagine the exhilaration on both sides.) Polygamy is not the point, nor is our old grim discredited monogamy. The point is slavery and endowment. You sell her to

{ 301 }

a rich person for a lot of money; you sell him to a lonesome pecunious widow. Here is your future, your nest egg. You live on this money, a substantial amount we would hope, but the point, really, is slavery, not money.

"'Doris,' you ask. 'What about Doris?' Yes, I am tired of her. There's no real poetry left to her. She has thickened and clotted. Hardly ever do I ever penetrate that loose gummy old valley of hers that I am not dreaming of some tight little frisketta, with hair flicking, black, like a horse tail. I, of course, numb the socks off old Doris, too, and she is ready to be sold into slavery, chewing on the tether, chomping at the prick — ho! — that now only dully feeds her. I am ready to go in there, in there to serve and to wait, even mourn, under some master. Who has not had voluptuous dreams of being, yes shivering dreams, of being persecuted, being scolded, being made to sing while you work?

"Whoever brings the best price, I tell you. We are waiting. I've had it with the land of the free. That fool Nathan Hale. Patrick Henry, my God, sure, *they're* interesting, they had stories. But we don't, most assuredly. We have had too much freedom, we should be horrified by it. All good people are eventually horrified by freedom, no? Let us lead you now, Doris and me, across the desert back to Egypt. For promised land, for bite of the whip again, for galley ship belowdecks, for ecstatic captivity — truss and collar, whistle while you crack a rock! For salt mines! I sing of thee. Here is manhood, womanhood. Here is character. Be somebody, I adjure you. Be a slave!"

They came and got him, this old mayor, shouting from his porch, just a few loiterers and one aimless millionaire across the street raking his yard, listening to him.

Of Doris — there was no Doris, of course. She had died years ago, smothered in jewels and furs, with a face-lift that wore well into death. Her coffin was so light coming out of the hearse that the men grabbing it almost tossed it in the air. For Doris was light — a thin old fashionable woman, without, really, a care, so well had the mayor provided.

So it was a very sad thing when they led him off — still haranguing — to the house of the rich and insane, his grown children smiling.

Hey, Have You Got a Cig,
the Time, the News,
My Face?

H IS DREAMS were not good. E. Dan Ross had constant night-mares, but lately they had run at him deep and loud, almost begging him. He was afraid his son would kill his second wife. Ross often wanted to kill his own wife, Newt's mother, but he was always talking himself out of it, talking himself back into love for her. This had been going on for thirty-two years. E. Dan Ross did not consider his marriage at all exceptional. But he was afraid his son had inherited a more desperate fire.

Newt had been fired from the state cow college where he taught composition and poetry. Newt was a poet. But a friend of Ross's had called from the campus and told him he thought Newt, alas, had a drinking problem. He was not released for only the scandal of sleeping with a student named Ivy Pilgrim. There was his temper and the other thing, drink. Newt was thirty. He took many things very seriously, but in a stupid, inappropriate way, Ross thought. There were many examples of this through the years. Now, for example, he had married this Ivy Pilgrim. This was his second wife.

The marriage should not have taken place. Newt was unable to swim rightly in his life and times. The girl was not pregnant, neither was she rich. If she had made up that name, by the way, Ross might kill her himself. He could imagine a hypersensitive dirt-town twit leeching onto his boy. Newt's poetry had won several awards, including two national ones, and his two books had been seriously reviewed in New York papers, and by one in England.

Ross did not have to do all the imagining. Newt had sent him a photograph a month ago. It was taken in front of their quarters in the college town, where they remained, Newt having been reduced in scandal, the girl having been promoted, Ross figured. Ross was a writer himself. He was proud of Newt. Now he was driving to see him from Point Clear, Alabama, a gorgeous village on the eastern shore of Mobile Bay. Ross and his wife lived in a goodly spread along the beach. He worked in a room on the pier with the brown water practically lapping around his legs. It was a fecund and soul-washed place, he felt. He drove a black Buick Riviera, his fifth, with a new two-seater fiberglass boat trailing behind. It was deliberately two-seater. There would be no room for the girl when they went out to try the bass and bream.

He saw ahead to them: The girl would be negligent, a soft puff of skin above her blue jeans, woolly "earth sandals" on her feet, and a fading light in her eyes, under which lay slight bags from beer and marijuana and Valium when she could get it. Newt's eyes would be red and there would be a scowl on him. He will be humming a low and nervous song. He will be filthy and misclothed, like an Englishman. His hands will be soft and dirty around the fingernails. He'll look like a deserter on the lam. This is the mode affected by retarded bohemians around campus. Cats would slink underfoot in their home. Cats go with really sorry people. If anybody smokes, Newt and Ivy will make a point of never emptying the ashtray, probably a coffee can, crammed and stinking with cigarettes. Somebody will have sores on the leg or a very bad bruise somewhere. They will have a guitar which nobody can play worth spit. A third of a bottle of whiskey is somewhere, probably under the sink. They'll be collecting cash from the penny bowl in order to make a trip to the liquor store. This is the big decision of the day. Old cat food would lie in a bowl, crusted. Shoes and socks would be left out. Wherever they go to school or teach it is greatly lousy, unspeakably and harmfully wrong. This was his son and his wife, holding down the block among their awful neighbors in a smirking conspiracy of sorriness; a tract of rental houses with muddy, unfixed motorcycles and bicycles around. Somebody's kid would sit obscene-mouthed on a porch.

E. Dan Ross, a successful biographer, glib to the point of hackery (he prided himself on this), came near a real monologue in his head: Your son is thirty and you see the honors he has won in poetry become like cheap trinkets won at a fair and now you know it has not been a good bargain. A bit of even immortal expression should not make this necessary. It should have brought him a better woman and a better home. Your son has been fired in scandal from a bad school. Newt must prevail, have a "story." These poets are oh, yes, insistent on their troubled biography. The fact is that more clichés are attached to the life of a "real" writer than to that of a hack. Every one of them had practically memorized the bios of their idols and thought something was wrong if they paid the light bill on time.

When I talk to my son, Ross thought, it is comfortable for both of us to pretend that I am a hack and he the flaming original; it gives us defined places for discussion, though I have poetry in my veins and he knows it, as I know damned well he is no real alcoholic. The truth is, Newt would drink himself into a problem just for the required "life." Nobody in our family ever had problems with the bottle. It is that head of his. He did not know how to do life, he did not know how to cut the crap and work hard. He did not know that doomed love would wreck his work if he played around with it too much. There is cruelty in the heart of those who love like this. There is a mean selfishness that goes along with being so deplorable. You will say what of the life of the spirit, what has material dress to do with the innerness, the deep habits of the soul, blabba rabba. Beware of occasions that call for a change of clothing, take no heed for the morrow, Thoreau and Jesus, sure, but Newt has no mighty spiritual side that Ross, has seen. Newt's talent, and it is a talent I admit, is milking the sadness out of damned near everything. Isolating it, wording it into precise howls and gasping protests.

Newt swam in melancholy, he was all finned out for tragedy, right out of the nineteenth century, à la Ruskin, wasn't it? Look deep enough into the heart of things and you will see something you're not inclined to laugh at. Yeah, gimme tragedy or give me nothing. My heart is bitter and it's mine, that's why I eat it. He would squeeze the sadness out of this Buick Riviera convertible like it was a bright black sponge. Ross agreed that his son should win the awards — he was good, good, good — but he could make you look back and be sorry for having had a fine time somewhere. You would stand convicted in the court of the real for having had a blast at Club Med, or for seeing the hopefulness at a christening. Ross had been offered university jobs paying four times what his son made, condo included. But Newt's readers — what, seventy worldwide? — rejoiced in the banal horror of that. They were, doubtless, whiskered Philip Larkinophiles in shiny rayon pants, their necrotic women consorts sighing through yellow teeth. The job Newt had thrown away, his allegiance to the girl for whom he had thrown it all away, had paralyzed him. There *must* be love; it has to have been all worthwhile. Ross took an inner wager on Newt's having a pigtail. He now sang with a punkish band. Odds were that he had not only a pigtail but some cheap pointless jewelry too around his wrist, like a shoelace.

Ross intended to talk his son out of this Ivy Pilgrim. A second brief marriage would go right into the *vita* of a modern poet just like an ingredient on a beer can. No problem there. Lately his son had written "No poems" in every letter, almost proudly, it seemed to Ross. But this was more likely a cry beneath a great mistake. In the back seat of the car were a CD player and a superior piece of leather Samsonite oversize luggage, filled with CDs. It was not a wedding gift. It was to remind Newt, who might be stunned and captured in this dreadful cow-college burg, that there were other waters. Sometimes the young simply forgot that. The suitcase was straight-out for him to leave with. Ross was near wealthy and read Robert Lowell too, goddammit. And "The Love Song of J. Alfred Prufrock" was his favorite poem. Had poetry done any better in this century? No. There were inklings here and there, Ross thought, that his boy was better than Eliot, if you take away the self-prescribed phoenix around his neck, this thing with women. Newt had a son from his first wife, a college beauty who had supported his melancholy. Already Newt was at odds with his seven-year-old son, who was happy and liked sports and war toys. He cursed his ex-wife and raised her into an evil planetary queen, since she sold real estate and had remarried a muscled man who had three aerobic salons. But Ross recalled the time when this woman was the source of Newt's poems, when it was she and Newt against the world, a raving dungeon teasing the eternally thirsty and famished.

This little Ivy Pilgrim had to be a loser and Newt would kill her one day. He had threatened his last wife several times and had shot a hunting arrow into his estranged house. Ross projected seeing Newt in the newspaper, jailed and disconsolate, Ivy Pilgrim's corpse featured in his bio, Newt not remembering much, doomed forever. Then bent on suicide. Or a life of atonement, perhaps evangelism. Or teaching prison poetry workshops, a regular venue for worthless poets nowadays.

Everett Dan Ross (given, not a pen name; how he despised writers who changed their names for whatever reason!) could see Ivy Pilgrim in the desolate house. Hangdog and clouded, nothing to say for herself. It made him furious. He predicted her inertia, a feckless, heavy tagalong. The bad skin would tell you she was a vegetarian. At best she would be working a desk out of a welfare office someday. Or "involved" in an estate settlement (meticulous leeching of the scorned dead). One always appreciated those who gave attention to one's son, but she would have a sickening deed to him, conscious that they were a bright scandal at this dump of a college ("Oh yes, they don't know what to do with us!") in the Romantic vein. When the truth was, nobody cared much. They might as well have been a couple of eloped hamsters. She was a squatter, a morbid lump, understanding nothing, burying him with her sex. She'd favor the states of "laid back" and "mellow," as if threatened crucially by their opposites.

Ross, through life, had experienced unsafe moments. He knew where Newt's melancholy came from. It was not being sued by that true hack whose biography Ross had done. It wasn't Ross's fault the man was too lazy to read the book before it came out, anyway, though Ross had rather surprised himself by his own honesty, bursting out here at age fifty-two — why? Nor was it the matter of the air rifle that always rode close to him. Nor was it a panic of age and certain realizations, for instance that he was not a good lover even when he loved his wife, Nabby. He knew what was correct, that wives liked long tenderness and caressing. But he was apt to drive himself over her, and afterwards he could not help despising her as he piled into sleep for escape. She deserved better. Maybe his homicidal thoughts about her were a part of the whole long-running thing. The flashes of his murderous thoughts when she paused too long getting ready to go out, when she was rude to slow or mistaken service personnel, when she threw out something perfectly fine in the trash, just because she was tired of it or was having some fit of tidiness; even more, when she wanted to talk about them, their "relationship," their love. She wondered why they were married and worse, she spoke this aloud, bombing the ease of the day, exploding his work, pitching him into a rage of choice over weapons (Ross chose the wire, the garrote, yes!). Didn't she know that millions thought this and could shut up about it? Why study it if you weren't going to *do* anything? She did not have the courage to walk out the door. *He* did, though, along with the near ability to exterminate her. She also called his work "our work" and saw herself as the woman behind the man, etc., merely out of cherished dumb truism. But none of these things, and maybe not even melancholy, could be classified as the true unsafe moments.

Especially since his forties, some old scene he'd visited, made his compromises with, even dwelled with, appeared ineffably sad. Something beyond futility or hopelessness. It was an enormous more-than-melancholy that something had ever existed at all, that it kept taking the trouble to have day and eyesight on it. He felt that one of them — he or it — must act to destroy. He would look at an aged quarter — piece of change — and think this. Or he would look at an oft-seen woman the same way. One of them, he reasoned, should perish. He didn't know whether this was only mortality, the sheer weariness of repetition working him down, calling to him, or whether it was insanity. The quarter would do nothing but keep making its rounds as it had since it was minted, it would not change, would always be just the quarter. The woman, after the billions of women before her, still prevailed on the eyesight, still clutched her space, still sought relief from her pain, still stuffed her hunger. He himself woke up each morning as if required. The quarter flatly demands use. The woman shakes out her neurons and puts her feet on the floor. His clients insisted their stories be told. He was never out of work. Yet he would stare at them in the unsafe moments and want the two of them to hurl together and wrestle and explode. His very work. Maybe that was why he'd queered that last bio. The unsafe moments were winning.

Ross's Buick Riviera, black with spoked wheel covers, was much like the transport of a cinematic contract killer; or of a pimp; or of a black slumlord. There was something mean, heartless and smug in the car. In it he could feel what he was, his life. Writing up someone else's life was rather like killing them; rather like selling them; rather like renting something exorbitant to them. It was a car of secrets, a car of nearly garish bad taste (white leather upholstery), a car of penetrating swank; a car owned by somebody who might have struck somebody else once or twice in a bar or at a country club. It was such a car in which a man who would dye his gray hair might sit, though Ross didn't do this.

He kept himself going with quinine and Kool cigarettes. All his life he had been sleepy. There was nothing natural about barely anything he did or had ever done. At home with his wife he was restless. In his writing room on the pier he was angry and impatient as often as he was lulled by the brown tide. Sleeping, he dreamed nightmares constantly. He would awaken, relieved greatly, but within minutes he was despising the fact that his eyes were open and the day was proceeding. It was necessary to give himself several knocks for consciousness. His natural mood was refractory. He'd not had many other women, mainly for this reason and for the reason that an affair made him feel morbidly common, even when the woman displayed attraction much past that of his wife, who was in her late forties and going to crepey skin, bless her.

It could be that his profession was more dangerous than he'd thought. Now he could arrange his notes and tapes and, well, *dispense* with somebody's entire lifetime in a matter of two months' real work. His mind outlined them, they were his, and he wrote them out with hardly any trouble at all. The dangerous fact, one of them, was that the books were more interesting than they were. There was always a great lie in supposing any life was significant at all, really. And one anointed that lie with a further arrangement into prevarication—that the life had a form and a point. E. Dan Ross feared that knowing so many biographies, *originating* them, had doomed his capacity to love. All he had left was comprehension. He might have become that sad monster of the eighties.

Certainly he had feelings, he was no cold fish. But many prolific authors he'd met were, undeniably. They were not great humanists, neither were they caretakers of the soul. Some were simply addicted to writing, victims of inner logorrhea. A logorrheic was a painful thing to watch: they simply could not stop observing, never seeing much, really. They had no lives at all. In a special way they were rude and dumb, and misused life awfully. This was pointed out by a friend who played golf with him and a famous, almost indecently prolific, author. The author was no good at golf, confident but awkward, and bent down in a retarded way at the ball. His friend had told Ross when the author was away from them: "He's not even here, the bastard. Really, he has no imagination and no intelligence much. This golf game, or something about this afternoon, I'll give you five to one it appears straightaway in one of his stories or books." His friend was right. They both saw it published: a certain old man who played in kilts, detailed by the author. That old man in kilts was the only thing he'd gotten from the game. Then the case of the tiny emaciated female writer, with always a queer smell on her—mopwater, runaway mildew?—who did everything out of the house quickly, nipping at "reality" like a bird on a window ledge. She'd see an auto race or a boxing match and flee instantly back to her quarters to write it up. She was in a condition of essential echolalia was all, goofy and inept in public. Thinking these things, E. Dan Ross felt uncharitable, but feared he'd lost his love for humanity, and might be bound on becoming a zombie or twit. Something about wrapping up a life like a dead fish in newspaper; something about lives as mere lengthened death certificates, hung on cold toes at the morgue; like tossing in the first shovelful of soil on a casket, knocking on the last period. "Full stop," said the British. Exactly.

Ross also frightened himself in the matter of his maturity. Perhaps he didn't believe in maturity. When did it ever happen? When would he, a nondrinker, ever get fully sober? Were others greatly soberer and more "grown" than he? He kept an air rifle in his car, very secretly, hardly ever using it. But here and then he could not help himself. He would find himself in a delicious advantage, usually in city traffic, at night, and shoot some innocent person in the leg or buttocks; once, a policeman in the head. Everett Dan Ross was fifty-two years old and he knew sixty would make no difference. He would still love this and have to do it. The idea of striking someone innocent, with impunity, unprovoked, was the delicious thing — the compelling drug. He adored looking straight ahead through the windshield while in his periphery a person howled, baffled and outraged, feet away from him on the sidewalk or in an intersection, coming smugly out of a bank just seconds earlier, looking all tidy and made as people do after arranging money. His air rifle — a Daisy of the old school with a wooden stock and a leather thong off its breech ring — would already be put away, snapped into a secret compartment he had made in the car door which even his wife knew nothing about. Everett Dan Ross knew that he was likely headed for jail or criminal embarrassment, but he could not help it. Every new town beckoned him and he was lifted even higher than by the quinine in preparation. It was ecstasy. He was helpless. The further curious thing was that there was no hate in this, either, and no specific spite. The anonymity of the act threw him into a pleasure field, bigger than that of sexual completion, as if his brain itself were pinched to climax. There would follow, inevitably, shame and horror. Why was he not — he questioned himself — setting up the vain clients of his biographies, his fake autobiographies, some of whom he truly detested? Instead of these innocents? They could be saints, it did not matter. He *had* to witness, and exactly in that aloof peripheral way, the indignity of nameless pedestrians. He favored no creed, no generation, no style, no race. But he would not shoot an animal, never. That act seemed intolerably cruel to him.

Assuredly his books raised the image of those he wrote about. Ross had developed the talent long ago of composing significance into any life. He had done gangsters, missionaries, musicians, politicians, philanthropists, athletes, even other old writers. He could put an aura on a beggar. Then with the air rifle, he would shoot complete innocents to see them dwindle. He would swear off for months but then he would come back to it.

It had happened often that Ross was more interesting than his subjects. He was certainly not as vain. Writing his own autobiography would not have occurred to him. But there was a vain and vulgar motive in everybody he depicted: *look at me,* basically. The ones who insisted on prefaces disclaiming this howling fact made him especially contemptuous. It was not hilarious anymore, this "many friends have beseeched me to put down in writing," etc. Blab, blook, blep. It was astounding to Ross to find not one of his biographees conscious of this dusty ritual in their own case. *Their* lives were exempt from the usual flagrant exhibitions of the others. His last chore on a porcine Ohio hack writer — the suer, as Ross called him — a sentimental old fraud who'd authored one decent book a century ago when he was alive, then rode like a barnacle the esteem of the famous who suffered him the rest of his life, dropping names like frantic anchors in a storm of hackism and banality. Ross had to pretend blithe unconsciousness to the fact that the man "was ready for his story to be told," and had sent friends to Ross to "entice you to sit down with shy, modest X." Ross also had to watch the man get drunk about seventy times and blubber about his "deep personal losses," his "time-stolen buddies." The depth of his friendship with them increased in proportion to their wealth and fame. Ross kept a bland face while the obvious brayed like a jackass in the room. The amazing fact was that the man had lived his entire life out of the vocabulary and sensibility of his one decent book. There seemed to be no other words for existence since 1968, no epithets for reality outside the ones he'd bandaged on it twenty years ago. He'd written his own bible. Most of all he adored himself as a boy, and wept often now about his weeping then. Ross gutted through, and one night, as it always did, the hook fell out to him gleaming — the point of the biography: history as a changeless drunken hulk, endlessly redundant; God himself as a grinding hack. The sainthood of no surprises. The Dead Sea. This truth he sedulously ignored, of course — or thought he had — and whipped out a tome of mild hagiography. This was his fifteenth book and sold better than the others, perhaps because it celebrated the failure of promise and made the universal good old boys and girls very comfortable. The hack was a Beam-soaked country song.

The fact that Ross himself was a sort of scheduled hack did not alarm him. There weren't many hacks of his kind, and that pleased him. He dared the world to give him a life he could not make signifi-cant on paper and earn some money with. So didn't this indicate the dull surprise that nobody was significant? Or was it the great Chris-tian view — every man a king? Ross had no idea, and no intention of following up on the truth. Years ago he had found that truth and the whole matter of the examined life were overrated, highly. There were preposterous differences in values among the lives he had thrown himself into. Even in sensual pleasure, there was wide variance. He himself thought there was no food served anywhere worth more than ten dollars. No woman on earth was worth more than fifty, if you meant bed per night. Others thought differently, obviously. The young diva who put pebbles in her butt and clutched them with her sphincter (she insisted he include this) — well, it was simply some-thing. It made borderline depraved people feel better when they read it. Also, when would the discussion about love ever quit? He could be deeply in love with most of the women in every fashion magazine he'd ever flipped through. The women would have to talk themselves *out* of his love, stumble or pick their noses. Usually he did not love Nabby, his wife, but given an hour and a fresh situation he could talk himself into adoring her.

What he loved was his son.

What was love but lack of judgment?

So if God judged, he was not love, eh?

This sort of stuff was the curse of the thinking class. You went away to college and came back with such as that to nag your sleep till you dropped.

Best to shut up and live.

Best to shoot anonymous innocent citizens with an air rifle and shut up about it. The delicious thing was that the stricken howled and bore the indignity as best they could, never to have an answer. He saw them questing through the decades for the source of that mo-ment. He saw them dying with the mystery of it. Through the years the stricken had looked up at the top of buildings, sideways to the al-leys, and directly at passersby. Once he had looked directly at a po-liceman, beebeed, rubbing his head and saying something. Twice people had looked deeply at Ross and his car — another year, an-other Riviera — but Ross was feigning, of course, sincere drivership. What a rush, joy nearly pouring from his eyes!

In Newt's neighborhood his car was blocked briefly by some chil-dren playing touch football on the broken pavement. They came around and admired his car and the two-seater boat towed behind as he pulled in between dusty motorcycles in front of a dark green cottage, his son's. Already he wanted away from it, on some calm pond with the singing electric motor easing the two of them into cool lily-padded coves, a curtain of cattails behind their manly conversation. They had not fished together in ages. Newt used to adore this beyond all things. Ross had prepared his cynicism, but he had prepared his love even more. The roving happy intelligence on the face of little Newt, age eleven, shot with beauty from a dying Southern sun as he lifted the great orange and blue shellcracker out of the green with his bowed cane pole — there was your boy, a poet already. He'd said he had a new friend, this fish, and not a stupid meal. He'd stroked it, then released it. You didn't see that much in the bloody Southern young, respect for a mere damned fish. He'd known barbers to mount one that size, chew and spit over it for decades.

They seemed to have matched Ross's care in his presents with (planned?) carelessness about his arrival. This sort of thing had happened many times to Ross in the homes of celebrities, even in the midst of his projects with them. Somebody would let him in without even false hospitality: "Ah, here is the pest with his notes again," they might as well have said, surprised he was at the front door instead of the back, where the fellow with their goddamn mountain water delivered.

The girl indicated somebody sitting there in overalls who was not Newt, a big oaf named Bim, he thought she said. Yes, there always had to be some worthless slug dear to them all for God knew what reasons hanging about murdering time. Bim wore shower shoes. He did not get up or extend a hand. Ross badly wanted his cynicism not to rise again, and made small talk. The man had a stud in his nose. He dressed like this because the school *was* a cow college, Ross guessed. It was hip to enforce this, not deny it, as with Ivy League wear, etc.

"So where do you hail from, Bim?"

"Earth," said the man.

Drive that motherfucking stud through the rest of your nose, cool-ster, thought Ross. Ross looked straight at Bim with such bleak amazed hatred that the man rose and left the house as if driven by pain. Ross stood six feet high and still had his muscles, though he sometimes forgot. There wasn't much nonsense in him, and those who liked him loved this. The others didn't. He might seem capable of patient chilly murder.

"I don't know what you did, but thanks," said Ivy Pilgrim. "He's in Newt's band and thinks he has a title to that chair. Can't bear him."

"Bimmer has a fine sensitivity. Hello, Dad." Newt had entered from the back. There were only four rooms. "Where'd Bimmer go?"

Newt did not have a ponytail. He had cut off almost all his hair and was red in the face around his beard. He wore gold-rim glasses set back into his black whiskers, and his dark eyes glinted as always. His head looked white and abused, as just shoved into jail. The boy had looked a great deal like D. H. Lawrence since puberty. Here was the young Lawrence convicted and scraped by Philistines. But he didn't seem drunk. That was good.

"I don't believe Bimmer liked me," said Ross.

"He moves with the wind," sighed his son.

"Mainly he sits in the chair," said Ivy Pilgrim.

Ross looked her over. She was better than the photograph, an elfin beauty from this profile. And she wasn't afraid of Newt.

"You have the most beautiful hair I've seen on a man about forever. That salt and pepper gets me every time," she said to Ross.

"Thank you, Ivy." Watch it, old man, Ross thought. Other profile suggests a kitten, woo you silly.

"What instrument does Bimmer play?" he asked.

"Civil Defense siren, bongos, sticks," said Newt seriously.

"So you're in earnest about this band?"

"I've never been more serious about anything in my life." Since Newt was twenty, Ross was wary of asking him any questions at all. He'd get the wild black glare of bothered pain.

Who could tell what this meant? Though with his bald head it seemed goony and desperate.

Ross was parched from the road. He sat in Bimmer's chair, big and tweedy. The place was not so bad and was fairly clean. There were absolutely no books around. He wondered if there were a drink around. He'd planned to share some iced beer with Newt, by way of coaching him toward moderation, recovering what a man could be — healthy in a beer advertisement. He was throwing himself into the breech, having lost the taste for the stuff years ago.

"I'm either going to sing or go into the marines," said Newt. Was he able to sit still? He was verging in and out of his chair. *Acasthia,* inability to sit, Ross recalled from somewhere. It was a startling thing when one's own went ahead and accumulated neuroses quite without your help. Ross looked at the girl, who'd come in with a welcome ginger ale, Dr. Brown's.

"Newt remembered you liked this," she said.

This was an act that endeared both of them to him. At last, a touch of kindness from the boy, though announced by his wife.

"Well, I need a splash with mine," said Newt. He went to the kitchen and out came the Rebel Yell, a handsome jug of bourbon nearly full. However, this was histrionic, Ross was sure. Newt did not look like he needed the drink. He had affected the attitude that a man of his crisis could not acknowledge ginger ale alone. Ross, having thought more than usual on the way up to Auburn and presiding too much as father to this moment, sincerely wanted to relax and say to hell with it. He wasn't letting anybody live. The marines, singing? So what? Give some ease. He himself had been a marine, sort of.

Where was it written in stone, this generational dispute? Are fathers always supposed to wander around bemused and dense about their young? Wasn't it true old Ross himself had nailed the young diva, weeping runt, with her heavy musical titties bobbling, right in the back door? While Nabby, loyal at home — source of Newt right in front of him — was shaking her mirror so a younger face would spill out on it? Not very swell, really, and his guilt did not assuage this banal treachery. Old, old Ross, up the heinie of America's busty prodigy. Awful, might as well be some tottering thing with a white belt and toupee, pot, swinging around Hilton Head. What a fiend for one of Newt's poems, but really beneath the high contempt of them.

"So how's the poetry-making, anyway, sport?"

Newt was tragic and blasé at once, if possible, gulping down the bourbon and ginger.

"Nothing. It's the light. Light's not right."

"But you're not a painter, Newton. What light?"

"He means in his *brain*," explained Ivy.

"My love for Ivy has killed the light."

Newt had to give himself his own review, this seriously? Good gad. Save some for the epitaph.

"I like it that way," Newt added hurriedly, but just as direly.

Ivy seemed upset and guilty, yearning toward Ross for help. "I didn't want to be any sort of killer."

He liked this girl. She had almost not to say another thing in her favor. *She* had the pigtail, pleasant down the nice scoop of her back.

{ 317 }

"Well, can't we open the shroud a little here, Newton? Look outside and see if you can see a little hope. Maybe some future memories, son."

Newt shuffled to the door and looked at the car and boat a whole minute, too long. Ivy got Ross another Dr. Brown's. The last thing Ross might say in a hospital room someday in the future, nurse turning out of the room: "Nice legs." Good for little Ivy. Would it never stop? Ross had long suspected, maybe stupidly but as good as any genius, through life and his biographies, that women with good legs were happy and sane. Leg man as philosopher. Well, Nabby's seemed to persuade mostly joy out of the day, didn't they? Even given the sullen, jagged life he sometimes showed her. Get out of my skin and look, he thought: Was I ever as, oh, *difficult* as Newt myself? Probably, right after he'd fired himself from the war, though he hid it in Chase's house in San Pedro.

"So what do you see, Newt?"

"No wonder Bimmer left," said Newt.

"Now, can you explain that?"

"Bimmer's father is a man of . . . merchandise."

Hold off, *hang fire*, with Henry James. Ross cut himself off. With a new enormous filtered Kool lit — stay with these, and you've got at most twenty-five years, likely; we don't have a clumsy century of discord to work it out, Newt, for heaven's sake — he thought, Don't give me that *merchandise* crapola, young man. I bred you in Nabby. You know very well my beach house and all of it could burn up and not impress me a great deal, never did. Let's take off the gloves, then. *I* came here.

"Is that why your man Bimmer dresses like a laid-off ploughboy? Missing the fields and horse shit over to the back forty?"

Newt smiled. Maybe this was the real turf, here we were. The smile was nice, at last, but why did he have to destroy his head? His son's hair was black and beautiful like his used to be.

"So let me declare myself and your mother finally. The quick wedding, there wasn't any time for presents much."

Ivy went with him to the Riviera. She saw the CD player inside and gave a gasp of pleasure. It was the piece of luggage full of CDs she wound up with.

"This wonderful suitcase. I'll bet you want us to get out of this dump p.d.q.?"

Ross felt very mean for his previous plans for the bag.

"Where are *you* from, Ivy?"

"Grand Bay, close to Bayou La Battre. Right across the bay from you. The poor side, I guess. But I loved it. And I'm not broke."

"Fine. Very fine." Unnecessary, but necessary, on the other hand. She'd won him.

"So there we are. Boat, motor, the player. And *voilà!* (Ross opened the bag, nearly a trunk). Some late wedding music."

"Must be fifty discs there!" cheered Ivy.

"Thought you and I might break in the boat and pursue the finny tribe this afternoon," said Ross, brightly.

Christmas in May, he was feeling, was really an excellent idea. Look down, son.

Newt barely glanced into the suitcase.

"Fishing? That's pretty off the point, Dad."

"Oh, Newton!" Ivy jumped right on him.

"What's..." Don't, Ross. He was going to ask what *was* the point, you bald little bastard?

"I've promised the kids I'd play some touch with them. Just about to go out there. Then there's the band tonight. You can come with Ivy if you want."

"Newt takes the band very seriously," said Ivy. This seemed to be a helpful truth for both the men. Ross forgot Newt's rudeness. Or did he *know*? What part of loony Berryman or Lowell had he researched? Newt glanced at Ivy dangerously. This brought Ross's nightmares right up, howling. This was the feared thing. His son seemed to want to beat on this strange idiot who'd just opened her mouth.

Ross couldn't bear it. He went out with a fresh Kool and the remains of the ginger ale and stood in the yard near his sleek Buick, gazing through some cypresses to a man-provoked swamp behind the hideous cinder blocks of an enormous grocery, some kind of weeds native only to the rear of mall buildings, ripping up through overflowed mortar on the ground.

Here he was back in "life," shit, man with twenty-five years to go, wearing a many-pocketed safari shirt next to a pimp's car. What did an old American man *wear* rightly, anyway? Fifty-two *was* old. Cut the hopeful magazine protests. You spent half your time just trying not to look like a fool. What intense *shopping*. Hell, shouldn't he have on a blazer, get real in a gray Volvo? Disconnection and funk, out here with his killer Kool, pouting like a wallflower; son inside wrecking the afternoon with bald intensity. Back to his nightmares, the latest most especially: Ross, as an adult, was attending classes in elementary school, somehow repeating, but bardlike, vastly appreciated at the school by one and all for some reason, king of the hill, strolling with the children, glib, but why? The school was paying him a salary while he was doing what? But at the school gate he was in a convertible with two girls, and two men — one of them Newt — jumped in the car and rammed long metal tongs through the skulls of the girls. Their screams were horrible, the blood and bone were all over Ross. Then policemen appeared and drove metal tongs through the skulls of Newt and the other man. The screams of Newt were unbearable, loud! He'd awakened, panting. Ross almost wept, looking at the back of that grocery now. But it was a dry rehearsal, with only a frown and closed eyes.

Ivy touched him on the arm. "Sometimes you've just got to ignore him. I'll go fishing with you. Please, I'd love to. And I love everything you brought. Thank your wife, Nabby, for me."

Marriage was a good cause, thought Ross. On a given day chances were one of you might be human. Was D. H. Lawrence a rude bastard, even into his thirties?

He saw the kids gather and Newt go out as the giant weird quarterback. The day was marked for gloom but he was going to have something good out of it. He did not want to watch his son play football. But thanks, Lord, for providing him with the dread image: Newt had once embarrassed him playing football with young kids.

He was home from graduate school — Greensboro — at Christmas. He was invited over to an old classmate's house in Daphne. Ross came later to have a toddy with the boy's father. It was another big modest beach house with a screened porch all the way across the back. They took their hot rums out to the old wooden lounges and watched Newt and his friend quarterback a touch game with his friend's nephews and nieces, ages five to twelve. Ross was pleased his boy cared about sports at all. It was a stirring late December day, cool and perfect for neighborhood touch, under the Spanish moss and between the hedges. But then Ross saw his contemporary staring harder out there and when Ross noticed, things were not nice. Newt was hogging the play and playing too rough, much too rough. He smashed the girl granddaughter of this man into the hedge. She didn't cry, but she hung out of the game, rubbing her arms. Then Newt fired a pass into the stomach of a boy child that blew him down into the oyster shell driveway. The kid was cut up but returned. Newt's friend implored him and the children were talking about him, but he remained odd, yes, and driven. Ross was looking at something he deeply despised seeing. He did not want to think about the other examples. They called the game. The children came up on the porch hurt and amazed, but gamely saying nothing around Ross. They were tough, good children, no whiners. In the car home, he said to Newt, "Son, you were a mite fierce out there. Just kids, *kids.*" Newt waited a while and came back, too gravely: "You want me to smile all day like a waitress?"

This *fierceness,* off the point, that was it.

So they drove around and Ivy, who did not change from her short skirt and flowered blouse to go fishing, directed him through town to pick up Newt's bounced checks — this tavern, that grocery, the phone company. Ross didn't mind. He'd expected financial distress and had brought some money. With some irony of kinship he'd brought up a fairly big check from Louisiana State University Press to sign over to Newt. This concern had published Newt's books. Ross had just picked up a nice bit of change from a piece of his they were anthologizing. Christ, though, the kid might make something out of it. But not a kid. He was thirty. Newt's sister Ann was twenty-eight, married in Orlando, straight and clean as a javelin, thanks. Ivy Pilgrim (her real name) wanted to know all about Ann and Nabby. Then they did go fishing.

Auburn had some lovely shaded holes for fishing in the country. Erase the school, and it was a sweet dream of nature. Ross, a Tuscaloosa man, could never quite eliminate his prejudice that Auburn U should have really never occurred, especially now that it had fired his boy. There had been some cancerous accident among the livestock and chicken droppings years ago, and, well, football arose and paid the buildings to stay there and spread. These farmboys, still confused, had five different animal mascots, trying to get the whole barnyard zoo in. Ivy was amused by these old jokes, bless her, though he really didn't mean them. She was in architecture, hanging tough. How could Newt have attracted *her*? he thought, instantly remorseful.

She thought Newt would return to his poems soon. Improbably, she *understood* his books and wanted him to move on to — pray for rain! — some *gladness,* bless him. The poetry had won her over, but as a way of life it sucked wind.

"Newt is proud of you and he wants to be glad," she said.

"Honestly?"

"Honestly."

Once he had been to an inspirational seminar with one of his clients. The speaker was a man who had been through unbearable, unlucky, unavoidable horror. He told the crowd he intended never ever to have another bad day. He just wouldn't. He was going to force every day to be a good day. Ross was heeding the man now. He was glad he'd remembered. He concentrated on Ivy, who was a good fisherman. She had sporting grace. They caught several bluegills and one large bass. There was never any question but that she'd clean them and put them in the freezer, since Ross was buying her supper.

"I suppose, though, Newt is casting around for other work?"

"It's the band, the band, the band. He writes for it, he sings. He says everything he's ever wanted to say is in the band."

Ross had noted the late gloomy competency in American music, ever a listener in his Riviera. Electricity had opened the doors to every uncharming hobbyist in every wretched burg, even in Ohio. You could not find a dusthole without its guitar man, big eyes on the Big Time beyond the flyspecked window, drooling, intent on being wild, wild, wild. America, unable to leave its guitar alone, teenager with his dick: "Look here, I've got one too." He saw Newt, late-coming thirty, in the tuning hordes, and it depressed him mightily. As witness the millions of drips in "computers" now. Yeah, toothless grizzled layabout in the Mildewville Café: "Yep, my boy used to cornhole bus exhausts, he's now in computers." Look down at a modern hotel lobby, three quarters of them were in "computers," asking the desk clerk if the sun was shining. His daughter's husband, a gruesome Mormon yuppie, was "in computers." Then Ross's ears harked to the Riviera speakers — something new, acoustic, a pro-tolesbian with a message. Give people a chance, Ross corrected himself: you were a G-22, Intelligence, with the marines in the worst war ever, by *choice*, dim bulb in forehead. Whole squad smoked by mortars because of you, put them on the wrong beach. A gloomy competency would have been refreshing, ask their mothers. I could have stayed home and just been shitty, like the singer Donovan, hurting only music.

Back at home, she showered while Ross set up the CD player with its amazing resonant speaker boxes. What a sound they had here with Miles Davis. She heard it while the water ran. Ross was excited too. In his fresh shirt, blazer, trousers and wingtips, he emerged from his own shower, opened the mirror door of the medicine chest to check Newton's drugs, and caught Ivy Pilgrim sitting naked on her bed, arms around her breasts, sadly abject and staring at the floor. Ross looked on, lengthening the accident. This is my daughter, my daughter, he thought, proud of her. The brave little thing.

There was a great misery she was not sharing with him. Doomed or blessed — he couldn't know — he froze at the mirror until she looked over at him in the reflection and saw him in his own grief. Ross felt through the centuries for all chipper wives having to meet their in-laws. Holy damn, the strain. She was such a little lady, revealed. He smiled at her and she seemed to catch his gratitude instantly. Oops, slam the mirror. Nice there was nothing ugly here. I won't have a bad day, I won't. This was the best of it, and later he thanked the highway rushing in front of him for it.

The place was a converted warehouse rank with college vomit, beer in Astroturf, a disinfectant thrown contemptuously over it. The spirit of everywhere: spend your money, thanks, fuck you. Chicken-yard hippies, already stunned by beer, living for somebody right out of suburban nullity like them, "twisted" on his guitar stroking: "He don't *give* a damn." Couple of them so skinny they looked bent over by the weight of their cocks. Ivy had quit beaming. Since the mirror there had been an honest despair between them.

Newt and his truly miserable band came on, tuning forever as the talentless grim do. Ross was sorry he was so experienced, old. He could look at the face and bald pate of the drummer, comprehending instantly his dope years and pubic sorriness, pushed on till damned near forty, no better on drums than any medical doctor on a given Sunday afternoon with the guys. Then came Bimmer, a snob in overalls, fooling with his microphone like some goon on an airport P.A. system. Then a short bassman so ugly he *had* to go public. The sax man could play, but he was like some required afterthought in a dismal riot of geeks. Then there was a skinny man near seven feet tall who just danced, male go-go. What an appalling idea. Then Newt, not contented with the damage he'd done on backup guitar, began singing. He was drunk and fierce, of course. The point seemed to be anger that music was ever invented. It was one of the ugliest episodes Ross had ever witnessed. He smiled weakly at poor Ivy, who was not even tapping her foot. She looked injured.

At the stage, Ross saw the chicken-yard hippies and a couple of their gruesome painted hags, hateful deaf little twats who might have once made the long trip to Birmingham. They loved Newt and egged him on. This was true revolt. Ross wondered why the band had bothered to tune.

He had had dreadful insights too, too often nowadays, waking up in a faraway hotel with his work sitting there, waiting for him to limn another life. The whole race was numb and bad, walking on thin skin over a cesspool. Democracy and Christianity were all wrong: nobody much was worth a shit. And almost everybody was going to the doctor.

"Professional help" for Newt flashed across his mind, but he kicked it away, seeing another long line, hordes, at the mental health clinic, bright-eyed group addicts who couldn't find better work waiting inside. Ross had known a few. One, a pudgy solipsist from Memphis, had no other point to his life except the fact he had quit cigarettes. A worthless loquacious busybody, he'd never had a day of honest labor in his life. What did he do? He "house-sat" for people. But the fellow could talk about "life" all day.

Then things really got mean.

Newt, between sets, red-eyed, hoarse, angrily drunk, drew up a chair ten feet away from Ivy and his father, muttering something and bearing on them like some poleaxed diagnostician. Ross at last made out that Newt was disgusted by his blazer, his shoes, his "rehearsal to be above this place."

"This place is the whole world, sad Ross-daddy. You won't even open your eyes. There's nowhere else to go but here! No gas, no wheels, no—" He almost vomited. Then he walked his chair over to them, still in it, heaving like a cripple. He was right in their faces, sweat all over him.

"Good-looking pair, you two. Did you get an old touch of her, Pops?" He reached around and placed his hand over Ivy's right breast. "But I tell you. Might as well not try. You can't make Ivy *come*, no sir. She ain't gon come for you. Might as well be humping a rock, Rosser!"

Crazy, mean, unfinished, he laid his head on the table between them. The sweat coming out of his prickly head made Ross almost gag. Then he rose up. His eyes were black, mad. He couldn't evict the words, seemed to be almost choking.

Ross handed over the endorsed check and stood to leave.

"What are you going to do for work, son?"

"S'all that bitch outside says. Job, job, job."

"Well, bounced checks, bounced checks, bounced checks is not your sweetest path either." He hated Newt. An image of Newt, literally booted out the window by an Auburn official, rose up and pleased him.

"Shut up, you old fuck," said Newt. "Get home to Mama. And remember, remember..."

"What? Be decent, goddammit."

"Let the big dog eat. Always fill up with supreme."

Ross looked with pity at Ivy. Given the tragedy, he could not even offer to drive her home.

Outside the turn at the Old Spanish Fort, Ross knew he would lie to Nabby. All was well in Auburn. Save Nabby, God, he asked. She was a fine golfer, in trim, but all those days in the sun had suddenly assaulted her. Almost overnight, she was wrinkled and the skin of her underchin had folds. The mirror scared her and made her very sad. Ross, for all his deskwork and Kools, and without significant exercise, was a man near commercially handsome, though not vain. There was something wrong with the picture of a pretty fifty-two-year-old fellow in a Riviera, anyway. In the mirror, he often saw the jerk who'd got eleven young men mortared over there — a surviving untouched dandy. A quality in all of Ross apologized and begged people to look elsewhere.

Newt, by the way, had married somebody much like his mother. Small, bosomy, with slender legs agreeable in the calf. Probably he wouldn't kill Ivy. Ross would make a good day of this one, be damned. It was only midnight. Nabby was up.

He caressed her, desperate and pitiful, wishing long sorrowful love into her. She cried out, delighted. As if, Ross thought, he were putting a whole new son in Nabby and she was making him now, with deep pleasure.

Newt had left some books in the house a while back. Ross wanted to see what made his son. He picked up the thing by Kundera with the unburdening thesis that life is an experiment only run once. We get no second run, unlike experience of every other regard. Everything mistaken and foul is forever there and that is you, the mouse cannot start the maze again; once, even missing the bull's-eye by miles, is all you got. It is unique and hugely unfair. No wonder the look you see on most people — wary, deflected, puzzled — "What the hell is happening?" Guy at a restaurant, gets out of his car and creeps in as on the surface of the moon. Ross liked this and stopped reading. There would be no Newt ever again, and whatever he'd left out, fathering the boy, it was just botched forever, having had the single run. Forgiven, too, like a lab assistant first day on the job. And then Ann, not a waver, twice as content as Ross was, almost alarmingly happy. She was the one run too. He could call Ann this instant and experience such mutual love it almost made him choke. There was the greedy Mormon, her husband, but so what? You didn't pick her bedmate out of a catalogue.

The old hack suing E. Dan Ross backed off, unable to face the prospect of any further revelations on himself the trial might bring. He called up Ross himself, moaning. He was a wreck, but a man of honor too, a First Amendment champion after all. Ross, who'd never even hired a lawyer, felt sorry for what the erupting truth had brought to both of them. He feared for his future credit with clients. But the hack was invited on television, in view of his new explosion of hackery, a photo album valentine to every celebrity he'd let a fart off near. He became a wealthy man, able to buy a chauffeur who took him far and wide, smelling up the privacy of others.

For months they did not hear from Newt, only two cards from Ivy thanking them for boat, motor, luggage and Newt. This sounded good. Around Christmas they got a letter from Newt. He was in the state asylum in Tuscaloosa, drying out and "regaining health and reason." The marriage was all over. He was smashed with contrition. There'd been too many things he'd done to Ivy, unforgivable, though she'd wanted to hang in right till the last. What last nastiness he had done was, after her badgering, he'd written her a poem of such devastating spite there was no recovery. It was a "sinful, horrible thing." Now he still loved her. She'd been a jewel. He was a pig, but at least looking up and out now. He pleaded with them not to visit him. Later, out, when he was better. He still had health insurance from the school and needed nothing.

> ...And Dad, the boat and motor was wonderful. Bimmer stole it, though. He proved to be no real friend at all. I ran after him down the highway outside the city limits with a tire tool in my hand. They say I was raving, my true friends, and they brought me up here. True. I was raving. No more "they said." Please forgive me. I'm already much better.
>
> Love, Newton

Nabby and he held hands for an hour. Nabby began praying aloud for Newt and then blamed the "foreigners at Auburn and all that dreadful radioactivity from the Science Department." Ross was incredulous. Nabby was going nuts in sympathy. Have a good day, Ross, have a good day. He walked out to the pier, into his writing room, and trembled. For no reason he cursed the Bay of Mobile, even the happy crabs out there. What could a man take?

Then, next week, another blow lowered him. Chase's wife called and told him Chase was dead. He'd taken a pistol over to Long Beach, threatened his ex-wife, and was killed in a shoot-out with the police. God have mercy. Chase was a policeman himself.

Ross recalled the street, the long steep hill down to Paseo del Mar from Chase's house, with thick adobe walls around it. Ross had needed the walls. He was badly messed up and stayed that way a month, having fired himself from the war, G-22, all that, after he misdirected the Seals to a hot beach and got them mortared. Chase met him in a bar and they stayed soaked for five weeks. Chase was a one-liner maniac. All of life had a filthy pun or stinger. Ross thought it was all for him and appreciated it. But when he got better and wouldn't drink anymore, Chase kept it up. Ross needn't have been there at all, really, he found out. Chase became angry when Ross quit laughing. Not only were the jokes not funny anymore, Ross knew he was witnessing a dire malady. Chase kept hitting the beer and telling Ross repeatedly about his ex-wife, whom he loved still even though married to Bernice, a quiet thin Englishwoman, almost not there at all but very strong for Chase, it seemed to Everett D. Ross, before he was E. Dan Ross. Ross heard of vague trouble with the woman in Long Beach and the law. But Chase was selfless and mainly responsible for Ross's recovery, giving him all he needed and more. Chase had also adopted a poor street kid, a friend of his daughter's. He was like that. He would opt for stress and then holler in fits about it. When Ross told him he was leaving, taking his rearranged name with him back to Mobile where his wife waited, hoping for his well-being, Chase went into a rage and attacked him for ingratitude, malingering, and — what was it? — "betrayal." Not of the Seals. Of Chase. It was never clear and Chase apologized, back into the rapid-fire one-liners. Chase was very strange, but Ross had not thought he was deranged. The shoot-out sounded like, certainly, suicide, near the mother of his children. Too, too much. A man Ross's age, calling happily to the ships at sea around L.A. Harbor over his ham set. Raving puns and punchers.

The very next day he heard that a classmate of his, the class joker, had shot himself dead in a bathtub in San Francisco. Wanted to make no mess. Something about money and his father's turning his back on him. Ross could not work. He stayed in his pier room rolling up paper from his new biography — of an old sort of holy cowboy in San Antonio. Talked to animals, birds, such as that. Four wives, twelve children. The balls of paper lay in a string like popcorn on the meager tide, going around the ocean to California where the dead friends were. Ross thought of the men not only as dead but as dead fathers. Children: smaller them, offspring of grown pranksters, gag addicts. Ross thought of his air rifle. His classmate, last Ross had seen of him, right before he went over to Vietnam, was in the National Guard. He did something hazy for athletic teams around Chicago, where Ross last saw him. It didn't take much time. His real life work was theft and happy cynicism about others. Bridge could level anybody with mordant wit. He'd kept Ross and others howling through their passionate high school years. Once, on a lake beach in late April, a class party where some of the girls were in their bathing suits sunning themselves, first time out this spring, Bridge had passed a couple of lookers and stopped, appreciative, right in front of them: "Very, very nice. Up to morgue white, those tans." The boys howled, the girls frowned, mortified. Given everything by his psychiatrist parents, Bridge still stole, regularly. Ross heard he'd been kicked out of the university for stealing a football player's watch from a locker. Bridge was an equipment man. He deeply relished equipment, and ran at the edge of athletic teams, the aristocracy in Southern schools. In Chicago, he'd taken Ross up to his attic. Here was a pretty scary thing: Bridge had stolen from his unit a Browning .30-caliber machine gun and live ammo and enough gear to dress a store dummy, stolen somewhere else; he had set the dummy behind the machine gun among a number of sandbags (the labor!) so that the machine gun aimed right at the arriving visitor. Ross jumped back when the light was turned on. Bridge, Bridge. Used to wear three pairs of socks to make his legs look bigger. Used Man Tan so he was brown in midwinter. Children, money and booze. Maybe great unrepayable debt at the end.

Ross knew he was of the age to begin losing friends to death. But more profound was the fact that he was not the first to go. Fools, some thirty of them from his big high school in Mobile, had gone over to Asia and none of them was seriously scratched or demented on return. It was a merry and lusty school, mental health or illness practically unheard of. What was his month of breakdown? Nothing. What was he doing, balling up the hard work and watching it float off? Nothing.

His son in a nut ward, Nabby collapsing, he took down a straight large glass of tequila and peered strongly across the bay to where Ivy Pilgrim had grown up. Did she have to be all disappeared from Newt, forever? A smart young woman, very sexy, plenty tough, endowed, couldn't cure him. He missed her. Ross, frankly, was glad Newton didn't want him at the asylum. But he sat down and wrote him a long letter, encouraging his strengths. The tequila gave him some peace. He took another half glass. His friend, Andy the pelican, walked into the room and Ross began talking to him, wanting to know his adventures before he opened a can of tuna for him.

He confessed his grief and confusion to the pelican. The absurd creature, flying bag, talked back to him: "Tell me. It's rough all over, pard. Lost my whole family in Hurricane Fred." One thing about the sea, thought Ross, sneering toward it, it doesn't care. Almost beautiful in that act. Maybe we should all try it.

Next thing they heard, Newt was visiting his sister in Orlando. She and her husband lent their condo at New Smyrna Beach to him. He was sunning and "refining his health" at pool and oceanside. He was working on poems and didn't know how he felt about them. Walker, Ann's husband, came by frequently and chatted. He liked Walker a lot. He wasn't going to impose on them forever. The world was "over there" and he knew it. Ross and Nabby's music was helping, thanks. Especially Bach. Had they ever listened to the Tabernacle Choir? Glorious. Newt said that he wanted "excruciatingly to walk in the Way." Grats extreme too for the money. He was just beginning his life and would be reimbursing everybody soon. "Truly, though, people, I like being poor and I am going to get used to it."

Ross had written himself neutral. He rewrote what he had thrown to sea, it didn't matter, there it was all back and the life of the saintly cowboy wrote itself. He wrote twenty pages one night, nonstop, and recollected that he could not remember what he had said. When he read the pages, however, they were perfect. The words had gone along by themselves. Ross seemed not to have mattered at all. His mind, his heart, his belly were not engaged. Entailed was a long episode of murder, rape, and the burning alive of a prized horse. A short herd of people were killed, the cowboy wounded in the throat.

It was some of Ross's best writing, but he had not particularly cared. Even hacks sometimes cared, he knew. This business was too alike to the computer goons he despised. Ross was bleak. He'd just gotten too damned good at his stuff. He was expendable. Nothing but the habitual circuitry was required.

Otherwise, it was a good year. Nabby did not say any more insane things. But she badly wanted a face-lift. Felt sure she was falling apart and would not show herself near sunlight. Back in her room the ointments overblew the air. She kept herself in goo and almost quit golf. They had had separate rooms since Newt went to the asylum. She felt ugly. Ross felt for her deeply. This emotion was a constant tender sorrow and that was what he had instead of the eruptions of love and homicidal urges. It was much better, this not too sad little flow. Their love life was much better, in truth. A sort of easy tidal cheer came over Ross, fifty-three. He was appreciating his years and the pleasant gravitation toward death. It had a sweet daze to it. He could look at his tomb and smile, white flag up in calm surrender.

Why not a face-lift, and why not love? Things were falling together even though he was a disattached man. He rushed to finish the book before the old cowboy died. Blink, there it was. The old man's children read it to him and he liked it very much. They told Ross his eyes, like a robin's eggs, brightened. He blessed the author. He had never thought his life made any sense. He had never meant to be famous or read about. He wished he could read. By far he was the most pleasant subject Ross had ever worked with.

Nabby, fresher at the neck though a little pinched at the eyes after her face-lift, wanted the children to visit over Thanksgiving and have a family portrait made. They'd not heard much from either of them lately. Newt was teaching night classes at a community college in Orlando. He had his own place.

But when Nabby called he could hear his daughter was not right. Something had happened. The upshot was Newt had converted to Mormonism, very zealously, and had simply walked out of town and his job and his apartment, without a word to anyone. Nobody knew where he was. He had destroyed all his poetry two months before. He left everything he owned.

Ross could see his wife, blank in her new face, holding the phone as if it were a wounded animal. She cradled it and stroked it. Ross had never seen an act like that. Ann's voice continued but her mother listened at the end, when Ross took the phone, as if death were speaking to her directly. Ann's husband, Walker, came on and detailed the same version.

"What do Mormons, new Mormons, do?" asked Ross.

"There's no place, like a Mecca, if that's what you mean," said Walker.

"I mean how should they act?"

"It's inside, Ross. They affirm. They attend. They practice. They study. A great deal of study."

"What *did*, damn it, Mormonism — or *you* — do to Newton?"

"He wasn't raving. It's not charismatic."

"Would he be in some fucking airport selling flowers?"

Walker hung up. His reverent tongue was well known. All told, he was a Boy Scout with a hard-on for wealth; the boy so good he was out of order. He wouldn't even drink a Coke. Caffeine, you know. When Ross lit a Kool, Walker looked at him with great pity. Ross hated him now, smug and square-jawed, wearing a crew cut. He saw him dripping with a mass of tentacles attached to him, dragging poor Newton into the creed, "elders" spiriting him away. The cult around Howard Hughes, letting him dwindle into a freak while they waited on his money. Clean-cut international voodoo. Blacks and Indians were the tribes of Satan, weren't they? Ross always rooted against BYU when they played football on television. Sure. Hardworking, clean-limbed boys next door. Just one tiny thing or three: we swallow swords, eat snakes, and ride around on bicycles bothering people for two years. Nabby lay on her bed with her new face turned into the pillow. Ross petted her, but his anger drove him out to the pier again, where for a long time he searched the far shore for the image of his lost daughter-in-law, Ivy, naked and in grief, hugging her breasts.

So. The colleges wouldn't have him anymore. There goes that option. He had a great future behind him, did Newt.

"Destroyed his poems." Right out of early Technicolor. Have mercy on us. What kind of new Newton did we have now? Fig Newton, Fucked Newton. He tried hard again not to detest his boy. He tried to picture him helpless. Mormons probably specialized in weak depressed poets. Promise him multiple wives, a new bicycle. But more accurately Ross detested Newton for the sane cheer of his letters. What a con man, cashing Ross's ardent checks. Venal politician. Ross could hit him in the face.

From Ann he had heard that Ivy was at home with her father, who was sick and might die. They'd cut a leg off him just lately.

Ross wanted to take the form of Andy the pelican and fly over there to her.

This did not feel like his home right now. He did not like Nabby collapsing again, especially with her expensive new face. He reviewed his grudges against her. Five years ago, at the death of his father — an ancient man beloved by everyone except Nabby, who thought he was an awful chauvinist who loved to be adored too much: true — she had not shed a tear until later in the car when she told Ross some woman had alluded slyly to her sun wrinkles. She began cursing and crying for herself, his father barely in the ground. Ross almost drove the Riviera off the road. He said not a word all the way home from Florida. Nabby, jealous of the dead man who'd upstaged her own dear plight; the funeral a mere formality while huge issues like sun wrinkles were being battled.

Feeling stranded, he'd driven over to Bayou La Battre four days later. He didn't call ahead. The Pilgrims lived just off Route 90 in a little town called Grand Bay. A healthy piece of change from the old cowboy's book had just arrived. He was anxious to spend money on something worthwhile. How impoverished were the Pilgrims? The mother had been a surprise. He'd not told Nabby about it, for the first time in his life with her.

Their home was neat. On the front were new cypress boards, unpainted. The house was large and the yard was almost grassless, car ruts to one side, where he parked behind a jeep with an Auburn sticker on the rear window. Over here you got a sense of poor Catholics, almost a third world, some of them Cajun and Slavic and Creole. He'd always loved this country. Most of your good food came from these people; your music, your bonhomie, your sparkling black-eyed nymphs. Upland, the Protestants had no culture. If anything, they were a restraint on all culture, especially as it touched on joy. He thought of Newton, now even odder than they were, beyond them, in a culture of how much crap can you swallow, unblinking, and remain upright. Close by was the great shipyard at Pascagoula, where Ivy's father had worked. You threw a crab net in the water and thought of submarines the length of football fields close under you, moving out with fearsome nukes aboard. Almost a staggering anomaly, these things launched out of the mumbling-dumb state of Mississippi.

Ivy and one of her brothers, also a painter at Ingalls, met him at the door. They were very gracious, though mournful. It didn't look like their father was going to make it. An hour from now they would go back to the hospital in Mobile. Surprising himself, Ross asked if he might go with them, drive them. They thought this was curious, but would welcome a ride in his Riviera, which the brother thought was the "sporting end." He had a coastal brogue. Ivy had got rid of hers. Maybe it would not go with a career in architecture. Ivy looked radiant in sorrow. When he mentioned Newt, the brother left for the back of the house, where it smelled like Zatran's spices and coffee.

"I've heard a few things, none of them very happy. I'm afraid I don't love him anymore, if you wanted to know that," she said.

The finality hurt Ross, but he'd expected it. He did not love the boy much either.

"He was in the shipyards 'witnessing.' My brothers saw him. Some security guys took him out of the yard. He had a bicycle. He told my brother he was going to places around large bodies of water."

"Did he have 'literature'?"

"The Book of Mormon? No, he didn't. You'd know that Newt would be his own kind of Mormon or anything. He'd stretch it."

Ross recalled his hideous singing.

"Did you ever think of Newt's age?" she asked him.

Ross went into a terrible cigarette cough and near-retching, reddening his face. Father of Newt, he felt very ugly in front of her; a perpetrator.

"His age. Thirty-one. Jesus Christ was crucified at age thirty-three. A Mormon is a missionary, all the males, for two years." Ivy revealed this much in the manner of a weary scientist. The evidence was in: cancel the future.

"You figured that out, Ivy. Do you...How...Would you like him dead?"

"Oh no, Dan!" She was shy of using his first name, but this brought her closer to him. "A friend of mine from Jackson, big party girl, said she saw him at the Barnett Reservoir north of the city. He was 'witnessing' outside a rock and roll club and some drunk broke his ribs. The ambulance came but he wouldn't get in."

"He rode a bike to Jackson, Mississippi?"

"I suppose so. Don't they have to?"

At the hospital he was useless, pointless, and ashamed of his good clothes, a pompous bandage on his distress. He smoked too much. He looked for a Book of Mormon in the waiting room. One of the nurses told him no flatly and looked at him with humor when he asked if there were one around. An alien to their faith, he was being persecuted anyway. The world was broken and mean.

The only good thing about the trip was the sincere goodbye hug from Ivy in her yard. She was on him quickly with arms tight around his neck, not chipper anymore, and she cried for her father, him and Newt, too, all at once. The strength of it told him he would probably never see her again. So long, daughter. I will not have a bad day, will not. He crashed into early night.

In Mobile, on Broadway beneath one of the grandfather live oaks "bearded with Spanish moss" — as a hack would write — Ross beheld a preacher, a raver, with a boom box hollering gospel music beside him on the sidewalk. He was witnessing through the din, screaming. Heavy metal would be met on its own terms. Three of the curious peered on. It was a long red light. Ross unsnapped the chamber, lower left, where his air rifle was hidden. He badly needed to shoot. But for that reason, he did not. He saw it was in there oiled, heavy with ammo, *semper fidelis,* a part of his dreams.

The next option was to buy a tramp and hump her silly. Make a lifelong friend of her. Nice to have a dive to dip into, young Tootsie lighting up in her whore gaud. Calamity Jane. Long time, no see, my beacon. Miserable bar folks withering around their high-minded big-time copulation. Relieve himself of wads, send her to South Alabama U, suckology. Nabby bouncing dimes off her face back home, considering a mirror on the ceiling and her own water tower of ointment.

He cruised home, shaking his head. He was having another bad day, and the clock was up on legs, running.

The next day he set out for Jackson, got as far as Hattiesburg, saw a bicycle shop, hundreds of bikes out front, sparkling spokes and fenders under the especially hired muttering-dumb Mississippi sun, and grew nauseated by chaos. Too many. He'd never find Newt, going on one mission from one large body to the next. He feared his own wrath if he found him. Two more years of life for him, if you listened to Ivy, who might know him better than Ross. Newt's conversion still struck him as elaborately pretended, another riot of fierceness. In Salt Lake City, he would have turned Methodist. What was he "witnessing" — what was his hairy face saying? He wouldn't sustain. He was a damned lyric poet, good hell, having a crucifixion a day, maybe even broken ribs, but chicken when the nails and the hill hove into view.

• • •

They did not know where he was for nearly a year. Minor grief awoke Ross every morning. Nabby almost shut down conversation. Some days he woke up among his usual things, felt he had nothing but money and stuff, was crammed, pukey with possessions — its, those, thingness, haveness. One night in April he tore up a transistor radio. Nothing but swill came out of it, and he always expected to hear something horrible about Newton. He dropped his head and wanted to burn his home. The men he'd got mortared called to him in nightmares, as they had not ever before. The tequila, nothing, would help. The murdered men begged him to write their "stories, our stories." Their heads came out on long sprouts from a single enormous hacked and blasted trunk. He got to where he feared the bed and slept on the couch under a large picture of him and Nabby and the kids, ages ago. Everybody was grinning properly, but Ross looked for precocious lunacy in the eyes of young Newt, or some religious cast, some grim trance. He fell asleep searching for it.

What was religion, why was he loath to approach it on its own terms? You adopted it, is what you did, and you met with others you supposed felt as you did, and you took a god together, somebody you could complain to and have commiserate. Not an unnatural thing one bit, though inimical to the other half of your nature, which denied as regularly as your pulse out of the evidence of everyday life. For instance the fact that God was away, ancient and vague at his best. Also there was the question of the bully. Ross had never been a bully. Better that he had been, perhaps. He had never struck a man in a bar or country club. Ross's mother was a religious woman, aided in her widowhood by church friends and priest, who actually seemed to care. He had never bullied her. Rather the reverse. She'd used the scriptures to push him around, guiltify him. There was no appeal to a woman with two millennia of religion behind her. Ross suddenly thought of the children Newt played football with, or *at,* hurting them, oppressing them. A thin guy, *he* was the bully, as with his little wives. A lifelong bully? Bullying the happiness out of life. Bullying his parents — a year and a half without a word.

When Ross was in his twenties, he went to Nabby's family reunion up in Indiana. Most of her relatives were fine, scratchy hill people, amused by the twentieth century, amused by their new gadgets like weed-eaters, dishwashers and color televisions. They were rough, princely Southern Americans. Ross thought of Crockett and Bowie, Travis, the men at the Alamo. But then the pastor of the clan came on board, late. It was Nabby's uncle, against tobacco, coffee, makeup, short dresses, "jungle music" and swearing. Stillness fell over the clan. The heart went out of the party. That son of a bitch was striding around, quoting the prophets, and men put away their smokes, women gathered inward, somebody poured out the coffee, and he was having a great time, having paralyzed everybody before he fell on his chicken. So here was Newt? Indiana preacher's genes busting out, raiding the gladness of others.

They received a letter, finally, from Newton, who was not too far from them, eight hours away in Mississippi. He was superintendent of a boys' "training school" and taught English. The school had a storm-wire fence around it, barbed wire on top, armed guards, and dogs for both dope and pursuit at the ready. Tough cases went there. Sometimes they escaped out to the county and beyond to create hell. Parents had given up, courts had thrown in the towel and placed them here, the last resort. Occasionally there were killings, knifings, breakages; and constant sodomy. A good many of the boys were simply in "training" to be lifelong convicts, of course. Much of their conversation was earnest comparison of penal situations in exotic places, their benefits and liabilities. Many boys were planning their careers from one joint to another as they aged, actually setting up retirement plans in the better prisons they considered beds of roses. A good half of them never wanted outside again. The clientele was interracial, international and a bane to the county, which was always crying out for more protection and harsher penitence. Newt wrote that he had to whip boys and knock them down sometimes, but that "a calm voice turneth away anger," and he was diligently practicing his calmness. He was married yet again. His wife was pregnant. She was plain and tall, a Mennonite and recovering heroin addict, healthy and doing very well. This love was honest and not dreamy. Newt apologized for much and sent over twelve poems.

They were extraordinary, going places glad and hellish he'd never approached before.

Ross cried tears of gratitude. His hands shook as he reread the poems: such true hard-won love, such precise vision, such sane accuracy — a sanity so calm it was beyond what most men called sanity. He raised his face and looked over Dauphin Island to the west, taken. Nabby trembled the entire day, delirious and already planning Christmas three months ahead. Newt was bringing his wife over to meet them and visit a week, if they would have him. He invited Ross to visit him at the school as soon as he could get over. His voice on the phone when Ross called seemed a miracle of quiet strength. He made long, patient sentences such as Ross had never heard from him before. Ross would leave that night.

His brand new navy blue Riviera sat in the shell drive. It was a sweet corsair, meant for a great mission: nothing better than the health and love of the prodigal son. Bring out the horns and tambourines. Poor Ann. There was no competition. All she was now was nice, poor Ann. He wanted to pick up his wealth in one gesture and dump it on Newton.

Outside Raymond, Mississippi, he pushed the hot nose of his chariot into a warm midmorning full of nits, mosquitoes, gnats and flying beetles. His windshield was a mess. Ross was going silly. He felt for the bugs and their colonies. Almost Schweitzer was he, hair snowier, fond, fond of all that crept and flogged.

They were very stern at the gate, sincere cannons on their hips, thorough check of the interior, slow suspicious drawls rolled out of the lard they ate to get here. While they repeated the cautions three or four times — about stopping the car (don't) and watching his wallet ("hard eye if I's yoo") and staying some lengths away from everybody, they acted as if Newt were a great creature on the hill ("Mister Ross he fonk nare boot cup, nard").

Ross had not been searched thoroughly since the war, when at the hospital they feared briefly for his suicide, and in a strange way he felt flattered by these crackers taking the time around his own domain. Only when he was driving up to Newt's house did he go cold, as splashed with alcohol. They'd missed the air rifle, which he had forgotten was there. Then he fell back, silly. It was an *air* rifle only. There would have been no trouble, only shy explanation about its presence and the snap compartment, where there should have been, if he were mature he supposed, a sawed-off pump for danger on the road. The times they were a-changing, all the merciless ghouls prowling for you out there, no problem. A shotgun would be easier to explain than a Daisy. Over here was the *home* of the peacemakers racked across the rear windshield, handy to the driver. Could always be a fawn or doe out of season to shoot, Roy Bob. Over here they considered anybody not in the training school fair gubernatorial timber.

So this was Newt's new job, new home, new Newt. He'd not said how long he'd been here. A job like this, wouldn't it take a while to qualify? But this was the Magnolia State. He'd probably beaten out somebody who'd killed only two people, his mother and father; little spot on his résumé.

Some boys were walking around freely, gawking at his car. This must be how a woman felt, men "undressing her with their eyes," as that Ohio tub of guts might "inscribe." Those kids would probably tear this car down in fifteen minutes. My God, they had skill-shops here to give them their degrees in it. Ross noticed that almost every boy, whether gaunt or swaybacked, chubby or delicate, had on expensive hightop sneakers. Crack and hightops were probably the school mascots. But he saw more security men than boys outside. He'd glanced at the Rules for Visitors booklet: no sunglasses, no overcoats, no mingling with the student body. Do not give cigarettes or lighters if requested. Your auto was not supposed to have a smoked glass windshield or windows, but they had let him through because he was the father of "Mister Ross."

At Newt's WPA-constructed house, like the house of a ranger in a state park—boards and fieldstone—Ross hugged his son at the door, getting a timid but then longer hug back. His wife was still getting ready. They had just finished a late-morning breakfast. There had been trouble last night. Three boys cut the wire and escaped, APBs were issued, the dogs went out, and they were brought back before they even reached Raymond, where they were going to set fire to something.

Ross was thinking about the appearance of Newt's pregnant wife. Why had he thought it necessary to describe her as "plain" in his letter, even if she was? It was something too deliberate, if you worried the matter. Revenge? Against Ivy, his first wife, his mother? Ross's handsome world scorned? He hoped not.

She, Dianne, was very tall, taller than Newt by three inches and close to Ross's height. She sat at the dining room table, very long and big-stomached, about seven months along. Her father had run this place before Newton. He was retiring and Newton, well, was right there, ready, willing, able—and with (she placed her hand over Newton's at the salt and pepper shakers) the touch of the poet.

Ross did not want to ask his boy the wrong questions and run him away. He was gingerly courteous—to the point of shallowness, he realized, and hated this. It made him feel weak and bullied and this couldn't go on long. But Newt was forthright.

"Not just the broken ribs over at the reservoir, Dad. I was saying my thing at Tishomingo, on the boat dock, and her" (he smiled over at Dianne, who looked fine although a bit gawky—old romantic history a-kindling) "boyfriend, this tattooed, ponytailed 'ice' addict, stabbed me with a knife right in the heart."

"You're not telling me —"

"Right *in* the heart. But Dianne knew, she was once a nurse and still will be when she gets her license back. She wouldn't let me or anybody pull it out. The knife itself was like a stopper on the blood."

"That's true," said Dianne. "He went all the way to the hospital with it still in him and you could see it pumping up and down with Newton's heart. They helicoptered him to Memphis."

"She followed me in a car, without her boyfriend." Newt giggled. "She was strung out, violently sick herself, but drove all the way over, couple hundred miles."

"The love got me through, don't you see, Mr. Ross? I was already in love with him, like a flash. It pulled me through the heroin, the withdrawal. I sat out there in that waiting room, sick as a dog. But there is a God, there is one."

"Or love. Or both, sure," said Ross. "He stuck you for being a Mormon, Newt?"

Newt still smiled at his father. He looked much older, used, but his grown-out hair was long, like a saint's or our Lord's, thought Ross. Now the spectacles gentled him and he seemed wise and traveled, much like his new poems.

"Pa, don't you know me? I was Mormon, I was Jew, I was Christ, I was Socrates, I was John the Baptist, I was Hart Crane, Keats, Rimbaud. I was everything tragic. I'm still outcast, but I'm almost sane."

His son giggled and it was not nervous or the giggle of a madman. It was just an American giggle, a man's giggle — "What the hell is going on?" — full-blooded and wary.

"You love these boys? I suppose they're helping you back to... helping you as..."

"Hell no, I don't love them. I hate these bastards. It might not be all their fault, but they're detestable vermin and utter shits, for the main part. I love, well, five. The rest...What you find most often is they've been spoiled, not deprived. Like me. Nobody lasts long here. They try to love but it gets them in a few months. Dianne's father lasted, but he's the meanest, toughest son of a bitch I've ever met."

Dianne assented, laughing again, about this paternal monster, just a solid fact. The laugh surely lit up that plain face nicely.

"Come eat with me in the big hall and I'll show you something," said Newt.

"Is this a bad question? What are you going to do? Stay here *because* you hate it?"

"No. I'll do my best. But I'm in fair shape for a job up at Fayetteville. They've seen my new work and I guess they like post-insane poets at Arkansas. Actually, a lot of folks like you a lot when you straighten out a little. The world's a lot better than I thought it was."

Ross considered.

"Newt, do you believe in Christ?"

"Absolutely. Everything but the cross. That never had anything to do with my 'antisocial' activity. I'll still holler for Jesus."

"I love you, boy."

"I know it. Last month I finally knew it. Didn't take me forever, is all I can say."

"Thanks for that."

"There's some repaying to do."

"Already done. The new poems."

Dianne wept a little for joy. This was greatly corny, but it was magnificent.

In the big hall, eating at the head table among the boys, Ross got a drop-jaws look at real "antisocial" manners. Guards were swarming everywhere, but the boys, some of them large and dangerous, nearly tore the place apart. They threw peas, meat, rolls, just to get primed. Two huge blacks jumped on each other jabbing away with plastic knives. A half grapefruit sailed right by the heads of Ross and Newt. It had been pegged with such velocity that it knocked down the great clock on the wall behind them. Whoever had done it, they never knew. He was eating mildly among them, slick, cool, anonymous, wildly innocent, successful. Right from that you could get the general tenor. Unbelievable. Newt and he were exiting when a stout boy about Newt's height broke line and tackled him, then jumped up and kicked him with his huge black military-looking hightops. Newt scrambled up, but was well hurt before the guards cornered the boy, who'd never stopped cursing violently, screaming, the whole time. With their truncheons the guards beat the shit out of the kid and kept it up when he was handcuffed and down, maybe unconscious. None of the other boys seemed to think it was unusual. They neither cheered nor booed.

Newt wanted him to sleep over so they could go fishing early the next day. He knew a place that was white perch and bass heaven. Dianne insisted, so he did.

They did fairly well on the fish, again in a pond so dark green and gorgeous you could forget the training school and human horror everywhere.

"I guess, like I heard anyway, you went to bodies of water because, well, because what?" Ross asked.

"Because in the South, I figured, the men who change the world mostly go fishing?" He laughed at his father with the flyrod in his hands, so sincere. "They want *out* of this goddamned place."

Next morning he left them cheerfully, driving out, but then, as he neared the gate, he circled back — out on his own hook, cautious in the car with smoked windows. He had seen what he wanted, set it up, had found his nest. There was a place in the parking lot for officials and staff that the Riviera nestled into, uniform in the ranks of autos and pickups, as you might see in a big grocery lot. Behind his smoked window he was unseen. Sixty feet away was the entrance to a shop or snack bar. Anyway, a lot of the boys were gathered there, allowed to smoke.

Ross unsnapped the compartment and withdrew the Daisy. My, it had been months, years. Thin, tall, lumpy, sneering, bent, happy, morose, black, white, Indian. It didn't matter. He rolled the window down just a tad, backing up so the barrel wasn't outside the window.

He began popping the boys singly, aiming for the back of their necks and, if lucky, an ear. That was about the best pain he could inflict. A boy leapt up, howling, holding his wound. He got another right on the tit. Did he roar, drop his cigarette, stomp and threaten the others? Yes. He popped another in the back of the head, a hipster with tattooed arms mimicking sodomy. Many of them were questioning, protesting, searching the trees in the sky and other inmates.

Ross rolled up the window and watched them through the one-way glass.

That's it, lads. Start asking some big questions like me, you little nits. You haven't even started yet.

That Was Close, Ma

HEY, THANKS, that one got us right in the morale, ho boys! Viciously imagined. Woodoo the Arab couldn't have done it better.

That one, again! Very close and nasty, old friend. We had you in the scope very early. Oh Vicksburg, Vicksburg! I am, personally, the Fall of the West. Hang all your hopes on my demise. Our Commander — may he strut and fuss still — we knew he had liquor, even women and Claussen's dill pickles. And an indoor croquet set for him and his harem. But it's plain old checkers he really loves. Nobody beats him.

We don't fire so many as the others over there. What we fire are bigger and fewer. They are not precision strikes, but who has precision anymore? Think of a television with a lime-green screen and sucking squares on it. That's what's here in the buried trailer.

It is so sandy and dry, as you know. People, you would gasp, the amount of Oil of Olay I keep on. Truthfully, most of us are bored nuts. Whatever oddness was in us has been exacerbated. How we torment each other in our cabin fevers. The periscope out of this bunker sometimes reveals their minions, scuttling distraught after a big one of ours comes in. Knocked-over anthill, that's about the perspective exactly, though I know it fits a bit neatly, which one must always suspect. Even were you here, words would be difficult, believe me. All the real experts in both language and ballistics were killed off long ago. We're third stringers just like you reading this, Ma, though a scrub can star every now and then, you must know. Sometimes a missile gets through and something perishes.

I am in love with Naomi Lee, the girl at the end of the trailer. There's no doubt about that, this is not mere propinquity. She's a prisoner of war from the other side, but she has been turned around by our food and happiness. You might say groomed, in fact, for the Commander, who is insatiable. Against the probable, I hoped a scrub like me might win her over before the croquet and the lusting began. They said he might have one of the women right on the spot, in the middle of a match. They have to wear, anyway, sort of hospital gowns, open in back, with knee-length chamois boots, like the elegant Sioux brides of old. The old fox was quite a nostalgist, his twelve-year-old scotch and the rest. Wears twin bone-handled Uzis at his hips as if face-to-face combat with the enemy was imminent. Of course he was third rate too, maybe fifth, but some like an antiqued fool at the top, neck-deep in the fat of the land.

We imagine he could hit no better than the discredited sheriffs of the Old West, and we imagine he required so many women because he never got it right, he fouls it up time after time — the Uzi of sex.

We have none, exactly, most of us. All we have is proximity, and except for the grief-provoking converted pupil, Naomi Lee, what would you expect? Like nuns or worse, these military girls — crooked, drab, haunted wallflowers, baritones, third string on the pep squad. You hoped maybe for sylphs with wit and charm. Nugatory. Look at us, the men. So funked by eccentricity and awkwardness we've got to make reservations to masturbate. Trailer joke, don't blame me. My own courteous mild looks are a mask for veteran apathy. The sad eyes shouldn't throw you, there's not really much there.

Well, hope still goes out, hypersonic, like some of our big ones. Maybe I could do something to make Naomi Lee take notice. She might be moved by pity, some accident I could get myself into right before her eyes. Lean back on the floor, nonchalant Dilaudid cigarette in my lips, a desk spindle driven deep in my thigh. Bring out the vast hidden nurse in her, one could hope.

That one didn't even explode, sand nits.

Came right by the periscope, you could feel it, cracked the glass. You could have stopped this screed entirely, all our spiteful monkery, everything. We the pale and buried, however, live on, and someone bounds out to repair the scope, that kid mechanic stunned by one Louis L'Amour book after another, over in the corner like just another monitor but with freckles and tennis shoes. More Oil of Olay for me. One can at least resist going lizard in this confinement.

I declare, when a rare hit on us is "registered" — something of us or ours is blown apart, gore running down some piece of wall, hairpieces thrown about, fur and brains and dermis all smoky, splatted in a square acre, paper and wires around — it finally has less effect, less moment, than a good hunk of gossip. Weird surpassed by the other weirdness, every gimp and drudge thinking himself of course

plainly normal. Rumors about the "war" flash and burn like cigarettes, but gossip, such as the piece about Corporal Vigoro embez-
zling bugles, of all things, stays and haunts and exhilarates. Poor
Vigoro had a case of the old "liberal arts" education some summer
years ago in Northern Ireland but under a Catholic lecturer. History,
guilt, atonement, all that, and he *believed* it, we found out. Vigoro
was driven mad by the lack of history here (his lawyer claimed, anyhow) and to his tiny cell he took these regimental bugles, labeled
them per date, and set them around in a flow of tradition — reveille
and taps since, well, I guess twenty-two years now — while the
armies' worst troops have been lobbing spite back and forth across
the line. Our desiring their trees and water, their desiring our plat-
inum and zinc, the two curing damned near everything nowadays.

Gossip must always have the venereal, for sure. I use the more
clawing longer word because it is accurate as opposed to the pathetic
sex between nobodies which of course succeeds furtively on the line
as in all times. *Venereal* has a downwardness to it, supposing eminence at one time. Like Colonel Devin and Marie, who was nothing
but a floorsweep, not even a Sand Engineer. A big weasel crunching a
sardine, essentially. But it brought him down direly when discovered.
Sure he *leads* still now, but really he's just bait for our getting a position on the other army. They put him out there on a dune, high on the
line, in all his garish officer's rig, ordered to curse the other side from
nine till five every night. Their audios pick him up. It's well known the
other side is more passionate and impetuous than we are. "Real" men
with a religion and something to prove over there, so here comes a
shot at him occasionally. We can beam in quite immediately on the
muzzle flashes and sometimes get off at them before they run.

Discipline is random but enormous here, like a god.

Then there is, call it subgossip, pretty constant, about one of us
fallen over, gone dead. I don't mean shot or poisoned. I mean six or
seven times a year someone's ghost will just be given up, he will keel
over, no apparent pathology at all. Some call it boredom, some call it
lack of dreams. The insane Vigoro called it lack of history. Maybe the
constant ozone of the overworked hot wires, though medical instruments can't find the damage. Some say waiting for the direct hit on one
for a number of months can kill you dead as the thing itself. It is a mystery but with no special passion attached to it. The bodies are shipped
back to the relatives — if there are any — under a shameful aegis rather
like medical discharge. Deep mental things are not much tolerated up
here, and every exercise we do pretends to making us more and more

superficial. The perfect soldier is barely even skin-deep, but tough as bleached hide in what remains. If there was much to us originally this might be resented, but in reality one enjoys floating in this smooth democracy where only violent eccentricity disturbs.

I have delayed a little in the above to reckon with the other gossip about my only one herself, Naomi Lee. I can't decide whether the information is appalling or simply phenomenal. Above, I might have gone into the matter of drug gossip too, but it's so perennial and so morbidly obvious that I will only say there are good ones up here, sneaked from the labs of old dear street wizards back home, so sublimely avant-garde the detectors cannot outrun them. There seems little doubt the Commander himself stayed popped on lucille. They say he adored French music, and, yes, with lucille I'd say he adored French music about twice as much as humanly possible. He was twice the tradition, he himself, that we all need here and there's no reason for us to commit inner culture individually. It isn't disallowed, but it would only disaffect us more. For isn't it a given that culture drags you flat away from wherever you are and that is its main point? For instance, I am not at all the Fall of the West nor is this remotely Vicksburg. We are not slaves. We all elected to come here. We are not brainwashed, nor patriotized by loud gatherings and flags and raving dumb career men. I suspect half of us would perish straight out if dragged back to the Motherland, Ma, that overpopulated horror of money and smart women. I *fear* money, personally. This land has its charm and a crashing missile is a rousing spectacle, especially reaching out those phosphorous tentacles under the moon. *There's* my money, there's my interest, their soldiers racing outward like happy diminishing fireworks. They go to heaven over there. Over here we don't, having already enjoyed the perfect bliss of killing others under a staggering Oriental twilight. One of them, more persistent or heroic than the rest, will run way out in the desert from the conflagration, a dark streamer against the sand. These sights are really moving, Ma. We call it "Really Lighting Up a Loser," clap each other on the back, losers all, and gain another chevron. Esprit de corps? You might wonder, but yes, sometimes on a rare night. We gather together and together perhaps we are worthy brutes after all. The team is given a chevron apiece. In the old days I believe they stopped at three and called it Sergeant. But that's been dropped. Nobody is of any rank whatsoever until there has been a kill, and the number of chevrons awarded is theoretically endless. With my nine years, both my sleeves are covered. It is a satisfying

parity with the airmen and their insufferable aces. How I hate it
when they drop in to visit the trailer, swaggering and patronizing us
buried sandlings. My sleeves cause a second look, I'm glad to report,
as I hope they will with Naomi Lee as she converts to us. I've not
pushed these emblems on her. A creep, I still have tact. You don't
know what bosom connections to her people remain, though she's
dropped her religion, gossip says. The chevrons, blue with white
lightning on them, were the brainstorm of our Commander. I have
never said the man was all bad. The meritocracy of "The Few, the
Proud, the Fliers" was too long observed. We moles need our whiff
of glory, too.

There are technical awards also, for refinements on the missiles by
individuals. These modifications, since the money and time are endless, can always be made even by the weakest trembling nerd as often
as the temperature and barometer change, and a true mod can be im-
plemented almost within the day. There was a sort of desert hurricane that lasted a week, so fierce everybody on both sides ceased
shooting altogether. But on the seventh day we got off something,
turreting almost 180 degrees, into 200 mph of wind, that boo-
meranged right in the gale east down the track and fell on them from
the rear, out of fuel but perfect, presenting itself as mere debris and
creating a lot of fun like something fired on them by God back home.
We could hear it and all the secondaries blow, even through the
storm. This sentimental piece of genius came from Willard Niles,
shyer than a monk and afflicted with spina bifida. Had I not been
particularly bored and despondent — and in love with Naomi Lee,
more honestly — I could have taken out the board and worked it myself. The award is a black chevron upside down, and poor Niles —
quietly so far to the political right, this cripple, that he could bite his
own tail, pathetically remote even from the rest of us socially dim
lights — was rolled in to blush at a banquet in his honor, the Commander himself in attendance, with (damn it) a shocked warm eye
on Naomi Lee, who did some native acrobatics to Moorish music on
the dial straight from the enemy's radio orchestra. Her movements
were gracefully allied to a whole dance. I could only hope the others
were not as agitated as I. I pleaded for the rest of the men to be as im-
penetrable and dumb as they looked. But I could see even the women
admired her. Our world has nothing even tentatively like that meditative dance and contortion. Everybody was charmed and stilled by
it and cast into another sphere. Suddenly it made you hate to kill
them, kill that. She may have dropped her god, but now, with her

elastic limbs, even in that sexless jumpsuit and boots, you were sorry
for it. You guessed — I thought, please, only I could guess — that she
was apologizing and explaining for leaving him. I am not at home in
the world where women offer their dance and prostration to divinity,
leaving themselves in a trance of submission. The thing she was
doing — it didn't last all that long — was so delicate, natural, say inevitable, I became a meek visitor to that world. The adjectives go on,
Mother, you must notice how I am grabbing around for them like
buoys in a sea — the sea, nine years from it — not very much like me,
but you must see it's clear I do have a heart, I've detected it, it's
pumping unusual things from me, this whole piece of writing, for example. Naomi Lee — I'm melting in my own blather like a lib arts
sophomore from yesteryear, goony on metaphors. She converted *me*.

They may have debriefed important secrets from her. I don't
know, that's another team responsible to the Commander directly.
But the thing she gave freely is what really slew. I am not going to
write some long code to you about my feelings because I want it out
in bright Mother Tongue on the page: I would, I believed, kill the
Commander for her. I'm a fool, a traitor and insane. I would kill *you*
for her, Ma, hang me, the only mother and the only letters I get. Even
at this older presumed cautious age, with a few liver spots yet, near
my ears. My hair grayed and my front tooth cracked, as you know,
from that direct hit three years ago. With Naomi Lee, though, I'm
back to the tidy. I will not burn her up with modifiers. She's beyond
all that, all that blur, and much beyond photography. To my father
I'm sure you were once beyond that too, and he would have killed
me for you. This would have been the heart's necessity. I salute you
and Father for your brilliant monogamy. Believe me then that when
she quit the dance I almost fainted. The Moorish music was over,
and their hilarious hallucinative propaganda began, from "Bedouin
Bob Smith of beautiful Portland, Oregon." Nobody noticed it even
to laugh, except me. The banquet was withdrawn, all was level
again, but I listened to the voice of *their* convert, old Bedouin Bob.

"Water and miracles, my friends. We are still here despite all your
gloomy attacks. We are still laughing, we are still dancing, we are
still having our God. Did you think we had nothing all these centuries on this poor land? How long, how long, soldier, has it been
since you've seen the smile of a child? Or the water? Have you, lately,
walked on the very fire of missile exhaust to the grateful home of
God Himself? We have. We smile at you and give thanks. Today:
Hug somebody close to you and feel the dry hurt in them. Today:

Come to us. Come to us. Take all the pain away." Then somebody clicked it off. We blended and resumed boring each other utterly.

Now, I've not gotten here through this procrastination because I'm lazy or proud of my words. The act I certainly never heard spoken of over here, our world, not even in wild publications. It didn't belong. In our discussions, which you were good at and never too fastidious for truth, it never came up. You were plainly scientific with me. We know that's one of the reasons I am here. I've known bald science forever. The women have their own decorum, and I'm clear on the morale of that, but certain things get through every epoch or so, certain...Well, here I'm getting shy, dear Ma. One of the little drab nunoids had noticed my special eyes on Naomi Lee's dance, and about a month later, tugged on my sleeve. We were outside the trailer, alone, taking the air and having the twilight, a boiling orange one, I recall. Tangerine. I've been a hack poet lately, copying patented scenery right off the postcards. The little woman I thought accidentally with me was a Christian, British.

She had been a missionary among the foe several years. I heard she was of a utility to us that was wearing thin. But she was an honored patriot and they hated sending her home. Be rather like *kicking* a nun. Her knowledge of morals, rituals and religion over there was profound but obsolete. She was aging swiftly. She prayed for the enemy, but that wasn't so uncommon. Intermarriage — our drab females and their opportunists — had been almost rampant a couple decades back. Maybe she'd had something romantic over there, and our missiles connected her to it. This is morbid and probably plain wrong, though rapt, a condition to which all poetry leads at last, no? Anyway, this little woman kept a hint of emergency about her. She still gasped when we saw contrails from our side or theirs arc over the sky. For years I'd looked right through her. She might have been a stand of silicone.

"I had to tell you about Naomi Lee. Only you. It's very precious and I'd not seen it in a long time."

"How's our prisoner doing?"

"Not so much doing as what she *did* the other night among the women in our end of the trailer. Your men's bunks were quiet. All of you were asleep. Two women had the scope duty."

The woman smiled, like your telling me about the Northern Lights years ago. She seemed so serene, so waked up.

"A pure native, of a type so innocent and sincere, so unselfconscious, so generous —" She was going on with those adjectives I've vowed not to try. On the page, from me, they'd lose their reverence and join the herd, the ordinary. "— and we women do hurt for something else, for God's sake, more than you men, I think. I don't mean mere geography. Geography and history would put her up in the mountain temples, I guess, but she seems almost prereligious, as though made before their god first joined their bodies, the very dawning. She's happily sworn off her god. I've wondered about that, but I believe her real gods were earlier, even before the Prophet, so perhaps she's just renewed herself with *them*."

A conversation of this length among us was already near preposterous and I was numbed.

The little woman held back now, having got me deep. This Christian wasn't without her dramatic sense, I tell you. You could imagine her wooing the heathen.

"So what did she do?"

"We're so blamed careful and close-kept over here. We forget or doubt there are any secrets to know, damn us. They burst out in our dreams and then are promptly destroyed by the breakfast bacon."

"You want me to beg, Miss Rawling?"

She giggled.

"Then yes, I beg."

"All righty. I'm turning red and glad you can't see it. This thing, this creature, who has never uttered one vile word, never anything *like* a curse — chaste, docile, schoolgirlish — heard one of the girls mention something about the lack of pleasure in all this sand. She, Miss Lee, found us curiously deprived, it seems, forgetting her own acrobatic gifts. Hadn't they remembered the easiest thing? 'Why, it's so simple!' our darling said. She didn't care whether they kept the lights on, but they were cut, and out came the flashlights, nearly all the women gathered around.

"She got up on the map table, got rid of her boots, then pants, then drawers. I swear, it was all so innocent, so girlish, so much in the spirit of 'us girls around the campfire' that nobody said a word and nobody left. Race, creed, religion, proclivities — all hypnotized. This Naomi Lee — wow! as they used to say — raised her legs to behind her head, steadied herself on her hands, dropped her neck to herself, and promptly, with her tongue, well, finesse, finis! With full moans, not quiet. Moments later she raised her face, eyes closed and perfect bliss in her smile. Finally she said, 'And that is "The Lonely Woman." Didn't you know, my friends?' We all felt very strange.

There was, believe you me, please, nothing *wrong* with it. Though for us it was impossible."

Flat enormous tangerine moon hurled on the dry face of the little woman, I there cold.

"Really, why did you tell me this?"

"To appear worldly, I guess. I supposed it would be something you'd like. I was the anthropologist more than the missionary, never admitted. Also I'm in love with her. I thought we'd be friends in that."

"Well, this will take time...to adjust to. But thank you, I guess."

"Isn't that exactly like us, now? Whereas she was instant. And happy. One remembers these are the people we are killing."

So, Mother, it's now on the page. You tell me low or high or simply *alien*. I still can't decide. I'm not right about it, despite what's happened since. Are *you* all right about this? Should I have told you? Naomi Lee is...a savage. I hesitate to attach something else to her. I'm afraid of an attitude about it.

What remains will be told in a sickness, and more briefly.

Yo, that one cut off the lights, neighbors!

We'll be digging up or spending a great deal of time on phantom imaging if this keeps up. Honestly, I'd quit caring whether we were hit or not, but with Miss Lee I am a whole different rocketeer, with all passion as has not been flattened by this clerkish trade. There are more scrupulous ways to find them and shoot them, I suppose, though the neap of my creative tide passed years ago, I suspect, along with my brown hair.

Naomi must not perish.

She is innocent, not a real part of them or us. I saw her at dinner, eating a hard roll for a long time. She was dainty and near reverent toward the thing. You could tell she had once starved. I could barely stand it. I saw that she was looking to save the rest of her meal, but there was no way politely to do it. Her eyes flew around, defeated, though a pleasant smile stayed on her. The little English she has is halting but precise.

The trailer suddenly shook from a very nearby one. Sand and lead rain fell into the dinner. That was it for all of us. We jumped up to stations.

They are grooming her to actually shoot, so she stands right by me now, and I am watching her doubly. That is, on the instructions and for her true eyes. Does she really want to pull the trigger on her old friends? Is she going to be this complaisant all the way? We've not got a zombie here, after all. The trigger doesn't match with the dance and acrobatics and her general tenderness toward others, including me, though I want more than the *pro forma* from her, in my mediocrity, in my priestliness. Now I yearn to be a wealthy surgeon or the like, knowing dance, customs, or even how to have recreation. So in truth I see her triply: How is her inner bosom reckoning with me? How do I move, what do I say? I'm sick when she's there.

It sounded grim and hideous, but one day it got out clear:

"I love you, Miss Lee."

She seemed shocked and maybe stunned. But she looked full on me, a brave one. It occurred to me she might be, after all, a lover of *women*. Then I would be just some vocal piece of rubbish beside her.

What was she, thirty, forty? She quit smiling.

"These times...do not seem fervent for that, sir."

Fervent. My savage. I dwindled, dilapidated. But she looked full on me, wishing for a change in herself, I hoped. Then she punched in and fired a missile.

We had a medium one not much smarter than a howitzer round set for her, on the level of those old F-5 fighters they sold the Egyptians years ago, almost idiot-proof. In fact, I flew an F-5 myself — rickety and leaking — for my furlough last year. It brought me to a big lake with tame baboons romping all around it.

There were women and wild fruit, buffalo steaks, liquor, more music than you could stomach, in bright air-controlled tents like beach umbrellas. For the buried like me, wouldn't you know about the females. Bibliographers out of some cave back West or the far Orient, perhaps retarded or idiot savants. Such an orgy of synthetic tedium. I finally, at last, lost my virginity just to break it, like some involuntary dufus on the ski slopes. Both the woman and I were horrified, wishing we were drunk or, better, rightly human. This dreary patriotism probably made her yearn for her adventures in the Singapore Archives. For me, I wanted back at the scope and board, and cut short my leave when the postman came the next day with one of your letters, dear Ma, and he scared the lights out of me. I mean the postman, not your letter. I was certain it was some message of doom from a great authority somewhere who knew about my feeble atrocity the night before. Real guilt, so unlike me, was at my heels like snapping turtles. I wanted my bunk dreams back, the minor terror of the soldier's twenty-four-hour day. Back here I was not much, but I was distinct, not a foul heavy liquid as with the woman.

With Naomi Lee it would not be like that.

I promised my letters would be briefer. Length would indicate a weak selfishness, but it is hard to avoid.

The Commander himself was in back of us, watching, without my knowledge, the next morning. This was the day I had hoped for an opening in her bosom, some sign, some exotic signal from her punching through our technical statuary. My bunk had given me no sleep. My head refused to sweeten me with a dream of Miss Lee. When I noticed him I went frigid. The truth is we would rather be evaporated by a hit than face his wrath. Our forces knew their Commander. He's younger than I. He did not rise so quickly for nothing. He laughs wildly and rebukes wildly. Besides the venereal colonel, witness Thurman the klepto who had to drive into no-man's land in a Rover with a fluorescent bull's-eye painted on it. It took them a half hour, but a mere cannon finally caught him.

The way he put his hand to her waist (she leapt toward the console), the way he was dressed today — suave in individualized camo, almost like a rich citizen sportsman; the lack of flamboyant accouterments; his hair freshly oiled under the beret, stars in a cluster at the peak, cigarette in a holder — I dreaded to know what I knew. She was for *him*, all this having to shoot and know the general ropes, it was to bring her over to him, grooming her for the right day, not far off, when her dance would be required for him alone. He had gone to some lengths to subtlize himself so his handsomeness could be seen in relief. Already he looked a softer, more tactile man. I was even sicker. That thing in my heart, old near-ossified ball, went to a cold oyster.

When she faced him, I doubt she knew all that. She did not seem wooed at all, but rather frightened. I've no idea what he said to her, because my ears pounded. What she said at the last — "I believe I am making satisfactory progress, sir" — could have been said to me, and I took pleasure in her flatness. He walked off.

I went into an anguished study — what to say? what to ask? — and could not find the thing until late evening at the end of the watch.

"Miss Lee. What is it here you *miss* the most? The thing you can't get anymore. Is it...something important?"

I was happy she was caught out, actually pausing to think, not looking timid about it either. It thrilled me she was giving something from my voice this much time. Her pursing Mediterranean lips withered me. Murdering for her, a rocking thought, flew around my brain again.

"I believe certainly it is my cup of hot river-root tea. Ceruba. It's rare and hard to make, but I know how." The memory of the tea brought a fine glow on her face. I panted.

"How could I get it for you?"

She laughed. "It's impossible. The roots are on the banks of that little stream in no-man's land. Very mined. Very barbed wired. Very...self-homicidal. *Suicidal.* Either for them...or us."

That night one of theirs took our whole periscope off and we were optically blinded. A spitting thunder for a second, and then the missile came down into supply behind us. Several were killed back there, and we'd have to wait a whole week for the periscope. The feeling was we'd simply dig up and go fairly soon. It was propitious.

The next morning I was spelled and I drifted back among the wrecked trucks, jeeps and rovers. I wasn't far from the Commander's bunker itself. Above the steps you could see where his HQ sign had been knocked over by the blast. I went over and straightened it. I was about the only one out there. The weather was moderate and there were even some oasis gulls about. I envied them and saw them flying over no-man's land, in the direction of that little stream, I supposed. The map showed it forty miles down the track.

Yes, one of the Rovers was untouched. The morning was hurrying along when I remembered I am ground blind at night. This accelerated me, though the time was ample.

I hadn't even a pistol. What was the use, except for myself? I remembered I chuckled just about all the way over, holding up the little shovel as if it was a grave threat to them. I was out of there and doing forty in some lucky tight sand. As I romped down some loose monumental dune, I was still chuckling. Naomi Lee's description of the tree and the roots sang in my head like an avowal of love, despite the fact that she ran through it as if reading the back of a cereal box. Wounded by a mine, I'd still spade myself to death before the heathen swarmed me. I imagine my chuckle became maniacal. Out there where time forgot, for good reason, I wondered what god would hand over this dry pointless filth to anybody. It was almost a poor joke graphic on a computer screen. "Fuck you" went with it.

Things livened up near the stream, however. They began shooting at me. Nothing attached to it, no men or artillery snouts, but several smack-downs in clusters of antipersonnel. You believe this? I was flattered. I felt enormous. They were using up a magnificent storm on me. That stuff was devastating all around me, weaving back and forth, me chuckling. Maybe they hit mines too. I was quite the sand man. Thinking of it, like him, nobody could find me. I was a dream.

The barrage was so dead-on me and panicked, they walked it right down in front and blew gaps in their own wire. I motored through this to the edge of the cut and looked down at the mini-trees on the stream. The water was gasping along through a crooked ditch, the bank a black-green like you never see out here. My friends the gulls were yapping like a mutiny of proprietors. Up on the farther bluff across the way, at last I saw the foe with my eyes. They were shooting at me with hand weapons and, flattered, I just stood there, nicks and pops and spurts from the little water around me. There was almost a tender closeness here, at last, at last. Poor, but each man with a different headwrap — burnoose, turban, beanie, bits of an angry sunset. Dead was no concern, but wounded was, so I went down with my spade and almost straightaway saw the signs she described and started chopping into the loam under the weedy Ceruba.

I got several goodish chunks and overdid the haul, as a good Westerner would, so I was really burdened and flapping when I went back up the bluff. They'd almost stopped shooting. Then there was no shooting at all when I made the top and saw them all, just waiting there with near-melting gun barrels, simply looking at me. Above my head I raised one Ceruba root. They knew exactly what it was because they began cheering. I held the root aloft, still in a chuckling dream, and here they continued hurrahing and pumping their guns. Quite a tribute from those wild dry throats. It was an acme in my existence. I wish I could remember it better. Shrill calls scattering the gulls. I enjoyed their great politeness in not firing at me anymore, so my trip back was unhurried, the only hazard being my pitiable blind self-esteem, which caused a near disaster off the backside of a running dune about halfway home.

Altogether I guess the enemy have done a fair job, given their poverty and lemmingward cause. The longer we stay, the better they like it, I think. Spiritually they are here forever, and our people certainly aren't. Except, that is, for fixtures like me, hired out of no place, no history, no real biology, even. The war has never concerned me, as war, so I should be the last trusted voice about whatever gallantry is ascribed to anybody. Until I found the roots for Naomi Lee, I was assured that deaths in our trailer would barely count anyway. They would not be killing anybody at all, only emptying their precious ammunition.

Sure, there was hell to pay back at the trailer. The Commander stopped my Rover with his foot and was apoplectic, especially when he saw the roots and knew their purpose. I was a filthy dwindled thing when I arrived. Nobody could believe I was alive. The surgeon almost refused to let me go, positive I had shock or concussion. Or was cuckoo. That diagnosis has not been lifted to this day. After all, I could be dreadfully harmful, even with my small powers. I was watched.

Naomi Lee was very charmed, very incredulous. She saved making the tea until I could sit with the regular crew — regular as wallpaper. We all had a cupful. It was black and licoricelike, with maybe a note of ginger thrown in. Nobody liked it like she did, going away in a swept trance, smiling for an hour. We were courteous and for her I was determined to be as exotic as she liked, in my characterless way. On the other hand, there was something in me now. Something to me. I could feel it. It was not quite wanton, or *diamondlike,* but something new was there.

Perhaps you can buy love, perhaps your desperation can bring a treasured bosom close to you. The old dusty library tales might still be fetching around with reality, having their stubborn fun with us of thick hides and brains in our skin. Naomi Lee gazed, hypnotized. She'd always been there for the old tales, I guess, and couldn't help herself. I was amazed by her look and unsettled. Close to indecorous it was. The Commander sat right beside me, now my supposed winking avuncular, when he saw how Naomi Lee was stuck on me. I could tell he was trying to turn it all into a trivial prank, with him as the generous honcho who, out of his sternness, couldn't help but forgive this human folly as a boost to morale. He treated me as if I'd got some nostalgic disease like mumps, as this would enlarge him and make him beloved in his inconsistency. Especially to her.

He was looking harder at her all the time.

What a vicious bust to him that she watched only me, having something wordless, savage and long with me. He blew up and left. I was extremely frightened and wanted her to be more subtle.

"You are so watched. I am so happy in you," she said next dinnertime, so softly as to be under the clack of the plastic utensils.

"It's not just..." *Happy in me.*

What was I allowed to dream in that? Was this the definite thing? The avowal? The victory? "They watch me for bad things, not just for good," I told her. She ought to know.

{358}

"Pretty soon I am called to dance personally for him, tomorrow I think. I hate this. Do you think, my root-finding man, there is another way to be a patriot over here?"

I was torn up.

"I could dance badly, couldn't I? I could be clumsy...ugly."

"No you couldn't," I said.

The periscope gone, the radar practically asleep except for incoming, the night shift halved, with Willard Niles and that little chess monster Beckett insuring the pall of the evening, I lay in my bunk staring at a flat white tile right above me. It was nothing, perfected. I do not want to urge this analog, Ma, having testified too redundantly, I know, to the flat nullity of everything and almost everybody here already. But I found the answer right there, staring at the absence, the square, the sweet open atmosphere if you looked at it right. Tasting better than fresh cold milk. Here I'm making hay of the color, collapsing into poetry again, but I am exhilarated. Forgive me. Perhaps I was not all traditionally in love yet, because I was thinking perfectly, and one isn't supposed to do that. I cave in, really, to old bald science. Thanks, Ma. My air is the ozone of hot console wires.

After midnight I sneaked out to the boards. I never sneaked at anything before. Like a baby on Christmas morning, then, I sneaked. As I didn't when a baby on Christmas morning, Santa Claus evicted as an irrelevance long ago by you and dear Dad, Ma.

The things that create a traitor are probably very simple, aren't they, Ma, despite all those massy rooty espionage books nine hundred pages long we so adored. And our nostalgia for "pure" intellect — what a laugh to me now. We imagine that old villain out there knocked pale by his own IQ score, jacked off by "pure" mathematics.

Good, nobody was up and I changed all the imaging along the line, six trailers east, nine right, so we seemed to have a breakdown of false targets. And they'd know it immediately. Then I corrected them quickly, but doubled the image on the Commander's bunker — an underground palace, really — so it would look hot and new and real. I knew he was at home, playing checkers and looking in the mirror for blemishes that might annoy Naomi Lee.

Thirty minutes later they hit him with at least three huge ones direct. Right through the square nothing. Bunks fell down in our own place.

When the generator popped us back on, I looked down the hall to the women's quarters, where the females were swarming and falling over one another. I waited and waited.

Then she came out at last, looking perfectly miserable like the innocent bystander she was, in a white slip, barefooted. She was anxious, with her hand to her mouth. Then there was an aisle in the bodies and she all at once beheld me, wretched me, renegade me, and she smiled, horror still on her face.

Nicodemus Bluff

T HAT OLD WOMAN has money, we know. The old withered dugs used to teach high school. They say she even taught me thirty years ago, but I'm not sure as I was mostly away on drugs. One thing about my body or blood flow or whatall, I'm twice as put away as anybody else on a drug, always have been. I declare that I stayed away from the world thirty years and more. So when I saw the old woman on her porch chair as we ran by—running out the drugs of three decades—I just saw a new crone, not somebody I'd ever known. She was sitting there taking up space and money, the green leaves of the tree limbs reaching over her head looking like money itself. Say she used to teach me. I wonder what.

They stood me up and walked me when I was on those ludes and reds. No man ever liked a lude or red better than this man. They walked me around the high school halls and set me on the benches and showed me food, I guess, in the cafeteria. It is amazing what I never knew, amazing. I accompanied people. I was a devoted accomplice, accompanier, associate, minion, stooge. The term *et al.* was made for me. But I can't remember how. We would be in church or jail. I would just look around and take stock of the ten-foot-or-so box around me and see what was in it, my "space," yes really. Couldn't tell you further what was out there. It could be bars or a stained glass picture of Saint John baptizing Jesus Christ in the Jordan River, boulders and olive trees hanging over the water.

What I wanted to be away from I believe was the memory of my father and his friends years ago at the deer camp in Arkansas. Something happened when I was out there. My father died that next week, but even so he still seemed to hang at the border of my space—the bars, the church window, that ten-foot cube—bloody and broken up and flattened in the nose, a black bruise on his cheekbone because of what happened to him with those others years ago down in the swamps.

We used to be better folks even though my father's people had nothing. There was hope then of rising in the community. My mother was a secretary to a wealthy lawyer in town. It's vague how you get to be "somebody" here, but mainly it has to do with marrying the right woman. Acts of kindness or neighborliness do not really count. I have seen people do acts of kindness over and over and although they get smiled at and thanked with a "Much obliged" — this doing for folks and making them "much obliged" is funny, don't you think? What really made esteem was not acts of kindness but money, clothes, car, house, posture, lawn. We knew, though, that we belonged on the edge of being respected "gentlefolk" (not my term but Dr. Debord's, the preacher friend and chairman of the Sociology Department at the Methodist college in town who helped me for a while. My mother had an easy gracious manner and dressed well naturally although she was not of moneyed people. She was a person of "modest understated grace," Mr. Kervochian told me once, wanting me not to forget what a valuable woman she was, so I'd have something to get up in the morning for. I run around the block again and again, gasping "success, success."

It was hard for Dr. Debord to get me to admit the story of my father Gomar. It was tough and deep, but in talking it up Dr. Debord believed I would get better and be about my work at the animal shelter. My father that week was among those new acquaintances he hoped would be his new and lasting crowd — up from the failed farmers, the beer-for-breakfast mechanics, loiterers and petty-thieving personnel who were his people. Yay for him, some people said, as my father tried to bring himself up into genteel society. I think most people approved of his rise. In the old days the whole county knew each other, don't doubt it, and you might have thought there was some god placed in an office with account books where he let out the word on the social worth of all citizens hereabouts, keeping tab on these as they rose, fell, or simply trod down the rut left by prior generations; the word went around and was known.

But at ten years old what did I know when my father and the rest of them were out at that lodge? I did not know my father had borrowed heavily from Mr. Pool and that was why we had a nice house, lawn, two cars, even a yard man who rode a riding mower, a Negro named Whit who was nice to me. Whit cut himself chopping down a tree for us and I recall thinking that his blood might be bluer and was surprised. Why do people live here at all, I ask. They must know this is a filthy, wrong, haunted place. Even the trees that are left look wrong or wronged, beat up. The red dirt is hopeless. The squirrels are thin and there is much — you can't get around it — suicide on the part of possums, coons, armadillos and deer who tried to exist in the puny scratch but could not, deciding then to leap out on the highway. There are no stories of any merit to come out of this place. The only good woods are near the base of the little mountain. (Let me tell you something about all the drug pushers around here. They are no mystery to me. They aren't a new wave of punk. They are just country sorry, like my father's people. Someone had a house and land and saved the woods at the west base of the little mountain (805 feet). This person would shoot trespassers, hunters and fishermen (there was a deep black pond in the middle). Nobody went in. The woods were saved. They were thick and dark with very high great oaks and ashes and wild magnolias, even bamboo, like nothing else around. Thicker, much, even than the woods over at the deer camp near the Mississippi River in Arkansas, with sloughs and irrigation ditches where the ducks come down too. You also could catch winter crappie in the oxbow lakes if you could sit still in the cold. (Allow me to express myself about those woods near the mountain here. They were owned by a doctor who was an enormous dealer in drugs. Well I know.) The only thing better I would ever see was the marijuana plantation at the state university where they grew it legally for government experimentation. I saw that plantation once driving by with somebody when I was seventeen and almost came out of my cube of space to get them to stop the car. (No, I could never drive; didn't learn to drive until I was twenty and that was when I finished high school too. All of this delay, I believe, is because of what they did to my father.)

My father then had these acquaintances: a banker, an insurance man, a clothing store owner, a lawyer (employer of my mother), an owner of a small company that made oil pumps for aircraft engines, a medical doctor. Then there was Mr. Kervochian, a druggist, who turned out to be the kindest, and the one who told me the whole story years later when he was dying of pancreatic cancer. My father — we had the lawn, the porch, the two cars, the nice fishing boat, the membership in the country club — I say again was lent heavily some money by three of these men. They told him it was a new kind of loan they were practicing with, a way to help really deserving men from the county who wanted to better themselves. It was agricultural rates interest, very low. It was "special" money on collateral of his personality and promise; and it entailed his being close by to aid these men at some business schemes; close by like at beck and call, said Mr. Kervochian. My father would get nice things immediately and pay it off so that he could enjoy the good life and pay along for it, not waiting until he was old like many men did, left only a few years to enjoy their station and bounty after a lifetime of work. They liked my mother and they thought my father was admirable the way he tried to sell real estate out in the country where the dead farms were. He knew them when they were dying and could be had.

He managed to get Mr. Pool and Mr. Hester a piece of land from a crazy man for almost nothing. The man went down to Whitfield, the asylum at Jackson. The land they used for turkey houses. That's where I came in: at age ten I went out there twice a day on my bicycle to feed and water the turkeys. I had a job, I was a little man. I was worthy of an invitation to the deer hunt. Everything was fitting together. My father had some prestige. He was arriving and I was well on the way to becoming a man of parts myself.

I can't remember why I was the only boy out at the deer camp in Arkansas. But I went along with my father, Gomar, and had my own gun, a little .410 single shot, for the delta squirrels, very fat, if I saw them, which I did but could not hit them much, at age ten. Something would happen when a live squirrel showed up in the bead at the end of the barrel. The squirrel would blur out and I'd snap the gun to the side, missing all of it. I think I embarrassed my father. A boy around here should be able to shoot at ten. The rest of them weren't hunting yet. They were in the lodge drinking and playing cards. I could hear the laughter getting louder and how it changed — louder and meaner, I guess — while I was out in those short stumps and wood chips on the edge of the forest. I remember seeing that cold oily-looking water in a pool in one stump and felt odd because of the rotten smell. They didn't know why I was frowning and missing squirrels out there and had gone back in to laugh harder, drinking. I could smell the whiskey from where I was and liked it. It smelled like a hospital, where I was once to have a hernia repaired.

The large thing I didn't know was that my father owed all this money to the three men, and he was not repaying it on time. I thought they were just his new friends, having them in this sort of club at the lodge, which was as good as a house inside or better with polished knotty pine walls and deer heads and an entire bobcat on a ledge. Also a joke stuffed squirrel with its head blown off, as I couldn't do out there smelling that rotten water, standing in the wet leaves in rubber boots made for a man, not my own, which I was saving for dry big hunting. I remember in December everything was wet and black.

They said flash floods were around, water over the highway, and we were trapped in until the water went down. Then it began to get very cold. I went inside, without much to do. I came back outside with a box of white-head kitchen matches and started licking them on the head, striking them and sailing them out so they made a trail like rockets, then hit and flamed up before the wet took care of them. I thought the future belonged to rockets — this had been said around — and I was very excited to get into the future. My father was providing a proud place for me to grow and play on our esteemed yard. One night I was watching television, an old movie with June Allyson. Her moist voice reached into me and I began crying I was so happy — she favored my mother some. But my father owed all this money, many years of money. It seemed that two of them, Mr. Hester and Colonel Wren, weren't that anxious about it. But the banker, Garrand Pool, who owned the lodge, was a different kind.

The trouble was, Mr. Kervochian told me, as he was dying, that my father thought he had considerably reduced the debt by getting that piece of land from that insane man for almost nothing. This provided grounds for a prosperous turkey farm for the men. Twenty or more houses of turkeys it would be. My father supposed that he had done them a real turn, a very handy favor, and he felt easy about his lateness of payment. He assumed they had taken off several thousand dollars from it and were easy themselves. He thought things had been indicated more than "much obliged." It was riling somebody, though. Just the money — considerable — wasn't all of it. Something else very terrible was mixed in.

I didn't catch on to much except their voices grew louder and here and there a bad word came out. My father asked me to go back to my bunk in another room. There wasn't anything to do back there but read an R encyclopedia. I could read well. Almost nothing stopped me. My father could read but it was like he learned the wrong way. He took forever and the words seemed to fly off on him like spooked game. He held his finger on the page and ran it along like fastening down the sounds. My mother taught me and I could not see the trouble. I was always ahead of the teacher. I felt for my dad when I saw him reading. I knew this feeling wasn't right, but I wanted to hold his hand and read for him. It almost made me cry. Because it made me afraid, is what it did. He wasn't us.

The terrible thing mixed in it was that my dad was good at the game of chess and vain about it. He had no degree at all — I don't believe he had finished high school, really, unlike such as Mr. Pool, who had college and a law degree. He had never played Mr. Pool but he had whipped some other college men and he was apt to brag about it. He would even call himself "country trash," winking, when he boasted around the house, until Mother asked him to quit, please — gloating was not character. But Mother did not know that my father, when he played chess, became the personality of a woman, a lady of the court born in the eighteenth century (said Mr. Kervochian). The woman would "invest" Dad and he would win at chess with her character, not his own man's person at all. Mr. Kervochian took a long time explaining this. The chess game, as it went on, changed him more and more into a woman, a crafty woman. He began sitting there like a plain man, but at the end of the game he couldn't help it, the signs came out, his voice went up, and his arms and hands were set out in a sissy way. He was all female as the climax of his victory neared. He would rock back and forth nervously and sputter in little giggles, always pursing his lips. It wasn't something you wanted to look at and those he defeated didn't want to remember it. It unnerved them and made them feel eerie and nervous to have been privy to it, not to be talked about. I didn't know what was going on, with the noise out there in the great "den" of the lodge. Mr. Hester and Colonel Wren, the doctor (Dr. Harvard) and the oil pump company owner (Ralph Lovett), with Mr. Kervochian just leaning near them, drinking, were playing poker that night. Only two of them had gone out to hunt a little in the rain and vicious cold but come back. My father and Mr. Pool were at the other end playing chess very seriously. My father's feet became light, tapping on the floor as with princess slippers. All through the other quiet I heard them.

Mr. Kervochian, dying of cancer, told me it was not clear how my father's change came about or even where he learned to play chess, which was a surprise — his chessmanship — unto itself. He was not from chessly people. They were uneducated, sorry trash; even my grandmother Meemaw — a loud hypochondriac, a screamer — had failed on the farm and in town both and lived between them, looking both ways and hating both of what she saw. But Gomar, my dad, knew chess, maybe from one month in the army at the time of the Korean conflict, after which he came back unacceptable because of something in his shoulders (as he said when I asked him once). My mother looked at the floor. She hated war and was glad he'd never been in one. But I wanted him to have been in the war. Mr. Kervochian believed somebody in the service taught him, but where he came in contact with the "woman" he does not precisely know.

But early on he was playing chess with the circuit-church-riding minister at the church near Meemaw's home. Sometime somewhere the woman in him appeared. It was a crafty, clever, "treacherous" woman; a "scheming, snooty, snarling" woman, rougher than a man somehow in spitefulness. She knew the court and its movements and chess was a breeze for her. She'd take him over about midgame or when things got tough. It would lurch into him, this creature, and nobody could beat him. He beat a college professor; a hippie who was a lifetime chess bum who lived at a bohemian café; a brilliant Negro from New Orleans; two other town men who thought they were really good. Something was wrong, terrible about it. He wasn't supposed to be that good.

He might have picked up the woman who inhabited him from somebody in the army, or from that preacher, whose religion had its strange parts, its "dark enthusiasms," Mr. Kervochian said, weakly speaking from his cancer. We don't know, but it led to that long rain of four days at the deer camp, the matter of the owed money, and Mr. Pool, the banker, who professed himself a superior, very superior chess player.

Voices were short but loud and I heard cursing from the "den" where the men were. They were some drunk and angry about the rain. When I peeped out I saw the banker looking angrily into my father's face. My father's face was red, too. He saw me at the door and told me to go back in the other room.

I said, "Daddy there's nothing to do." He brought our guns over to me and said, "Clean them," without looking at me. Then he shut the door. It was only me, the R volume of the encyclopedia and the guns with their oil kit. I went on reading at something, I think Rhode Island, which was known for potatoes. I could hear Dr. Harvard complaining and very concerned about the rain cutting us off, although we had plenty of food. I recall he wasn't drinking and was chubby with spectacles, like an owl, looking frightened, which wasn't right. I didn't like a doctor acting frightened about the weather. My father and Mr. Pool were in a trance over the board of pieces. Mr. Kervochian was drinking a lot, but he wasn't acting odd or loud. This I saw when I cracked the door and peeked again. Mr. Kervochian had a long darkish foreign face with heavy cheek whiskers. He stared out the window at the white cold rain like a philosopher, sad. He liked big-band music — there was some he had brought on his tape machine — and I learned later that he wrote some poetry and might be a drug addict. He seemed to be a kind man, soft, and would talk with you — or me, a kid — straight ahead. He never made jokes or bragged about killing game like the others, my father too. I remembered he had given me a box of polished hickory nuts. They were under the bed and I got them out and started playing with them.

The thing was, Mr. Pool did not believe any of my father's chess victories. Something was wrong, or fluked, he thought. It couldn't be that a man from my father's circumstances could come forth with much of a chess game, to Mr. Pool, who, with his law degree and bankership, hunting, golf and chess, thought of himself as a "peer of the realm," Mr. Kervochian said later. "A Renaissance man, a Leonardo of the backwater." There was a creature in Mr. Pool, too, Mr. Kervochian said, hoarse and small because of his cancer. Mr. Pool owned the lodge and midway ("in medias res," said Mr. Kervochian) in his affairs he began thinking to own people too. He had a "dormant serfdom" in his head. His eyes would grow big, his tongue would move around on his teeth, and he would start demanding things, "like an old czar." Thing was, there was nobody to "quell" him when he had these fits. He did pretty much "own" several people, and this was his delight. People were "much obliged" to him left and right. Then he would have a riot of remembering this. He would leer "like Rasputin leching on a maid-in-waiting." Mr. Kervochian knew history. Pool was "beside himself" as the term had it: "himself outside the confines of his own psyche." Like he was calling in all his money and the soul attached to it. I could hear they had been talking about money and Mr. Pool was taking over all the conversation. My father's point was that the purchase transfer from the old loony man was worth a great deal as a piece of work and should make some favorable patience about the loan on Mr. Pool's part. But I didn't know all that, what their voices were saying. I knew hardly anything except for the strange loudness of their voices with the whiskey in them, which was an awful thing I'd never heard.

I knew my father wasn't used to drinking and did not do it well. Once the last summer when he was coming up in the world, he had bought a bag and some clubs, some bright maroon-over-white saddle golf shoes, a cart, and took me with him to try out the country club. I remember he had an all-green outfit on. This was the club where those men who were his new group played; but this was a weekday, a workday, and he wanted to come out alone (only with me) because he'd never played. So he rolled his cart into the clubhouse and we sat in a place with a bar. He began ordering glasses of whiskey almost one after the other. I went around here and there in the chairs and came back and sat, with him looking straight at me, his ears getting red and his eyes narrowing. I didn't know what was happening but the man behind the bar made me think everything was all right, saying "sure" and "certainly" when Daddy wanted another glass of whiskey. But then he, my father, wouldn't answer me at all when I asked wasn't it time to play golf. I wanted to chase the balls and had several on the floor, playing.

"You know, really. You're not supposed to bring your bag in here," said the barman, kindly.

My father looked like he didn't know what the man was talking about. I pointed at the golf bag and said, "He means your club bag, Daddy."

"What?" He looked at me, whining-like at me.

Then he drank another whole glass and something happened. I watched my father fall to the side off the chair, knock over the golf cart and bag, and hit the floor, with his golf hat falling off. I got up and saw he was really down, asleep, at the other end of his saddle shoes, maroon and white. He had passed out.

My mother came from the office of the lawyer to pick him up after the barman called. I sat in the chair and waited for him to wake up while other people came in, not helping, just shutting their eyes and looking away. I was awfully scared, crying some. It wasn't until a long time later I learned (from Mother) that he was afraid to start playing golf and embarrass himself, although there were just a few people at the course. He wasn't sure about the sticks or the count. My mother whispered this to me but I never understood why he'd go out there at all. My father, I say, had no whiskey problem, he just couldn't drink it very well and hardly ever did. My mother I don't think had any problems at all and she had high literacy and beauty.

At the deer camp the weather would not quit. I can't recall that kind of cold with that much rain. One or the other usually stops but on top of the roof the roar of water kept up and my window outside was laid on by a curtain of white, like frost alive. They were quiet in the "den" for a long, long time. I imagined they were all asleep from drinking the whiskey. I liked imagining that because what was out there was not nice. I'd seen it, even if they were only playing chess, a game I knew nothing about, but it looked expensive and serious, those pieces out there, made of marble, a mysterious thing I knew my father was very good at.

Mr. Kervochian knew the game and had watched Mr. Pool defeat many good players around the town and in big cities. Mr. Pool wore a gray mustache and looked something like an old hefty soldier "of a Prussian sort," said Mr. Kervochian. You could picture him ordering people around. You could feel him staring at you, bossing. He'd hardly looked at me, though. I was not sure, again, why I was the only child out there.

It got late at night but the lights were still on out there. I had gone to sleep for a while, dreaming about those polished hickory nuts and squirrels up to your hips. When I peeped out I saw all the others asleep, but Garrand Pool and my father, Gomar, were staring at the board without a sound. They had quit drinking but were angry in the eyes and resolved on some mean victory, seemed to me. It was fearsome. The others in the chairs snoring, the rain outside. Nothing seemed right in the human world I knew. Then Mr. Pool began whispering something, more hissing maybe, as grown men I knew of never did. Pool was saying "Stop it. Stop that. Stop that, damn you!" This made my father's body rise up and he put his hand down and moved a piece. He stiffened to a proper upright posture with shoulders spread back, and then this light queer voice came from him. I didn't know, but it was the woman overcoming him. Even in his wrist — thinking back — you could see a womanly draped thing. His fingers seemed to have become longer. Now this was another evil: Mr. Pool knew nothing about the woman and thought my father was mimicking him. He seemed to be getting even angrier and I shut the door. Let me tell you, it was odd but *not* like a nightmare. Another kind of dream, maybe even more wicked and curious, a quality of dream where the world was changed and there was a haze to it, and you couldn't get out by opening your eyes. It made you weird and excited, my father's voice and posture and hands.

"Now hunt, old toad," he had actually said to Mr. Pool, jangling high-voiced like a woman in a church choir.

So I had to open the door a crack again.

Mr. Pool stood up and cursed him and told him something about "deadbeat white trash." But my father said something back shrilly and Mr. Pool I thought was coming out of his skin.

"Don't you mock me with that white-trash homo voice! I won't stand for it!"

The other men woke up and wanted to know what was happening. Nobody had had any supper. They ate some crackers and cheese, commented on the steady rain, then went back to their rooms to sleep. My father and Mr. Pool had never halted the chess and paid no attention to anybody else. I was very sleepy and lost-feeling (in this big lodge, like something in a state park made for tourists). I lay there in the bunk for hours and heard the female voice very faintly and was sick in my stomach through the early morning hours. Ice was on the inside of the window. I could feel the cold gripping the wall and a gloomy voice started talking in the rain, waving back and forth. It wasn't any nightmare and it was very long, the cold wet dark woods talking to me, the woman's voice curling to the room under the doorjamb. Another whole person was out there playing chess, somebody I never knew. A woman and, I thought, somehow sin were in the lodge. Without a dream I was out of the regular world and had prickly sparking feelings like they had put you in a tub of ice and then run you through a wind tunnel.

At daybreak they were still at the game. Garrand Pool had started drinking again. He was up looking out a kitchen window and my father was leaning over studying the board, cooing and chirping. Mr. Pool was going to say something, turning around, but then he saw me in the doorway and stopped, coughing. When my father turned in the chair, I didn't recognize his face. It was longer and his mouth was bigger. His eyes were lost behind his nose. I was very glad he didn't say anything to me. He hurled himself back then as if my eyes hurt him. I shut the door again. I felt cold and withered.

Soon there was a knock on the door. It was Mr. Kervochian. He told me to dress up, that it was cold out, it had quit raining, and he was going to take me out, bring my gun. In a few minutes the two of us walked by Mr. Pool and Daddy, frozen at the board, not looking up. Mr. Kervochian brought me some breakfast out on the porch — some coffee (my first), a banana and some jerky. It was hurtfully cold while we sat there on the step. I could smell whiskey on Mr. Kervochian, but he had showered and combed his hair and had on fresh clothes. My boots were new and I liked them, bright brown with brass eyelets. I felt manly. I think Mr. Kervochian was having whiskey in his coffee.

"Let's go about our way and see what we can see, little Harris," he said.

"Don't you want your gun?" I asked him.

"No. Your big shooter's all we need."

I picked up the .410 single, which was heavy. He told me how to carry it safely. We walked a long time into the muddy woods, down truck tracks and then into deep slimy leaves with brown vines eye-high. I tripped once, went down gun and all with shells scattered out of my coat pocket. Mr. Kervochian didn't say anything but "That happens." We went on very deep in there, toward the river, I guess. How could cobwebs have lived through that rain? They were in my face. Mr. Kervochian, high up there with his thermos, could float on the leaves and go along with no danger, but I was all webby. He began talking, just a slight muddiness in his voice because of the drink.

"He used to have a colored man out here with us, like successful Southern white men have at a deer camp. A happy coon, laughing and grinning, step and fetch it. Named Nicodemus, you know. Factotum luxury-maker. Owing so much to Pool Abe Lincoln's proclamation didn't even touch him. Measureless debt of generations. Even his pa owed Pool when he died."

"Mr. Kervochian, what's happening with my daddy and Mr. Pool back in the lodge?"

"Old Pool's calling in his debts. He always does, especially with some whiskey in him. He's that kind, perfect for a banker, gives so gladly and freely, then when you don't know when, angry about the deal and set on revenge. Gives and then hates it. One of those kind that despises the borrower come any legal time to collect."

"Are they playing for money? Is that why they're so mad?"

"They could be, a lot of money if I heard right, whatall through their whispering. I don't know for sure. It's a private thing and you can be sure Pool's not going to let it go."

"It's like nobody else's in the lodge."

"Let's hunt. Tell you what: there's got to be big game down by the river."

We walked on and on. Cold and tired, stitch in the side, sleepy, was I.

We were on a little bluff and then there was just air. He caught me before I walked out into the Mississippi River. It was like a sea and I'd almost sleepwalked into it, that deep muddy running water. "Watch ho, son!" he said. Then I was pulled back, looking at our home state across the big water.

"You've got to watch it around here. Something's in that bluff under us. It's haunted here. This would be a very bad place to fall off."

The river was huge like a sea and angry, waves of water running. "Why is it haunted?"

"Nicodemus is under the bluff, son."

"That colored man? Why?"

"Old Pool and Colonel Wren."

"Are you drunk now, Mr. Kervochian?"

"Yes, son, I am."

"Please don't scare me."

"I'm sorry. Pay no attention to me. I can get sober in just three minutes, though, boy."

We walked back toward the lodge very slowly, the Nicodemus place behind me and the chess game going on, I guessed, ahead. We saw two squirrels, but again, I missed them. I didn't care. Mr. Kervochian said I was all right, he wasn't much of a hunter either.

"You know, all under our feet are frozen snakes, moccasins and rattlers, sleeping. All these holes in the ground around us. Snakes are cold-blooded and they freeze up asleep in the cold winter."

I didn't like to think of that at all.

Then it began raining all of a sudden, very hard, as if it had just yawned awhile to come back where it was. We were already stepping around ditches full of running water.

"Little Harris, there is a certain kind of woman," he all at once said, for what? "A woman with her blond hair pulled back straight from her forehead, a high and winsome forehead, that has forever been in fashion and lovely, through the ages. And that is your mother. Like basic black. Always in fashion. Blond against basic black and the exquisite forehead, for centuries."

I said nothing. We stopped and saw through the forest where Mr. Hester and Colonel Wren went across a cut with their guns, out trying to hunt but now caught by the rain, heading back to the lodge. We didn't say anything to them, like we were animals watching them.

"She used to come in the drugstore for her headaches. A woman like that in this town, I predicted, would always have some kind of trouble. That nice natural carriage, big trusting gray eyes."

"It's raining hard, Mr. Kervochian."

When we at last returned to the lodge my eyes were hanging down out of their holes I was so tired. There were empty plates on the bar of the kitchen and nobody in the chess seats, just empty glasses and cups on the table. Dr. Harvard said they had left off the game and finally gone to bed, thank God. He peered at the rain past us beyond the doorway and commenced fretting, almost whining about the weather and the thunder and when were we ever going to get out of here, the way the roads were flooded over. There was no telephone, and so on. To see a grown medical doctor going on like this, well, it was amiss, ugly. It changed me. I went right on to bed and was out a long time.

When I woke it was late into the day and going out I saw Mr. Pool and my father were sitting there again, at it after their nap. They looked neither left nor right. My father suddenly gave a yelp, shrill, and I thought Garrand Pool had done something to him. But he was only making a move with a chess piece that must have been a good and mean one, because Mr. Pool cursed and drank half a glass of whiskey.

Mr. Kervochian took his place at the window with a new glass. He looked out into the weather as if he could see a number of people, all making him melancholy. Colonel Wren and Mr. Hester were all wet. They threw more logs on the fire and got it really blazing. They talked about more poker. Nobody knew quite what to do with all their big grown-up bodies and eyes and ears trapped in by the rain these days. Dr. Harvard nagged himself asleep again. The insurance man, Mr. Ott, came tumbling in the door holding his hand. He had cut it on an ax out there chopping wood. The blood was all over it and when he put his hand in the sink it dripped down in splotches around the drain. They woke up Dr. Harvard and he was in the kitchen with Mr. Ott a long time. Then he went out in the rain to get his bag. Mr. Ott needed stitches. I was fascinated by this, sewing up a man. Dr. Harvard worked over Mr. Ott for a long time. Every now and then Mr. Ott would cry out, but in a man's way, just a deep *uff!* I looked over at my father and Mr. Pool. They had never even looked up during the whole hour.

Then Colonel Wren said he was going to have something, damn it all, and went outside with his gun, where in late evening it was just sprinkling rain. Everybody had read all the magazines. I found an old *Reader's Digest* Condensed Book and went back to read something by Somerset Maugham.

It put me to sleep although I liked the story. I guess it was after midnight when I heard them making more sound than usual. I went out in my pajamas. The men at the poker table were high on beer, maybe, but they were very concerned about Colonel Wren. It was raining, thundering and lightning, and he hadn't returned. One of them called him a crazy Davy Crockett kind of fool. Mr. Kervochian, sipping at the fireplace, put in, "Closer to it, Kaiser Wilhelm the Second. Shot ten thousand stags, most of them near tame. Had a feeble arm he was trying to make up for."

Then who comes in all bloody and drenched, with a knife in one hand and a spotlight in the other, but Colonel Wren. He was tracking mud in and shouting.

"There's breakfast out on the hook, by God!"

We went to the door past Mr. Pool and my father, frozen there, and saw a cleaned deer carcass hanging on a board between two trees. In all the rain it showed up sparkling in the spotlight beam.

"That's just a little doe, isn't it?" said Mr. Kervochian.

"That's all the woods gave up, help of this spotlight," said Colonel Wren, very loudly. "It'll eat fine. Come that liver and eggs in the morning, partners, we'll have an attitude change here!"

I won't say again that my father and Mr. Pool paid no attention to any of this, and didn't do anything but play and take little naps for the next two days straight.

After breakfast around eleven that day, I drove out with Mr. Kervochian and Dr. Harvard to check the roads. We looked out of the truck cab and saw wide water much bigger than it used to be, the current of the creek rushing along limbs and bushes. It was frightening, not a hint of the road. Dr. Harvard was white when I looked at him. Later Mr. Kervochian explained that every man has a deathly fear and that Harvard's just happened to be water.

There was more poker and big-band music on Mr. Kervochian's tape player, with now and then a piece of radio music or weather announcement. But the next two days they argued mainly about Killarney Island. Colonel Wren said he knew the deer were all gathered there from all the flooding. And that there was an old boat, they could go out in the Mississippi and shoot all the deer they wanted. The rain shouldn't stop them. This wasn't a goddamned retirement lodge, they were all hungover and bitchy from cabin fever. He wanted to start the expedition.

"Our old boat should be right under Nicodemus Bluff," he said. There would be nothing to rowing out there.

I looked over at Mr. Kervochian. The others were arguing about whether that old boat was any good anymore, the river would be raging, it was stupid and dangerous. Mr. Kervochian, looking with meaning at me, said that was hardly any hunting at all. The deer on that island, which was only fifty yards square, would just be standing around and it would be nothing but a slaughter.

"You couldn't shoot your own foot anyway, Kervochian," said Colonel Wren meanly. "You're an old thought-fucked man." Then Wren looked down at me. "Sorry," he said.

But early the next morning we were all ready to get out of the place. Except for you know who, at it, in another world. Mr. Pool suddenly won a game, but he just got tight-lipped and red in the face to celebrate. I didn't want to look at my father's face. When Mr. Pool said "Checkmate, Gomar!" it sounded like a foreign name in the house.

I went along with them, taking my gun. Mr. Kervochian took a gun and his thermos. The rain was very light now in the early morning. The plan was, when they got to the island, Colonel Wren was going to scare a deer off the island just for me. It couldn't swim anywhere but almost right to me on the shore, and I could blow it down. I wanted to do this. A deer was larger than the squirrels and I wasn't likely to miss. So there I was at ten all bloody in my thoughts, almost crazy from staying in that lodge around that chess tournament that who knows when it would end, both of them looking sick when I could stand to look at them.

We tracked that long way out to the bluff. They went down and found the boat and set out with the paddles, three of them. Mr. Kervochian stayed with me. He seemed to either care for me or wanted a level place to drink. With all these people the bluff didn't seem that fearsome, so I asked him what about Nicodemus, what happened?

"You can't tell this around, little Harris."

"I wouldn't."

We watched them flapping and plowing the water, heading left and north to the island, just a hump out there a half mile away.

"Looking at it several ways, it's still a wretched thing. The man was full of cancer. Owed Pool a lifetime's money. Couldn't afford a hospital. He asked Pool to shoot him and so they did. I don't know which one."

"He'd been with them—"

"His whole life. You could blame Pool for the cancer too. The way he gave, then hounded. Nicodemus, that man, still wanted 'to keep it in the family.'"

They were hollering now out in the tan water, paddles up in the air. Something was wrong with the boat. They turned it around and headed back in. You could see the boat was getting lower in the water. The going was very slow and there was a great deal of grief shouted out. They must've been up to their knees. I heard Mr. Kervochian laughing, but my sense of humor must not have been attuned correctly. The river to me looked like the worst, fiercest place to drown. They came back under the bluff, their guns underwater and their throats stuffed with rage.

Then of course the rain came on, half-strong but mocking, and you could feel the sleet in it. The wet men said almost nothing, flapping back through the woods. It took forever.

There was a shout ahead, a cackling. Down the cut I could see some motion in those stumps in the edge of the lodge clearing. The cackling and now a yipping called at us through the last yards, a stand of walnuts where on the ground you crunched the ball husks of the nuts with your boots.

Mr. Pool was beating my father on the neck with a hard pepperoni sausage. It was a long pepperoni. He kept whacking it down. But my father, holding his hands over his head and trying to dodge, kept cackling and yipping. Thing was, he was laughing, down on his knees, fingers on the top of his head, knee-walking and sloshing through the pools. It was there where the water lay rotten-smelling in the tops of the stumps, putrid and deep back in your nostrils.

"It's all mine, free and clear. I won it, I won it!" my father was shrieking, in that woman's voice.

He couldn't know we were standing all around him. He was shrieking at the ground. Mr. Pool didn't know we were there either. He hit my father again. The pepperoni stick made an awful fleshy thunk on him.

"You trash scoundrel. Stop it, stop it!"

Then Mr. Pool drew around and saw us all, me especially. He hauled my father around facing me, on his knees. Garrand Pool was a big man and my father had gone all limp. His face was cut, his nose was smashed down. He looked horrible, the rain all over his face, and his face long, his mouth hanging down agape, as if frozen in a holler.

"Show him. Talk for your son. Let him see who you are."

I went up close to stop Mr. Pool. I was right in front of my father. He came up with his face, and you could tell he didn't want to, but couldn't help it. He spilled out in that cracking, cackling female voice, "I won! I won!"

Then Mr. Pool just thrust him off and he fell on his face out there in that stinking water.

What Garrand Pool had done seemed awful, but my father almost canceled it out. Nobody could make a direction toward either one. I know how they felt.

The next morning we left. Dr. Harvard was terrified, but the water had receded some and the tall trucks whipped right out through it and to the highway.

He couldn't even look at me for days when we got home. He was all bandaged up and sore. I never saw my father full in the face again. His face would start to turn my way, then he'd shake it back forward.

Nobody, I heard from Mother, ever bothered us about payments of any sort ever again while she was a widow. We had the house, the nice lawn, the two cars, a standing membership in the country club, which I only used to get loaded at and fall in the pool over and over again, swimming underwater long distances full of narcotics until my wrung-out lungs drove me to the surface.

My father never got it right at the country club either, you see. The next week after the deer lodge he was walking at twilight down the road next to the golf course. The driver of the car says he swerved out suddenly right into the nose of his car. They didn't find any alcohol in his blood, and none of it made much sense unless you had seen his eyes trying to call back that terrible woman's voice, pleading right at me.

The extra money my mother had, her legal secretary's salary free and clear, was in a way my downfall. She did not know how not to spoil me, and I always had plenty of money, more money than anybody. And Mr. Kervochian felt for me deeply, truly. I will never blame him. He was of that certain druggist's habit of thought that drugs are made to help people through hurtful times. You wouldn't call him a pusher because he meant only the kindly thing. He saw I was numbed, shocked and injured, so he provided plenty of medicine for me. He gave some to my mother too. She wouldn't take hers, so I got it and took it. I went back and he was always a cheerful giver. Later, he even came down to the jail and brought me out after I'd been taken there, accompanying somebody, some group, somehow an accomplice, just lugging there and nearly keeling over in that racing little sleep I loved. Never did I fight or even complain much.

My mother never remarried. Her looks, her high brightness and carriage, you would have thought she could have a number of prominent handsome men, but she was the kind of woman, I found out — maybe there are a few of them — who don't want but just the one marriage. They are quite all right going along alone. I was shocked, I believe when I was eighteen or thereabouts, only slightly nembied in the kitchen, when she told me she actually had loved my father very much. Then I was confused even a bit more when she said, "Your father was a good man, Harris."

"He *was*?" This confused me, as I say. I'd hated him for being on his knees with that voice at the lodge, I'd hated him for being killed, and I was angry at him through his brother, his own country-trash brother, when I saw him at Dad's funeral in a long-sleeved black silky shirt with a gold chain on his chest. His own brother in not even a suit.

Soon I needed some more drugs and went by Kervochian's.

"My mother said my father was a good man. Is that how you saw him, Gomar Greeves?"

"Gomar?...Well, Harris. Frankly, I just don't know. I hadn't known him that well. But he was probably a good man."

Later, but before he got sick, Mr. Kervochian, sharing a lude with me, began trying to have a theory, like so: "This state is very proud of its men's men. Its football-playing, tough rough whiskey-drinking men. But I tell you, you calculate those boys at the Methodist college who come by the store here. At least *half* of them are what you call epicene—leaning toward the womanly. The new Southern man is about half girl in many cases, Harris. Now that means their mothers raised them. Their fathers didn't get into it at all. So these men, maybe Gomar was a country version, the woman came—"

"I don't want to hear that, any of that." I was thinking of that awful Meemaw.

"But it was—I watched and heard closely, closely—a brilliant courtly woman who invested him, a spirit—"

I just walked off.

Of course I returned for drugs. He told me two things about Mr. Pool and one about Colonel Wren, but I hate to repeat them because here my testimony gets pushy toward life's revenge, but I'll say the real fact is, Kervochian didn't have to tell me, I saw Pool plain enough around town. The man began losing his face. It just fell down and he got gruesomer and gruesomer and at last just almost unbearably ugly. He went and had galvanized electric facial therapy—five hundred dollars at the beautician's, but nothing would save him. The last time I saw him in a car windshield he was driving with nought but two deep eyeholes hanging on to a slab of red wrinkled tissue. He had got strange, too. He had women out to the deer lodge. His wife found out about it and went over and burned it down. Then Colonel Wren, whom I never saw again, did a thing that got him "roundly mocked," said Mr. Kervochian. Wren was a veteran of Wake Island, where the U.S. soldiers had bravely held off a horde of Japanese before they were beaten down, the survivors going to a prison in China until the end of the war. Wren wrote a long article for an American history magazine, telling the true story, in which he figured modestly and with "much self-deprecation." Then in the next issue in the letters section there was a long letter from a man who was a private at Wake with the others. He went on to say how modest the then Captain Wren was, too modest. He had exposed himself to danger over and over, carrying wounded in one arm and firing his .45 with the other, etc. The letter was signed Pvt. Martin Lewis, Portland, Oregon. All was fine until somebody found out Wren had written the letter himself.

"In his seventies, old Wren. Pathetic," smacked Mr. Kervochian.

None of these happenings raised my spirits and I am putting them in only in memory of Mr. Kervochian, who died such a long painful death, but had explained nearly the whole town to me before he passed on.

When we lap that old woman's house and see her sitting there, on her porch, grand car to the side, safe and nestled in, blasted dry with age, I still say over and over, "Success, success," to my running buddy. Forever on — maybe I'll get over it — I hate a good house, a lawn, the right trees, I despise that smart gloating Mercedes in the drive, all of it. Early on, I moved out of our house, way back there, thirteen or fifteen or something like that. I believe I moved into a shack, maybe I even lived once in a chicken shack. I have missed a great deal, but as the drugs run out with each kick and step, I am beginning to see the crone, once my teacher, go back in time. My legs are pushing her back to a smoother face, a standing position, an elegant stride, a happy smile, instructing the young cheerfully and with great love.

Now there is something for tomorrow. What are women like? What is time like? Most people, you might notice, walk around as if they are needed somewhere, like the animals out at the shelter need me. I want to look into this.